SOUTHERN JUSTICE

by

Sam Eakin

Relentless Capital Company, LLC

This book is a work of fiction. Names, characters, places and incidents are either the product of the author's imagination or are used fictitiously. Any resemblance to actual persons, living or dead, or to actual events or locales is entirely coincidental.

Cover designed by Justin at Jensen Design Co.

Published by: Relentless Capital Company, LLC

ISBN: 979-8-9916951-0-7 (eBook)
ISBN: 979-8-9916951-1-4 (Paperback)

Version 2024.10.09

SOUTHERN JUSTICE

Table of Contents

Prelude

Foster Landeaux stared angrily at Mack the bartender, "Where the hell is she?" he demanded.

Mack shrugged an apology as he fiddled with the cash register and pointed to the end of the bar. Two bar stools stood empty, tipped against the scarred railing, waiting for occupants.

Foster scowled. She was late, which pissed him off. But then, she didn't know him, nor did he know her. He was an officer of the law and always on time. He never waited on anyone—especially a local hooker. He walked the length of the bar, stood the stools upright and shook the rainfall off his blazer, trying to ignore the raucous voices of a dozen G.I.'s attempting to harmonize "Back in the USSR" with an old jukebox. He turned to drape his coat over the back of the stool, intentionally displaying his holstered gun to command respect among the rowdy military crowd.

The Drop Zone Bar was rank with the stench of rotting pine, nicotine, and the sweat of hardened young men ready to go to war. Its plank walls, crudely striped in red, white and blue were plastered with Uncle Sam's official recruiting posters. Square-jawed soldiers stood next to steely gray tanks and fighter jets, juxtaposed against psychedelic images of Jimi Hendrix, the Statue of Liberty and a giant can of Campbell's soup. Such were the mixed voices of the Sixties that no one quite understood. The "DZ" was by far the most popular hangout in Leesville, Louisiana, a blip on the road just outside the guarded gates of Fort Polk, a massive army deployment base for Vietnam-bound soldiers. Fort Polk secured southwest Louisiana like an occupying force.

Foster took a seat at the scarred bar, pulling a starched white handkerchief from his coat pocket to mop the moisture off his face. His nostrils flared at the musky smell of the bar. He stifled his disdain for military bases and their bars. Down deep he felt a pang of guilt that he quickly quashed. After all, he was white, the only son of a Louisiana Sheriff who wasn't about to let his kid get drafted to fight a useless war in Viet Nam. He watched the crowd of young recruits with a stony face. How many would die face down in a rice paddy on foreign soil? "Better them than me," he muttered to himself.

His "guest" made her grand entrance forty minutes late, unrepentant and unhurried. A stunning young mulatto, she walked fearlessly through the open doors into a crowd of gawking eyes that devoured her black knit miniskirt and matching ponytail. A sudden clap of lightning lit her profile, searing her curves into the minds of leering G.I.'s. Even the jukebox fell silent to the sound of high heels on the wood floor. She strode purposely toward the bar, stopping midway to shake off a big black umbrella, snapping its closure and hoisting it over her shoulder in a military stance. Erect, with her chest thrust out, she glanced at Mack, who responded with a quick nod toward Foster as he set two beers down to spot her mark. The mulatto walked to the open bar stool like a racehorse looking for a gate as Mack receded back to the cash register, his services rendered.

She thread a delicate arm with a dangling bracelet over Foster's shoulder, bracing herself without introduction as she slid smoothly onto the bar stool, tugging her scant hemline down in a show of modesty befitting the intrigue of their encounter. Foster appreciated the smooth southern ease with which she had maneuvered her target, but he was impervious to the bait.

The mulatto laid a gold cigarette case on the bar in front of her. She turned to Foster with an alluring smile and a silky voice. "You've been stalking me for a week," she said. She cocked a perfect eyebrow and tilted the pretty head with indifference as she pulled a cigarette from its case. "To what do I owe the pleasure?" she asked, then "And can I expect more?"

"Stalking or pleasure?" he parried.

"Your call," she replied coolly.

"Good to meet you also," Foster countered with a curt nod and swig of beer. "But 'stalking' sounds a tad conceited, don't you think?"

"Lots of men stalk me. It's kind of fun, actually."

"Well, it's good to know I'm that memorable," he responded.

"Give me a break, Whitey," the silky voice took on a sharp, cynical edge. "You're the only guy in a coat and tie for a hundred miles. That starched shirt looks like your mama just ironed it." She held her cigarette up expectantly for a light. Foster obliged her with a flicker from his lighter before two willing soldiers stumbled over themselves to do the same.

"You're either a Fed investigating something on the base or another horny cop looking for a freebie. So, talk fast, Whitey. I got work to do," she said with a wink.

"What a shame, I was hoping we could do some business together," Foster deflected her barrage while he pretended to watch the jukebox crowd, now trying their luck off key with "Johnny Be Good."

She blew smoke into the heavy air as she looked over Foster's short hair and strong frame. He could certainly hold his own against any of the locals. "You got a room?"

Foster closed his eyes and shook his head, dismissing the question with a heavy sigh. "Not that kind of business," he responded in a harsh voice, visibly exasperated by her youth. "Real business," he tried again, "for real money," he emphasized real in a brusque manner to make his point.

The mulatto shot him a disbelieving look and chugged her Dixie, setting her bottle down hard on the bar. Foster watched her intently, looking for a shadow of the past that he had been searching for. He had finally found his target, but he knew she was too cynical to accept his story without credentials. He considered his next move and decided to start over.

"Think of me as a talent scout," he offered. "I came to make you an offer." His jaw tightened, his lips parting in a rare smile.

"A talent scout with a gun. Good help must be hard to come by."

"So it is. And I'm looking for a very special talent," he said decisively.

She blew smoke into his face with a tease, the pouty lips intentionally pursed in the air to ignore his response. He couldn't decide if it was a show of nervousness, arrogance, or ignorance, from a siren fifteen years his junior. It didn't matter. Patience was not one of his virtues. It was time to close the deal.

"And just what kind of offer were you going to make me, Whitey?" she asked, staring at the ceiling, aloof and unconnected.

"Big money, if you can perform," Foster said in a determined monotone.

"I perform all the time for the right money, but you better tell me why the hell a white boy in mama's shirt shows up in po-dunk Leesville instead of N'Orleans?"

It was a legitimate question but not one Foster had expected, nor one he would answer. He had counted on the purity of money and a ticket out of this dreary town to gain her attention. For her scant years of experience, she was damned savvy. Of course, survival was a great teacher. He took another swig of beer, choosing his next words carefully.

"We don't compete with the New Orleans mob, and we don't need them," he said matter-of-factly.

"So, tell me, where are you from, Whitey?" she asked with renewed curiosity.

"We run a place in Bumkin, out in the middle of nowhere. By choice," he added with a smirk.

His guest rolled her eyes at the name of the infamous one-stoplight town in south Louisiana. Bumpkin was famous for antique shops and speeding tickets.

Foster continued, unabated, pressing to keep the conversation on track. "I'm looking for new girls who like playing with rich guys." He motioned toward the military crowd, "Nothing like this crowd."

"What kind of 'rich guys' go to Bumkin?" she giggled in disbelief while she blew nicotine into the air.

"The kind that don't want to be found; the kind who go to a place where their friends are in total control and there are no surprises," he said in a serious tone that got her attention. "Oil men, plantation owners, lovesick insurance salesmen, crooked politicians, you name it. We cater to them all. Don't you know?" he jested, attempting to lighten the mood, "Bumkin is the best spot topside of God's green earth." He chuckled at the Chamber of Commerce slogan. "Actually, it's kind of true - but only if you know the right people."

Her eyes narrowed as his message took hold. "And let me guess, they're all white?"

"Does it matter to you?" he asked.

"Not to a half-breed, Whitey, but you already know that," she shot back defensively. "But then, I've never worked for a bunch of rich white men and their bitches. I don't know that it would work out."

"What do you have to lose? Got family here?" Foster asked, knowing well the answer.

"Forget that Whitey, I was dumped on the welfare system in diapers. I'm a disposable girl like all the others you hire, I got nuthin' here and nuthin' holding me back. But I sure ain't lost nuthin' in Bumkin."

"Maybe...," Foster said offhandedly as he pulled a folded piece of paper from his shirt pocket and spread it on the bar in front of her. He tapped it with a manicured forefinger to draw her attention, "...or maybe not," he said pointedly.

The death certificate for Meadow Williams, born and died September 23, 1947, in Bumkin, Louisiana lay in front of her. She read the paper in disbelief, her mouth open, as she quietly looked at Foster in a state of shock. "I *am* Meadow Williams," she said with defiance.

"I know," Foster said calmly, finally getting the response he wanted.

"How...?" the young woman's edgy voice trailed off, replaced by a teenager looking for answers she had never found.

"Join up and find out." Foster said without sympathy. He would have preferred to keep her in the dark about her past, but he had to capture her attention.

Meadow recovered quickly, "What do I have to do?" she asked.

"Fall in love," Foster said quickly, prepared for the obvious question.

"There must be more, Whitey, I do that every day," she challenged him.

"Only one guy, a black man," he explained, suddenly serious. "I pay his tab for your services. You keep it quiet and gather information while your living expenses are covered. When I get what I want, you get a big bonus. Then you can go wherever you want."

"What's a "big" bonus, Whitey?" her voice was caustic, disbelieving.

"One hundred thousand dollars."

The mulatto threw her hair back and guzzled her beer. Her amber eyes grew bigger. She bit her lip, eyeing Foster while she weighed her options. He wasn't worried. Money and history always won the day in Louisiana.

"Why me, Whitey?"

"Because you have a cover story and no history. You have a reason for being there, but you don't exist on paper. It will make the job easier."

"I could also disappear and no one would ever know," she note, her suspicious nature rose to the occasion.

"You've got the best insurance there is."

"Like what?" she asked.

Foster pulled out his wallet and flipped it open on the bar to reveal the gold face of a Deputy Sheriff's badge from Avignon Parish. "You're in protective custody," he quipped. He drained the last swallow of his beer and slid off the bar stool while she inspected the badge. Foster pulled on his blazer and picked up his wallet. He leaned over to plant a kiss on the mulatto's neck for the benefit of the lingering G.I.'s.

"Let me get this straight, Whitey," Meadow blurted out, ignoring the kiss. "You run a whorehouse out of the Sheriff's Office?"

Foster stepped back to look at her with a laugh and a wicked smile. "Welcome to Louisiana," he said.

Meadow grabbed his arm impulsively before he could leave. "Can I find my parents?" she asked in a strained voice.

"Not if you stay here," he replied. The hook was set, it was time to reel her in. Foster plucked five one-hundred dollar bills out of his wallet and placed them on the bar. The mulatto watched with astonishment as he tore each bill in half, one at a time. He placed half back in his wallet, then rolled up the other half tightly, placing the roll down the V-neck of Meadows sweater, nestled snugly between two perfect hemispheres that shone like beacons in the dim light of the bar. "You get the other half when I pick you up at noon tomorrow," he stated confidently.

The wide eyes took in Foster's bravado with a girlish smile. She pulled out the roll of torn cash and looked at him with curiosity, "What's in it for you?"

"Money, love, and satisfaction."

"And what if I back out?"

"We both lose. No guts, no glory, Meadow," Foster responded with finality. He winked at her, fastidiously straightened his tie and walked out, anxious to get to his car before the storm got worse, and glad to put the Drop Zone bar into his rear-view mirror.

Chapter One
Summer's End, 1969

"**D**ammit!" Sally Callahan yelled to herself as she slammed down the phone. Then she counted backward from ten. It was a habit that had served her well over time.

Outside, young Burton Callahan drifted slowly on an old porch swing, his bare feet hanging over one end, his face buried in a pillow beneath the pages of *Plato's Republic*. It was the last book his mother had imposed on him for the summer. He lurched up from the blast of Sally's voice reverberating down the hallway of the Cajun cottage.

"Bam Callahan! Front and center young man!"

Plato fell to the floor with a thud as Bam sat up to get his bearings. He already knew the issue. How had she found out so quickly? His mother's resources never ceased to amaze him. Careful not to let the screen door slam behind him, Bam walked toward the hum of an electric typewriter that sounded more like a swarm of angry bees. He knew she was still mad about his last car wreck and the bra the mechanic found in the wreckage. Why would a mechanic, of all people, care? It wasn't even his daughter. Still, he didn't need another "incident." The last week of summer was alive with bikinis, beer, and rock 'n roll, and he had locked up a hot date with Angela.

Bam tucked his shirt tail into his Levi's as he walked toward his mother's small office. Sally would never accept a plea of ignorance. He would go for denial of responsibility, to be distinguished from denial of the incident itself. He would also call it an "accident" this time. Incidents were bad. He cleared his mind, then stepped unassumingly into her office. The afternoon sun streamed through the sheer curtains, softly illuminating his mother, an elf in a flowered dress, with the ever-present cup of steaming green tea near at hand.

Sally swiveled around, searing him with her most intimidating scowl. "Tell me about it. All of it. Now." The anger in her staccato command overrode her southern drawl, which was not easily done.

Bam hated this part. How much did she really know? How pissed off was she, really? "Mom, it wasn't my fault!" Best to get in the first salvo.

"Who else could blow a hole through the Canton's garage roof with a chemical reaction?"

"Clay Mansfield," Bam said it so defiantly he almost believed himself.

"No damn way," Sally responded angrily. "That football jock can't spell NFL. Try again," her voice rose an octave as she got a second wind.

"Nobody was hurt," Bam tried to deflect the issue.

Her eyes burned through him. "Again, young man. From the top!"

"Damn" was the strongest cuss word his mother ever uttered. She was definitely headed into the stratosphere. Bam thrust his fists into his jeans and submitted to the greater power. "Okay, ...so we had an old car battery and some acid lying around, and I mentioned that combining the two would produce hydrogen. Clay said I didn't know what I was talking about, I think he was just showing off for his buddies." That was simple enough, wasn't it?

"How many times, Bam? How many times before you learn to walk away from a dare?"

Bam fell quiet. It wasn't a dare. It was proof. "I told Clay that all he had to do was put a match to the tube to find out, and I was right!" Bam said with a triumphant grin.

Sally shook her head in disbelief. "Why in the world would Clay do such a numbskull thing?" she asked.

"'Cause he's a jock," Bam answered.

"That is the one thing we agree on so far, young man." Sally rubbed her temples and closed her eyes. "Did it ever, even vaguely, occur to you that setting off an explosion could create problems?" ...then a frightening thought swept over her. "Oh my God,—if any of their help had been injured all hell would break loose in this town. You'd be the first Louisiana kid accused of inciting a race riot with a Molotov Cocktail!"

"It wasn't a Molotov Cocktail, it was a bell jar, and this isn't Chicago or Boston, Mom," Bam said seriously. "No one here would ever think of that."

"Of course!" Sally slapped her head in feigned surprise. "Real riots only get organized in the North, we just lynch people in the Deep South. Don't kid yourself, young man. Schools are about to integrate, and you are setting off an explosion. People are scared Bam, and they do crazy things when they're scared."

"Clay won't say anything, Mom! He peed in his pants when the bell jar blasted off!" Bam couldn't contain himself and burst into laughter at the memory.

Sally pivoted away from Bam to face the window. The improbable image of a six-foot basketball player peeing down his leg at the site of a rocketing bell jar, whatever the hell that was, blasting through the roof, was a bit too much. She tried to hold onto a serious tone while she quelled an ignoble laugh. Bam sensed he had earned a slight reprieve and seized the moment. "I'm sorry, Mom." It was his last, best ploy, delivered with the innocent look of true contrition.

"You could have killed someone this time, Bam."

"No, ma'am," he responded. "Clay was the one who lit the fuse." He said, smiling to himself as he looked down at his boots.

Sally could feel her anger rise at his ambivalence. "You were complicit Bam, no way around it. You will report this entire escapade to Judge Jim immediately, then you will apologize personally to the Cantons. And you better figure out how you're going to pay for the damages to their roof."

With a penitent nod, Bam turned and strode back down the hallway. Sally could hear the screen door slam against the house to register his frustration. She watched her fair-haired teen head toward town on foot, with little sign of remorse. She refilled her teacup before returning to her next paper on Southern plantation history. Squirrels played on the mimosa tree outside her window as the last of its summer blossoms floated away on the August heat. The season was changing, as was life in the small town around her.

1967 had already been a year like no other, inside a decade like no other. The growing pace of change in the South was hitting her family in ways she had not anticipated. The unexpected Court order for integration had hit Avignon Parish like a bombshell, then the Ku Klux Klan burned crosses on her front yard like she was personally responsible for it. Now a new whites-only school had been hastily thrown up by the local landed gentry, mostly cotton and cane planters, splitting the parish along racial lines to assert their influence. Public education was falling into chaos.

The aristocracy that controlled the State was pushing back hard to secure their political control with harsh rhetoric that Sally hadn't heard for decades. Beneath the economic veneer lay hidden fears of embarrassing family genealogies that traced back to the mixed racial coupling of past generations. To make bad matters worse, her scholarly credentials were in increasing demand to cleanse the histories of powerful families who wanted to hide their ancestral heritage. There was no way in hell she would play that game but southern tradition was hard to fight.

Sally was becoming a lightning rod of social conflict caught between two racial factions, not that it was all that unusual for her. Reporting the real facts had always been her job, first as a journalist, then as an academic. But this time it was different. The black population she had long championed was itself getting organized and funded. Both sides wanted to stack the deck of history in their favor to influence The Great Society government largess. Integration was no longer simply about society and skin color; now it was about money. Big government money. And no one was more credible than a native farm girl; a white, female, academic who literally wrote the book on Louisiana black history. Now, after twenty years of books and editorials, integration had suddenly made Sally politically "correct." Everyone wanted her to rewrite their story but Sally's history wasn't for sale at any price.

Sally despised politics, as well as her unexpected role as a local arbiter of the integration order she had fought for. Her new status consumed her time with phone calls from frantic neighbors and friends looking for comfort about their own children growing up in a fractured, diverse world where everything was changing, even the foundation of history itself. Not that she minded soothing the fears of locals, or even a good fight for that matter, but she was a scholar, she had books to write. She wasn't a social worker or a news commentator. Who the hell had time for politicians or demonstrations? Besides, real history couldn't be changed. It was history.

The political pressure was unavoidable in a rural community. She would be asked to deliver validation for everyone, from the local Teachers Union to the Daughters of the Confederacy, even the local synagogue. Better her than some Yankee historian misrepresenting the South, but white politicians were anxious for her to weigh in on their side. They better be careful about what they wish for. Her history had a way of humbling everyone it touched.

The only good news was that a hundred years of racial prejudice, denied by two world wars and a Great Depression, could now bubble to the top of a new social consciousness, fueled by a sea of television screens that were slamming the South into a new reality. Technology was changing society on a scale never before possible. It made her shiver. The slow pace of the South couldn't—wouldn't keep up. It would inevitably respond with its own brand of political rebellion.

She hadn't seen this sort of visceral racial fear since she grew up on her family's plantation during the Great Depression. It was fueled by the same prejudice she had fought against all her life. Integration was going to be a crash course in chaos for public education. It was overdue, but instant integration was also overwhelming. The Federal Judge didn't understand that a legal brief wasn't the same thing as an instruction manual for educators.

Bumkin itself was exuding its own wave of rumors and tension that festered like a big hurricane over the Mississippi Delta. The town folk were hunkered down behind closed doors, expecting the worst. But the fear of integration lacked the respect which nature demanded. It bred paranoia fed by images of riots in faraway cities and redneck violence closer to home. A bayou of fear was bleeding onto a sea of white graffiti and coarse epithets appearing on public walls. Bumkin was slowly becoming a powder keg of anxiety fueled as much by fear of government intervention as racial conflict.

All she needed now was for Bam Callahan to light the fuse on another explosive incident. That's what an over educated kid got you in a boring Southern town. Thank the Good Lord, she had finagled a way to ship him off to college early, if he didn't kill himself first. Now she could get back to work. She had books to write.

Chapter Two
Quinine

Deputy Quincy Tremblay Jackson pumped the brakes on his new Ford sedan, painted with the big, black & white stripes of the Bumkin Police Department. He slowed to a crawl on the muddy back road, then turned onto a thin asphalt strip he occasionally missed in the darkness, stopping on a decrepit cypress trestle bridge to take in one of his favorite scenes. The ivory moon hovered above him like a giant cue ball, its perfect sphere mirrored in the liquid ebony of the stagnant bayou below. The contrast was not lost on Quinine. Everything was black and white in bayou country.

He followed the bayou road until his headlights fell beneath a canopy of large oak trees. Jumbo raindrops bounced off the asphalt like glitter in his headlights. The big car crept slowly beneath long strands of moss, like a scene borrowed from a cheap horror movie. Generations of his ancestors, both black and white, had since drained the waters of Bayou Hauffpower for irrigation. The bayou was an old riverbed for the Mississippi River that fed into the Atchafalaya. Once a navigable waterway, it was now just a trickle of its former self, occupied by alligators and their prey.

Quinine pulled to a stop and opened a pocket-sized bottle with an amber label and scarlet letters: Genuine Quinine Cough Syrup. The elixir calmed his anxiety, which occurred often, especially in the company of women, which did not. His habit got worse after he took on the Bumkin Police Department night shift, eighteen long years ago. Like most cheap miracle remedies, Quinine syrup was little more than flavored alcohol with a strong bite to ensure it would be used sparingly and sold for its mythical medicinal value. Quinine Cough Syrup allowed Avignon's inhabitants to get through another day of poverty and ignorance, and Southern Evangelicals to justify an occasional nip of alcohol.

The Sheriff allowed Quincy his "cough syrup" so he wouldn't have to fire him for alcohol abuse on the job. The farce forever changed Quincy Tremblay Jackson into "Quinine" Jackson, but he embraced the job as his destiny on the wrong side of the tracks, and soon became the Sheriff's most trusted bag man. It was a shotgun marriage of convenience, of course, as Quinine had never known a life of choices.

Quinine lit a match in the darkness and checked his Timex, with five minutes left to kill. He had to be on time for the Saturday night pickup or there would be consequences, even after a decade of faultless service. He drew a deep swig of his addiction, wincing as the sweet red syrup with the kick of rye whiskey scorched his throat. Handling cash always made him nervous, and the thought of this tired ritual dominating the remainder of his life was depressing. He found his favorite radio station on the dial to let the Supremes lighten his mood while he waited.

His mind wandered to the metallic vibrations of oil rigs, pounding like a migraine that held the great marsh hostage, pulsing with the ebb and flow of oil that pumped wealth into the pockets of his white cousins. He gritted his teeth with a quick sneer, but he had long since given up his disdain. There was no escape from his cousin's influence; it surrounded him and everyone else. The oil was black, but the power was all white. The night was his only escape.

Quinine tightened the cap onto his cough syrup and tucked it under the sun visor. He put the car in gear and drove deeper into the Atchafalaya Swamp, following the canal system that had connected bayous with railroads for more than a century. Two miles later, he came upon the abandoned carcass of the Basin Canal Company, a weatherworn tin sign standing like a sentinel at the intersection of nowhere and paradise, tipped toward a flashing pink neon sign that announced "The Spot" in the darkness with an electric buzz. Quinine allowed himself a wry grin. This was the busy intersection everyone looked for, once they admitted what they were looking for.

The Spot was the biggest secret that didn't exist in Louisiana. Sadly, it wasn't classy like the old New Orleans bordellos where Quinine worked as a young doorman. It was, rather, the kind of cheap, new, luxury that belonged to the sixties. Modern in looks and garish in colors, it was a "hunting camp" with "social entertainment," an ambiguous term famously attributed to Huey Long during his reign as the "Kingfish." Nonetheless, Quinine did not believe The Spot to be without social merit; it was in fact a safe haven for errant husbands, bleary-eyed truckers, and drunk teenage boys. The Spot kept the night safe for white strangers and the backwoods private for everyone else.

Quinine made his way down a final dark tunnel of weeping willow trees. The long fronds swept the rooftop of his car like a thousand delicate ropes that formed a natural camouflage.

The sound of "Good Golly, Miss Molly" soon interrupted the distant thump of oil rigs as Quinine approached the gaudy pink neon sign. He could see a bevy of half-naked girls on the lodge deck, dancing for the pleasure of a rowdy male crowd. The night was still young.

Behind the rollicking deck and a dozen "working" trailers, Quinine counted two Lincoln Town Cars and seven pickups, then he caught the reflection of Foster Landeaux's unmarked sedan. Unexpected, but not surprising. He was, after all, a member of the "lucky sperm club" of life. Quinine was not.

Foster was born into the police force that Quinine had labored hard to enter. Unpredictable, and unliked, Foster was still the boss's son. He had escaped the discipline his father was well known for. The Sheriff had always covered his son's ass, but he still didn't trust him to deliver the Saturday night cash bag into his personal mail chute. Only Quinine held that "honor," at half the pay, which still irked Foster. Quinine couldn't figure Foster out. He was an aggressive officer, always well groomed, who seemed to like the ladies, but he was always alone. Of course, Quinine had no room to talk, but he had an excuse. He was a black lawman.

Quinine caught his breath and refocused on his mission to make the pickup and drop off the money. He flashed his dimmers twice toward Trailer

"A" and idled the police car at a safe distance, although the vast majority of the regular patrons knew Quinine by name. The door swung open on time at the stroke of midnight. Elton, the night manager, was right on time.

Quinine blinked his headlights for confirmation when an apparition burst from the trailer, jerking him out of complacence: a long-legged mulatto girl in blue jean shorts and a wet t-shirt splashed through shallow puddles in her bare feet, like a young colt running toward him in the rain. Quinine fumbled to unlock the door as she frantically knocked on the window.

The song of the cicadas and the clatter of raindrops filled the car briefly as she slid inside, giggling like a schoolgirl on a secret rendezvous. Quinine grabbed his gun handle as the waif pulled the door shut. An awkward silence filled the car as she looked at him innocently, squeezing long black strands of hair, wiping away rivulets of water from her lovely face.

Quinine was dumbstruck. He clenched his jaw and watched in silence while she pulled a worn leather money pouch from a plastic bag, immediately handing it to him. Then she fished out a hot wrap of boudin, the Cajun sausage that was a prized snack for common folk.

"Flash your lights quick so Elton knows I gave you the bag!" she squealed anxiously.

Quinine said nothing. He unzipped the bag to confirm its contents, mentally weighing the cash, then he flashed his lights with hesitation, his normal procedure broken, with Foster's car nearby. He didn't believe in coincidence, but he had little choice. His first duty was to protect the cash.

"I told them they should trust me by now," she complained. "Hell, I've been here six months!"

"I'm glad they did," Quinine replied sincerely. He assessed his new passenger in the darkness while he secured the money bag under his car seat.

"You in a hurry?" she asked. "I needed a break and Foster said you deserved some company." She rubbed her feet together and took the liberty of turning the blower up to get more heated air. Still shivering, she placed her back against the car door and wiggled cold toes under Quinine's khakis while she rubbed her arms furiously. Quinine tried not to stare at the wet t-shirt that clung to a bulging chest. She was the picture of young femininity, cuddled against the car door, too close for his comfort. She was a woman in demand, certainly used to being sought after. He knew it, and he knew she knew it. Why would she want his company?

"I've got a little time," he finally answered uneasily. "What can I do for you?"

"Nothin'. Just some nice talk for a change."

"That I can do," Quinine nodded. A man scarred by history and occupation, he was still gentle by nature. "What's your name?"

"Bambi."

"Right. And I'm Malcolm X. Let's try your real name" he said sternly. "I got a feeling you already know mine."

She paused. "I got to trust you first." Her accent wasn't Cajun. He could hear a twang of west Louisiana redneck in her voice. He nodded without comment, found his bottle and tipped it back. It was definitely time to steady his nerves.

"That stuff don't make you jittery?" she asked.

"No, woman. You make me jittery," he blurted, then looked away, embarrassed by his own honesty, not knowing what else to say. She looked twenty at best, barely more than a girl, and less than half his age.

She motioned for the bottle and giggled as he passed it over. "All yours," he said with a smirk. She nabbed a quick, scorching sip and began coughing uncontrollably, beating her chest as tears came to her eyes. "You make this stuff?" she wheezed.

"No, woman," Quinine patted her ankle for comfort. "It just kills a cold and keeps me alert," he lied.

"I'm surprised it hasn't killed you yet," she groused. "Is that why they call you Quinine?"

He shrugged a silent admission.

"Tell me your real name?" she pressed.

"Have to trust you first," he jabbed back, not quite kidding, just then realizing neither of them claimed a name of their own.

"Well, let's see if this helps," she said, handing over a link of boudin and punching in the car lighter. She pulled a marijuana joint out of the bag and held it up enticingly with raised eyebrows.

"I can't," Quinine stammered.

She shut him off with a flat palm in his face. "Yeah, yeah, I know, it ain't legal, like that money I just handed you was," she scolded his hypocrisy. "Don't you ever break the rules?" she teased with a come-hither look as she lit the joint.

"I'm a policeman."

"And I'm cold" she volunteered, pushing her feet underneath him for warmth.

Quinine checked his mirrors, certain no one could see them in the downpour. He eyed the young siren, an impossible dream he could never imagine to land in his car. A fine mulatto was the *crème de la crème* of the racial hierarchy, mythical bed partners in high demand. White men always wanted darker women. Black men always wanted lighter women. It didn't matter what women wanted, it was always about what men couldn't have.

His instincts warned him that she couldn't be real… but how bad could she be, really? He tried to convince himself that she was sent by the Sheriff in recognition for his years of service. Finally, he shifted against his door and pulled the cinnamon-hued legs into his lap to stroke painted toenails and soft skin.

"How did you end up in the middle of nowhere?" he asked.

"Maybe I'm just getting paid while I'm looking for a good man," she suggested with a twinkle in her eye.

Quinine chuckled with an unconvinced look; he'd known too many miserable prostitutes in the course of his duties. "This is a hard row to plow," he advised in a voice that shed neither shame nor blame about her occupation.

"At least it's a well-paid row," she shrugged. "Believe me, my story has no laughs and few choices, it's nothing anyone wants to hear about, so it really doesn't matter. How about you?" She offered him the joint, its tip glowing red in a small cloud of sweet-smelling smoke.

Deep down he felt a kernel of honesty emerging from this unlikely conversation of shared misery. He knew it was an illusion, but he welcomed an understanding stranger into his depression. "We share that history," he acknowledged with a nod and a light drag from the weed. "I got nothing to brag about either. Nothing to offer a cute girl like you."

She tilted her face in a sympathetic manner and shoved his shoulder with her foot. "You want an older woman?" she jibed, wiggling her legs underneath his long torso for more warmth and attention. Quinine felt his inhibitions dissolving from the narcotic rush while he massaged her leg. He rubbed her leg cautiously, waiting for rejection as he rubbed legs still cold from the rain.

"Girl, how long you gonna stay a whore?" he dared ask. It was a shock to him more than her.

"Well, that depends on what I get, and what they take," she responded without hesitation.

Her words shattered Quinine's sanguine mood with a sobering thought: he could <u>never</u> get more than they took from him. It would always be so. His life had already been bought and sold.

The mulatto pointed in the direction of the stashed moneybag. "And what about you? How long are you going to stay a whore?"

Quinine jolted, his eyes blinking at the accusation. "Maybe forever," he finally admitted softly, more to himself than to her. He had never considered himself that way. But there it was; glaring evidence of his own prostitution. Nobody had ever stuck that mirror in his face. He had never confronted raw honesty, and he fought back the anger that came with it. Suddenly he felt alone; his honesty was better hidden in the night. "What have they taken from you, girl?" he asked.

"My childhood," she said, averting her eyes. "What did they take from you?"

"My land. Then my life," he stumbled, barely able to speak the words. His fear had suffocated the truth too long. It was unspeakable, a world he couldn't discuss.

"How much was it worth?"

"The land or the life?"

"The land," she said caustically. "I already know the value of a black cop's life."

"More than I would ever want or need... millions," he admitted, grieving a lost future more than a disappointing past.

She fell quiet, letting the puzzle of Quinine's life fall into place, trying to empathize with his defeat to get more answers. "Why don't you take it back?"

"'Cause dead men don't need no land," he said matter-of-factly, "and I want to live," Quinine said with unexpected conviction.

Until he heard himself say it, he had never been sure that living really mattered. His life was a restricted state of survival that began with sunrise over Bayou Hauffpower and ended with sunset over Bayou Boeuf. But he was here, now, cozying up with a fiery, young woman full of innocent questions, herself just another slave to a common master, searching for freedom and safety.

Pounding rain filled the silence of the big car with a rhythmic ebb and flow from shifting winds. She listened to the radio with her eyes closed as Jimi Hendrix's guitar roiled over the humid air.

Quinine wondered if she was thinking anything close to what he was thinking, too shy to presume it possible. She sensed his mood and suddenly cupped his chin, pulling his face toward her, inviting his move. Gently, he bent to kiss her, felt her yield with unexpected tenderness, her passion awakening the man he had lost. Suddenly he wanted to devour her, to ease her broken past, to set her free from the captivity they shared.

"I want to know your name," she whispered in the steamy darkness.

"Quincy," he whispered back. "My name is Quincy."

"Quincy. I like that. That's a name with history. What's the rest of it?"

"Don't ask. You don't want to know."

"What happened to trust?"

Trust. It was yet another luxury Quinine had long lost, but perhaps one Quincy could still claim. Quinine was little more than a gritty shadow of Quincy, a stillborn character lost in a story he could never tell. It took a velvet night only a dark swamp could yield and the touch of a strange woman to release the story of Quincy Tremblay Jackson. His was a story painful to admit to a stranger, however willing she was. It seeped out slowly, void of forethought, spilling into the ink of the night without fear of reprisal, gradually turning into a torrent of vindictiveness and despair propelled by decades of suppressed anger which permeated Quincy's every pore.

The mulatto pulled him close, interrupting his anxiety as he wept. "Take a breather, Quincy," she whispered, handing him another joint. She spoke his given name respectfully like the white Sheriff who relied on his judgment and the inhabitants of the shanty town he protected. She knew he had value. "Go on," she urged, listening to his every word.

The drizzle abated, then amplified again as the hours passed. With the weight of history lifted and the mellow fragrance of marijuana surrounding them, the conversation gradually turned to shared stories of lost friends and old lovers, and the abandonments and betrayals that marked their lives.

Quinine fell quiet, ashamed of venting his emotions like a child who had talked too much during class. He watched tiny beads of moisture slowly finding their way down her tussled hair, dripping between the swell of thinly covered breasts. He admired that she listened to him, quietly. She was a hard woman to find.

"Trust me now?" he asked, finally void of things to say. "Tell me your real name."

She smiled in the darkness, nodding with understanding as she took off her t-shirt and pulled him to her. "My name is Meadow," she whispered in his ear. She had learned as much as she could for tonight. It was time to close the deal. "Let me teach you about trust."

Chapter Three
Judge Jim

By eleven a.m., young David Tremblay finished his morning drill as Managing Partner in his law firm, "checking the output" of three legal secretaries who actually did all the work before he headed out the door. Judge Jim Keys watched his "Junior" partner step out onto Main Street through the blinds of his office window. Tremblay walked with the manicured look of a busy lawyer headed for court. Judge Jim knew better. He was headed for an early lunch and drinks at the country club, not to be seen again until the following morning. Outside the window, an irksome wooden sign swayed gently over the sidewalk outside the law firm entrance:

Tremblay & Keys
Attorneys-at-Law

It was a lie, of course, bought and paid for by the Tremblay family, like everything else in town. Judge Jim could only take comfort that it was no different than most advertising. There had never been a Tremblay at the helm of Judge Jim's firm: not at its outset and certainly not now. His titular young partner, who also just happened to be the titular president of Bumkin Bank & Trust and Dynasty Oil, had never produced one damn brief or rendered one damn opinion of any kind. The Judge would never risk letting David write his own legal documents. Hell, he was barely a legitimate lawyer at all; his law degree had been "obtained" from an obscure Northern college following a contribution from the Tremblay Trust, discreetly arranged by Judge Jim.

Thus, it had been throughout the entirety of David Tremblay's misspent youth. He was smart enough to understand the cost of his mistakes, and selfish enough to avoid responsibility. Any screw-up of importance Judge Jim had quietly swept under the Tremblay family "rug," so it didn't disrupt the balance of nature in Bumkin or the Tremblay family. Fortunately for all, the family "rug" extended for miles in all directions.

The Judge passed his hand through his shock of silvery, white hair as he considered the issues at hand. To think, he had both covered for the young hell-raiser and mentored him to create an independent life of his own with infinite possibilities, a life that could escape his father's controlling personality. The world had been his oyster. Then, unexpectedly, at age thirty-five, the kid decided to play Prodigal Son and return home to cash in on his family's fortune rather than make his own. Now he stood to become the kid's gopher, his seniority forever overshadowed by the name of the third-generation pretty boy he had created. Insufferable. Unforgivable.

Judge Jim was no longer willing to bear the indignity of it all. But then, he had yet to come up with a plan for the lucrative exit he deserved. Where would he go? For all its petty problems, he would be hard pressed to find a more comfortable position with greater security and clout than Judge of Bumkin and caretaker of the Tremblay fortune.

He rose from his leather club chair and opened his carved walnut wet bar. It was one of those days. He was wealthy and well respected by any reasonable standard, but only within the limits allowed by the Tremblay family. He was not as rich or as powerful as he thought he would be, or should have become, for that matter. It made for one hell of a mid-life crisis. He had all the trappings befitting a southern judge, from Deacon at First Baptist Church to Director of Bumkin Bank & Trust. He had a public service pension courtesy of "the family" and had socked away plenty of money to get his kids through LSU and beyond. It was all very legitimate, for the most part. Contrary to the belief of Yankee lawyers and Hollywood filmmakers, Southern judges didn't need to be corrupt to get rich. No, that was the job of the Sheriff. Besides, Judge Jim had always preferred women, whiskey and power, mostly in that order.

He poured a nip of Southern Comfort to help him analyze his situation, then fell back into his chair and took in his elegant surroundings. It was all quite nice, but it was no longer enough. He wondered when it had become insufficient. It just happened, he surmised; unplanned and unwanted, like so much of life. He knew that David Tremblay would be a continuing problem but in fairness to the kid, he could sell igloos to Eskimos. His genteel mother had spoiled him rotten. She had in fact molded him into an extremely effective front man for the law firm, knowing no one else would ever employ him. Of course, he admitted to himself, his willingness to "manage" David had translated into growing legal fees for himself from the Tremblay largess.

The kid had natural good looks and a silver tongue that could easily separate little old ladies from their money, all of which had benefited the bank, the oil company, and ultimately the law firm. David was pleasant, well-spoken, and impeccably dressed—as much the polar opposite of his coarse father "Bubba" as he could possibly make himself. Understandably so, the Judge nodded in his silent thought.

The problem was that the kid had never earned a damn dime of his own. Judge Jim held far higher regard for Bubba Tremblay's accomplishments and loyalty to money than David Tremblay's education and social manners. Bubba was no rocket scientist, but he knew what he didn't know, and he hired Judge Jim to cover his uneducated redneck ass on all the rest. With Jim at his side Bubba had held onto the family fortune and even grown it, surviving decades of boom-and-bust cycles, not to mention untold scores of women.

At the end of the day, Bubba commanded the respect of the community as a successful planter in his own right. In his own weird way Bubba remained personally attached to "his" town and generously supported the community, unlike his effete son. Bubba wasn't afraid to get his hands dirty.

But, it was a new era, the Judge mused with a melancholy sigh. "Planters" like Bubba were dinosaurs in the New South, no longer revered as powerful figures that once defined the Old South. A "planter" was now just another wisp of history, an arcane word reserved for a particular genre of southern farmer whose heritage was embedded in land that surrounded everyone else.

Ironically the Cajun and black communities still accepted the power, privilege, and abuses of the shrinking, white, aristocracy of planters. Theirs was the "old money" that tethered everyone to a treasured past and a security blanket that was now under assault by a federal government.

Jim became part of the myth thirty years prior: flattered to be recruited out of LSU law school and honored by the recommendation of Bubba's granddaddy, legendary "planter" David Tremblay, Sr, who had established the Tremblay dynasty while he was Grand Wizard of the Ku Klux Klan. Power shifted with generations, but it was still tied to the land. As a much younger lawyer, he was honored to have the modest name of Keys representing the biggest family fortune in Central Louisiana. He had been an heir apparent, effectively controlling the estate. Now he woke up in midlife as an elected Parish Judge, a lawyer for "the family" and caretaker of an estate filled with the last generation of aristocratic fools that came with it. To think, he could have written his own ticket, played with the big boys in New Orleans. His lot seemed to be a much smaller part of the universe now.

Judge Jim always knew that he faced a tectonic shift when Bubba retired from old age or passed away from hard living, the surer bet. Now he had to manage Bubba and keep David's nose clean along the way. But working with David wasn't like working with Bubba. The kid didn't listen, and never would. His insecurity and glitzy lifestyle didn't sit well with the local folks either. He sure as hell wasn't one of them, and it was only a matter of time before they abandoned him. So, who was the real front man? Jim sighed at the obvious answer to his own question.

The grandfather clock chimed on the half hour, stirring Judge Jim out of his most private thoughts, reminding him of his appointment with young Bam Callahan. Not the first, and not the last, he would wager. He mentally scrolled back through the call from his old high school sweetheart, Sally, and the script she had handed him, just like the good ol' days. The arrangement was implicitly made without admission, as only a Southern gentleman such as Judge Jim and a Southern woman such as Sally could make; Sally would continue referring to him as a capable and hardworking public servant in her weekly newspaper column and Judge Jim would scare the hell out of young Bam, once again, without inflicting serious humiliation. They had always worked well together growing up, the curious journalist and the analytical lawyer.

This time around Judge Jim had more than a passing interest in seeing Bam's rough edges smoothed over in very short order. His daughter's growing appreciation for young Bam had not gone unnoticed. Angela had inherited her mother's good looks, and her father's hormones; he had no doubt that Angela and Bam were a train wreck waiting to happen. They were both smart, hotheaded teenagers with too much time on their hands, not unlike his and Sally's own youth, he reminisced with a fond grin. What goes around comes around.

"It's Mr. Callahan, Your Honor," the secretary announced over the loudspeaker. Judge Jim wiped his shot glass clean with a napkin, set it into a cubbyhole in his roll-top desk, then tossed a stick of gum in his mouth. It was time to scare the hell out of Bam Callahan, for more reasons than Sally needed to know.

Bam entered the Judge's chambers slowly, taking in the musky, leather-bound books and hand-hewn bookcases that made everything feel so … official. He admired the twelve-foot ceilings with high-beveled transoms, and the leaded-glass window that refracted sunlight across the Judge's desk. To the right, a panoramic view of Main Street followed Hwy 71 into the horizon, looking like a road to nowhere. It was a scene right out of "Perry Mason," a drama Bam liked to watch, but not one he wanted to be in.

Bam quietly took his seat in the familiar, red leather chair facing the Judge's desk. He gripped the lion-claw armrests he figured had been rubbed smooth by prior occupants nervously fearing their own verdicts. He knew the drill. Judge Jim maintained an intimidating silence, reading his notes and ignoring his prey as he gradually lowered his eyeglasses precariously to the tip of his nose. Then he slowly unbuttoned his cuffs and rolled up his sleeves on each arm, as if readying for a boxing match, his suspenders stretched tight against a barrel chest that filled an immaculate starched white shirt. The Judge's chair squeaked under his weight as he glared over his glasses at his quarry. Bam felt a sudden sense of déjà vu roll over him. It was going to be long visit.

The intercom buzzer interrupted the silence just as Bam was about to speak. The Judge held up a single finger motioning Bam to sit and remain silent as he punched the phone.

"Bubba's on the line, says it's urgent, I couldn't get him to hold off," the secretary apologized. The Judge looked annoyed. Bam thanked the Almighty for the interruption.

"Put him through." The Judge punched off the speakerphone and swiveled around for privacy, his chair screeching under the weight of its cargo. Not that it mattered. Bam could hear every raspy word shouted by the angry caller, easily recognizable by anyone in town as Bubba Tremblay.

"You get an answer from Quinine?" Bubba barked.

"He doesn't want to sell," the Judge responded coolly. "He has no reason to sell."

"I don't care," Bubba roared, causing the Judge's big shoulders to rise at his impertinence.

"Bubba, why does it matter? Dynasty is already capturing all of the oil."

"Have you seen the price of Dynasty stock? It's tripled. Sooner or later that nigger is gonna wake up and cause me problems. If I buy it now, I can sell it back to Dynasty for twice what it's worth in stock. I need to lock it up."

"Leave it alone, Bubba," the Judge pleaded.

Bam could hear the raspy voice turn indignant. "Don't tell me what to do, counselor. I make my own damn decisions and this here is a business matter-- I'll handle it my way. It don't appear I can count on my esteemed law firm to get things done like I want anymore."

The Judge tightened his grip on the receiver for a long moment after Bubba abruptly clicked off the line. He swiveled back around, to scrutinize Bam, who was admiring the grandfather clock, pretending not to be listening to the conversation.

"Ah, Bam. What can I do for you today?" Judge Jim asked, arching his bushy silver eyebrows. He was a gregarious man who genuinely enjoyed meeting people from his community under any number of circumstances and infractions. His meetings rarely involved criminal issues, but justice inevitably had to be delivered for the public welfare, especially in an unsettled era where the patience of the court was regularly challenged, and parents were increasingly hard to find.

"Mom asked me, well…," Bam gulped. "Mom suggested…" He stopped and gave up, then spit it out all at once. "Actually, Judge, Mom instructed me to tell you about a problem I had, uh, actually a problem I guess I kind of made at the mayor's house."

Judge Jim's voice deepened. "Yet another problem, young man? When did we last have to visit? What this time?"

"Well, it's different from the others, Judge," Bam stammered. "There's no car wreck, or missing pumpkins."

"And I would hope, no misplaced ladies' apparel?" the Judge said with a stern look. He remembered independently confirming that Angela had truly been at her aunt's that weekend.

"No, sir. That either," Bam stammered.

The slightest of smiles crossed Judge Jim's face. He delighted in the range of violations that occurred in the small town over which he presided. It was a true testament to American innovation. "Okay, Bam. Tell me the story. The whole story."

Bam gradually regained control and recited the story of a chemical experiment gone awry. Judge Jim grunted at the climax, having trained himself never to diminish the seriousness of an infraction. Bam finished the story and hung his head for the expected onslaught.

"Do you realize you could have hurt someone, Bam?"

"No, I don't think so, Judge, there wasn't enough hydrogen to really hurt anyone."

"Except maybe you, and Clay, not to mention the building, and any domestics who happened to be around."

"Well, yes, sir. Maybe so," Bam conceded.

"Do you realize you destroyed someone's property?"

"Yes, sir, I do. But not intentionally." Bam made a point of his intention.

"Now Bam, if you had been caught vandalizing a house and damaging the property of others, what would you expect that I would do?" the Judge looked piercingly over the rim of his glasses.

"You would make me pay for it," Bam said glumly.

"You bet your sweet ass I would, son," the Judge snapped.

"But Judge, it was not deliberate, and I didn't ignite the hydrogen, I just made it. Actually, I only directed the making of it. It was just science."

Judge Jim leaned back in his squeaky chair, staring at the ceiling, letting the youngster hang out to dry in silence while he contemplated Bam's position. A pertinent legal point had been made. Bam had only done what he set forth to do, without intent to damage the people around him. Bam was too smart to strike a match to hydrogen. And he could have reasonably assumed that Clay, being older, should have known better. What was that boy thinking? Nevertheless, it was time for Bam to learn responsibility. The squeaks from his chair subsided until the silence of the office contained only the swishing of the ceiling fan.

"Judge, I really didn't think Clay was that dumb!" Bam offered for the record.

Judge Jim folded his hands on his desk and squared his shoulders, leaning forward. His stretched suspender straps made him look bigger than he was. "Maybe so, Bam, but you were in charge. You started the process. You knew the risks. But, you do make a point, which is duly noted. And, I understand that it wasn't your intent to ignite the hydrogen. But that in no way lets you off the hook. It was your experiment that allowed some other numbskull to strike a match. Now Bam, I want you to remember that there will always be an idiot in the crowd who will screw things up, no matter what you do, or how well you plan. Contemplate this lesson for the future because it is sure as hell going to cost you today. I will confer with Sheriff Franklin and let your mother know how the fines will be assessed." There was unmistakable finality in his voice. Bam knew the session was over. There would be no appeal.

Judge Jim sat back calmly, letting the drama of the moment soak in. The moment after sentencing could inspire a rare epiphany for teenagers. He wanted this one to be especially intense.

Bam spoke up, "I presume damages to the property will be spread between Clay and me. It would only be fair that way, Judge."

It was a fair retort, but unexpected. Was the boy growing up, or was this a cagey diversion?"

"That's fair, Bam, and so it is." He slapped his hand on his desk like a gavel, ending the session, ready to rise out of his chair.

Bam didn't budge. "How about I resolve my half of the damages directly with the Cantons?"

"And what about Clay?" the Judge asked.

"That should be between you and Clay, Judge. He screwed up my experiment, so he should pay his share of the damages to the Cantons also."

Curious, the Judge asked, "How do you figure that would work, Bam?" as he looked over his eyeglasses.

"I think David and I should jointly pay a third, Clay and his buddies should pay the rest. If the insurance pays up, then we should give our share to the science club at school?"

Bam was getting way to familiar with court negotiations, the Judge thought. "I will consider the offer and communicate my decision to your mother. Rest assured that if I find you here again there will be serious consequences," he said to drive home his point, waving off the incorrigible little shit, his patience at an end.

Bam still didn't move, slowly lifting his hand to get the Judge's attention, "Just one other thing, Judge," Bam dared in an apologetic voice. "If I work this out with the Cantons, how about we just keep all this between us? I would rather Mom didn't have to read about it in the newspaper."

The Judge gave him an angry look, then he let out a boisterous laugh. "Ok Bam, you want to make this 'man to man?' We will try it this one time. But it damn well better stick. Settle up with the Cantons and stay out of the newspaper. Now get your ass out of here."

"Yes, sir." Bam stood and shook Judge Jim's hand. He wasn't sure whether he should thank him for his time or express remorse for past sins. He didn't really feel grateful, but not wanting to be disingenuous, he decided to head for the door. As he reached for the brass doorknob the Judge's voice befell him.

"I commend you for your honesty, Bam. Coming forward takes guts and I don't see any other participants here to fess up. One other issue does come to mind, Bam."

"Yes, sir?" Bam stood at attention.

The Judge looked down at him over his glasses. "This integration order is going to be rough going for everyone in town and I have little doubt that your mom is going to be in the middle of it. Not everyone on our side of the tracks agrees with her view of integration, as you know. You need to keep your head down and stay out of trouble or there will be hell to pay for both of you."

"Mom isn't looking for trouble, Judge," Bam replied, unsure of the Judge's remark.

"She doesn't have to, Bam. I've known your mother for forty years. Trouble finds her quite naturally, and it doesn't need any help from you. Smart people always attract conflict, Bam. It's people who don't do anything that never have problems."

"Yes, Sir," Bam said, ready to agree with anything the Judge said as he fought to understand the weight of the message. Bam thanked him again and pulled the big door shut to leave the chambers.

Judge Jim turned back to look out his window, his thoughts returning to the Tremblay family issues he had to face. Bam had actually been a welcome diversion from far more difficult decisions.

The Judge watched Bam cross Main Street to head home. He was satisfied he had communicated a message that would stick with him after he left Bumkin for greener pastures. The kid was too smart to hang around town - or to return. The Judge took another sip of whiskey and wished he would have been as smart.

Chapter Four
Meadow

The stale air smelled faintly of motor oil and two working bodies, soaked in their own wetness. Meadow leaned against the back door of the police car, making sure not to let the cool air out or the mosquitoes in. The bloodsuckers were so thick around the swamp you could hear them buzzing outside the window. All eight cylinders of the engine hummed in unison, laboring to convert tropical moisture into cool air as the bayou fog outside engulfed the car.

Satisfied, she watched Quinine recover from their lovemaking. It was always best to keep the local authorities satisfied, she mused. Not that she minded. Now that all her clients were white, she found an unexpected comfort with a black man whose intimacy she did not have to measure by the hour. She knew Quinine lived for their weekly rendezvous, as she did in an odd manner. Every session was like the chapter of a new book full of clues, the unfolding of a map that got her closer to the treasure. Her motivations now required brains, unlike her commercial ventures. She liked the suspense; capturing a man's heart was far more difficult than his other parts.

"What were your parents like, Quincy?" she asked innocently as she cuddled into his arms.

"Just hard-working people," he reminisced. "My father was a farmhand, mostly worked for the Tremblay's. He was tall and light skinned, with hair kind of like yours. My mother was darker skinned with long braided hair, she just took care of kids. How about yours?"

"I don't really know," she said, holding up her charm bracelet. "All they left me is this," she said, holding up a bracelet that dangled from her wrist. "Nothing else."

Quinine fingered the oddly jagged bracelet. It was bright silver and heavy, obviously hand crafted and expensive, unlike anything he'd seen before.

"I must really trust you, Quincy," she smiled. "I almost never wear it, but today is my birthday."

"Today?" he asked, surprised, and guilty for not knowing.

"All day long." She smiled.

"How old?"

"Twenty-one and a few hours," she said proudly.

"You're just a baby," he said in earnest. "My baby." He kissed her forehead in response. Meadow's eyes slowly gazed down toward the money bag at his feet.

"Don't you ever wonder about that bag?" she asked aloud.

Quinine jolted, staring at her sternly in the darkness. "Girl, I don't know what you are thinking, and I don't ever want to know. Whatever is in it belongs to the Sheriff, and it better be in his mail chute by sunrise, or we will both pay a price."

"I was just askin'," Meadow shrugged, surprised by his response. "It's been getting bigger, like lots of things around here lately." She giggled and tweaked his nose. "You said I could ask you anything," she teased.

"No, I don't wonder about the bag. Not anymore," he replied in a calmer voice.

"How long you been handling money for the Man?" she wondered out loud.

"Going on thirteen years? Why?" he asked, somewhat annoyed.

"'Cause we all work for him. You know that as well as I do."

"How do you know that, woman?"

"Oh silly, my 'daddy' told me," she giggled again, then added wistfully, "If I had one."

"Everybody got one," Quinine responded sympathetically. "Sometimes they are just hard to find. Have you ever looked for him?"

"I still am." Her words were soft and sorrowful, and Quinine left them unquestioned. "I'm just hoping you're gonna stick around a while to be my Big Daddy. I think about you all the time."

Quinine pulled her to him. Meadow flinched and unconsciously whelped with pain. She rolled to her side and moaned, clutching her arm as Quinine sat up and pulled her hand away from the tender spot to inspect it, uncovering a deep bruise she covered in her nakedness.

"Who hit you?" he demanded, his voice deep with a manliness she had not heard before.

Meadow waved him off without comment. Violence was an occupational hazard for her, at times hard to distinguish from rough pleasures that came with the job. Another adrenaline rush was just second nature in the daily art of survival.

"Tell me," his police officer persona demanded.

"It's nothing. Nobody, Quincy," she reiterated." Nobody worth worrying about. I have a customer who can get a little out of control, that's it."

"Tell me, who."

"Oh, he just starts ranting. He's wacko," Meadow said dismissively. "Don't worry, I can make him stop."

"What's his name?" Quinine asked in a way that said he already knew.

"Leave it be," she begged.

"Red hair?"

Meadow was caught off guard. Her eyes widened and Quinine caught it. "Why are you covering for him?"

"Because he pays well. I keep a knife under the bed when I am with him," she confided. "If he hits me again, I will slit his throat."

Quinine sat up, stone-faced. He heard a steely edge in Meadow's voice he had never detected. The cop in him recognized a statement of premeditated fact, spoken like a schoolgirl assuring her older brother she could stand on her own. He stroked her hair with a calm hand and a rigid jaw, while his heartbeat raced. "Listen to me. Bubba must never know about us."

"How do you know him?" she asked with a tremor.

Quinine's eyes burned with vindictiveness.

"How?" she repeated. "Tell me, baby."

"His name is Cameron Tremblay, Jr. Everyone knows him as Bubba. He is my second cousin."

Meadow blinked in disbelief. Now she got it. Now she knew why she was here. "Bubba Tremblay is your cousin? How can that be?

Quinine sighed with dismay. "My grandmother lived on the General's plantation. I guess she had to pay the rent somehow."

"The General?"

"General Cameron Tremblay, Sr., Bubba's father. He called himself, "General." His real title was Grand Wizard of the KKK. He was never no real General," he said with disgust.

"Bubba must be rich," she said, knowing the answer full well.

"Too stinking rich. And too stinking powerful," Quinine sneered.

Meadow pressed him for more, anything to add to the fragmented information she had extracted from Bubba and Foster, even the stupid white sluts at The Spot. "Does Bubba know ya'll are related?"

"Of course he does. Everyone in the whole damn parish knows. We had the same great grandfather. Mrs. Sally Callahan even documented it for one of her books." Hard bitterness crept into his voice, then he added, "But no one will admit to it."

Meadow's eyes twinkled in the night. Foster's plan was far better than she anticipated. "So that land you told me about, Bubba stole it from you?"

"He didn't have to. The Tremblays just use the land like it's their own and steal the oil because I can never fight them."

"How can that be?" she asked, genuinely curious. It was clear that Quinine had never shared his circumstances, let alone a woman's sympathy. She had to keep him talking. The missing piece of her treasure map was coming into view.

Quinine became angry. "They own the town. They own the judge. They stole the oil from my father. He didn't read or write. He probably didn't know what was going on, just another nigger who died a poor man because he was helpless. They would throw him a bone to keep him in line, then intimidate him so he wouldn't create any more trouble. He finally threatened to find a lawyer; that's when we found his body in the bayou. He left me the original deed, but they probably have their own forged copy. It don't matter no way, a lawsuit would just produce another dead nigger."

Meadow placed her head on Quinine's chest and hugged him while she considered his story and pieced together Foster's actions. He had pimped her out to two warring lovers that only a mulatto could share in order to confirm the information, while he kept her blind to the obvious. She knew there was still more to the story. There had to be. White people never shared the truth with the hired help. And she hated them for it.

In the distance Meadow saw a slight spray of light flash through crooked Venetian blinds that hung on the back door of the trailer. She knew Foster was watching, waiting anxiously to learn the whereabouts of Quinine's deed. But he had badly underestimated the hired help. Not that it mattered anymore, Meadow smiled to herself. There was no love lost between Quinine and Foster. Quinine was hers.

Meadow grabbed Quinine and kissed his cheek. "Quincy, we need to leave, I want *us* to leave, and I want to be with you. Please," she pleaded in a helpless voice.

Chapter Five
Trigger

Gil Winchester dropped his battle-worn leather carry-all on the floor of his new office, taking it all in. It was laid out just like he had wanted. He had arrived on an aged twin engine puddle jumper just two hours earlier. It was his first day on the job. His favorite rocking chair had replaced the big executive desk chair. A shiny new bronze nameplate rested on his desk, announcing him like royalty: Superintendent Gilbert Winchester, PhD. He walked over to his stereo, pushed in his favorite Bob Dylan tape and stopped to pick up the nameplate, holding it up so he could admire it in the light. Then he threw it in the trashcan unceremoniously and plopped down in his rocker.

He wailed with Dylan at the top of his lungs, "Everybody must get stoned…" Throwing his hands behind his head and rocking at full throttle, he took time to enjoy the moment. Life was outta sight! He enjoyed the staff snickers at his distinctly California attire, his fake emerald cufflinks and a hunter green, silk shirt that made his gold sports coat look like it matched his straw blonde hair. It was all loud and stylish, just like Gil Winchester. He knew he was a shock; no, he knew he was shocking, but they would learn to love him.

His flashy attire already fueled gossip around Avignon Parish. He dressed for his audience, his students, especially his black students, who really dug his loud colors and hip music. He really didn't give a shit what the grownups thought. Like all kids, Avignon kids were suckers for advertising and Gil was a living billboard for the perks of a good education. Gil walked the walk for "his" students. They wouldn't have to settle for a life of denim coveralls on the farm. He was there to help them escape, just as he had.

Gil loved that fate had delivered him back home, just in time to oversee integration, like an earthquake, smack dab in the middle of the Old South. There was a tectonic change coming in the land of plantations and the KKK. He loved, no, he *relished* a good fight. And what a just cause! He was the local son, returning to a third world country known as Louisiana, like a young warrior returning to the battlefront against overwhelming odds, armed with a new doctorate and the counterculture energy of Berkeley still flowing hotly through his veins. No one else could pull this off. Hell, no one else in their right mind would try. And only Sally Callahan could have made it happen. For a historian who avoided politicians like the plague, his mentor had proven her political skill by lining up the local votes he needed to win the position. She had put her reputation on the line and effectively scared the hell out of the Board by threatening to write about their incompetence, even as she explained that the sixties required a younger generation of leadership. Now it was show time.

The intercom beep interrupted Gil's frenetic rocking. He stretched forward to unleash the voice of his secretary, Marge Bordelon, a high school classmate of his twenty years earlier. "Your guests are here, Dr. Browning," she said in a professional manner.

"Show them in, Marge," Gil opened the door to welcome his guests. Sheriff Franklin Landeaux, Deputy Quinine Jackson, and Reverend Hezekial Allen filed through the door, each shaking the Superintendent's hand with perfunctory, if disingenuous, congratulations.

After dispensing with the normal pleasantries, Gil got straight to the point. "Gentlemen, this is my first day in this office and there is nothing more important than addressing the drug problem in our schools. I am under immediate pressure to develop a drug education and enforcement plan as part of the Integration Order for the "Powers That Be". I need your firsthand view of the problem so I can get to work. Where do you think is the best place to start?"

Three faces looked at each other, then stared at him blankly. Finally, the Sheriff spoke up, looking at the Superintendent with the worn face of a seasoned police officer. "What drug problem?"

Gil stared back in disbelief. "The drug problem we hear about on the news every day," he responded somewhat cynically, trying not to be a wise ass.

The Sheriff gave him his best hometown grin. "Dr. Browning, you must be thinking about California news; we don't even have a television or radio station in Bumkin. The Bumkin weekly newspaper is the best news we have and it gets filled up with school pictures and local sports. We don't have a drug problem. I don't honestly recall that we have ever made a drug arrest in town," the Sheriff said. Then he added, "You're living in Mayberry now, Dr. Browning. The only problem we have is implementing a Federal integration mandate on short notice. Just ask these guys." The Sheriff nodded to the Reverend and Quinine.

Browning suddenly remembered he was back in the South. The very Deep South. He rocked back in his chair and looked out the window to get his bearings. He couldn't tell these guys that he had already met with the black school principal to make sure he had the real scoop. He already knew the magnitude of the problem. Now he knew the magnitude of the deception. This wasn't Mayberry, this was the damn Twilight Zone. How could this be? He rocked forward and looked seriously at Hezekial and Quinine. "Gentlemen, do you agree with the Sheriff? You don't see any drug use in the black community?"

Quinine spoke in a slow, calm voice. "Can't say I've made any drug busts on my shift, Dr. Browning. My time is mostly spent on speeders, petty theft and fistfights on the other side of the tracks, down at the "Black Cat" saloon."

"And what about you, Reverend? You don't find any of your parishioners using illicit drugs?"

Hezekial filled his office chair fully, decked out in a bright green sports coat, yellow shirt and a matching tie that competed with Browning's dapper attire. He inhaled deeply and spoke in the deep, articulate voice of a black preacher who chose his words carefully. "Dr. Winchester, my flock is mostly composed of hard-working families, the majority led by struggling, single mothers who are working to get out of poverty every day. They are too busy raising families to deal in drugs, and too poor to afford them. Certainly, there has always been alcohol abuse among the downtrodden. As intelligent people, we might assume that there could be a drug problem of some sort, but I am confident that it is highly controlled by the good Sheriff. As I am sure you understand, I am also restricted to what I can say due to the confidential nature of my pastoral service. I must first protect my parishioners. If and when the Sheriff advises me of drugs being distributed in the black community, I'm sure he will provide us all with the facts, and I am equally confident Quinine will exert every effort to remove that plague on our side of the tracks." Hezekial closed his commentary quietly, succinctly, with an apologetic smile that bowed to the white authority seated in front of him.

Browning nodded contritely, more to himself than to his guests. It was not at all what he had assumed, but in retrospect, he shouldn't have been surprised. He reminded himself of the old teaching adage; every time you "assume" a fact, "u" make an "ass" of "me."

"Well, it appears we have one less problem than I was expecting," Browning surrendered without further discussion. "I'm clearly jaded by my experience in California, gentlemen. Organized gangs exploited the working poor there, then they started dealing drugs into schools. Today, Northern California's largest employers are large marijuana farms that saturate the urban centers and are aggressively moving into rural America. And that doesn't even include hard drugs which are on the rise. I sure would hate to see that trend find its way into our Parish."

The Sheriff shook his head in disbelief. "I've been told stories about that," he said sympathetically. "Fortunately, we're just not big enough to attract that kind of problem," he said in a dismissive tone. Quinine sat quietly with no comment. Hezekial looked down at the floor. Not yet ready to throw in the towel, Browning asked the obvious. "How do you think Bumkin has avoided the problem, Sheriff?"

Franklin tightened his lips with a homey smile as he considered the question, "I'd have to give credit to First Baptist Church. The folks there have gone out of their way to support Hezekial's Mount Zion Church across the tracks, so we can build a solid Christian community to protect our kids."

Browning stood up to end the meeting without further ado, extending a hearty handshake to thank each of his guests. "Now I know how to proceed with the Federal Judge, Sheriff. Thanks for taking time to visit. I'm sure we will all be seeing each other again in the near future."

The Sheriff put on his Stetson and tipped it silently in acknowledgement as he departed, his entourage following him out the door. He punched his intercom. "Marge, get Sally Callahan on the line for me."

Two minutes later Marge put Sally on the line and Gil picked up the phone. "Hello Sally, how are you?"

"Good, Trigger, tell me how the new Superintendent is doing?" Sally asked with a hint of pride in her voice.

Gil winced at the old nickname he had tried to leave behind. "Kind of confused right now. Sally, I need some local history."

"Tell me about it," she said without hesitation.

"Sheriff Franklin just told me there was no drug problem in Bumkin; apparently, never has been. Can you believe that?"

"Of course, what's odd about that?" Sally deadpanned.

"Okay, I'll bite. How so?"

"Because Franklin doesn't investigate drug offenses across the tracks and white drug abuse is confined to special social "licenses," shall we say? Places like The Spot, or through his son, Foster. It's all very controlled."

"His son? Wow. 'Controlled' was the exact term Hezekial used, but he said it in a different context."

"Or maybe you heard it in a different context," Sally commented. "Anyone would have to know some local history to understand what he meant."

"I get it, Hezekial didn't want to contradict the Sheriff," Gil mused.

"He can't afford to," Sally said. "Mount Zion is always in hock to First Baptist Church, beholding to the Deacons of the white church, which is controlled by Tremblay money."

"Translate that for me, Sally," the Superintendent asked.

"Well, I'd say it means that Hezekial gets to keep a nice Cadillac and a steady job so long as he and his flock mind their own business and stay on their side of the tracks. That doesn't mean that Hezekial doesn't work hard for his church or his people. Just that he has no real choice in an incestuous community under control of a few white people - all with the last name of Tremblay."

She continued as her former student listened intently. "Meanwhile, Quinine runs interference on the black side of town with a 'blind' eye, while the Sheriff and his buddies control drugs and prostitution discreetly. Welcome back, Trigger. There is absolutely nothing new about any of these shenanigans. It's been that way for generations. And in some ways, it's not a bad system," the historian confided. "Everyone knows the rules and everything is managed to an acceptable level of social injustice. Different people call it different things, Trigger: some would call it effective community policing, or others would call it racial containment. And don't get indignant, the only difference between California and Louisiana is one of scale." Sally was as blunt and analytical as ever, as was Trigger.

"You know that arrangement will go to hell quickly with integration," he said.

"Absolutely, Mr. Superintendent. You should have figured that out before you signed up for the job. The Civil War eliminated slavery, but it gave birth to austere segregation of a second class of citizens. Civil Integration stands to finish the job the Civil War started about a hundred years ago. But you now have a hundred years of alcohol, drug abuse, poverty and ignorance ingrained in the black population by a welfare system engineered over generations to create a dependency—and a black voting bloc for Democrats."

"That's what I'm inheriting?"

"Everything from early pregnancy to illicit drug use, welfare fraud, and declining moral standards. Obviously, that doesn't mean that there aren't good students, good teachers and smart people also, it just means that they have been forced to live in a segregated world, and they migrated from a different culture anyway. Don't dismiss that you're also getting great athletes and musicians out of this mix. What else would you like to know?" Sally asked whimsically.

"You know I can't have drug dealers in my schools," Trigger responded angrily.

"Of course not, Trigger, but if you are depending on local law enforcement to keep them out of your new school system, you are going to be sadly disappointed. The Sheriff isn't prepared or motivated to deal with real conflicts; he tickets speeders and keeps black people on their side of town. And, speaking of conflicts," Sally quickly segued before Gil could speak up, "if you don't know already, Bam couldn't get Principal Greely on board for an early college transfer, so he negotiated his own deal directly with the Dean. Greely is madder than hell, apparently he didn't want to get upstaged by the college."

"Bam undertook that himself?" Trigger asked.

"I didn't have a clue until the Dean told me. That's what an overdose of independence and hormones does to young males," Sally said wistfully.

"Greely must feel that Bam is getting special consideration because of your position with the university," Gil mused.

"Bam shouldn't want to get ahead?" Sally's hackles were raised. "Maybe he should be content to trap nutria rats on Bayou Boeuf for the rest of his life." Her voice had an edge Gil knew not to test. "Greely doesn't care about Bam, he cares about pandering to the feds," she concluded.

"You are objectively correct, of course, Sally," Trigger spoke in a soothing voice, "but you are not politically correct. The Integration Order means we are forced to weigh opportunities as a zero-sum game. If Bam gets an opportunity, it's now perceived as an opportunity that a minority student loses. Everything has to be equalized."

"Trigger Winchester, 'political correctness' sounds like a damn Berkeley oxymoron to me, and you're the moron. If I ever hear that nonsense again, I will tell the school board I made a big mistake. If you don't have the balls to manage a tough issue without spurting meaningless gibberish to justify a political policy, your days back in the South will be numbered. This isn't Berkeley, Trigger, this is the real deal. You are back in the Deep South where a bureaucratic response gets treated like a liar's insult."

Trigger knew she was right, as usual, but he had to move the conversation forward; the last thing he needed was a fight with Sally. "Greely retired from the Army. I expect that he has too much military pride to negotiate with a teenager," the Superintendent offered.

"Why don't you tell him he should be *praying for* the Dean to take Bam off his hands," Sally laughed. "It's just a matter of time before Bam will require your intervention, Trigger. I've got to get him out of Bumkin before something else blows up."

Her use of the word "require" kind of pissed Gil off, but as a practical matter, Sally had every right to make the demand. Thank God she had taken an interest in a brash, young history student way back when. He could do no less for her.

"If it's any comfort, Sally, I think Greely is a real prick. But in fairness, integration has changed the rules for everyone; we are all paranoid about hitting targets and measuring integration more than measuring education. It's like being blamed for political 'crimes,' in the goddamn Soviet Union."

"Trigger Winchester, there are better ways to express your sentiments."

"That's part of the problem, Sally. Southern manners can't survive both integration *and* the sixties. No one listens to 'please' or 'would you mind?' anymore. Our southern world of congeniality is falling by the wayside, Sally. We've been thrown into a world of caffeine and shock therapy."

"Not me," Sally lit into her former student. "Go lay that line off on someone who will put up with it, Trigger. You can't be a schoolteacher with a foul mouth! Pretty soon you will have a school full of foul-mouthed kids who can't read and don't follow instructions."

"So, I just need the balls to defend the King's English, right?" Trigger commented wryly. Gil smiled over the phone at Sally's hearty laugh, one that could awaken the most resistant student to new possibilities. It felt odd to be her peer.

"If it blows up between Bam and Greely, you know I'll be there," he said. "In the meantime, I need you to speak at the Rotary Club meeting. It's my turn to get a speaker next week and you're the best I've got."

"Marge called me last week, she figured you'd forget. What's my topic?"

"I don't know, something historical and relevant," he said. He knew there was little chance she hadn't already drafted a speech and edited it thoroughly.

"I'm sure I can manage that."

"Thanks, Sally. Next Tuesday, noon at Jimmy's place."

"Flossie's fried chicken?"

"I hope so," he laughed. "It always brings in a crowd."

"See you then, Trigger."

Before she hung up, Gil had to ask, "One last thing, Sally? Why don't you consider calling me Gil? It's my grown-up name."

"No chance, Trigger," Sally said bluntly, without recourse.

He sighed. "Okay, then at least tell me who can give me a reality check on the drug scene in the Avignon Parish Schools system?"

"That's easy, call Bam Callahan. He's on the ground floor. See you at Rotary."

The line went dead. Gil smiled at the thought of getting ground floor information from a student. Bam would be a natural source. He placed the phone in its cradle and buzzed Marge. "Thanks for covering my backside with Sally, she's good for the Rotary speech."

"That's my job description, Trigger," Marge chided. "You also have another decision to make. The 'Big Dog' legal consultant appointed by the court, Mr. Ethan White, called to make an appointment with you about the court order, on the same day as Rotary."

"That soon? Okay, I'll bring him along for lunch." A prolonged hush, uncharacteristic of Marge Bordelon, befell the phone.

Trigger knew the drill. "Speak up, Marge. What's on your mind?"

"Dr. Winchester." Her uncharacteristic formality always telegraphed a sensitive matter at hand. "Mr. White is, I believe, well, I think, well, actually, I know, that Mr. White is a black person. In fact, I think he is a black lawyer. In fact, I am certain that he is a black, Yankee lawyer, from Boston."

"Well, at least he's not a Philadelphia lawyer," Trigger joked. "You know I don't give a damn what color he is, Marge! Why does it matter?"

"I am very aware of your liberal leanings, Dr. Winchester," she replied tersely, "but I doubt that the rest of the Rotary Club has ever had the pleasure of visiting the Berkeley campus, or ever meeting a black Boston civil rights lawyer."

The light bulb flashed in his mind. Marge was dead on. He had forgotten how to navigate the incestuous South, where everything was connected, and common sense could alter logic. But he was already stuck. What else could he do? "Screw 'em, Marge, they gotta grow up sometime, just like the rest of us."

"Certainly, Dr. Winchester," she feigned. "And I am just so certain everyone will be very appreciative of your efforts to introduce them to their first female speaker and only black Yankee lawyer in attendance on the same day," Marge continued. "May I come enjoy the fireworks?"

"I would enjoy your company, if you really want to attend," Gil challenged her.

"Thank you for your chivalry, Sir, but on second thought, the Bumkin Rotary does not allow female members. I will be content to clean out my desk drawers," her sarcasm filled the phone.

"Your day will come, Marge."

"Sally Callahan will make it happen, *Trigger*," Marge responded curtly and quickly clicked off the speaker. Gil ignored the prescience of his secretary and returned to a mountain of paperwork, happy to have one less thing to worry about.

Chapter Six
Advance Notice

L evi Epstein, Publisher of the *Bumkin Record*, pounded on his old Royal typewriter, rewriting a canned press release about the prospects of another losing season for the New Orleans Saints, wishing he could come up with a new angle. He was doing his best to balance local interests with the flood of civil rights reporting that permeated local news. He preferred to let the daily newspaper deliver the bad news of social turmoil; his weekly got to stick to the "feel good" stuff. The phone interrupted him in the middle of his local sports summary. Levi pushed his horned-rims up onto his forehead and picked up the receiver. "Epstein."

"It's Buggy, Levi. You might want to get to Rotary early today. And bring an extra notepad."

"How come?" the journalist asked.

"Gil Winchester's office made a last-minute reservation."

"And?"

"Seems he's bringing a Negro to Rotary."

Levi shook his head, trying not to laugh at Buggy's attempt to be racially sensitive. He wasn't malicious, he was just Southern.

"And what would the name of this Negro be?"

"Can you believe this? It's Mr. White. He's a black Civil Rights lawyer from Boston, coming to hear Sally's talk at Rotary. When Reverend Hudson found out, he up and invited Hezekial Allen so the other black dude wouldn't feel alone." Buggy was breathless.

"That *is* interesting," Levi confirmed.

"I'll hold you a seat. And don't forget to mention "The Palace" when you write that headline. This here's going to be a humdinger." Buggy hung up.

Levi abandoned his article mid-draft, threw on a worn-out sports coat and shouldered his camera bag, then waved good-bye to his assistant on his way out the door. Outside, he checked his thinning hair in the showcase window where pedestrians sometimes watched operators run the web press. Further up the street he could see a "local" traffic jam forming at The Palace already. He struck out on foot in the mid-day heat.

Sally was the first columnist Levi had hired when he bought the failing paper. He had almost fired her after Joey Stephens, the head of the local John Deere distributorship, stormed out of his office because Sally wrote about his family tree. There were the Stephens, and the Stephens; a black and white family with the same name—and the same genes. She cost Levi an advertiser, but within weeks his subscriber base doubled because everyone wanted to see what she would say next. "True southern stories were better than the National Enquirer," she assured him, and she was right.

Genealogy remained as close to a cottage industry as Avignon Parish could support, sprung from a culture steeped in biracial history with a hundred years of gossip and lies that came with it. Incest, economics, and intrigue still sold newspapers and Levi knew that fearless Sally Callahan was still the best truthteller you could find. Levi wondered what the body count would be today. If the parking lot at The Palace was any indicator, a lot of other folks were wondering the same thing as he caught up with Sally.

Sally looked up as he held the door for her. "Looks like everyone got in early today, Sally. Nothing like a little racial unrest to attract a bunch of men and make a history professor a hot ticket," he joked.

"Come join the party, Levi," she said as she walked through the door. Levi followed her, the only Jew following the only woman at Bumkin Rotary Club. Sally reminded him of that lone oak tree she wrote about that stood out in her father's cotton fields, visible for miles and just waiting for lightning to strike when the next storm rolled up.

Chapter Seven
Showdown In Black And White

Sally gave every planter who produced cotton, corn, cane, or soybeans within thirty miles a good southern hug. They were all lined up in their overalls and jeans in plaid shirts at the very back of the big room, seated at long picnic tables with cheap red-checkered, vinyl tablecloths. The merchants who supplied them, the bankers who financed them, the insurance agents who insured them, and the lawyers who fed off of them, all sat in their own pecking order closer to the front of the room. White-collar professionals, including the high school and grade school principals and the local agricultural agent, all claimed the front table. To the side sat the preachers, Reverend Hudson, and his black counterpart, the eloquent Reverend Hezekial Allen. It was an unexpected pleasure for Sally to find Hezekial in the room, another historic first. She joked with the preachers, both friends in the odd mix of southern life.

Henry Bordelon, the local State Farm representative and the perennial master of ceremonies for the Rotary Club, welcomed Sally with a big hug as she sat down next to him near the podium. With slicked back hair, spotless white shoes and a matching white belt, Henry could well have passed for another preacher. "Thanks for coming, Sally," he half whispered. "Trigger, that is *Dr. Winchester,*" he exaggerated, "said to tell you he'd be a tad late and that he's bringing an important guest from out of town. "By the way, what's our topic today?"

"Why Henry, it's "integration," of course! What else could it possibly be?" Sally smiled and winked.

"You're a brave woman, Sally. Are you ready?" he quipped.

"Henry, since when have I <u>not</u> been ready for this crowd?" Sally laughed. She had grown up with, or was related to, more than half of the room's occupants and knew the rest as neighbors, with exception to Principal Raymond Greely, Bam's high school principal. Greely sat quietly with military rigidity near the back door, just behind the preachers, guarding two empty seats. She figured one was for Trigger, his boss, the other for his mystery guest.

Bubba Tremblay and his entourage of planters and good old boys who backed his all-white school huddled together, their intolerance already laid bare in a small town where there were no secrets. They already knew that Sally was an ardent supporter of the public school system; her parents had sent nine children through college along with scads of grandchildren, courtesy of public schools.

Sally felt a little isolated as she surveyed the room of old white men, then reminded herself that Flossie was cooking up fried chicken in the kitchen. She made a mental note to stifle her own prejudices about rednecks and the plantation system testosterone in this speech. The problem was men. Black and white. When had any of them taught a kid, much less a child of another color? If it weren't for their wives and daughters who they didn't allow in their organizations, these guys would still be living in caves.

"Sally," Henry whispered. "Think I should go ahead and let go of Judge Jim's seat?"

"I'd say so, Henry. He's always a no-show for a 'Big Talk' whenever he can be," she said knowingly. Their lifelong friend, the Judge, referred to town meetings with Sally as "Big Talk" meetings where neither truth nor politicians could find a place to hide. Judge Jim avoided them whenever possible.

The sweet smell of fried chicken and biscuits had filtered into the dining room by the time Buggy opened the door to signal Henry that Flossie was ready to serve. Then he made a quick dash to the mop closet to correct a serious oversight; he forgot the flag. Henry called the meeting to order with the hollow clack of a worn wooden gavel. After a carefully worded prayer from Reverend Carl, all in attendance dutifully faced the entryway where Buggy was still locking the American Flag into its sprocket. He stood straight and slowly backed up against the wall, his hand solemnly placed over his heart in unison with the crowd as they began "I pledge allegiance to the flag of the United States of America…"

Trigger entered through the back door mid-pledge and quickly snapped to attention. Behind him a distinguished-looking black man stepped through the entryway and stood quietly, producing a brief lull in the Pledge of Allegiance. Sally picked up the volume as she watched the black man stand with his hands by his side. She said a short prayer that he would cover his heart in true Southern tradition. For a brief moment she thought she saw a slight smirk on his face as he stood stoically with his hands at his side. She watched Bubba's sneer at their new attendee. Not a good start, Sally thought.

Henry stood at the podium to welcome the newcomers in attendance. "Dr. Sally Callahan doesn't need any introduction to us local folks, but Dr. Gil Winchester is—"

Bubba's raspy voice rang out from the back of the room. "That's no "Doctor," that's "Trigger" Winchester!"

Bubba's boisterous exclamation broke the tension, much to Sally's relief. The black man next to Gil turned and mouthed, "Trigger?"

Gil stood to face the crowd of locals, trying his best to enjoy the humor of the moment. "It's *Dr.* Trigger to you boys, and don't forget it." Everyone laughed as he shifted into a more commanding voice as the senior educator of Avignon. "I would like to introduce my guest today, Mr. Ethan White. Mr. White is an attorney from Boston with the Department of Justice. He is visiting with us about our interpretation of the court order for integration of the Avignon Parish School System."

Ethan White rose slightly and gave a customary nod to his newfound southern peers. Sally and Henry stood, applauding loudly before the silence of a begrudging applause from the planters became deafening. He was a stately, trim man, with athletic shoulders and a square jaw. Thick glasses framed a high forehead and short hair that gave him an academic demeanor. But his expensive, blue pinstriped suit, starched white shirt and maroon tie screamed "lawyer."

Bubba Tremblay sat in his overalls, freshly stained from early morning work in his cane fields. He eyeballed the two "suits" from across the room. What was the damned Justice Department doing here from Boston anyway?

"Sooo..." Henry segued nervously.

"We are honored to have Dr. Sally Callahan, who we all know. I am happy to say that Bumkin made it through its first week of integration without incident, so it's a good time for Sally to speak to us about the history of integration. Give Mrs. Sally a big welcome," he urged, relieved to have a white speaker, even if she was a woman.

Sally gently pushed Henry aside with an assertive nod. She didn't need to wait for a patronizing applause to take over. She spent the first fifteen minutes walking through Reconstruction, the Emancipation Proclamation, and ultimately the formation of a Democratic black vote to provide welfare to the freed slave population. She reminded her audience that Louisiana had one of the lowest slave populations of any southern state, just 21,000 by the end of the war, compared to Virginia and the Carolinas, with hundreds of thousands. But Louisiana, Mississippi and Alabama became the bastion of the Confederacy and that still haunted them today.

The Jim Crow laws gave the South "separate but equal" rhetoric to control the purse strings of black education and institutions in the South behind the invisible wall of railroad tracks. But in fairness to the South, Yankee racism against the Irish, the Chinese and the Italians forced them to segregate into their own communities, no different than black populations after the emancipation.

"Despite media attention to the contrary, the South does not have a monopoly on prejudice; our history just makes us a bigger target. Black and white television coverage of racism in the South delivered cheap content and easy ratings to networks in big northeastern markets. The South is like watching a foreign country to many of our own countrymen, and we are still guilty by historical association with slavery. Today's reality is that all free ethnic populations segregate themselves, no different than the burrows of New York or Boston, where the Chinese and the Irish and the Italians have their own communities."

Sally ignored Gil's wince at her dig into Northern hypocrisy.

"And herein lies a new layer of conflict. Bussing as our only option works in dense urban areas but it is impractical in the rural South. Yet we read about violent riots in Boston, Chicago, Newark, and L.A. over bussing while the television networks ignore a peaceful transition over most of the South."

Mr. White glared at Sally. He had expected a cool reception in the South, but this was an assault. He had been set up. Attending a speech to a redneck audience by a white, female academic in the South was not what he expected. All this local crap was a waste of his time. These people had to play by new rules.

Trigger sat stoically, ignoring White's glare, praying that Sally would tone down her "lecture." Greely gulped his water freely, calculating a rush for the restroom before the shit hit the fan.

Sally continued to deliver both sides of the new reality to her crowd. "We deserve what we get, gentlemen; the sham of "separate but equal" is all too transparent where the black vote accounts for 33% of the electorate. We cannot have two states in one, just as South Africa will ultimately have to abandon apartheid for the same reason. If we don't give truly equal opportunity to all our citizens, violence that Northern cities are facing today will seep into our own urban areas. It is time to integrate, gentlemen. The only question is how do we do it?"

Bubba spoke up without introduction. "But Mrs. Sally, we should not be forced to integrate!"

Sally quickly responded: "Bubba, I will fight for your right to send your kids to the school of your choice. And, I understand your pitch; it is true that humans of every color, just like animals of any stripe, do not naturally tend to commingle. So, as a practical matter, change is ultimately up to the culture, not the laws ... or the courts."

Bubba's crowd began to clap and started to give Sally a standing ovation, but she quickly held up an angry palm like an old schoolmarm quelling the emotional surge of her ungainly students. "I didn't say that I agreed with you, Bubba," she said bluntly. "Government and laws are the very difference between civilization and animals, because they serve the interest of the greater good."

"But the guv'ment is *making* us build a new school to protect *our* culture," Bubba bellowed.

"No, Bubba, you are making your own choice to disassociate from other citizens of your own country, for your personal beliefs, which is your right. You are electing to become your own isolated minority."

"That's 'cause the minorities are getting better treatment in this country than the majority," he announced, his big face getting red, his fist hammering the table.

Trigger closed his eyes and prayed he would wake up in a new place. He couldn't believe what he was hearing. Sally had managed to piss off White *and* Bubba at *his* invitation, in the same speech. What had he been thinking?

Sally drove home her latest point. "Well, Bubba, the value of being a minority depends on who you talk to. The prejudice against white women like myself in the workforce is visceral. I make about half of what male professors make, and I teach more students by far than they do and publish more books. If we want women to continue to add income to the middleclass we all need, women's rights will also have to change."

Bubba was speechless. What rights did women have?

As if on cue, Flossie tiptoed up behind Sally, wrapped an arm around her shoulder and set a mug of tea on the podium. Sally stopped and gave her a warm hug in return with a silent exchange that exemplified the contradictions of the South in front of everyone and their God. Bubba squirmed uncomfortably as the two women of different races expressed their affection, while White studied the situation, confused by the contradictions of the South. Sally sipped her tea and resumed without a flinch.

"Fortunately, gentlemen, there are always extraordinary individuals from every race who overcame obstacles and made tremendous cultural leaps for society."

Her voice exceeded the low drone of the single window air conditioner, filling the room with history as her audience sat motionless. Sally went on to cite the names of unknown black scholars, scientists, and writers never seen in public history books or recognized by an oblivious white culture. Women and men whose names only a scholar would identify from years of research and interviews. The silent angels and social servants of a minority culture who fought prejudice with their science, intellect, words, and human dignity.

"Despite their racial challenges," she continued, "these remarkable people prevailed to the common good of our state and our country. History says that rare people of this caliber will ultimately prevail in any society," she concluded, "because they are right. These were black men and women who built schools and hospitals, formed insurance companies and colleges, conducted medical research, and went to war for our country. Why should these people be excluded from our history books because of their color?"

Trigger almost wept with relief. She had brought her presentation full circle, from the gates of hell back to the gospel of Sister Sally. Now she had the entire room nodding in agreement.

Bubba Tremblay listened intently with a dismissive smile. He loved Sally, just as he loved all spunky women, even when she was wrong. Sometimes he felt like she was preaching to him because everyone here who mattered any knew he was their leader; he was The Man. He didn't pretend to have much of an attention span, or even the vocabulary to go with it, but then, he never really needed it. People around him had always done what he told them.

Bubba sat silent and respectful as Sally paced the room before he finally intervened. As the most vocal supporter of segregation and the financial cornerstone of the entire Town of Bumkin, he had an obligation to intervene, to be heard. He represented real people, not just a couple of suits from the guv'ment. Any damn fool who read the Good Book knew this day of guv'ment interference against the Chosen was the beginning of the end. And Bubba was damn sure he was one of the Chosen. Why else would the Tremblays own their own church? It was time for the righteous to stand up and be counted. And here was dear, smart Mrs. Sally with all her degrees, agreeing with him. If the blacks had just stayed separated like all those foreigners did in Yankee cities, in the China Towns and the Little Italys, then there wouldn't be any problem, now would there? He didn't see any court orders for them Chinese to invade the public schools. Those people stayed to themselves because that's what made them happy, and it was sure as hell what made Bubba happy.

Sally looked up at the big Coca-Cola wall clock. Every restaurant she ever spoke in had one; there must be a million of them out there, its red second needle relentlessly ticking away in circles against a white clock face, with Coca-Cola branded in red. It was time for her to sum it all up so Levi could make his deadline and she could get home.

"Like it or not, the black culture is a big part of our country. And just like the white culture, it also has a seedy side. Better education is the only hope for both. Unfortunately, integration isn't simply about exchanging virtues, it's also about exchanging sins, and both sides have plenty to share. It would be naïve for us to believe that only the good traits of our two cultures will survive integration. Our best hope for managing the process for the best outcome is to slow it down. It's happening way too fast for educators, students, or parents to plan. The school system isn't doomed because of integration; but our students will be if teaching is politicized. We just need more time to think it through."

Sally stopped to eyeball her audience, letting her silence invite a class of mutes to ask questions, knowing they were hesitant to do so. Trigger breathed deeply and released a deep sigh. It was dicey at first, but in the end, Sally had verbalized the social stalemate that haunted the South, with a black Yankee lawyer and preacher in the backdrop, and what could any of them say? Everyone got the message. Maybe she even educated his new best friend, Mr. White, and maybe White would tell the Powers-that-Be in Washington that there was hope for the South after all … and that Trigger Winchester was the man to make it happen.

In the back of the room, Bubba Tremblay raised his big right hand, revealing the strong sunburned forearms of a working man. Apprehension seized the room.

In the front of the room, Henry just wanted it to be over. A racial slur, or one of those dumbass, offhanded comments that Bubba was famous for was the last thing he wanted to hear. No one ever accused Bubba of being lazy or stupid, he was just "jackass" dumb in that peculiar Southern way that was reserved for landed gentry.

Bubba stood to his full height, holding his baseball cap in hand. His red hair gleamed under the florescent light from a fresh sheen of Brylcreem. His khaki pant cuffs still held the soil from an early walk in the fields to inspect his crops. "Mrs. Sally, you seem to be saying this whole thing is one big damn mistake put upon us by the federal guv'ment." Grunts of consensus followed in unison from his peers; real men in the South hated the federal government. Hell, everyone hated the guv'ment.

Sally's eyes narrowed as she focused on the classroom bully she grew up with a lifetime ago. He wasn't much different in adulthood. She had tried to feel sorry for Bubba in the past, but the truth was she just didn't like the racist S.O.B. back when, and she didn't like him any more today. She had never understood how natural selection hadn't caught up with Bubba yet.

"No, Bubba," she responded calmly, "I didn't say that at all. I said, in a nutshell, that integration is a right and necessary, but the implementation stinks. High schools get more time to put together a football schedule. Throwing everyone together without any preparation only serves to reinforce our fears. Our lack of preparation undermines the value of the entire effort. We need more time." She replied in a respectful manner. Even Neanderthals deserved Southern hospitality.

"But this country don't have no more time, Mrs. Sally," Bubba ranted, oblivious to Sally's point. "That's why we have to save this country ourselves. It's up to people like you an' me. That's how democracy works. Us citizens have to protect ourselves." Bubba knew his way was the American Way. He was sure George Washington would have done the same thing. After all, George owned his own slaves.

Sally actually sympathized that Bubba had a sincere sense of duty, maybe even a genetic sense of divinity, in his misguided way. But she really didn't give a rat's ass about Bubba, his money, or his school. She knew that he would lead an outflow of funding and support that would dilute public school efficacy. Sally could see a deteriorating, divided, and disorganized public school system in the future as clearly as she saw Bubba's swarthy form in front of her.

"Bubba," she said earnestly, "I applaud your right to build another school, and I'm happy that a 'poor cane farmer' wants to ensure the future of our democracy," she offered with thinly veiled sarcasm. "But you and your buddies aren't any more educators than the lawyers who have taken over the school system. It simply won't work. You don't know *how* to teach."

Sally could hear Trigger gagging on her words. She momentarily regretted her reference to lawyers, but screw it, she thought, it wasn't her idea to bring a lawyer to the party. She continued to focus on Bubba. "You and your buddies don't have the time to build a new system any more than the public school system has the time to reinvent itself in three months. In the meantime, we will only deplete the value of education for everyone's children because the legal system didn't have the common sense to integrate in a graduated manner. This is a hundred-year-old problem; it won't get cured in one school year," she concluded.

Ethan White finished his fried chicken and placed his elbows on the table, cupping his chin in his hands while he grit his teeth. He listened closely to the exchange taking place in front of him between an educated white historian who hated lawyers and a southern redneck who hated black people. Prejudice took many forms in the South, he knew, but he didn't expect to find them all in one room, all at once.

"Ah must respectfully disagree with you, Mrs. Sally," Bubba defended himself, his voice getting louder. "There are those of us who feel we have to take a stand now, even at significant personal sacrifice." Everyone needed to know that patriotism was expensive for Bubba.

Sally feigned sympathy. "Bubba, Southerners took a stand against the rest of our country a hundred years ago on this issue ... and we lost." The back of the room inhaled, like their hands had been slapped in school, their heads shaking in disbelief. Everyone knew the Yankees had stacked the deck. Sally cut the conversation short with a curt nod that told Bubba it was time for him to sit down like a good student.

Henry Bordelon contemplated the political fallout of integration in his town as Sally spoke to her peers. Sally was dead on right. At the end of the day, all they needed was more time. Bubba wanted to stop time like a captured memory; Sally just wanted to slow it down so everyone could get on board; the Feds wanted a fast forward to put it behind them.

Integration was a great, high profile issue for a progressive Rotary Club President like Henry to tackle as a springboard into the mayor's race. All he needed now was a progressive Rotary Club. But Henry was a pragmatist; he knew all this bullshit would ultimately be procrastinated right out of existence, in true Southern fashion. Normally, it would take the town leaders only one good game of Bourre down at the Golden Nugget bar, until the morning light of reality would dawn in the recesses of Southern cerebellums. Reaching a consensus was easy, but it would take time, and liquor.

Things just didn't get done quickly in the South, like it must happen up there in Yankee land, Henry thought. This was probably just how the Civil War got started: the Yankees wanting to get things done too damn fast with Southerners that were too damn stubborn to move quickly. What the hell was the judge thinking? Full integration overnight, with no warning? The white flight out of the small town alone would kill its future.

Trigger caught Henry's eye, held up his wristwatch and pointed to it: time to cut the crowd loose. Most of these fellas had been given more to think about in the last hour than they had contemplated in the last decade.

Trigger knew there wasn't any lack of brainpower sitting in the Bay Room. That was one of the great misperceptions of the South. Some of the smartest men that he had ever met were sitting in this room. Wall Street would be lucky to have many of the planters as commodity traders. They might be selectively ignorant, but they were far from dumb. The good news and the bad news was that they were all from Louisiana. To a man they loved their simple life and their state just as it was, and there was little motivation to change. Others should be as lucky.

He had begun to breathe easy, but Trigger was ready to take his gains and leave. Sally got the Big Talk into the open, like no one else could have. It would roll all over town and take some time to sink in.

Just as Henry rose to adjourn the meeting, a deep, new voice sprang from the back of the room. Trigger noticed that the stately Mr. White was standing up to be recognized. Trigger looked nervously at Greely, who shrugged, also surprised. Mr. White's voice held that deep baritone quality that only large black men seemed to produce, but it carried a northern accent that had never before been heard at The Palace. "Dr. Callahan." Mr. White made his audience suspicious with enunciation articulated like he was in a Shakespearean play. His voice was calm and factual. "How can you suggest that the black man give the segregationists more time? The red man gave white men more time and their culture was virtually obliterated."

Sally considered the question. "Mr. White," she tried to put his name in the back of her mind, "are you complaining about segregationists or about white men generally?" she asked earnestly. Gil twitched. Greely smirked. Bubba jerked with anticipation as a new plot unfolded. He knew Sally would bite back, no matter your color.

Sally picked up. "Mr. White, we live in the here and now. There is little else which I, or anyone else, can do about the red man, the westward expansion of the white man, or the enslavement of the black people, over the course of the last two hundred years or so. There is even less that our children can do. All any of us can do is learn from those tough lessons and try to make this a better world going forward. But all of our children, black, white, yellow and red, are going to pay a high price because the educators who know them best, who teach them every day, haven't been given the time to develop *their* plan for twelve years of *education for an integrated audience.* The unintended consequences of our cure can be as bad as the problem we created."

Mr. White was visibly tense. "Come now, Dr. Callahan," he began. Gil shuddered and closed his eyes. Patronizing Sally was like snuggling with a moccasin: the bite would be so fast that the patient would die standing. "The real issue here is that integration could mean that *your* children will suffer for a generation or two while the black man tries to reach equality. You people don't want your children to have to pay the price our children have long paid."

Sally was enraged and mentally tried to count backward. White had just insinuated that she was a bigot! Bubba snickered with an I-told-you-so grin. Trigger leaned forward on the table, head in hands. Greely watched attentively. Henry shook his head. Levi held his pen ready to vigorously memorialize Sally's counterattack for his next article. Mr. White had just walked into their swamp and was now hopelessly up to his ass in alligators.

"The difference between you and me, Mr. White, is that I work in a classroom, and you work in a courtroom. Maybe you could enlighten us on all of your teaching experience in public schools? Your legal system may force change, but it cannot guarantee results. Only educators can do that, and only if they are allowed to do their job. If the court order gave teachers time to transition, it is possible that even folks like Bubba here could be convinced to give the public school system a try rather than diluting our collective effort."

Henry was unsure whether Bubba was going to jump out of his seat to kiss Sally or to accost White. He signaled him with a stern look to stay in his seat. The rest of the crowd were already looking to find a fast exit. Henry jumped up hurriedly to close out the meeting, "Well, Mrs. Sally," Henry interrupted, "We want to thank you for speaking to us today. It's time to adj…"

White's voice overrode Henry's diplomacy as it boomed throughout the room, "So, Dr. Callahan, since your son can get into college early to avoid the effects of integration, don't you think that the public school system should allow black students to do the same thing?"

It was a low and unexpected blow. How did he know? Sally looked at Gil, his face flushing a brilliant red. Then she stared at Greely as he made a quick exit through the back door. She instantly understood. What a snake, Sally thought. Not that it mattered. White had just picked a fight about her kid. He was dog meat.

Sally looked around the crowd of men, half out of their seats, but enamored by the prospect of a face-off between their steel magnolia and a black Yankee lawyer. Reverend Hezekial, the only other black man in the room, sat erect, quietly watching the intensity of the unfolding drama play out from his corner seat.

"Sit down, gentlemen," Sally demanded coolly. "We have more to talk about." The crowd dropped back into their seats, leaving Sally and White standing like two boxers in their opposing corners.

"Mr. White, as you apparently know, my son Burton, who happens to be white," she added with emphasis, "has for some time attended college classes with the consent of the college dean. What would be your concern, Mr. White?"

"Technically, Dr. Callahan, there is nothing wrong with the arrangement, but the high school has to focus its resources on getting fair treatment for all of its students. This is not about your son, Dr. Callahan. This is about resources and policies that favor white children. Principals like Mr. Greely can't take time away from the immediate task of integration just for the benefit of a few students. Besides, let's face it," he said in his best courtroom voice, "this is a privilege that you have been able to obtain for your son. Perhaps you can tell me how black children can get this same opportunity?"

Sally didn't blink. "Send me the students who qualify, and I will help them get the same options, whatever their color, Mr. White," she shot in a blistering response. "But, if your definition of integration means that individuals cannot excel so you and your cronies will define education in your infinite wisdom, Bubba's school is going to do better than I thought." Bubba let out a whoop in the back of the room.

White stood his ground, morally flattened but visibly unfazed, a black icon of authority surrounded in a room filled with white supremacists, two preachers and a mad woman. His mission was to establish black participation as a policy in this godforsaken town. It was the first of many that he would have to deal with. He might as well start now. No one here was ever going to accept him anyway.

"Then I am to believe, Dr. Callahan, that your son is simply a special needs case? Or is this just another opportunity that blacks should be content to wait for, like you want them to wait on integration until the educators can approve their own plan?"

It was a trick question of course. Burton Callahan was indeed a special case. But Sally had her fill of White's manipulation. Two could play that game, and he was in her town. "Mr. White, I just spoke about the remarkable, gifted people that your race produced and who have enriched our entire country. Do you believe for one moment that any of those remarkable people would want a student of any color denied an opportunity because of his color? Is that your answer to integration, to become the racist that you are trying to eliminate by restraining motivated people who aren't black? Or, perhaps you are scared that your new education system will not produce such remarkable people?"

White began to stutter, then Sally belted him again.

"And one last thing, Mr. White. Don't ever accuse me of being racist. I have done more for the black cause in this region than you and your buddies in Boston will ever accomplish. In my childhood, white women weren't any better educated than black women. Women in general had no labor value on a plantation. My father was as poor as you have ever been, he died penniless because he sold his farm to put seven girls through college, all of whom are public school teachers. I've lost as many jobs to white men from discrimination as any black person you can name. So, understand this, Mr. White, being black doesn't give you a monopoly as the target of prejudice any more than Yankees have a monopoly on education."

The moan of the air conditioner once again filled the quiet room. The chill inside the room belied the raging heat outside. White stood speechless amid an audience of good old boys who watched him squirm in silent delight. Trigger grabbed White by the arm and pulled him toward the outside door. Sally used the awkward silence to thank her audience with a chuckle. "You can go home now boys, class is over."

Bubba swaggered out with obvious delight. He pulled on his LSU baseball cap with a big smile. "Boy howdy, this here's the best show we've had in this town since that New Orleans stripper's car broke down," he broadcast with glee. On the other side of the room the Reverend Hezekial Allen sat in silent contemplation of the opportunity that the Almighty had just delivered to him. Levi Epstein was already out the door, headed for his typewriter.

Chapter Eight
Purgatory

Greely burst into the Principal's offices with a sour face and quickly poured a cup of coffee.

"How did Rotary go?" Lucery Butts asked.

"I'd say Sally Callahan embarrassed the black guy from Boston, big time. He called her out about getting privileges for that son of hers and she called him out as a lawyer trying to tell everyone what to do without knowing his ass from a hole in the ground. She won but he ain't about to let it go. What's new since I left?"

"I've kept my door shut," Lucery said tartly. "You are going to have to regain control over the halls, there is a constant ruckus."

"Any fights?"

"The coach scared them off, but I am still scared."

"Keep your door locked and don't tell anyone I'm back," Greely said. He walked into his office and slammed the door shut.

Lucery got up and locked the door for the third time since the morning bell. They were like an invading force that had surrounded her private space. Her first week of school felt like a month of imprisonment.

Marge Bordelon's call from Trigger's office had only confirmed what Lucery had already figured out. It was a conspiracy. There was no other answer. Why else would that liberal Superintendent Winchester allow a black Yankee to join the Bumkin Rotary Club meeting? A Yankee lawyer, of all things! It would be like her, a born-again Baptist, going to a Catholic mass. Principal Greely was shocked but there was nothing to be done. She knew Marge's cousin, Henry Bordelon, the new President of Rotary, didn't have the guts to kick the black lawyer out of the meeting. Hell, Henry would try to sell him insurance first.

She patted her puffy cheeks with both palms to wake herself up, then sank down on her inflated seat cushion, doing her best to contain her panic attacks. What business did a black lawyer have coming to Bumkin? Hadn't they done enough damage? When would it end?

Thank God the end of the First Week from Hell was almost over. She needed more caffeine to keep her alert. She wrapped her pudgy hands around her Fatty's Barber Shop fiftieth anniversary coffee mug. There were only two hundred of them ever produced. Her scarlet red fingernails tapped nervously against the thick ceramic cup, as she contemplated her future. She couldn't accept that she had been cast down among the devils and misfits of society and into the Pits of Purgatory for no reason. On second thought it couldn't be Purgatory; that was for Catholics. Real Christians like Southern Baptists got to skip that part. The Catholics had to pay the price for being liberal. Everyone knew real Christians didn't dance, or drink alcohol. The Catholics needed to throw out those Italians that ran their church.

Of course, she conceded, it wasn't like she wasn't being paid well during her penance on earth. She was now the Senior Support Assistant to the Office of the Principal of Bumkin High School, a title so impressive it required two nameplates end-to-end on the front of her desk. She had risen quickly from a nameless assistant when the Integration Order came down. No one else wanted the job of course, but her new position came with a three thousand dollar raise that was a decent bribe, so she wouldn't take early retirement in the middle of the big transition. All in all, it was bearable, but she was miserable. At least she was better paid; miserable, but better paid, miserably. She made no secret about her misery, of course; she even knew the students had started calling her "Mizery" Butts.

Greely was a tough, Christian soldier, but the man couldn't find his ass with both hands if she wasn't there to help him, which was probably best for everyone. He reminded her of Grand Daddy Butts. He would ride off on his horse ready to kick ass so his boys could keep the white race pure; meanwhile her grandmother ironed those pointy sheets of his. Now there was a man. He demanded respect, and respected tradition. He was proud to be a Captain in the Invisible Army, the Knights of the Ku Klux Klan. She remembered him telling her that mixing races wasn't natural. It would lead to another civil war. And here it was, happening right in front of her, just like Grand Daddy said.

Southern manners had been obliterated by black language. There was no respect for elders or authority. The blacks even wanted to have their own kind of English, if that's what it was. She couldn't understand a word they said, much less tell them apart.

It had taken a hundred years since the War of Northern Aggression for smart people like Grand Daddy to establish a natural order of segregation where everyone knew which side of the tracks they stayed on. All of a sudden it was illegal, without warning, without rifle shots, without gossip. No nothing. It made no sense. A judge and a bunch of Yankees were just taking over, making new laws. Even so, the KKK was still legal, still free to meet at Curl's barn on Wednesday nights, right after Church dinner. They still marched in the streets of Big Prairie in full sheets to protect their rights. They still burned those big crosses at the cemetery on their weekend rallies. Her Daddy and brothers still attended the secret meetings that women and kids weren't supposed to know about, playing war with the Grand Wizard in the Piney Woods, or whatever they did to prepare for the End Times.

If the KKK was still legal, how could segregation be illegal? Had her cousin Billy Paul paid the supreme price fighting Communists in Vietnam last year just so the country could integrate? Billy Paul was turning over in his grave. He would never let her rest. Thank God she had found a stone mason to preserve his legacy with a Rebel Flag etched into his headstone. It was the least she could do to let him know it was all going to work out.

Mizery downed two pills with a swig of coffee to calm her nerves. She needed time to think. Everything was happening too fast. Her Daddy had told her that the KKK had gone "Corporate" after Grand Daddy had died. He joked that David Duke had brought them out of the closet, just like all those queers in California called it. Not that the KKK had any queers in its closet, of course. But if the queers could open their closet, so could the KKK.

Mizery rose to check her door lock as another ruckus erupted among a gaggle of boys in the hallway. She leaned against the doorway in a cold sweat, pressing her head against the frame, her pulse pounding furiously. The clock on the wall told her she was just forty-five minutes into a long school day. She couldn't live this way. She wasn't safe. No one was. The black gangs were aggressive, taking greater chances all the time. And those girls? Their sexual language embarrassed Mizery in ways she could never explain, even to Reverend Carl. Babies without fathers were more common than ever. She shuddered at the thought.

Her Grand Daddy would never tolerate such unchristian activity. She knew he and his boys had even delivered local justice on bad white men who treated their own women wrong. He kicked them out of the Klan and made them an example, just like they weren't no better than the blacks. The Klan was still the only way for common folks to get justice.

She took heart knowing the Invisible Army were still out there. They would protect White People or die trying. Now was their time to save the day. The streets weren't safe for women of means like herself to even go to work anymore. There were still regular Saturday night brawls and killings at the honky-tonks across the tracks. In the good old days, it didn't matter, but now those characters were coming across the tracks. Students talked about marijuana, drugs, and guns openly at school now. They even sang about it!

There weren't no telling how many black whorehouses were still out there. Well, maybe not, she caught herself. As much as those people liked to screw, they probably didn't need established places like white folks. Down deep she sometimes worried when she found Wilber laid out on the couch after one of his all-night poker games, a smile plastered on his silly face like she hadn't seen in years. She didn't trust Wilber when he smiled, but at least she knew he was only drinking with a white crowd. She knew The Spot would never integrate; the Sheriff would never allow it.

She took her seat back at her desk, and asked herself quietly, "What would Grand Daddy do?" An epiphany struck her like a lightning bolt sent from Heaven above. Praise the Lord! The Holy Spirit invaded her mind and set her at peace. The pills had probably helped some. It didn't matter. She instantly knew what she had to do.

Mizery steadied herself in her chair with one hand as she leaned to one side, gripping her white vinyl handbag with sequined yellow daisies that lay at her feet. She clung to the edge of the desk and used her other hand to dig deep down into a secret compartment, plucking out the frayed business card Grand Daddy had entrusted to her before he passed into the Kingdom of God. She put on her reading glasses and held the yellowed, dingy card up at a distance, bringing it closer until the blurry text came into focus. She read it slowly to herself in a whisper:

Need Help? Call 1-800-IMWHITE.

She could feel Grand Daddy right there beside her, smiling, as she picked up the phone. She had to do something.

Chapter Nine
Magnolia

Magnolia Williams sat in padded silence in the plush back seat of the New Yorker Town Car as it glided back to the white side of town. She watched the landscape change from shanty town rentals to sprawling new urban homes, from brown and gray decayed wood to pastel porticos and prim gardens less than two miles away. The big Lincoln rumbled over the railroad tracks that tied two worlds together, or kept them apart, depending upon one's station in life. Maggie toyed nervously with the shiny pendant she wore for her birthday, trying not to attract attention.

Beverly Dillard sat rigidly behind the wheel of the big car, spewing an endless trail of gossip about her husband and their neighbors as she drove "Maggie" to work. It was a normal beginning to a long day of domestic work for Maggie. She stared enviously at the Italian silk scarf Beverly wore, wishing she could touch it, but she took solace that the best of clothes could never conceal the despicable woman who drove her to work each morning in a toxic cloud of lies and cigarette smoke. A woman with no breasts, skinny legs and no ass; a woman no black man would tolerate. A mouth like hers would starve across the tracks.

But Beverly did in fact pay her workers more than anyone else in town, and for good reason, Maggie had come to learn. The bitch had to bribe her employees and friends, even her Pastor, to put up with her. Maggie knew damn well Beverly chose her to parade around her parties and prayer luncheons because of her light skin. She made her dress like a white girl for business meetings, playing the role of black maid so she could act like a progressive socialite for the wives of the local aristocracy. The act didn't fool Maggie; Beverly would do anything for attention. And so, Maggie played her deftly, patronizing Beverly as her mentor around her white peers who slipped her handsome tips. They could only wish they had their own little "black girl."

Maggie remembered Reverend Hezekial consoling her to feel sorry for the wealthy, white woman who was so insecure that she had to pay for attention. He said churches got built by the guilt of people like Beverly. But Maggie could find no sorrow for the bitch. She was far more empathetic to her husband, Mr. Tom, the kind attorney whose oil money Beverly spent recklessly while he returned home dutifully every evening with a loving embrace for his wife. It made Maggie cringe. Tom still thought Beverly cooked all those home-made meals she left on the stove everyday with the corn bread he loved. Maggie prayed Tom would find a hot black mistress across the tracks who really knew how to treat a man right.

Beverly's shrill voice interrupted the hushed silence of the ride. "You were late again, Magnolia! I waited on that street for five minutes. No telling what could have happened to me in that neighborhood of yours."

"Yes, ma'am," Maggie replied, trying to hide her feelings against Beverly. She was sure her disdain was pure and without racial prejudice, although there was no doubt that Beverly was easier to hate for being hypocritical, white, and rich. She didn't outright claim a genetic superiority like some of her friends. Beverly was just a social predator, a woman who consumed Maggie's innocence for her own purposes, like a cat playing with its prey before the kill, leaving her carcass on display so other predators could admire her catch. Maggie knew Beverly expected her to remain her hostage until her children grew up. But she had her own plans. And long after her escape from Bumkin, Beverly would still be an ugly, white bitch with no ass, stuck in the outback of Louisiana.

Maggie rushed into the house as soon as the big car came to a halt and worked non-stop for the next eight hours to avoid any unnecessary contact with Beverly. She sorted the laundry, ironed Tom's white shirts, washed the dishes, waxed the kitchen floor, and cleaned the bathrooms. Then she started dinner on time for Tom's return. When Maggie finished, Beverly was asleep on her chaise, her claim to having slaved over a hot stove for her husband's favorite meal safe for another day.

Maggie was creeping out the door, headed for her weekly tea with Mrs. Sally Callahan and her own sister, Lee Esther, when the big hall clock sounded five chimes. Her fondness for Sally was an unspoken, sore subject with Beverly, who was always competing with Mrs. Sally, as if Mrs. Sally cared a whit about Beverly.

Suddenly Maggie remembered that Bam Callahan was visiting with Clyde, Beverly's oldest son. Maggie wanted to be long gone before Beverly woke up, but she didn't like leaving the two boys unattended. Not those boys. She crept down the long hallway with its thick Persian carpet and knocked on Clyde's door. "You guys all right?"

"Sure, Maggie," Clyde chirped.

"I'm leaving. Bam, I'm going to your house to see Mrs. Sally. You need to head home."

"Yep. Tell Mom I'll be right behind you, Maggie," Bam responded through the door.

Maggie caught a brief acrid smell in the air and hesitated for a moment. "You boys better get rid of that smell before Mrs. Beverly wakes up," she whispered.

"We're cleaning up now," Clyde assured her.

Maggie cut through Beverly's garden, casting all thoughts of her aside so she could enjoy a quiet walk through the manicured lawns and trimmed sidewalks. She loved walking under the venerable oaks along the bayou and fragile crepe myrtles that lined the boulevard.

At the end of the bayou, she fell in line with a parade of older black women who appeared on the street shortly after the five o'clock church bell rang at St. Rita's school. A chorus of black gospel voices followed them like a scene out of a Southern Mary Poppins movie. Cushy car rides were only available to domestic workers in the morning hours; the return trip was by foot.

Sometimes Maggie would attempt to catch gossip from the white side of town through her older peers but today it didn't matter. Mrs. Sally had convinced Maggie that she could forge a better life somewhere else just as her children had. She even helped Maggie apply for a part-time bookkeeper position at Reverend Hezekial's church. Lord knows that man needed someone to take care of his money, or the church's money. At times it was hard to tell who it belonged to.

Of course, Maggie had never expected her new job to turn into a passionate affair. Her cheeks flushed as Hezekial's image entered her mind … his body arched on top of her at the peak of their passion, his strong shoulders dripping with sweat. He was a powerful man. Women on both sides of the tracks looked for that kind of man. He could talk the talk and walk the walk with young and old alike. Her mother and grandmother idolized his ability to soothe their lives with unshakeable faith. The words of Reverend Hezekial Allen were all they had to hold onto in a world of raw strife. Not even Mrs. Sally could truly understand the importance of a black preacher to his flock.

It worried her that he was married, but Maggie was nonetheless proud that Hezekial was not part of the long history of male trash her sisters had bed. There just weren't enough men like him to go around. What was she to do? Hezekial was one of a kind on her side of the tracks; he had real cash money in his pocket that grew with every sermon. He owned his own church and rented it to the congregation, along with a late model Cadillac befitting a man of the cloth.

Maggie closed her eyes to recapture the feel of them fitting together, so unexpected, and so welcome. She wondered what the other housemaids would think if they found out "Hezzy" had become hers? She knew it was only a matter of time before he left for his "greater calling" and took Maggie with him to a better place. She wondered if his wife and three children would come along? It would only be fair, she reasoned, they deserved a better life too. Maggie was far from a selfish person.

Back at Beverly's house, Clyde and Bam worked feverishly to remove any trace of their activity. Beverly would wake up any minute. Bam mopped the floor stringently while Clyde wiped his desk with furniture polish to pick up any stray particles, then sprayed air freshener all over the room.

"Smells better, don't it?" Clyde asked triumphantly.

"Yeah, now it smells like gunpowder with lemons."

At least the powder spills had been scrubbed clean. The boys had resolved to get rid of their gunpowder mixtures after Bam got busted for his hydrogen experiment. His visit with the Judge scared the hell out of them both. Who knew this chemistry shit really worked? But their gunpowder had not enjoyed the success of the hydrogen production. They had the formula right, but they couldn't get it to combust, it just fizzled like a bad firecracker.

They had conducted their trials in the woods at the edge of town, but now it was time to clean house, literally.

"What do we do now?" Bam asked Clyde.

The older boy pointed across the street. Smoke billowed from piles of burning sycamore and cottonwood leaves as boulevard residents raked grassy yards covered with mounds of brown and gold autumn leaves. "Perfect timing!" Clyde grinned. "See all those trash piles burning? Nobody will notice the extra flames."

Bam nodded. They could dispose of the evidence on his way home. The trash piles were high enough to cover the flames and distributing their inventory in random trash piles made sense.

Six blocks ahead of them, Maggie bid good-bye to her friends as the boulevard merged into a single lane lined with modest, wood frame homes. Mrs. Sally had told her once that the intersection marked the transition of Bumkin from a turn-of-the-century railroad stop to a twentieth century town as clearly as trunk rings told the age of an oak tree. At the very intersection of the old and the new stood Sally Callahan's home.

Maggie stooped down to smell Sally's pink roses as she stepped into the front entrance, unconsciously grasping the chain she had inherited from her mother, Roberta, as it hung loose over her neck. It gave Maggie comfort that Roberta had walked the same path to Sally's door, undoubtedly admiring the same roses. Roberta had grown up with Sally Leland on the Leland farm, once part of the old Walnut Grove Plantation, but her good luck had ended there. Sally moved on to college. Roberta just kept giving birth to girls, each one from a different father. Six girls in all, not counting the one she had lost, all with their own individual skin colors.

Maggie's light skin was not unusual, but Beverly had taught her how to use her lighter color to her benefit in a perverse sort of way that distanced her from her family. She had seen first-hand how icily Beverly had dismissed Maggie's darker sisters, as though dark meant they were ignorant or cursed by Beverly's God. Hezekial had taught her better. Maggie wished for Beverly's damnation even as she asked for forgiveness from the God that resided across the tracks.

The "Grandmother" clock sitting on Sally's cedar mantle welcomed her with a single soft stroke at half past the hour. The modest cottage was a nondescript, simple house of white painted pine siding and red shutters, but the inside was pure Mrs. Sally, lined by books and antiques that led to a central kitchen where textbooks transitioned into cookbooks and a massive stove that was always producing good food. Maggie walked slowly, taking time to look at things she had never noticed before. She followed the household hubbub to a hand-hewn kitchen table made from cypress planks taken out of the old Leland barn, where Mrs. Sally grew up.

"Hey, chile!" Lee Esther's high-pitched voice resonated from the kitchen sink as her flowered apron caught the slosh from her dishwater. Maggie's eldest sister was as large as Maggie was small, and as dark as Maggie was light. She wiped her soapy hands on her backside, which would have done a linebacker proud, then grabbed her little sister with both arms, "Now you come give your Big Sister a hug." Maggie hugged the only real mother she had ever known. Lee Esther pushed her back and quickly focused her owl eye to the pendant around her neck.

"I get to wear it for my birthday," Maggie defended herself, holding onto the unique talisman Roberta had left her.

"Not till you leave home," Lee Esther said firmly. "And if you've got a lick of sense, you won't be thinking about leaving too soon. I just don't want to hear you scream when you lose it."

"Now, Lee, leave that pretty girl alone. Pretty girls need jewelry," Sally scolded Lee Esther in jest as she breezed in, tossing a history book on the kitchen table. She immediately poured hot water into their waiting teacups, as was their ritual. "Maggie, what was so important you couldn't have tea with us last week?" she asked.

"Church work," Maggie smiled, trying not to think about the special attention she had received from Reverend Hezekial.

"And how is the good Reverend?" Sally asked.

Maggie tensed, then changed the subject. "He said you gave all them men a real lesson the other day, Mrs. Sally."

"I'm glad someone was listening," Sally demurred, herself wishing to change the subject. The newspaper article would be out soon enough.

"How was life with Mrs. Dillard today?" Sally asked with a sympathetic smile.

"Aw, Mrs. Sally, you know better than to ask me about that woman! She is bad to the bone. There's nuthin' she does that I want any part of."

"Hasn't it gotten any better?" Sally asked hopefully.

"She treats me better in front of other white people now, especially when she has those church ladies over. But nobody asks about me. I try hard not to puke when I'm serving them coffee."

"She still makes you serve coffee, knowing you're allergic to it?" Lee Esther fumed.

Sally raised an eyebrow. She had her own thoughts about Beverly, but she had more important things to worry about. She sat at her tableside rocker with her tea in hand. "Clyde does seem to be a good boy, and he's very smart," she said. "He and Bam have become good friends, don't you think, Maggie?"

"I think Clyde is a good boy with too much time on his hands. He's a little crazy! They going to get in trouble if they keep working with those chemicals, Mrs. Sally. And Clyde needs to quit smokin'."

Sally held her expression despite her rising blood pressure, stirring her tea as she considered Maggie's statement. There was no better way to gather intelligence on her own children than in her own kitchen. Sally was a protector of the black community and they protected her and her children. She had a set of eyes in every home in town when she needed them.

"And what chemicals might that be?" Sally asked calmly, her voice slightly edgy. Be careful what you ask for, she reminded herself.

"I don't know, Mrs. Sally, but I heard them talking about gunpowder."

"Dammit!" Sally whispered between grit teeth. "Where in the hell would Bam get his hands on gunpowder?" Sally immediately raised a palm up in surrender. "I know, I know, it's a dumb question. Where in the hell would Bam get his hands on anything?" Sally rose to her five-foot height and marched over to the black wall phone, her fluffy pink slippers flopping against the brick floor. As she dialed the Dillard's phone number, Lee Esther scowled at Maggie for volunteering too much information. Frustrated by no answer, Sally sat back down to her tea. "Too late," she said. "I hope he doesn't kill someone this time."

"Don't worry, Mrs. Sally. They just bein' boys. They be alright," Lee Esther patted Mrs. Sally's arm with an earthy calmness only she could provide.

"I didn't know Clyde smoked cigarettes, Maggie," Sally attempted to resume the conversation.

"Cigarettes? No, Mrs. Sally, I'm talking *smokin'*. You know what I mean … he *smokes*." Maggie pinched her thumb and forefinger together and began blowing an imaginary puff from a marijuana joint into the kitchen air. She stopped suddenly, embarrassed that she was far too convincing to be innocent.

It finally hit Sally. "Ohhh," she said softly with a nod.

"I mean he smokes grass! Not them bad-ass drugs, Mrs. Sally, just grass." She giggled, proud to teach the teacher, without admitting guilt.

"You mean marijuana," Sally said, trying not to sound totally removed from common street knowledge. The motion of her rocker increased as she contemplated the consequences. "So, … how does Clyde get 'grass,' Maggie?"

"Oh, Mrs. Sally," Maggie playfully held Sally's hand, her large brown eyes twinkling. "You can buy weed anywhere in town! But Clyde's smart. He's got a patch of marijuana weed growin' right with the sunflowers in Beverly's own garden. He got his mother's green thumb, you know."

"What?" Sally abruptly stopped rocking. However much she disliked Beverly Dillard, she was in fact the best gardener in town, deservedly the "Garden of the Month" winner for years. Sally suddenly remembered Clyde working in the garden diligently over the last weeks. "Let me understand, Maggie," Sally clarified. "You mean to tell me that there is a marijuana plant growing in the Garden of the Month?"

Maggie's dark eyes widened like a child no longer able to hold onto a big, fun secret. "Right out in front of God and all those Garden Church Ladies!" They all burst out laughing. "Now, Mrs. Sally, you can't be telling' anyone you knows this!"

"Does Beverly know?" Sally asked.

"That crazy woman thinks they be poppies from South Africa."

"Clyde told her they were a new kind of flower that needed extra time to bloom. She's real proud to be the first one to plant them. Clyde even gave his plant a name so Beverly could brag on it - *Distractus Cannabis.*"

Sally took off her glasses to wipe away tears from laughter. She could imagine a gaggle of Bumkin's finest gardeners, bent over the Garden of the Month in their fine sundresses, admiring a marijuana plant! Maggie had made her day.

Lee Esther was the first to get serious. "Now, Magnolia Williams! Don't you get caught in the middle of no marijuana mess with them white Baptists! They do weird shit!" She stumbled on her words, then added, "Excuse me, Mrs. Sally."

Sally ignored the slip. She knew Lee Esther had a legitimate concern. "Now Maggie, tell me the truth, is Bam fooling around with that stuff?"

"No ma'am, Mrs. Sally." Maggie knew Bam would never do drugs. He had suffered from asthma as a kid. He hated hospitals, and drugs. But Sally knew Maggie would never rat on him. They had grown up together, a few short years apart, tied together by tradition, and history. Bam was as close to a brother as Maggie would ever have.

Just two blocks away Bam and Clyde moseyed down the boulevard, passing by the first burn pile as workers piled up cottonwood leaves. Clyde tossed the first gunpowder package into the small pile of burning leaves nonchalantly. The blue signature flames soon hissed like a big sparkler, no different from the last one, spreading noxious sulfur dioxide that quickly filled the air behind them. The boys walked ahead faster, never looking back.

"Same old problem," Bam shrugged. Clyde nodded sympathetically as they slogged forward and came up on another burn pile just up the block. Another toss. Once again, a blue plume spat out, this time belching forth sparkly cinders that scorched the boys' nostrils, with a thick blue plume that hovered close to the ground, smelling up the entire boulevard. Children quickly ran inside, pinching their noses and screaming for their parents. The boys ran before any adults came out of the houses.

"Anticlimactic," conceded Bam with disappointment. "I really thought we would get at least a pop out of that one."

"Me too," Clyde said. "I'm bummed."

The boys rounded the corner near Bam's house just as the setting sun was turning the horizon a dark crimson. Bored, Clyde eyed his wristwatch. "I've got to get back home before Mom freaks out," he said, tossing the last billet to Bam. "Why don't you get rid of the last one? Maybe we can figure out the right formula after the heat dies down."

"See ya," Bam nodded, and waved his friend off, looking about for a burning pile. Turning the corner near his home, he saw it in front of him: Sheriff Franklin's barrel. The Sheriff's trash bins stood out brazenly for its meticulous workmanship among lesser receptacles of trash can mediocrity. The Sheriff's personal trash barrel was designed and constructed by the town's engineers and machined to perfection at the expense of taxpayers. It had earned a photo in the *Bumkin Record* as the epitome of extravagance to the chagrin of the neighbors, whose rusted barrels now stood out like as many sore thumbs. A small fire still burned as the last clump of trash was efficiently reduced to ashes in the Sheriff's trash bin.

The Sheriff's patrol car was nowhere to be seen, his new truck parked nearby, a sure sign he was gone. Bam lobbed the remaining billet over his shoulder as he passed it. He could hear it clang against the bottom of the barrel just as he caught a whiff of Lee Esther's cornbread. Bam threw open the screen door, greeting Lee Esther and Maggie as he walked over to kiss his mother hello.

The shockwave shook the house like a sonic boom from the air force training jets at nearby England Air Force Base. Bam froze and quickly looked around with an allure of excitement. "What was that?" he asked with anticipation.

Lee Esther stood transfixed at the kitchen sink, watching out the window with her hands immersed in dishwater, her mouth wide open. "My oh my," she exclaimed as Maggie and Bam ran to her side. Two hundred feet away the Sheriff's barrel was skyrocketing upward, into its perigee. It rotated, as it seemed to levitate in slow motion, then plummeted back to earth.

Bam, Maggie and Lee Esther stood silent, breathing a sigh of relief as the barrel barely missed the Sheriff's pick-up truck. Bam exhaled at his good fortune, then the sound of bent metal hit the pavement, followed by the sound of shrapnel, like a rifle shot echoed by the sound of shattered glass. The rear window of the Sheriff's truck imploded into a thousand pieces.

Sally walked up behind Bam, pulling his head down so she could sniff his shirt. The pungent scent of gunpowder was not to be mistaken. Maggie held both hands to her cheeks in disbelief. Bam blinked and smiled shyly, his brain processing the unexpected success as he fought mightily to stifle the wrong response. "The biscuits smell great, Mom. Let's eat."

Chapter Ten
The Lodge

Foster propped his alligator boots on the pine railing of the outdoor deck at The Spot, the only fixed structure built to overlook the ancient Atchafalaya Swamp. He leaned back in a wicker chair and swigged his beer, careful not to stain his white starched shirt. He let a blue heron entertain him on a cypress stump just a few yards away. The elegant bird raised one regal foot in slow motion, then the other, striking a small bass silently with a lightning jab of its long bill without disturbing the silky black water of the basin.

Nearby he could see Meadow pace the interior of the bar with nervous energy. She sulked around in a Rolling Stones sweatshirt that had Jagger's famous rock 'n roll red tongue positioned just over a red G-String. She was definitely the new queen of the swamp. She knew he was waiting. It was time they talked. Things were moving fast now, almost too fast, for reasons he did not yet understand. He signaled Old Elton to bring him another beer and waited patiently under the shade of the old cypress tree.

Half-a-beer later, the rustic lounge was filled with a dozen local customers watching the LSU football game with a bevy of half-naked women. Meadow made a show of working the crowd while the other girls played along, but Foster could sense their resentment. She was an unqualified success at her new job, and younger than many of her peers.

Foster's upgrades to The Spot had gained him a newfound respect. His new "talent" received accolades from his father's peers, some of the most powerful people in the state. And Foster's meticulous attention to order and aesthetics were boosting The Spot's reputation.

It was common knowledge that Foster enjoyed cleaning out the old clientele with a heavy hand. The Spot was becoming a southern gentleman's hangout that appealed to better customers. His father, never a man to extend praise lightly, even commended him for staying professional and keeping his distance from the girls. Hiring the mulatto had been a real bonanza. She was a novelty who held a special attraction for Bubba, their most important customer. Word got around and business was pouring in.

Foster signaled Meadow to join him, knowing full well that she loved upstaging his authority in front of the other girls. Finally, she bounded over. "You lookin' for me?"

"No. You're looking for me," Foster said coolly, impervious to the show of long legs and a bare midriff.

"Ya think?" she shot back.

"Wouldn't surprise me in the least," he said.

Meadow dropped into the big chair next to Foster, waiting for his questions. Foster could feel his acrimony receding once Meadow gave him her undivided attention. They had become friends of an odd sort, comrades in a common pursuit who recognized each other's irreplaceable talents—and limitations. There was no doubt they needed each other.

"Fill me in," Foster asked in a subdued voice. "Think you can get it?"

"I can get anything," she said coolly. "Quincy is in love with me. He wants to elope."

Foster squelched his initial shock. Bubba would love that twist, he thought. Or would he?

Meadow drew down deeply on her cigarette. "I'm thinking about having a justice of the peace tie the knot. I'm sure your Daddy owns one or two."

"There is one we could depend upon," Foster asserted, sensing a subtle power shift in their conversation. Married to Quinine, Meadow could wrest control to half of the oil property that Dynasty Oil had been syphoning off for decades. Spouses were hard to get rid of under the arcane Napoleonic Code which governed the laws of Louisiana. He could end up on the outside looking in. He would have to be careful. "I'll set it up. Bubba wants his hands on that deed."

Meadow sipped her drink. "Fuck Bubba. Tell him he better come up with a better price. Fast."

Foster grabbed her forearm and pulled her onto the floor in one quick motion. Her head hit with a thud between his feet as he looked her sternly in the eye. "You and Bubba are getting along pretty well, just like you and Quinine. He's practically living out here with you. Don't screw this up. You'll come out fine if you stick to the rules."

"Don't give me that shit, Foster. We both know you only gave me half of the story." Her voice was suddenly angry. "Bubba ain't never done me no favors. He's a slob. I hate him. He deserves what it costs him."

Foster dismissed her outburst for the ploy it was. "Listen to me," he said sternly. "Don't attempt to negotiate with Bubba. You will fail miserably." He knew she was baiting him. Her special gift was extracting whatever she wanted from men of any kind, shape, or color. He also knew it was only a matter of time before she figured everything out, assuming his original gamble had been correct. "Stick to our deal - understood?"

"I'll deliver, but we both know this can't be a happy ending for Quinine. His land is worth millions and Bubba ain't gonna get it without my help. I need more than a hundred thousand for my piece of this action. I've got to put a lot of distance between me, Bubba, and Quinine."

Foster released her arm with a show of force he knew inflicted pain. "That may be harder than you know, but you are right about the property," he conceded, to put her at ease. He pulled her off the floor. She did not yet appreciate the leverage he held on anyone who got in his way. But now was not the time to exert it. The stakes were too high; he couldn't risk her bolting in a new direction to prove her independence.

"Bubba lied to me about the value of Quinine's oil. I wasn't out to disadvantage you. But a lot has changed with this integration shit going on. Someone bombed the Sheriff's house and Bubba thinks we are about to be in a war zone."

"So what,' Whitey?" she snapped, her voice rising over the din of the party, drawing stares. "That just means he needs me more than ever." She pushed Foster back into his seat and leaned over him, pretending that he was a playful customer, as she whispered. "I might be better off keeping my man Quinine *and* the property, if you know what I mean. The new price is a million dollars, or you can find someone else to do your dirty work with Bubba and Quinine."

Foster didn't blink. He slowly slid his hand around the back of her neck, grabbing a lock of hair, and pulled her to his face with a quick, painful jerk. "We will split whatever we end up with because we will both have to leave town. This game is far from over and any one of your girlfriends over there will be glad to take your position if you don't like it. Play your cards right and you might make more than a million. Play it wrong and Quinine might not be the only one making an early exit. Either way, that's my decision. Don't make me replace you, Meadow." His icy voice got her attention.

Meadow looked into his steely eyes. There was something different about him, something vulnerable. "How come you never told me Bubba and Quincy were related?" Meadow blurted out.

"Seemed irrelevant," Foster lied.

"Irrelevant to you, shithead," she whispered in his ear as she hugged him to keep the farce up. "I'm taking all the risk screwing Bubba and his black cop cousin. But you're just as scared of Bubba Tremblay as all these other assholes in town, and don't think I don't know it."

Foster played his role and hugged her closely. "You need me to cover that fine ass of yours," he explained calmly, almost apologetically. "We are both in too deep. One screw up and Bubba will kill us both. Shut up and listen to me. It's us against him. Get the deed and everything else follows."

Meadow said nothing while she straightened her sweatshirt and dragged on her cigarette.

"That's better," he said. "We have a deal. Like it or not, we need each other. I don't know why Bubba's in a sudden rush to get his hands on the deed. But I know he's more vicious and powerful than you or I will ever be. All that matters now is that his timeline is working to our advantage."

Meadow stared back at him until his silence forced an explanation. "Bubba's taking me to his cottage this weekend. It's a big deal. I can find out what we need to know."

"Good girl. And I'll get you that Justice of the Peace lined up for next week. 'Mrs. Quinine' should be able to get her hands on the original paperwork, no sweat. Find out where he's hiding the deed. It's probably somewhere in his dump."

"I already know," she interjected to prove her value. "It's in a lockbox at Bubba's bank. A black preacher knows the contents and holds the only other key… so far." She winked at Foster with a wicked smile.

"How hard will it be to get it?"

"It doesn't matter. I'm going to do whatever it takes. So, I guess you better protect me if you want your share." The slim vixen rose up over him and bent down, planting a long, wet kiss on Foster's lips, her breasts exposed under a sagging neckline as the local boys watched with envy. "I guess we're in this together," she whispered her concession.

"We are now."

Chapter Eleven
Early Departure

Across the railroad tracks Quincy finished boxing the last of his meager items. He twisted the top off his remaining bottle of Quinine and flopped down on his favorite leather armchair. His only armchair. The cracks in the leather outlined his body like a ghost that occupied the upholstery. Sweat from the toils of the day saturated his T-shirt and sank into the dry leather. So what? He was leaving it all behind.

Quinine looked around the austere "shotgun" house he had occupied all his life, now scrubbed down to its bare essence. He cleaned it up for the last time. Today was a test of his newfound commitment to do the unthinkable. He was leaving, not knowing where he was going, with a woman he really didn't know. He was finally breaking the chains of his past.

His little residence was sparse in the best of times. Now, in the glimmer of daylight streaming through the plank walls, it was virtually naked. The few items he had accumulated over a blue-collar lifetime were packed in four small boxes, sealed with duct tape, and stacked neatly by the back door. Quincy leaned into the familiarity of his leather chair and closed his eyes, hoping to catch any cool breeze that might find its way through the cottonwood grove out back.

A fleeting thought made him smile. His next house would surely be air conditioned if Meadow had any say in the matter, which he knew she would.

They would depart after his last pickup at The Spot so they could put as much road behind them as possible before his absence was missed. It was his nature to be prepared, especially given the risk he was taking. Strangely, he didn't feel the fear he expected, only the anticipation. Walking out of his old life didn't bother him in the least, as long as he could land far away with Meadow. He was like a spirit escaping its coffin, giddy at the prospect of a real life, with a real woman. Quinine would never take such a risk. Quincy couldn't wait.

Quincy took a final walk through the cabin, amazed at how little space he had occupied, and how little it mattered to him now. Just the thought of making a commitment to himself, let alone to another person, made him alive and spontaneous. Leaving the protection of four barren walls and a policeman's uniform gave him an intoxicating sense of freedom. He would never come back.

Quincy bounded to his feet, snatched the bottle of Quinine, and hurled it out the back door. He smiled at the sound of it smashing against the trunk of the big cottonwood.

Chapter Twelve
The Mart

Bam walked sullenly into the front of the EZ Mart, just ahead of his afternoon shift. He was glad to have a diversion from his guilt. The "Mart" was an innocuous box of glass and cinder block which guarded the strategic intersection of Main Street and Lexington like a beacon, luring locals and tourists alike with its twenty-four-hour supply of cigarettes, beer, and cheap wine, even lesser necessities like milk and gasoline. Free coffee and donuts attracted enough police officers to make shoplifting and loitering manageable in the small triangle, which was always congested. The EZ Mart also provided a steady flow of traffic ticket revenues for the City of Bumkin from "foreigners" with out-of-state plates who didn't see a precipitous drop in the speed limit just as they entered or left Bumkin.

Bam welcomed the rush of cool air as he entered the store. Then he saw dual headlines on the *Bumkin Record* newspaper rack: "Sheriff's House Bombed! FBI Suspects Racial Tension." Right beneath it "Dr. Callahan Rebuffs Justice Official; Says integration needs more time."

Bam stood paralyzed, his mind suddenly blank. He turned away, thankful he had a place to hide out as a responsible, working citizen. He expected Sally's willingness to play scared and ignorant for Levi Epstein and the Sheriff had been sufficient for them to conclude it was a racially motivated bomb. But he hadn't expected the FBI. He thought his "bomb" was just giant firecracker, but it was "symbolic" enough to become a warning "shot" from the likes of the Black Panthers, as the tale got spun out of control. The rumors sent tremors down the railroad track spinal cord of the town. As if the Panthers could even find Bumkin on a map, Bam thought.

But it was too late now, paranoia was rampant. If "they" were big enough to make a bomb, "they" had to have local operatives. How else could "they" have known? After all, blowing up the Sheriff's new trash bin was about as personal as it could get.

The only good news in Bam's life was that the specter of black militants had shifted blame away from him. The guilt was overpowering, but the sheer intensity of the unbridled racism now exposed was shocking. The white side of town *wanted* a bomb to blame black people, even as the black side of town *wanted* to embrace the notoriety of political retribution. Bam stared out the front windows of EZ numbed by tension and guilt. Then he realized there was nothing to see. Commercial activity in Bumkin had slowed to a crawl.

Bam realized he had lit a fuse on another bomb, just like Sally warned him, but he couldn't own up to it even if he wanted to, which he didn't. Only the Judge would believe him, but then he would be accused of a cover up. Sacrificing a young white boy wouldn't be enough to satisfy the town. It would only result in Bam being sent to boarding school, and Sally losing her job, or both.

Meanwhile, Sally had gone mute, but she couldn't hide the concern on her face. Bam knew she had come to the same conclusion, so she didn't ask, and Bam hadn't offered any explanation. But they both knew she knew. And they both knew better than to discuss it. It could only make a very bad situation much worse.

Timmy Michot jerked Bam out of his haze. He was the eldest son of Cajun neighbors, two years older than Bam. He lived just down the street; everyone lived just down the street in Bumkin. "What's the word?" Timmy asked.

Bam shook off melancholy depression and yelled back, "Thunderbird!"

"What's the Price?"

"Thirty Twice."

"Who's got the plan?"

"The EZ Man!" Bam concluded the chant half-heartedly.

He took an apron from Timmy and looked up at a bright green and red Thunderbird Wine banner announcing a sale. Cheap wine was a staple for the black community that was just a stone's throw across the tracks from EZ Mart. Even with the pall in traffic, it was going to be a hectic night. The boys high-fived their mantra, as Timmy directed Bam to take over the register shift. Timmy was due a quick toke of weed before the late shift started.

Bam had hustled a job at EZ Mart when he began dating desirable females, which required money. The Mart had turned out to be an engaging necessity, in the most unexpected ways. He got to buy cheap beer and view the latest Playboy magazines. But more so, he quickly became mesmerized by the intrigue of human activity in this epicenter of local trade. EZ was more of a bazaar than an actual convenience store, an intersection of commerce and culture that he had never before witnessed.

Southern Belles in expensive designer clothes, too embarrassed to buy Midol for their menstrual pains, preferred the anonymity of the Mart, standing in line next to street bums buying cheap wine to get them through another day. Newly baptized Evangelicals covertly bought alcohol "for medicinal purposes," while elected officials procured porn magazines in brown paper bags with their secretaries, primed for a midnight rendezvous. EZ shop brought to life the fringe of human behavior under cover of darkness. The free-for-all amazed Bam. It was a space equitably shared by every citizen, a communal place void of racial interaction. The Mart was a bastion of free enterprise, an island of equality for blacks and whites, and even a few Mexicans, living proof that Southern commerce knew no prejudice; consumers could be equally overcharged, regardless of race, creed or color.

Bam surveyed the parking lot, warily watching for a "get away" theft of gasoline by drivers in need of a tank of gasoline to get out of town. The parking lot was always frenetic, stacked full with consumers standing in line while truckers pumped diesel into their trucks and fumes into the air.

Bam watched Willie Johnson slide out of his beat-up work truck. Willie's truck was a local landmark, hand painted in discontinued baby blue paint discounted by the local hardware store. Willie eked out a living mowing grass and clearing tree limbs for white people to supplement his day job as the cemetery custodian. Everyone admired the hard-working jack-of-all-trades.

Willie put four disciplined children through college over as many decades. Sally had taught them all.

Ahead of Willie, Bam saw Deputy Quinine Jackson following Foster Landeaux into EZ. Quinine nodded respectfully to Willie but Foster refused to hold the door open for the older man as he entered EZ. Bam was suddenly enraged over the obvious slight to the dignity of Willie's dirty overalls by the white deputy who swaggered inside for a free cup of coffee. Bam was in no emotional state to ignore Foster's arrogance.

"Hello, Mr. Johnson," Bam acknowledged Willie to piss off Foster.

"Tell Mrs. Sally I'm reading about her in the paper today. I'm sure that man had it coming," Willie said, as he limped to the beer cooler.

"I'll tell her," Bam replied in a subdued manner.

"And how's the new job?" Willie asked.

"Just fine," Bam smiled, surprised how fast word had spread that he was "the man" on the night register. He never could have guessed the job carried unmatched power in Bumkin. The EZ register was an arbiter for the needy. Deferring payment for a loaf of bread or a six pack of beer commanded respect from EZ patrons. EZ was the local plantation "company store" that had never really shut down.

Willie placed a six-pack of Jax Beer on the counter and looked at Bam with an earnest smile. "Mistuh Bam..." he hedged; his forehead furrowed with concern.

"Please call me Bam, *Mr.* Johnson," Bam interjected for Foster's benefit. "How is Mrs. Stella?" Bam did his best to divert the inevitable request that he knew was coming, but he defiantly elected to take the bait while Foster and Quinine looked on.

"Stella is fine, but I am short on cash, and I have a brother coming to visit. I need a six-pack for tonight but all I have is food stamps." Willie ended the sentence matter-of-factly, his trembling hand extended with a ten-dollar food stamp printed in red ink. Willie's weathered face and dark eyes pierced Bam to the core. There was no chance he could turn him down.

They both knew it was illegal, but Bam had to ask the question, "Mr. Johnson, you don't have any cash at all?" he pleaded. The question came out harsher than he had meant.

Willie bowed his head. Reaching across the counter, he placed a strong, calloused left hand on Bam's shoulder, while his right hand pointed toward the dark, ramshackle main street across the tracks, now silhouetted against a crimson sunset. "Mistuh Bam, we are so poor over there, even our rainbows are in black and white."

The sadness of history poured over Bam. It just wasn't right. Nothing was right in his world. The pain in Willie's eyes was more than Bam could stand. He glanced at Quinine for direction.

Quinine stood next to Foster, letting his coffee cool. He allowed Bam the slightest of nods. Foster caught the contact and stared menacingly back at Bam, his arms crossed in an obvious warning. Bam ignored Foster and shook Willie Johnson's hand, implicitly approving the illegal transaction. He knew he was about to break the law. So did Quinine. So did Foster. Willie Johnson didn't care.

"This one is between us, okay, Mr. Johnson?" Bam smiled and rang up a cash sale, deliberately neglecting the register button required for food stamp purchases. Buying beer with food stamps wasn't illegal but selling it sure was.

"I appreciate you, Mr. Bam," Mr. Johnson said with a tired smile. Bam gave him change in greenbacks for a ten-dollar food stamp and a three-dollar six pack of Jax.

Willie ignored Foster's threatening glare with indifference only the elderly can muster. After he shuffled out the door, Foster confronted Bam. "A man could get in serious trouble doing things like that." You know it's against the law to cash food stamps. That's how bombs get made, because of people like you," Foster yelled.

Bam was speechless, disoriented. How did he know? Then he heard Quinine laughing. Foster turned to face the other Deputy. He had never seen Quinine so animated, so independent.

"What's your problem?" Foster challenged Quinine.

"I ain't got no problems. And neither do you if you don't make one. Who you kidding? You think Willie there is building bombs on food stamps? Why don't you go find another speeder?" Foster was visibly enraged, making fists, then gradually massaging the handle of his gun, ready for a fight.

Timmy interrupted, sliding off the bar stool behind the register. "Hey Foster, let's go outside a bit, we need to talk business." Timmy pulled a paper bag from under the counter and put his arm around the angry cop, leading him outside with an animated conversation about LSU football.

Bam looked at Quinine with new respect. "Didn't mean to create a ruckus."

"Young people never do," Quinine responded solemnly. "Doesn't mean you're intentions weren't good. I would have done the same thing for Willie."

Bam hung his head and let out a deep sigh. He thrust a bottle of red cough syrup into a small bag and handed it to Quinine. "Please take it. It's not a bribe, just a "thank you."

Quinine burst out laughing. "Mr. Callahan, we both know you're going to end up paying for this out of your own pocket, and probably that six-pack as well."

"It was my fault. Foster was doing his job."

"No, he's just a jackass, Bam, a white jackass," Quinine laughed.

"Sorry you have to work with him."

"Don't be, I've got better plans." Quinine grabbed his cough syrup and walked out the door. "Stay out of trouble, Bam."

Bam closed his eyes and shook his head. It was easier said than done. He looked out the big window and watched Timmy and Foster swap bags behind the patrol car. Timmy threw his bag under the driver seat of his old sedan, then locked the car door and returned to the store.

Bam apologized when Timmy returned. "Sorry, bro'." I didn't expect the hassle with Foster. What's with that guy?"

"He's a jackass."

Bam laughed, "Quinine said the same thing."

"Stay away from him. It wasn't about you. He was talking to me."

Bam scratched his head with a curious look, "What do you mean?"

"Foster wanted a bag of grass from me. He was pushing on you to hammer me into giving it to him. He didn't give a shit about you, or Willie."

Bam scratched his head, struggling with a sudden change of perception. "Wow! You mean you do *business* with Foster? He's a cop for God's sake!"

Timmy's silent stare left Bam with another answer he hadn't expected. "What's going on, Tim? I really don't care; I just need to know the rules."

"Don't worry Bam, no one will get in trouble. I'm just staying on the right side of the law," Timmy said with a sly grin. "Just don't sell beer for stamps, especially in daylight hours, especially to blacks. You know it's illegal. Some redneck dude will report you to the cops just because a guy like Willie is black."

"I got it. I never thought of it that way. But if there ever was a guy who deserves a break, it's Willie. Would you have said no to Willie?"

Timmy took his stool and balanced himself on shaky wood legs. "Can't say I would, but I sure as hell wouldn't have done it in front of Foster."

"Okay. But it's the tenth of the month."

Timmy stopped chugging his Coke and looked at Bam. "What the hell does that mean?"

"Well, about half of the business of EZ is in food stamps and most sales are in beer and wine. So, it follows that no one is going to find a small discrepancy for beer in favor of food stamps during the first of the part of the month." Bam slid into the academic mode he had inherited from his mother.

"So?" Timmy asked again, dumbfounded.

"Food stamps and welfare checks arrive at the same time. They must come in around the fifth because beer and liquor sales start going crazy about this time of month and increase until the end of the second week, come hell or high water. Between the tenth and fifteenth, they drop off because the cash is mostly used up, but they still have stamps for food."

Timmy knew he was stoned, and couldn't understand Bam, "*So?*" he prodded again, rolling his eyes.

"Sooo, … by the end of next week a lot of our customers will use their food stamps to buy beer, because they will have spent their cash, and legal or not, everyone finds a way to convert stamps to cash for beer and liquor."

Timmy looked at Bam with a blank stare. "Think of it this way, Tim. If I hadn't sold beer to Willie for food stamps, someone else would, but they would have charged him a lot more because then they would have to exchange the stamps. It's not that beer is illegal, like, say weed, you just can't use food stamps to …" Bam stopped in mid-sentence, then looked at Tim with a quizzical smile. An idea hit him between the eyes, as they were prone to do.

"Wow, I just got an idea. If EZ shop were to sell weed instead of booze, purely as a theory of course, I would sell it for food stamps between the fourteenth and the twenty-first of the month when there are more food stamps than cash available. That means that you, well someone like you, could sell weed for food stamps at a higher price. You could create a new "black market" for grass."

Timmy's eyes widened, as he began to catch on. "Bam, help me out here. You mean I could make more money selling weed for food stamps than cash?"

Bam popped open a Coke and nodded. "Yep, that's a fact," he said with conviction. "A lot more. You have to make the trades during the third week of the month and convert it back to cash by the first week of the following month."

"How would I do that?"

Bam pointed to the register as he rang up his Coke and watched the cash drawer pop open with a ring, "I'll bet you can figure that out pretty quick," he said with a wink.

Timmy looked at Bam, then at the cash drawer. Bam saw a light bulb click on in Timmy's clouded head. Timmy dug into his jeans and contributed a dollar for Bam's Coke. "Here's for your next Coke," he said with a grin. "Stick around till Lester shows up."

Timmy was mopping the floors two hours later when Lester showed up. He leaned the mop handle against a back corner of the building and whistled at Bam to get his attention.

"Whatcha need?" Bam asked as Timmy approached the counter. The store was empty but for the two boys and Lester. Bam could see Lester at the end of the aisle, his lean, slippery form listlessly moving from one foot to the other, one hand holding a big radio to his shoulder and his other holding a cigarette. Lester was in a constant state of dance, his feet in motion, seeming to be independent organs detached from the rest of an otherwise lifeless form, with a heartbeat and rhythm of their own.

"Bam," Timmy whispered across the counter. "Guess what?"

"What?" Bam asked.

"Lester has food stamps but he don't have any money. He's up for a deal to, uh, buy stuff I have, that he needs."

"Told ya," Bam said with a triumphant smile. "So, what's the hitch?"

"Well, he only has thirty bucks in food stamps, and he wants two 'dimes.' The brother needs change." Even Bam knew that a 'dime' bag of grass was $10.00. It was one of the few standards of the universe introduced during the Sixties.

Bam instantly understood. "Gimme the damn stamps," he demanded, putting his hand out and nodding to Lester matter-of-factly. Timmy turned and motioned to Lester to join them. He strutted down the aisle, his purple suede coat and matching cap rustling against the sound of thick, gold chains clanking underneath an open shirt and busted radio speakers. Only the whites of Lester's eyes revealed the presence of a human being beneath the costume and the boom box that glided toward Bam on dancing feet.

Lester stopped midway down the aisle to strike a disco pose. He took time to suck on a cigarette and blew out three perfect smoke rings, one into the other, then he bowed to an imaginary audience, deftly pulling a government envelope from his inside coat pocket. He slid the food stamps across the counter to Bam.

Bam knew Lester was rich by the standards "across the track." No older than Timmy, Lester was known to carry a large wad of cash he constantly flashed as verification of his status. He also knew that using food stamps for barter with a white boy was embarrassing for the drug dealer and presumed part-time pimp whose reputation relied on ready cash, so Bam tried to put him at ease. "How's your folks, Lester? My mom says your mom makes the best yam pie in the world."

A slight smile from Lester told Bam he had hit home. Bam punched the cash register and looked at Lester. "Just this once with me, never to be discussed. That cool?"

"You cool."

The cash drawer sprang open, offering real money for a profitable exchange. Bam took the stamps and held them up to the light to make sure they were real and properly signed, or at least well counterfeited. He put all thirty dollars into the register compartments and handed over six bucks' cash to Lester and twenty-two to Timmy. Bam looked at Lester and then Tim, who looked at each other with frowns.

"Two bags, twelve bucks each, Lester," Bam explained. "That's a four-dollar premium that goes back to the dealer for exchanging your stamps.

"You bad, Bam, you bad!" Lester exploded. "That's too much. His bags ain't worth twelve dollars!"

Bam quietly shut the cash register drawer and stared at Lester. "It isn't just twelve bucks, Lester. It's twelve plus a real cash rebate on your stamps. Where else are you going to get six bucks to buy more cigarettes and wine? We both know you're going to turn that twenty-four bucks into sixty bucks on the backside selling joints to your buddies across the tracks at higher prices, 'cause they don't have cash either."

Lester considered his options momentarily. "Ok, tha's cool, bro', tha's cool. I know you always gotta pay The Man," he said with indignity. The plantation never changed, only the times.

The price increase was hefty, but it was the same everywhere in Lester's world. They both knew Bam was right; no one else would give him change in cash. In the end, shit always rolled downhill. Lester would pass the cost onto less fortunate souls, keeping cash while holding on to welfare money he and his girls received from the government. Lester stifled his momentary animosity at The Man as he counted his cash, then it hit him. Lester looked up at Bam, then at Timmy with a bright smile. He suddenly saw possibilities he had never considered.

Timmy had the smile of an entrepreneur who had just received a 20% raise on an unexpected sale. Then he counted the money in his hand and realized he was short. "Say, what the hell is this, Bam? I got $22.00 and I should have $24.00. You shorted me!"

"You have to pay a "take" to The Mart," Bam replied curtly. "Good advice ain't free." It was actually his dad's saying, but Bam thought it fit the moment well. "That's a 10% commission to EZ."

Lester's ebony face turned into a huge grin of white teeth as he let out a whoop. "You gotta pay The Man too, Timmy! We all gotta pay The Man!" The thought of Timmy getting hit by the same usurious business practice made Lester's day. In the dirty little world of small-town drugs and poverty, it was good to know that everyone paid their dues. Maybe he could deal with this Whitey after all.

"Hey, Bam, I didn't know you deal, man. I'd brought you tons of business if I knowed you deal."

"I don't smoke. Don't deal either, Lester. I ain't seen no drugs here and I better not when I'm on shift. This gig is between you and Timmy."

Chapter Thirteen
Preachers

Hezekial Allen scoured the Bumkin weekly newspaper on his morning reprieve. His big, muscular frame filled up the small office deep inside the Holy Mount Zion Baptist Church. It served as a safe hide-away from parishioners for a few hours. He checked out the sports page peppered with pictures of high school football heroes and last weekend's scores in Avignon Parish, but his mind never left the front-page headlines. Sally Callahan had insulted a top civil rights lawyer, and someone had attempted to bomb the Sheriff's house, all in the same week. These were turbulent times.

Hezekial shook his head in dismay. At least Levi didn't pontificate on the bombing being racially motivated. Not that he had to. But Hezekial couldn't for the life of him figure out who on his side of the tracks had the talent to create a home-made bomb with that much explosive power.

Mr. White's black face stood out among white Rotary Club members on the front page. "That was no accident," Hezekial muttered, wondering if Mr. White appreciated the exposure, such as it was.

Hezekial truly loved Sally Leland Callahan. He knew the whole town did also. He had enjoyed tea at her kitchen table on many occasions, discussing, and sometimes fiercely debating, the black and white reality of the South, always in an educated and civilized manner. She was a woman ahead of her time, he thought, as he stroked his meticulously trimmed beard. It was a terrible shame that no local black woman could make the same claim. It was a sad irony that only a white woman had the credibility to champion the black people of Louisiana. Someday a black woman would rise to the occasion and Hezekial had no doubt Sally would help her get there, just like she had mentored Maggie.

He wondered what Sally had been like as a young woman. It wouldn't have mattered, he mused; white women just didn't get it, no matter how smart they were. In fact, that was part of the problem. Sometimes brains just got in the way of the physical attraction which was fundamental to survival for the disenfranchised. He had been with women of both races and there just was no comparison to the sexuality of black women. The sex drive of his race was as much a part of Southern tradition as the magnolias in bloom. His were just a more physical people. Hopefully, that would never change.

Neither did his white brothers in the ministry understand that physical exertion was a necessary release for poor people. Sometimes it was all they had to keep sane, to gain comfort. At least his people weren't hypocrites like those honky deacons at "First Bubba" Baptist Church across the tracks. White congregations shared the same bible as Mount Zion, but reality printed their doctrines from a different negative.

Hezekial glanced up at his Certification of Doctorate of Divinity from Oral Roberts University, hanging prominently on the office wall. He had thought about being a history professor at one time, but it didn't carry the power and authority of a Baptist minister in the South, not to mention the sense of purpose. Or the money, he conceded. There were few better paying jobs for a black man in the South than heading up a good congregation. He wouldn't be content to lecture history, he intended to make it. Besides, his chance of making a living as a black scholar was an impossibility. He was the wrong color and the wrong sex to be taken seriously.

What irony; only a white woman could get away with talking freely about black people to white people. White people only believed other white people for scholarly works. Any black scholar's history would become as politicized as a white man's history of black women. And it took a female to wield the sympathy of sexual prejudice, a new weapon of choice, as Sally had taught Mr. White. Only a white woman could make a claim as a repressed minority that could back off a black, court-appointed, Yankee lawyer in front of God and everybody worth anything for fifty miles outside of Bumkin.

Sally Callahan was a formidable proponent of an integrated world. Why White chose to challenge Sally on her home turf was a mystery to Hezekial. White must have felt above reproach but his arrogance did him little good. Little did he know that Sally Callahan was combative, passionate, and well informed about things she believed. She stood her ground and defended her truth.

Less than a year ago Sally would have been just a female southern scholar, lost among an academic bench of old men, and Mr. White would have been just a visiting bureaucrat relegated to his corner of the universe. Now they were the megaphones of two societies. Times were indeed moving too fast for Louisiana. Sally had made a valid point to that end. But times were not fast enough for him. Hezekial wanted his own megaphone.

Hezekial had watched comfortably from his corner seat at Rotary, munching on Flossie's fried chicken as Bumkin's white preacher and priest squirmed at the sight of another North-South confrontation. None of them had the balls to weigh in when that redneck planter Bubba mouthed off. Realistically, none of the planters had mouthed anything new for the last hundred years. They depended on the silence of their white churches to maintain a sanctimonious barrier for black people in the South. But that too was changing.

It had not escaped Hezekial that the Rotary meeting personalized the debate between two highly educated representatives of two different races *and* cultures. An educated argument meant someone had to be right, and someone had to be wrong, in Yankee terms. Right *or* wrong only existed north of the Mason-Dixon line. Right *and* wrong co-existed quite peacefully in the South for time without end. That was how Southerners avoided the time-consuming conflicts in life that Yankees fret about all the time. It was the only way arguments could be swept under the cultural "rug" in true Southern style. How else could the South "forget" about integration for a hundred years?

Hezekial looked back at the newspaper article, which was surprisingly accurate. It even noted that the articulate Rev. Hezekial Allen was unusually quiet throughout Sally's speech. Hezekial was surprised that his silence got noticed. But it was true that he had consciously elected not to assist his black brother. White was obviously unfamiliar with the psychology of lynch mobs in the South. He couldn't have defended White even if he had wanted to. Had he done so, he would have been found guilty of ganging up on the untouchable Mrs. Sally, who did, in fact, know one hell of a lot more about his race than he or White knew, or even cared to know, for that matter. Not that White would ever let it go.

It was offensive to Hezekial that he was expected to defend White because he was black, not because he was right. Well after Mr. White departed on one of those sleek jet airplanes back to Boston, Hezekial would still live as a black man among a bunch of redneck white people, still engaged in spiritual trench warfare, while White got to make proclamations from afar in his ivory tower, at government expense. Being black in Boston was not at all the same as being black in Louisiana, no matter how much White thought it should be. That, of course, was Sally's point: white educators of young children, most of whom were women, had more real sense of dealing with racism on the ground floor than any black lawyer in Boston ever could. Who but White would attempt to argue with that?

Hezekial remembered fondly that Sally once threatened to find a white ancestor in his background if he didn't hold up to his responsibilities at Mount Zion. Therein lay the problem for Mr. White and the opportunity for Hezekial. White never stood a chance against Sally. She relied on facts. White needed local representation to alter the playing field.

Hezekial ran his fingers under bright blue suspenders, stretching them against his thumbs while he peered out the window in deep contemplation. Here he was, leading the charge of Christianity at ground zero of poverty and ignorance. God had called him, and he had followed in the best tradition of his family. But he was better than this. God *required* him to be better. He knew he was destined for one of those big New Orleans or Atlanta churches, maybe even Washington, D.C. Churches where the congregation was counted in thousands, not mere hundreds. Where ministers had discretionary funds and retirement accounts, and the pipe organs were made of real silver and gold.

Those careers were increasingly being made with political headlines and television appearances, not in the squalid confines of local sin and salvation.

Religion was moving into the airwaves, where the beauty of salvation and the gloss of pageantry weren't overshadowed by the grime of poverty and ignorance. The new media was like his grandmother's oatmeal salve on a burn; it never healed a damn thing, but it sure made it feel better.

It was time for him to act. Time for him to establish his credibility with a wealthy white audience, not just poor blacks. Time to play offense for himself, not just defense for his race. He nodded slowly, letting his straps loose with a loud slap against his big chest to punctuate his conclusion. He grabbed the phone and dialed up Reverend Hudson at The First Baptist Church of Bumkin.

Across the tracks in the calm setting of First Baptist Church, Reverend Carl Hudson gently raised himself from a prayer stool that sat next to his roll-top desk. Polio from childhood had left him with a pronounced limp, and constant pain. It was part of his calling. At least he didn't have to wear the brace anymore. He spent his mornings behind closed doors in a plush office trimmed in rich red and gold and a fervent belief in faith and service.

Carl accepted his pain as penance for the rut in which he found his church was caught, the result of too much success and power. He asked God for a real, high profile challenge to mobilize his Christian soldiers against the sins of the world. He needed to keep the congregation of First Baptist Church occupied with God's will, distanced from the pitfalls which prosperity brought. He needed a worthy battle and a clear sense of duty, one that would pit the principles of right and wrong, good and evil, against each other with clarity. He needed a civil purpose that could define new boundaries.

Carl finished his prayers and returned to his desk, wondering where God would lead him next. He was a general in a broken body, but with significant resources, ready to charge into a new battle that would bring Christian light to the masses. Churches grew in focus and size during times of torment and upheaval; prosperity delivered a soft and indifferent culture that could rot from within. He knew in his soul that only a spiritual war could force a renewed sense of direction to a wealthy church like First Baptist. He also knew that the battle he saw rising like a thundercloud over the bayou wasn't the one he would have chosen. His congregation wasn't on the right side of integration, nor would they be in his lifetime.

A button lit up on his phone, followed by a ring that broke the serenity of the moment. He hung the heavy receiver on his shoulder as he held a pen in hand, ready to outline his next sermon.

"First Baptist Church," Carl said, trying to sound unperturbed by the interruption.

"Reverend Carl, this is Reverend Hezekial Allen. How are you this fine day?" Hezekial's smooth voice welcomed Carl over the phone.

"I'm fine, Reverend. To what do I owe this honor?" Hezekial had always refused to call Carl anything but Reverend, so Carl always responded in kind.

"Reverend, I am most concerned about the impact of this integration order on those of us who have flocks in Bumkin. It appears to me that Dr. Callahan's speech was a harbinger of difficult times."

"Reverend Hezekial," Carl responded, taking off his glasses and laying down his pen for what was surely a serious call with his fellow preacher. "We are all worried. It is going to be a slow, difficult process for everyone, but I did not find Sally's speech out of order."

"No, no, not at all. You misunderstand me, Reverend," Hezekial's voice lowered into the rich tone for which he was well known. "Her message helped to define the issues, but it neglected the reality which you and I must manage. Our churches will survive. But I am worried about the fallout on you and me if we don't take the right position in this firestorm, so we can help each other. Forced integration is not a message from God, this is a conflict among men," he proclaimed vociferously. "It is up to clergy to define answers within God's will for the common folk. The merger of our schools does not eliminate the tracks that divide us. Our congregations will be split more so between two opposing forces that already reside on either side of the railroad tracks. Both factions now want to be heard openly, Reverend. They will want the issues to be vetted. And they won't feel that it has been settled unless you and I challenge each other. We are like two unwilling boxers stuck in the limelight of a championship match."

After a pause, Hezekial continued. "If we don't individually lead our separate charge, our congregations will turn against us as unworthy leaders in a new world, and they will find someone else to be the megaphone of heaven's message."

Carl pulled out a drawer from his antebellum desk and propped his bad leg on it to reduce the pain. He closed his eyes, letting the black minister's words sink into his brain. Hezekial was right. Carl had been thinking of integration in biblical terms of right and wrong, a social obligation to correcting a human injustice. He had not considered the political dynamics of his own all-white congregation in the broader battle for the souls of Bumkin, Louisiana.

Like all men of the cloth, biblical translation was Carl's mission, but local politics was his job. Southern religion and Southern politics were suddenly becoming indistinguishable. Broadcast preachers like Jimmy Swaggart and Oral Roberts had literally stolen the microphones right out from under local preachers like Carl with a new evangelical message of neo-fundamentalism laced with a conservative message of prosperity and racial overtones. The broadcast ministries had remanufactured mass religion into sound bites which crossed all religious boundaries, and age. They cut out the local preachers as middlemen as surely as Walmart had hollowed out Main Street. Broadcast religion had become a cheap solution for protestant guilt, allowing parishioners to collect all the blessings of Christ at home with mail-in contribution of just ten dollars a week. Of course, more than a third of their checks bounced also. But nonetheless, wholesale religion was taking its toll, creating a new wave of unrest between black and white Baptist churches which scrambled to maintain the relevance of retail religion and the higher cost of brick-and-mortar edifices which they had to support.

The last thing Carl needed was another split in the religious marketplace. Who knew where integration would take his flock? How could he have missed this freight train, Carl asked himself? It was headed directly at him and his church. Caught off guard, he decided he best listen to his fellow preacher. He had little doubt that Hezekial had more experience in battling prejudice than he did.

"Hezekial, tell me exactly what you are saying?" Carl queried to get the conversation in full gear.

"All I'm saying, Reverend, is that prejudice and churches in the South are contradictions that reflect our culture and keep both of us in business. We do not serve anyone's purpose by dividing our churches, even though we may be at odds about the direction of the winds of change. In fact, sometimes it is only by virtue of *conflict* that we can pull our people into reconciliation. My people are like the Jews under Moses, Reverend, we have been lost in the wilderness of poverty for generations. And just like the Holy Bible tells us, even Moses couldn't contain internal conflicts among his people. Even mighty Moses could only redirect his people toward a common enemy to vent their frustration and reconcile themselves with the Almighty."

"Hezekial, our common enemies are ignorance and poverty."

"But Reverend," Hezekial cut him off, "people lost in the desert do not believe that they will ever overcome their hardship, and so they stay alive by fighting the enemy they can see, not the invisible plagues that influence us all."

Carl cleared this throat and slowly took another sip of coffee. This was too important to translate through a biblical analogy. The tough church administrator who had shepherded numerous emotional conflicts for decades hardened his voice. "Okay, Hezekial, this is Carl you are speaking to now, not one of your backwoods brothers. We are talking now about the *business* of the church, not our philosophical creeds. Cut the bullshit and tell me what you want from me this fine morning."

Hezekial's perfect white teeth shined through a wide grin, lighting up his office with delight at the breakthrough in this most important conversation. At the end of the day, business was the only thing that was as dependable as God. He cleared his throat and waited a poignant moment. "Reverend, it is an unfortunate truth that ignorance dominates both of our congregations at opposite extremes. Neither the poor nor the wealthy have time to be worried about social issues. We both know we live in a paradox. It is the wealth of racists and the passion of evangelists that defines and funds each of our churches and it is by virtue of this delicate balance that we, in turn, moderate their very existence. If we extricated the evangelists and the racists, both churches would collapse, left only with poor congregations and no hypocrisy to fight, no sin to expunge! Our mission would have no character and our foot soldiers would have no purpose or resources. Our backers would find a new church to dominate so their voices could be heard. We would be both left standing without any mission or resources." Carl remained silent as the sting of Hezekial's truth hit him in the gut.

"For Mount Zion to grow," the preacher continued, "I must become a visible champion to ensure that my people can truly realize benefits from integration. If I do not step up, the congregation will splinter and I will be a leader of half a church that will certainly fail, and hence no church at all. And who would win from such a loss? As we both know, Reverend, a Goliath cannot exist without a David. And if the First Baptist Goliath fails to acknowledge that it isn't being challenged by a lowly Mount Zion preacher, neither congregation will have any reason to surface in this racial challenge for equality and stability, and no boundaries will be established."

Hezekial's voice softened to a whisper. "But, in the alternative, if the racial elements of both churches are allowed to ignite and burn themselves out while we lead them toward a broader resolution, both churches will reap the benefits of renewal that only comes with the resolution of a major conflict. And the economic benefits that follow."

"There is only one problem here, Reverend," Carl responded. "I'm on your side on this one. My wife and I both really believe integration is the right thing to do."

"Of that I have no doubt. But we must keep that between us." His voice oozed years of preparation for his calling. "As you have already stated, Reverend, this is about business, not philosophy. If you take a philosophical stand for integration at First Baptist, the money interests in your church will abandon you, just as they are abandoning public schools to create their own system. Then you, too, would be left with half a church and unfortunately, Reverend, I know from personal experience that white congregations are even less forgiving than black congregations. Unlike black churches that fight poverty and ignorance for change, First Baptist lays claim to *wealth* and ignorance that has no need to change."

Hezekial let the troubling thought dangle on the phone before resuming. "A splintering of First Baptist church would rip our fair community apart, undermining the only two leaders capable of reconciling the two races philosophically." Hezekial paused dramatically. "That would be you and I, Reverend Hudson."

Carl sighed heavily into the phone. Hezekial's articulate monologue reverberated in his phone as he considered his new reality. "And so, you see, Reverend, in order to get God's work done, sometimes we must first dance with the Devil."

Chapter Fourteen
The Cabin

The darkness of strange bedrooms was familiar to Meadow. Still and guarded, she tried to gather her bearings, careful not to disturb the massive body next to her. Through a fog of pain and bruises, she focused on where she was. The old slave cabin was made of small rooms with high ceilings supported by overhead beams notched together on top of tree trunks, their cracks and crevasses covered with mud and moss that sealed the interior. In the twentieth century, it was a quaint environment of artistic appeal. A hundred years prior, it must have been a dreary, depressing place, Meadow thought. Her senses were filled with the smell of smoky embers, pine sap, and pain. She placed her fingers to her face and felt the swelling of broken blood vessels. Where was her bag?

Her fear of movement was so visceral she bit the back of her fist and held her breath while she slid slowly out of the canopy bed, standing naked in the middle of the plank floor. She quelled her fear and tried to piece together fragments of their pillow talk. She remembered Bubba began by telling her how he had moved the old cabin to the edge of the swamp for duck hunting, and how things had changed soon after he met Roberta. He didn't want to talk about it at first, but Meadow skillfully applied a night of hard sex, alcohol, and amphetamines to tease the real story out of him.

Little did the fool realize that the exquisite pleasure of the evening was all hers. He was but another a drunken teenager, like putty in her experienced hands. She remembered playfully calling him "Big Daddy" before she found an arrogant fool anxious to brag with a loose tongue in front of a loose woman. Now she had to recover her wits.

She felt her way silently to her overnight bag, verified that her stash of cash and drugs was untouched, and confirmed the cold steel comfort of her switchblade as she retrieved her cigarettes and lighter. She considered cutting Bubba's throat but decided it was not yet time.

Meadow walked over to an unusually large, single window, the only one in the bedroom. A majestic magnolia tree stood silhouetted against the rising sun. Meadow gazed transfixed as the broad dark leaves steadily gained definition, casting a long shadow over the golden, rolling meadow that surrounded it. She flicked her cigarette out the window and crawled back into the big bed and slowly caressed her lover. She knew what she had to do.

The big bloodshot eyes opened quickly, staring at her. "What do you want now?" Bubba asked with bravado.

"I just want to hear you beg for mercy, baby." she whispered honestly.

Chapter Fifteen
Dead-End Road

T he siren of the Bumkin police car whined eerily in the dampness. It took a while before the residents on Mable Street knew it was more than just another speeder trying to outrun a ticket in Judge Jim's court. The arrival of the Marksville police and the wail of the sole Cheneyville police car barreling off of the highway stirred the population to open doors and peer out of pulled blinds, curious that such a rare event would be taking place on the white side of the tracks. The sirens broke the nightly chatter of roosting starlings in willow trees and beckoned barking dogs to guard their porches.

Levi Epstein's trained ear woke him from a quiet slumber on his living room couch. He pulled on his tennis shoes and bolted out the door in one motion, grabbing his new, single-lens, reflex Leica on the way out the door. There was never much real news in Bumkin, but what news there was got covered by the *Bumkin Record*, Levi's weekly newspaper.

Levi hit the gas pedal of his '65 Chevy Imperial, rolled down the window, and punched in the car lighter. The car lurched onto the single-lane blacktop and headed toward the side of town that was inhabited by the middle-class poor, and hourly white farm hands. He came to a screeching halt when his headlights locked onto a small mob standing in the street, surrounding three blaring police cars.

The *Bumkin Record* didn't have competition in the classic sense of the word. It wasn't like Levi had to worry about getting scooped. No, the problem was always about preserving the scoop, not getting it. Headlines in small towns were made, not captured. Hell, as a practical matter everyone in town could get more first-hand details than he could print from Mike's Truck Stop before the night was over. Levi regularly bought Flossie's biscuits early in the morning at The Palace to find out what he had missed or didn't know from the night before.

The real trick was to get pictures of people at the scene before small-town cops screwed things up. Pictures were the essence of the *Bumkin Record.* He needed faces, lots of faces. Cops always redirected traffic and sent witnesses away before he got on the scene. Getting there first and getting lots of pictures was essential for the newspaper.

The rickety car jumped the sidewalk on the dead-end road with a painful screech from untended brakes. Levi landed just a few yards from the end of Bumkin's City Limits at a barbed-wire fence that marked the beginning of the Tremblay's cane rows. He yanked his camera out of its case and made sure his windows were rolled up to protect against a sure drizzle that was already starting. Levi spotted his quarry quickly, running up to Sheriff Franklin Landeaux and Officer Foster Landeaux, Bumkin's dynamic duo, father and son protectors of the people. They were pouring each other coffee from a metal Thermos while deputies redirected scores of locals away from the crime scene. Franklin filled another Styrofoam cup for Levi as the reporter caught up to him.

Levi was shocked to see the coroner, Dr. Hines, bent over in the back seat of Quinine's police car. The squad car sat parked at an awkward angle in an odd spot, on the wrong side of town. Levi could already smell real news in the air. He took the coffee cup and raised it silently in appreciation to Franklin. "What do we have here fellas, some sort of domestic violence?"

Franklin looked down at the reporter from his six-foot four advantage, almost a foot over Levi's balding head, with a big Stetson that made him look even taller. "No, Levi," the Sheriff said glumly with heartfelt sadness. "The body in that police car is Quinine himself." The Sheriff grit his teeth, his head shaking in genuine grief.

Levi was shocked. There weren't many murders in Bumkin; there weren't really that many people worth killing, and even fewer to steal from. More accurately, there weren't very many cases classified as murders in the bayou country. Most homicides were crimes of passion and cheap alcohol. The Bumpkin cops were not recognized for being overly inquisitive, but in their defense, the distinction between accidents and murder in the swamp was difficult to figure at times. Levi had recently covered the story of a Hessmer man lost while spear fishing underwater with his good buddy in the Atchafalya River. As diligently reported in the *Bumkin Record,* he got tangled in his line when he speared a big Gar fish that dragged him deep into the muddy river, never to be seen again. Nine months later the *Bumkin Record* announced the wedding of his good buddy to the insurance-rich widow of the deceased, or the unfound, depending upon one's perspective.

Levi pulled a Bumkin Bank & Trust pen from his pocket and began jotting down notes furiously. He placed his coffee cup on top of the police car to aim his camera. Franklin quickly put his hand over the lens, pushing it down before Levi could swing it up for a picture.

The Sheriff leaned over, whispering to the reporter, "We got a problem here, Levi. We need to respect the dead. I don't think Quinine or the police department would want you to print him in his current condition. Seems that one of the girls from The Spot was in the car when Quinine got shot. Foster had to capture the girl before she took off." The Sheriff's head motioned toward a long-legged mulatto girl being led into Foster's cop car by an unusually attentive deputy. She had a lot of leg, even at a distance.

Foster Landeaux snickered and turned away. He recovered with an earnest face and a solemn look to address the reporter. "Quinine was quite a man, and he had himself quite a girl there."

Levi's killer instincts as reporter had been dulled from years of local reporting about flower gardens and little league baseball. He had been writing filler for the Piggly Wiggly grocery advertisements more than serious journalism for the last ten years. Such were the economic realities of journalism in a small town. But deep down in his gut, he still hungered for a juicy front-page news article. His old news hound nose still remembered the day when he lusted after the story, not just the advertising that paid for it.

Levi nodded slightly to the Sheriff with understanding, dismissing the need for a camera with a shrug. The crime scene wasn't suitable for a photo anyway. Blood was good for police shots, but it only worked for black-and-white print when there were large enough pools of blood for contrast, like the famous shots of mob hits in New York. Levi wasn't about to pay the expense of a color print for a black victim and a mulatto suspect in a black-and-white cop car.

Still, beneath his shock and sadness, Levi sensed a story with immediate Southern intrigue: a black cop murdered by a mulatto hooker in the white section of town, all occurring in the swirl of politics and prejudice which integration had foisted upon his community. All he needed now was for Sally Callahan to say the hooker was a student of hers with a degree in black history. He stifled a laugh at his own dark humor. He would share it later with Sally.

Levi eyeballed the Sheriff, his neighbor, friend, and primary source of local news, with whom he shared the fine line between journalism, gossip, and speculation. He could hazard denying the request of the Sheriff to not print the picture, but he couldn't deny the request of a neighbor to do the right thing. There really was no telling what harm a picture of this scene might generate amid the current racial tensions. Nevertheless, there was a story here that had to be told. Levi scrutinized Quinine's car with a reporter's trained eye, scouring the scene while flickering red-and-white police lights refracted off the foggy mist from the bayou.

Quinine's uniform was strewn about on the grass, partially covering a telltale bottle of red cough syrup that must have slipped out of his breast pocket. That would have only happened in a scuffle, Levi knew. Bound leaflets of paper littered the ground. Crews of cops were shuffling about, making a disjointed attempt to pick up some of the evidence before it flew away.

Levi turned to the Sheriff. "How about just one shot at a distance, Sheriff? I'll frame the Doc to get a friendly face on film, nothing that exposes Quinine." The Sheriff nodded with exasperation, holding up a single digit to confirm the limits of his concession. Levi pointed the camera as Doc Hines backed out of Quinine's beloved squad car with great difficulty, exposing two bare, black feet oddly hanging out of the car door, toes down.

Levi subtly shifted the shot to exclude Quinines' feet and include Foster's cop car, where the girl was visible through the open window. Wet and haggard, she was still an unmistakable beauty. He framed the picture to include the girl's profile at the far right of his frame. A pile of clothes and paper were strewn over the foreground, with a grim coroner attempting to smile, despite his macabre surroundings.

Light from the flash bulb beamed through the darkness, capturing a relatively innocuous image for the lead story. Elections were coming up and pictures like this were in high demand, Levi knew. Payback for the front-page picture was as good as currency; Levi would extract inside information from the good doctor over coffee tomorrow morning. He capped the shutter on his camera and put it away, anxious to hear the rest of the story from the Sheriff. "So, tell me about it, Franklin," he probed.

The Sheriff shrugged. "Looks like there was something going on between Quinine and a hooker from The Spot. Pretty girl, barely an adult. It's a real shame she's pissed off her life like this. Foster got a call for help from Quinine and apprehended the girl after she had shot Quinine. That's all we know for now 'til Doc gets finished and we can write it up." His voice was somber and his message blunt: nothing more, nothing unusual. Under control. Classic Franklin.

"Any chance it's drug related?" Levi threw a curveball to watch the Sheriff's reaction.

The Sheriff glared at him for a moment with an official scowl. "You've been here long enough to know that everything is related in the South, Levi— and nothing in Bumkin is drug related."

Foster interjected himself with a hapless smile, proud of his role in catching a murderess. "She put up a hell of a fight, Levi. She even took a shot at me." Levi noticed that Foster was frightfully nervous. Levi tossed his cigarette butt on the ground and looked down to step on it as Foster blathered about his actions to preserve the peace. Levi noticed splotches of black mud spots on the cuffs of Foster's khaki pants. It was the same black mud that was on Quinine's tires. Atchafalaya swamp mud, still wet and gooey clay from the swamp. A lot different than the sandy loam of farmed cropland around town.

Levi's eye caught site of a business card blowing close by, odd for this side of town. He feigned listening to Foster's story as he stepped on his cigarette to put it out, deftly putting his foot on the card while he looked up to distract the Deputy. "Why in hell would Quinine be banging a mulatto hooker on the white side of the tracks, in his police car, on a cold, wet night?" Levi asked Foster bluntly.

"You know how those people are, Levi," Foster responded, his voice dropping an octave as he moved closer to make his point confidentially with an unusual display of concern. "Some people screw anywhere. It's a problem."

"How did you get here first?" Levi pressed.

Foster stammered, then got a grip. "Quinine knew he was in trouble, he called me on the radio, and I happened to be nearby."

"Are you telling me Quinine called you naked, with a hooker in his car?"

Foster glowered at Levi with a growing anger. "All I can tell you is that he was dead in the back seat and she was throwing on her clothes with a gun in her hand."

Levi eyed the son of his friend, the Sheriff. Even in front of his father, Levi wasn't going to cut Foster any slack. He could find nothing good about him, however desperate his father was to make him over in his own image. As far as Levi could tell, Foster was a street punk hiding behind the badge of his father. For a young Jew who had made his own way from New York to Bumkin to start a business, the incestuous nature of the South was as despicable as its racism. Foster wasn't dumb enough to be pitied or smart enough to be liked, but he was connected enough to be dangerous. Levi's reputation in the community had been built on objectivity, honesty, and fierce independence. Foster was everything Levi hated about the South.

Levi silently bent down, pretending to tie his shoe while he palmed the business card, then he slid it into his pants pocket as he stood up. He looked at the ruts in the grass and noticed that there were three sets of tracks in the grass adjacent to Quinine's car.

"You must have pulled right up to Quinine's car to save him," Levi said respectfully to Foster, pointing at the tracks.

"Yes sir, I did. But I was too late. I got my gun on her before she could shoot at me."

Levi nodded approvingly. "Smart move. So, tell me, who was the other guy?"

Foster looked at him with a glint of surprise. "What do you mean?"

"Who do the other tracks belong to?

"There weren't no other guy. You must be looking at tracks from the other police cars," Foster protested, his voice shaky. "Talk to them, Levi, I got to get back to work."

Levi looked up at Foster, twenty years his junior and six inches taller, barely able to contain his disdain. Finally, he said, "Thanks for the information, Foster, but it's Mr. Epstein to you. Let's not forget it." Levi delivered the verbal punch line with a hard glare. "Where is the other officer on call?"

"He's over there." Foster pointed in the direction of the captive. "Eddy came out to help me after I called in, *Mr. Epstein.*" Levi nodded curtly, leaving Foster in mid-sentence, fully aware of the conflict he had just created with the Sheriff. He walked around the Sheriff's car to visit Eddy Descant as the Sheriff's eyes bored a hole in his backside. Tough shit, Levi thought. This whole scene smells, and he's your kid.

Eddy leaned casually against the cop car, caressing his own coffee cup as he stood guard over the hooker, with a clear view of her cleavage. She had been put into the Marksville police department car for the time being. Eddy wanted to make damn sure that Marksville cops weren't trying to take credit for his prisoner, with good reason.

Levi bent over slightly to look through the back window of the sedan, its police lights still flashing with authority. The girl was crouched into the corner of the back seat. She could have been naked but for a blanket, stiletto heels, and a silver bracelet that hung from her wrist. Shapely, tight legs were splattered with mud and blood. She was visibly shaking from the cold air as she buried her chest into multiple jackets provided by deputies who were happy to share them.

Eddy was the youngest officer on the force. Levi had known his parents for years. "Heard you bagged a big buck this week, Eddy," Levi began.

Eddy's big smile confirmed a twelve-point buck was now in his freezer. "You got that right, Mr. Epstein." Eddy was born to be a local cop, Levi thought. Big, tough, a great shot, with a high school education, bubbling over without ambition. But, like many others, he was a fundamentally good, dependable person whose public service was not questioned. Eddy was one of the people who made America work, regardless of your color or politics.

Levi got straight to the point. "Also heard you had to back up Foster tonight. Did you catch any action?"

"No sir, Foster had her cuffed and in his car when I got here. 'Course, we had lost Quinine by then. I guess Quinine had a thing going … can't say I blame him if you know what I mean, but I shore hated to lose Quinine. He was a real man, Mr. Epstein."

Levi hadn't realized Quinine had commanded so much respect in the lower ranks of the small police department. He jotted down a note to use the quote as the lead in Quinine's obituary.

Doc Hines walked up to Levi to ensure that he would get his share of local press. Events like this had to be exploited for the coroner. He had never had any competition for his elected position of course, but he didn't want to start now. Always best to make the most of the opportunities when they came along.

Levi welcomed his friend. "So, what happened, Doc?" he asked.

The doctor peeled off his plastic gloves in a quick action and zipped his jacket to keep out the dampness. "Shot in the back of the head with his own gun, Levi. Quinine died instantly."

Levi scratched on his note pad. "So, I guess, since the girl is practically naked and I saw a clump of clothes without any visible blood stain, Quinine was naked also?" Levi deduced out loud.

"Now, Levi, you know the Sheriff wouldn't want me to comment on that. Besides, I gotta get home to Jenny." He smiled and slapped the reporter on the shoulder. "Make sure I get a good picture, okay, buddy? Re-election isn't too far away," he winked.

"Always do, Doc. How about coffee tomorrow?"

"Sure thing."

"Just give me a short statement in your own words," Levi requested, knowing the Doc couldn't ignore getting his name in print.

The lanky coroner stopped momentarily to collect his thoughts, scratching his chin. "Yeah, sure, Levi. Let's see now," he said, taking his glasses off to ponder his official statement. "Try this, Levi. Quinine was a man's man who enjoyed his work and died in action on the job. We're gonna miss him. Write that down. Truer words were never spoken."

Levi stopped his pen and looked up. "I didn't know you knew Quinine that well."

"I didn't. But I'm a doctor, Levi. I know a good man when I see one." The doctor walked to his car and departed, satisfied that his work was done.

Levi scratched his bald spot. Foster and the Sheriff had left the crime scene. Eddy and the paramedics were in charge of the cleanup. The remaining onlookers gradually headed back to their own homes, anxious to share tawdry rumors with family and neighbors. All the strewn paper had been picked up and the crime scene was dismantled in a surprisingly efficient manner before the oncoming rain fell.

Levi watched Dubey Smith, a local boy just out of paramedic school, commandeer the help of two other men, all working within the confined quarters of Quinine's back seat. They attempted to stuff his mortal remains into a body bag with dignity, but it just wasn't working. Quinine was a tall man. Three white paramedics had never clothed a dead black man on a cold slippery night, and no one really wanted to handle the evidence. They grappled with the bag and the body in an awkward show of hygienic persistence. Finally, the body was bent like a pretzel and forced into a position that allowed Quinine to be zipped into eternity.

The thinning crowd watched quietly in an acknowledgement of their own mortality as the body was placed onto a gurney and wheeled to the ambulance. The final shape of the body bag protruded in various ungainly directions as if it contained some ghastly, alien form frozen into an unnatural state.

Levi was curious. The crime scene made no sense and Foster's story made no sense. "Hey, Dubey!" Levi ran up to the younger man as he heaved the bag into the ambulance. "If Quinine was just killed, how could the rigor mortis set in that fast?"

"Because, Mr. Levi," he said solemnly with the utmost respect, "that's the biggest damn erection you could imagine. That was a real man." Levi raised his eyebrows in a newfound recognition of Quinine, not knowing how to respond. He turned and walked back to his car as he rewound the film in his camera, carefully marking the film casing with a felt tip pen, then slipping it into his pocket so he wouldn't lose it. Then, he felt the card he had picked up earlier. Looking around to ensure he was alone, he held it up to read under a streetlight, shocking himself as he softly mouthed the words:

Protected By:

Imperial Knights of the Ku Klux Klan
Protectors of the White Race
Call 800-ImWhite

Chapter Sixteen
Images From The Past

The storm had passed but the high humidity made the smell of fresh newspaper ink linger in Sally's kitchen. Sally held the newspaper carefully at its edges so as not to get ink on her fingers. She read the headlines out loud to Lee Esther and Maggie over afternoon tea, as was their custom. The front-page headline announced "Bumkin Policeman Murdered." It was followed by Levi's article that covered half the front page and most of the back page, along with memorable quotes about Quinine from just about everyone in town.

Of course, the article wasn't nearly as interesting as the gossip Lee Esther and Maggie confided about Quinine, which was more than Sally ever wanted to know. It was clear to her that the passing of Quinine had indeed created a genuine sadness in the black community, along with a new sense of pride. Rumors about his last moments on earth had increased Quinine's stature by epic proportions. Maggie giggled along with the older women, never letting them know that she had already received the inside story directly from Reverend Hezekial. She couldn't help but smile knowing the Reverend had been humbled by the revelation of Quinine's manhood. Gratefully, he had also been aroused by it, Maggie remembered with a devilish smile.

"Reverend Hezekial said he could only imagine the power of a woman who could kill a man and still leave him in a fit of passion! The Reverend said he had to tell that undertaker to modify the casket or to modify Quinine, so the casket could be sealed for church," Maggie blurted excitedly.

"My-oh-my!" Lee Esther exclaimed half in shock, half in awe.

Sally sat speechless, as she listened to the dialogue between her black sisters. It was the stuff of black legends that she had collected as a historian, but she had never seen it in real time. She knew that the casket story would only swell a newfound sense of pride within the black community, confirming a myth that everyone already believed.

"Well, at least he died happy, Mrs. Sally. I'll bet that his girlfriend was happy too!" Maggie volunteered in a manner that made the older women wince.

Sally handed the newspaper to Bam as he walked into the kitchen, drenched in perspiration from a five-mile jog after school. She immediately held her finger to her lips with a stern look to make Lee Esther and Maggie shut off any further reference to Quinine's body parts. The last thing Sally needed was to explain rigor-mortis erections to Bam. Not that it was anything he didn't know about. But Southern mothers didn't ask about things their sons already knew. It might lead to a conversation well beyond the ken of Southern maternal congeniality. That was what older brothers were for.

Bam had already heard the Quinine story at school of course, just like everyone else in town, but he was anxious to get the facts, or close enough, from the local newspaper. A good amateur photographer himself, Bam especially wanted to see the pictures. He read the headline and looked closely at the lead photo of Doctor Hines with the profile of the incarcerated woman leaning against the car window. A bracelet dangling on her wrist glinted from the cameras flash as she puffed on a cigarette.

Bam nudged Maggie playfully and pointed to the photograph. "Hey, she kind of looks like you!"

"You white boys, you don't know nuthin!" Maggie reacted angrily in jest, slapping Bam across the chest. "You think we all look alike! Well, I got news for you, Bam Callahan! All you white boys look the same and it ain't none too good either! And, you ain't got nuthin' on my man Quinine!"

Bam pulled the front page closer to his face for closer inspection. "What's all the trash on the ground?" he asked Maggie as he laid the paper out on the pine table.

"Looks like a shit load of food stamps if you ask me," Maggie said quietly so Sally wouldn't hear her cuss.

Bam gulped, making a mental link to the EZ Mart that he didn't want to think about. His voice turned croaky. "Are you sure, Maggie?"

"That there is food stamps, Bam. I know food stamps," she acknowledged with irrefutable experience in her voice. "Do you think that girl got paid in food stamps for doin' things?" A food stamp hooker was hard to believe, even for Maggie.

Lee Esther briskly walked over, snapping the paper off the table to see what the fuss was about. She grew quiet as she looked at the paper, her natural happiness abruptly vanishing as she eyed the photo. "Bam, you go get yo' shower now and Magnolia, you get on home. Don't be messin' with this stuff. This here is bad people. Go on, now. I got supper to cook."

An inexplicable chill quickly filled the room. Bam looked at Sally with curiosity. She motioned for him to do as instructed. Maggie fiddled with her necklace unconsciously as she looked at Lee Esther. Teatime was over. Maggie knew too well when Lee Esther was upset. But she usually knew why.

Bam quietly headed toward a hot shower, lost in his own world. He didn't know what had upset Lee Esther, but he did know that it was only a matter of time before someone would be asking why Quinine and his mulatto hooker had bags of food stamps in their possession. And he had an ugly suspicion he might know where they came from.

Left alone with Lee Esther, Sally silently extended her hand, palm up, to her friend and maid. The cook placed the rolled newspaper in her hand after a momentary hesitation. Sally opened the newspaper and spread it back neatly on the pine table in front of her, sipping the remainder of her tea while she scrutinized the front-page photo. Lee Esther returned to the stove, soon lost in the sound of catfish frying in the big cast iron pan.

Sally methodically inspected the image in front of her with the eye of a trained photographer and journalist. She was immediately taken aback with the profile of the young woman in the back of the police car. She did look like Maggie. In fact, she looked exactly like Maggie.

Chapter Seventeen
Snowball

Sally grabbed repeatedly for the bedside phone, finally tipping it off of its stand. She felt under her bed, found the cord, and pulled the receiver to her, lifting its cold metal gingerly to her ear with a groggy "Hello."

"Mrs. Sally, this here is Danny down at the station," a high-pitched voice squealed into the phone. "We got Snowball in storage over here. Can you pick him up as usual?"

"Do I have to?" Sally asked, her voice muffled by her favorite feather pillow handed down from her Grandma Sally, for whom she was named. It smelled as old and comfortable as it was. Silence, then she finally asked, "How bad is it?"

"Nuthin' much different than usual, Mrs. Sally. He smelled pretty bad from booze and all, and probably knew Jesse wouldn't let him stay in. But I 'spect he'll be cleaned up 'bout noon or so."

"You out of room again, Danny?"

"Yes, ma'am. We had a big night last night. More of this racial stuff goin' on. We got ourselves eight or ten new inmates who gonna be stayin' for a while."

Sally frowned. Bumkin didn't need any more headlines, but the jail was small and even a normal Saturday night honky-tonk brawl could fill it up. "Anyone hurt?" Sally felt obligated to ask.

"No, ma'am. Just a bunch of black folk having a ruckus," Danny replied matter-of-factly.

"Was Snowball part of the ruckus?" she queried.

"Snowball? Oh no, no ma'am. Snowball doesn't fight or fuss, Mrs. Sally. He just got on a run shootin' the bones and needed to sleep it off. He must'a done okay last night. He shore had a bundle of cash and food stamps on him and I need to hand it off to you before it disappears. I put it in the safe for him. He locked himself up good and proper in his cell, but I gotta get the cell emptied in case we get any more 'visitors.' Asides, Mrs. Sally, we got that black gal in here what killed Quinine. She takes up a whole cell to herself. You take a little time and we'll roust Snowball here shortly to start breakfast."

"Okay." "I'll be there by ten, Danny. Save me some biscuits."

"Will do, Miss Sally."

It wasn't unusual for Snowball to have a roll of cash on him from gambling, but she couldn't imagine him having food stamps. Snowball was too proud to ever use food stamps. Something was different. Then she realized why Danny needed her to get to the station before Snowball served up lunch. He was harmless among men, but he was legendary around women. He had his personal cell at the jailhouse with access to his own keys. Leaving Snowball in the lockup alone with a cute hooker, fresh from a winning streak with a load of cash and food stamps on hand, wasn't in Danny's job description.

"Get some coffee in him and keep him busy in the kitchen until I get there, Danny."

"Shore thang, Mrs. Sally. We'll have him fixed up decent by the time we see you," the deputy assured her.

"See ya soon." Sally hung up the phone and glanced at the alarm clock. She needed her morning tea. Danny woke her up at eight a.m. on Saturday morning to tell her that Snowball was still asleep. Great. She would have tea, Danny would suck up caffeine, and Snowball would sleep off a hangover, waiting for his chauffeur to show up. Sally shook her head as she pulled herself out of bed and plodded a path down the long hallway toward her favorite teacup, delicately laced with ivy like her grandmother's garden. Saturday mornings shouldn't start out this way, she grumbled to herself.

"Snowball" had been bequeathed to the Callahan family by her side of the family, the Lelands. He was one of those family heirlooms still only possible in the Deep South. The Lelands had always taken care of him like he was their own, which he was, like it or not. However politically charged that statement was in the midst of an integration order, it remained the honest and welcome reality between Snowball and the Lelands.

Snowball was a free spirit who enjoyed life by any standard of human measurement. He was too wily not to. She remembered her grandfather, Daddy Leland, saying that Snowball was the only nigger he knew who would have voted against the abolition of slavery. He made his living being a black man in a white man's world. He was a man of many talents: the best cook in the parish, a professional gambler, and an accomplished lady's man. Snowball could play Dixieland on a handsaw and mesmerize youngsters with stories about the Normandy invasion. No one could replace Snowball and no one wanted to, least of all the Callahans, or Snowball.

Support of Snowball was generally spread among her extended family in one form or another. Sally was his chosen custodian today, until he was fit to be returned to his wife Jesse. The Callahans were both caretakers and family for Snowball, as he was for the Callahans, although Sally was never quite sure who worked for whom where Snowball was concerned. However maddening, the historian in her knew the Saturday morning drill was a rich slice of Southern life that wouldn't last another generation.

Who else would handle odd jobs around the house, pick up groceries when she was sick, or cook for family get-togethers on a moment's notice? Even when she got mad at him, which was as common as not, she held a soft spot in her heart for Snowball. He was like a piece of history that would soon be lost, a vanishing breed of black man, and a dependable member of her extended family.

Sally put on her glasses and waited for her tea to boil, enjoying the solitude of a quiet home early in the morning. The cool mist from the winter night was just beginning to lift off the bayou into a bright, crisp day. She picked up the daily newspaper. A small headline at the bottom right corner of the front page of the *Daily Town Talk* from nearby Alexandria immediately caught her eye: "Woman held for Slaying of Bumkin Policeman."

The article looked like it had been lifted directly from Levi Epstein's account of Quinine's death in the *Bumkin Record*. It didn't attempt to do justice to the details of Quinine's circumstances that only the locals would appreciate. A story about the hinterlands didn't warrant a picture in the daily newspaper. But it did serve to assure the good citizens of Bumkin that they were safe from a fragile, 110-pound, unidentified mulatto female being held without bail in the Bumkin City Jail.

There was noticeably no mention of the girl's prostitution history or standing employment at The Spot brothel, let alone her weapon that was supposedly confiscated. No mention of where, when, or why, the classic reporter's questions. Hell, all they had to do was ask anyone on Main Street in Bumkin and they could have gotten more information than they put into print, Sally thought. Her reporter instincts screamed that something was deadly wrong. Someone had called in a favor with the publisher to make sure that their reporter didn't go past the Avignon Parish line to gather the detailed information that the murder of a local policeman normally warranted. Only the Sheriff or Bubba Tremblay had the stroke to stop the daily reporters from doing their job.

The teapot began to whistle as Sally picked out one of her signature cotton dresses. She realized that she had never had a tour of the Bumkin jail. It might just be a good time to make that happen.

An hour later, she walked into the barren, cinder-block walls of the Bumkin Police Station. It was painted a dull battleship gray that was void of appeal except for a caricature of the southern Sheriff from Alice's Restaurant hanging on the wall, the latest movie to slam southern culture. But the poster made it hard not to notice the nameless deputies walking around with potbellies and big guns, holding stale coffee in Styrofoam cups. Hollywood was missing out on a lot of raw talent, Sally mused.

The front-page picture from the most recent edition of the *Bumkin Record* was pinned to a cork billboard on the waiting room wall. The headline proclaimed Bumkin to be "The best spot topside of God's green earth." Underneath, Sheriff Landeaux and the mayor smiled as they broke ground for a big new outdoor sign proclaiming the Chamber of Commerce's famous slogan on the main highway to the south side of town. The town didn't have the money for a sign on the north side just yet.

Danny Ducote stirred inside a stainless-steel cage, sealed behind impressive bullet-proof, plate-glass windows that made him look like a bug under a magnifying glass. His perch gave the illusion that large numbers of people were attempting to break into, or out of, the Bumkin prison. No one could get past the thick, steel door that he guarded religiously with pen and paper. Except, of course, those people who were always exceptions to the rules, like Mrs. Sally Callahan.

Danny immediately stood up in conformance with his Southern upbringing and pressed a button underneath his desk to release the lock. The door opened automatically to admit Sally and he greeted her with a goofy neighborhood smile, never understanding that the illusion of his importance had just evaporated. "Mornin', Miss Sally," Danny said pleasantly.

"Is he alive, Danny?"

"Well, he's still laid out in his cell, Miss Sally, but he shore cooked up a great breakfast for me n' the boys. You know, I ain't ever seen someone who could cook with his eyes closed. He just got right up and walked into the kitchen, still drunk as Cooter Brown, and cooked up a great mess of eggs, bacon and biscuits. Even that female inmate gal asked for more. Next thing I knowed, he was back asleep." Danny handed over a saucer to Sally with two hot, butter-drenched biscuits covered in tin foil. Even Sally was impressed; the biscuits melted in her mouth. Must have been the military training, she figured.

"Did Snowball eat anything?"

"I'm not sure, Mrs. Sally. I'm not sure he was ever awake, now that I think about it."

"Where's Roy?"

"He's asleep underneath Snowball's bed. He always stays close to Snowball. You know, Mrs. Sally, I never knowed a coon could snore. And you know what else? Roy turned his nose up at scrambled eggs. Snowball said he only likes his eggs fried, sunny side up."

Sally shook her head. Never a dull moment, she thought. She pulled a small bag of vanilla wafers out of her purse that she always carried for Roy the

Raccoon, who would kill for vanilla wafers. It was the only way she could get the big raccoon to follow her when Snowball wasn't fully conscious. Snowball kept a pack of wafers in his shirt pocket so Roy could access them while he rode around town on Snowball's shoulder. They were quite an act. You had to love 'em.

"Let's go take a look," Sally said, walking deliberately toward the jail cell. She wanted to get into the cell quarters quickly to make her next request. Danny picked up the keys and followed obediently down the dark hall to the jail cells.

At the end of the dank concrete hall, in the only cell sectioned off by actual steel bars, Snowball Jacobs lay perfectly rigid on his regulation canvass army cot, hands folded neatly on his chest. He snored softly, his face the picture of contentment. Huge, ebony black feet jutted out the end of the thick wool army blanket, meticulously draped over a seemingly lifeless body. The letters on the blanket proclaimed that the body was the property of the U.S. Army, 606th Cavalry. The Army of General George Patton. At the end of the bed, Roy's large, fluffy ringed tail lay stretched out on the floor from beneath the cot, the source of a lighter noise that sounded like a baby snoring between Snowball's heavy heaves. Sally could see a metal plate on the floor in the corner with the remnants of a fried egg, sunny side up.

Sally's memory flickered back to the story of a young black army officer in World War II, twenty years earlier. General Patton had promised to jail the young officer, caught red-handed with a stolen pig on a spit in Southern France, at the end of the Normandy invasion. Snowball was unflinching, and probably drunk at the time. He convinced the general to try some of the pork before he went peacefully on to the brig, knowing that Patton himself had Louisiana roots. As the Cochon de Lait melted in his mouth, the general reconsidered, feeling that the brig would be a terrible waste of culinary talent. Better yet, the general's new personal cook had enough bullshit and Cajun French in him to procure food in a war zone, and he proved to be a useful translator for his staff.

Snowball would forever live off his general's legacy. He walked with the limp of a hero's wound sustained from a grenade for which the army sent him a regular disability check. Of course, the Leland family had long known that he had actually been stabbed in the leg during a brawl over a card game as he taught naïve Frenchmen how to gamble, Louisiana style.

Sally and Danny slowly encroached on the sleeping soldier. His snoring reverberated against the bleak, cement walls with the deep sound of satisfied intoxication. He was the blackest of Negroes, with short, cropped grey hair. He lay bare chested with the same red suspenders he always wore since returning from the war, a small patch of grey chest hair standing out against his ebony skin.

"Thanks for letting him keep his army gear here, Danny," Sally said earnestly.

"Ain't no problem, Mrs. Sally. We all knowed he served his country well, so we keep his gear in the hall closet." No matter where he was today, Snowball would always be a veteran from the real war, an American who had paid his dues. Danny crossed his arms and leaned up against the wall with a nod. "It wasn't like this here war we're fightin' in Vietnam, Mrs. Sally. That there was a man's war." Danny was happy to have missed out on both.

Sally turned to Danny. "Where's that girl you have locked up?"

Danny silently nodded toward the cell door thirty feet down the narrow hall and to her right. A small 12-inch by 12-inch window centered in the plate steel door offered the only possible view. She walked over and stood up on her toes, barely able to see over the edge of the window.

The mulatto sat on a feather mattress with plain cotton sheets. She played mindlessly with her bracelet in bored silence. Sally stared at her for a few long seconds. There was no doubt in her mind. She knew the features like those of her own children. The slim frame and long neck, the high forehead, the turned-up nose and high cheekbones. It was no coincidence. That girl was one of Roberta's children. The rumors she had dismissed for decades were true. Maggie had a twin.

"What's with the bracelet, Danny?"

"She done put up such a screamin' battle about that bracelet we jus' decided to let her hold onto it."

"What's her name?"

"She calls herself Meadow. We don't know what her real name is. Don't know if she even knows."

"I'm sure the Sheriff's buddies can help you out," Sally said cynically. She doubted that The Spot kept files on its working girls, but the Sheriff would know them by name.

"Now Mrs. Sally, it ain't my place to ask those questions. It may not be yours either, if you know what I mean." Danny was getting an uneasy feeling.

Sally settled back on her feet and turned to Danny with a demanding stare. "Okay, Danny, while you get Snowball up, I want to visit with this young lady for a few minutes," she said matter-of-factly.

Danny stood to attention and started scratching his ear, as was his habit when he panicked. "Now, Mrs. Sally, I don't know if I can do that without the Sheriff's permission!"

Sally's stare meant business and Danny knew it. She wasn't budging. She looked silently at Snowball resting peacefully on his cot and then back at Danny. The deputy instantly knew it was a lost battle.

"Now Mrs. Sally, that ain't' fair, you know I can't keep Snowball here, and I got to get permission from the Sheriff."

"And I've got to get home, Danny. With or without Snowball. You think the Sheriff is going to tell you to stand guard over me? I started first grade with Sheriff Franklin, knew him twenty years before he ever became a policeman. Now look, Danny," Sally changed her tactics, figuring she had sufficiently intimidated the young deputy. "I don't think this young woman has had any other women to visit her. She's just a child. She can't be much older than Bam. I'll check on her and be gone by the time you get sleeping beauty up and walking. He needs some coffee anyway."

"I think he's had plenty of coffee already. It don't seem to do much good."

"Then you better think of something fast, or I'm leaving him with you. Now open up," Sally said sternly, her teacher's finger pointing at the door to Meadow's cell. Danny inevitably succumbed to the willpower of the stronger individual. His shoulders drooped as he opened the heavy, steel door.

"You can't be more than 15 minutes, Mrs. Sally. Now don't press me." Sally gave him a dismissive nod, ignoring his hollow threat as she walked into Meadow's cell. Danny would get over it or risk Sally telling his wife about the private strip-poker game he policed at the Golden Nugget. The best threats never had to be voiced in a small town.

Sally had given a lot of thought to the girl sitting in front of her since she saw the photograph in the newspaper. It had been local gossip that Maggie had a twin sister at birth, but Lee Esther had never confirmed the circumstances of Roberta's death, or the loss of the other child. It also was clear that Lee Esther was trying to protect Maggie with a mother's love. It was all too much for Sally to ignore. Besides which, Sally carried the same burden of responsibility to Maggie that she did to Snowball. They were family. Responsibility or guilt? she asked herself. Maybe Southerners didn't know the difference.

Either way, Maggie had a right to know her sister was alive, and Sally had an obligation to Maggie's family that went back several generations. History was meant to be honored in Sally's world.

The Mulatto looked up hesitantly. She was immersed in the depressive loneliness that resided in the confined quarters of a small-town, dingy jail cell. A small town where both sides of the tracks had already convicted her of racial homicide. "Who are you?" she asked suspiciously of Sally, both defiance and fear in her voice.

"My name is Sally Callahan. You can just call me Mrs. Sally. I just came by to check on you, Meadow."

"Why?" It was an accusation as much as a question. The long legs curled beneath her while she sucked nicotine from a cigarette.

"I thought you might like a visitor," Sally replied in her friendliest voice. "Where are you from?"

"Up the road, at The Spot. You know that. The whole world knows I'm a whore."

"Even whores deserve friends," Sally responded without sympathy.

"Even black whores?"

"If you were a full black, you wouldn't be allowed in The Spot. The whole world knows that too." It was an unexpected statement that startled the prisoner. Female mulattos, especially pretty ones, held a different position from blacks in the local caste system. She wouldn't have been found in The Spot as a black woman. Sally hoped she could spur the mulatto into a discussion with the calm voice of an older, white woman, but she wasn't in the mood for jousting. She needed answers, and she needed them fast. Snowball would soon rise from the dead and she had things to do.

"So, I'm not a nigger, I'm just a police killer," Meadow said defiantly.

"Are you? I don't know that. Only the judge can decide that."

Meadow stared out the singular narrow window with a view of the police parking lot. "Don't matter none," she said quietly. "They going to 'lectrocute me just the same."

A Bumkin police car broke the silence as it parked just outside the jail wall. Sally and Meadow watched an officer pull himself out of the car through a thin window in the metal grating, his official clipboard full of new speeding tickets for the city coffers. Meadow began to shake uncontrollably. She shifted her feet to the floor and put her head down, trying to get control over her breathing as the lit cigarette fell onto the cotton sheets.

Sally immediately rushed to the bed and brushed the cigarette onto the floor. She sat next to Meadow and put her arm around her, pulling her inward on her shoulder, hugging her as a mother hugs a lost child.

Sally looked beyond the police car and saw Bubba Tremblay's unmistakable profile across the street. He sat alone, reading the morning paper in his truck. Sally figured he had spotted her car in front of the station. Or was she just getting paranoid? Regardless, she didn't have any time left to get information.

"What happened, Meadow? What really happened?"

"It's about the bag, Mrs. Sally. I shouldn't have asked Quincy to open it. It was full of money and food stamps. There was a phone number in it that scared him bad. We were gonna leave so we could be together, I just didn't know he was gonna take all their money. We pulled over to sleep on a road for a while 'cause he thought someone might follow us. Shore nuff, they had. They snuck up on Quincy and me. We didn't have no clothes on and the Big Man went crazy. He swung the door open and shot Quincy before he could get up, then he came on me like I was still hookin' at The Spot. That policeman over there," she pointed and hardened her gaze. "Foster, it's him. He watched Quincy die, then he shoved me into the Big Man's truck and drove Quincy's car back into town, with Quincy dead in the back seat. They acted like I shot him, and he had to defend himself from me."

Sally could hear movement. She had to get out now without getting Danny in trouble. She had more questions than answers, but Foster and Bubba didn't just show up at the same time for no good reason. "Do you have a lawyer, Meadow?"

"I don't trust no one, Mrs. Sally, 'specially lawyers."

Sally nodded. It was good advice, even if you weren't a mulatto hooker jailed by white men, accused of murdering a black cop in outback Louisiana.

"We'll talk some more," Sally reassured her, hugging her one more time before she slipped out the door and pulled it slowly back into position. She turned the key and palmed it as she walked down the jail hallway towards Snowball's cell.

Snowball was standing, somewhat shakily, folding his army blanket with care, gently placing it into the hall closet while Sally waited at the cell door. The steel security door at the end of the hall swung open unexpectedly behind them, spreading light down the dark passage. Sally could hear authoritative footsteps walking toward her, sure it was Foster Landeaux's swashbuckling gait, with Danny tagging behind. Sally intentionally kept her hands in front of her and her back to the approaching footsteps.

"I think we're just about ready to get on home, Danny," she said loudly, then turned abruptly and feigned surprise at the sight of Foster. "Well, hello Foster," she said. "You're up early for a Saturday morning, aren't you?"

"Just checkin' on things, Mrs. Sally. There's a lot going on in town these days." He looked into Meadow's cell window with a show of concern, lingering a moment to watch the Mulatto stretch out on the unbending mattress. His head jerked back when Meadow looked up and gave him the finger. Even in her current state, she was naturally sexy, and naturally defiant.

Sally searched Danny's face for expression, unsure whether he had told Foster that she had been into Meadow's cell or not. Then again, Danny didn't have the spine to fess up voluntarily. She winked at him to let him know she had the key in hand and received a visible sigh of relief.

In his cell, Snowball buttoned a brilliant white, newly bleached and starched shirt, laundered and hand pressed by a fellow inmate in appreciation for breakfast. He finished putting his belongings neatly on the closet shelf and shut the door with his usual panache, holding his head high even though the hangover from the night before still wracked his senses. He walked past Sally and up to Foster, grabbing his hand and shaking it profusely.

"Thank you for the hospitality, Mistuh Foster. You tell the Sheriff I done fed all the boys well this God's mornin'." Sally rolled her eyes. Daddy Leland was certainly laughing somewhere in heaven right now. He used to call it Snowball's "Mastuh" pitch; he served it best when he needed a loan or was lifting your wallet. While Snowball peppered Foster with platitudes, Sally sifted through the cramped quarters of the narrow hallway so that she was now behind Foster, with her back to Danny. She stifled a laugh at Snowball's sly manipulation of his white captors, enamored as she watched a master at work. She dangled the key quietly behind her back, until she felt Danny take it from her just as the small gathering broke up and headed out the security door.

"Let's go, Snowball, the day is still young," Sally proclaimed. Snowball walked gingerly ahead carrying his hangover behind dark eyeshades. He stopped for a moment so Roy could catch up, scurrying up his master's leg and taking his spot on Snowball's left shoulder.

Sally marched Snowball outside with Roy. She opened the car door for Snowball as Roy jumped onto the back floorboard where he was trained to ride. Everyone knew the drill. She shut the door after Roy settled in.

Snowball immediately flopped down on the back seat of the Rambler station wagon. He appeared to be in good shape and was conversant as only Snowball could be after costing his friends and keepers an entire Saturday morning. Sally drove quietly toward his "regular" house on the outskirts of Shirley Plantation. Jesse would be gone by now, departing without leaving one of her famous chocolate pies behind. It was a sign to let Snowball know she was pissed off at his latest foray, but the door would be unlocked for his return. Any winnings from the night before would be left in the cookie jar as a peace offering before Snowball went comatose on the couch. It was a well-rehearsed play and the entire town of Bumkin was a supporting cast.

Sally drove slowly, hoping that Snowball didn't throw up in her car. She turned onto a dirt road that traced the bayou to Jesse's neat cabin deep in thought.

"Mrs. Sally," Snowball's voice broke the silence of the ride like a ghost floating on her back seat. He was lying down, face up, staring through dark glasses and red eyes. His was a strange accent, a romantic mix of Cajun French, English, and black patois. "How you knowed dat girl in jail?" he quizzed without warning.

"I don't know her, Lawrence," Sally replied matter-of-factly, addressing Snowball by his Christian name as only she did. No one outside the Leland family and Jesse even knew his real name. "I just wanted to meet her. Why do you ask?"

"Dat's Roberta's daughter," he stated, a sad quality entering his voice. Sally's eyebrows rose as she looked at him in the rearview mirror. She had forgotten that Roberta was a peer of Snowball's, and God knew what else.

"Both of dose two girls, dey belong to Mr. Tremblay."

Sally slammed on the brakes. The automobile came to a screeching halt. Snowball tumbled onto the back floor of the sedan and Roy scrambled for cover under the front seat.

Sally took her foot off the brake and gently pulled over on the grassy ditch that lined the bayou. She turned off the ignition and turned around in her seat, leaning against the car door as she faced Snowball with a face full of concern. He clambered back into a prone position in the back seat, staring up at the ceiling with a somber look.

"Lawrence, why in the world would you say that?" Sally demanded, trying to contain her shock.

"I knowed it," he said, his arms covering his shades. This was a particularly bad hangover.

"How would you know?"

"You might be surprised what a drunk nigger can hear when he wants to, Mrs. Sally."

"And why haven't you ever told me?"

"You might be surprised what a drunk nigger can forget when he needs to, Mrs. Sally," he deadpanned.

Sally scowled at her black companion for a long moment, frustrated by his sudden honesty. "Okay, Lawrence. This stays between us. Out with it. There's a young girl's life at stake. What do you know?" It wasn't a question; it was a command from his senior officer.

Snowballs' eyes remained closed beneath his shades as he mustered his words. "Roberta and I growed up together, Mrs. Sally. We was close. Of course, she was wicked hot and always had lots of men but we were special-close. She told me she had been stayin' out in the ol' cabin on the Tremblay's farm during weekends. Then she moved there full time after Lee Esther got older and could take care of her children. She knowed full well she couldn't handle all her kids as well as Lee Esther did, so Lee Esther became their mom. Roberta just figured she was better off sending money to Lee Esther rather than be in her way. Mr. Tremblay would visit her regular back then. 'Course Roberta, she got 'round anyway and we all knew her. Black and white. But her and Bubba had a real thing goin', Mrs. Sally. They would get drunk and tease each other about themselves. Roberta taught him to smoke dope. She even taught him how to grow dope. Bubba, he really did treat her good till he knew she had twins. I think he really liked her. But Roberta wouldn't have an abortion 'cause they was his. He was the only man she really cared about," his voice trailed off.

Sally sat in stunned silence. "What happened, Lawrence? Tell me." Sally persisted.

"Last thing I remember was that Roberta tells me Bubba didn't want the twins around town, there was too much to go wrong. Then she died. Well, we all knowed she was murdered. He probably had one of his mad fits when she wouldn't do what he told her to. Next thing is Lee Esther is raising a new baby, Maggie, but no one knows what happened to the other girl. No one talks about it either."

"Are you sure, Lawrence, really sure?"

"Yeah, I'm sure Mrs. Sally. You see Roberta, she loved Bubba's cabin. It has a big magnolia tree dat growed in the corner of an open field. She would talk about sitting under the magnolia tree with Bubba and catching the breeze blowin' out over the meadow. She named one girl for the magnolia, the other girl was named for the meadow." His voice trailed off as he mercifully fell asleep.

Chapter Eighteen
Hezekial's Calling

Hezekial walked proudly into his office, his new fluorescent purple suspenders tightly stretched over a lavender shirt, tucked into his navy-blue, double-knit suit pants. It had taken him a week to locate the right phone number, but it was well worth it.

Leadership required effort and risk, although he saw no downside to his plan. If Ethan White had elected to ignore the whole affair, Hezekial could bring sympathy and understanding to his experience. If, on the other hand, White had left with a bruised ego, delivered from a white woman's unexpected knock-out punch, Hezekial could deliver a method for retribution.

Not retribution, Hezekial quickly corrected himself. Retribution belonged only to God. Humility. Yes, that was the issue, wasn't it? God's messengers should teach humility. And like all of God's messages, humility deserved to be spread around.

He glanced at his own Coca-Cola wall clock donated to the Mount Zion Baptist Church by the local bottler. It was eight o'clock; nine o'clock in Boston. They were so big they had their own time zone. Hezekial dialed the number as he read from the scrap of paper on his desk.

Twenty seconds later, the buzz of a distant ring made its way into a phone at Cleaver & Windrop, a small but politically well-connected law firm with decades of ties to the Democratic Party. A well-spoken secretary answered, "Cleaver and Windrop. How may I help you?"

"Dear lady, I would like to speak to Attorney Ethan White," Hezekial said in his best preacher's voice.

"Certainly, sir," she replied, her own voice smooth and responsive. She wondered if she would have the opportunity to meet the man at the other end of that wonderful voice. "One minute," she added, wanting to hear that voice again.

"Thank you, ever so much," he said before she put the call through. Hezekial wondered if she looked as good as she sounded.

Another deep, but more serious voice answered the phone a thousand miles away. Hezekial instantly recognized Ethan White.

Hezekial cleared his throat to sustain his most ministerial voice, toned down a little so as not to sound too black, too Southern, or too Baptist. "Hello," he offered, "is this Mr. White? I am looking for Attorney White who is advisor to the Department of Justice on integration?" It was a good intro.

"It is." The response was short and quick. White looked up from his reading table over a thick book of Supreme Court cases, momentarily rubbing his temple as he focused on the unexpected voice from the Deep South.

"Mr. White, this is Reverend Hezekial Allen of the Mount Zion Baptist Church in Bumkin, Louisiana." A slight pause. "I was a witness to your retort to Dr. Sally Callahan's speech last week."

"Yes, Reverend," his voice turned cool, almost suspicious in tone. "What can I do for you?"

"Attorney White," Hezekial had rehearsed since early morning, "I believe that the efforts of agents of our government, such as yourself, must be supported in the local communities they are seeking to change. I do not pretend to know what impact your visit had, or did not have, on your efforts to erase racism in our land. But, as we both know, education is the battlefront of a plague upon which there can be no exceptions to the eradication of prejudice. I would like to offer my help and that of my congregation, and we would like to solicit your help in the battle that we both must win." Hezekial returned the phone on the desk, freeing up his left thumb to stretch his suspender with the pride of the moment. He felt good, and when the preacher felt good, his message felt good.

Hezekial waited patiently as White calculated his response, thinking through the unexpected contact and the eloquence of his introduction. "How would you suggest that we help each other, Reverend?" Although his voice remained suspicious, it now offered a kernel of curiosity.

"We sir, require your guidance to this end," a silky texture always crept back into Hezekial's voice when he was on a roll, no matter how much he tried to quash it. "We are not adept at attempting such things on our own. I can only note that your expressed concern over the favoritism received by Dr. Callahan's son is certainly endemic to the bigger issues that haunt our community. Obviously, we both know it is symbolic, which the white population does not understand. It is a symbol of acceptance of the status quo, an unwillingness to embrace equality as it should be. We are all concerned. The members of Mount Zion are prepared to mobilize, to bring this matter into a local perspective, which requires action. Assuming, of course, that such an effort deserves greater attention from our leaders in Washington."

Hezekial allowed a momentary silence. The Reverend knew he was dealing with a federal bureaucracy and Yankeeland diplomacy was needed. If there was one thing Hezekial prided himself on, it was reading his audience. "Of course, we would have to find the precious resources necessary to dedicate to such a worthy effort."

White thought back to the sweltering summer day, the smell of southern fried chicken, and the heat of the exchange with Dr. Sally Callahan. A white Southern woman preaching to other white Southerners about black people. How could a white woman possibly understand the experience of the black race? "Reverend Allen, your concerns are our concerns. Allow me to introduce this to the appropriate people in Washington and I will get back to you." White's voice had become lighter, almost friendly, in the last thirty seconds. It brought a big smile to Hezekial's face as he sipped the remainder of his coffee.

"God bless you, Mr. White. My congregation and I will eagerly wait to hear back from you. God's warriors are at your service." Hezekial put the phone on the cradle and frowned after his excitement delivered a splash of coffee on his pants. No matter. Maggie had been after him to get a new suit. So had his wife.

In Boston, Ethan White turned to his assistant. "Get Washington on the line."

"Who was that?" the younger woman asked.

"A black minister in Bumkin, Louisiana."

"What did he want?"

"Money and fame," White said matter-of-factly, then returned to his law books.

Chapter Nineteen
Second Calling

Trigger Winchester pointed Bam and Clyde toward two leather chairs as they entered his office. They sat down, trying to calm their nerves.

The boys had been unexpectedly instructed to meet Winchester in his office that afternoon by Mizery Lutz, who took great pleasure in delivering the message.

They went home and sneaked out in coats and ties for the occasion, trying to look like wholesome students while they carefully avoided parents who might ask questions. They had agreed on the drive over that the call from the Superintendent's office was better than a call to Greely's office, where they both stood to be hung at high noon on the big oak tree.

Gil Winchester greeted the boys with a display of disgust for paperwork as he moved stacks of paper one-by-one from his desk to a nearby table, threw his coat on a hangar, and took his seat behind the desk across from the boys. He wore a black silk shirt with an expensive, cream-colored coat and matching tie today, cool by anyone's standards. He pulled his tie loose and rolled up his shirtsleeves after he sat down, then reached into a desk drawer and pulled out a small tape recorder that he placed in the center of the big desk.

Clyde and Bam looked at each other with wide-eyed apprehension. This looked like an interrogation. No one knew where they were. Bam wondered briefly whether the Sheriff had made a call to the Superintendent after their meeting but dismissed the idea quickly because he knew they had a deal. Everyone knew that a handshake among Southerners was as good as any written contract.

Winchester allowed his actions to garner the expected reaction, then opened the conversation. "Not to worry, gentlemen, I won't turn on this recorder without your agreement. You may not believe this, but you are minors; your recording wouldn't be admissible for court anyway. More importantly, I need your help."

Dead silence. The boys gulped.

Trigger waited for a calculated moment. "Here's the rap, boys. I need good, blunt information from you guys on this recorder that will help me get my school board off their ass in confronting the drug problems in our schools. No one will know it's you."

The boys sat stunned. Bam untied his tie. Clyde's big head bobbed back and forth as it always did when he was excited or stoned. "Would you repeat that, Mr. Winchester?" he asked with a polite demeanor that only Clyde could muster.

"Let me explain," the Superintendent said as he unleashed his charisma. "All these guys I work with on the school board are a bunch of old farts who don't have a clue about our schools. They are still living in the fifties with no idea of the changes that have occurred in the sixties. By the way boys, the fifties were when nobody smoked pot, girls didn't screw until you married them, and every healthy male wanted to enlist in the military."

The boys sat like statues, mesmerized by an educator whose voice blasted through them like a real person.

Trigger continued, "Here's the gig. You have to lay it all out, no bullshit, no sugar coating. Tell it like it is. I have to record you so the board will believe me, but your identities stay with me. No one else knows you're here That's why I called you out of class without any advance notice. If you have any problems with any of this, say so now."

Bam and Clyde shook their heads in a unison. This was a dream.

Clyde spoke up first. "You mean we can say anything, and no one will know it was us?"

"Your identity stays with me," Winchester said with assurance, holding his right hand up like a pledge.

"About anything?" Bam added.

Winchester didn't blink. "Anything."

"Nothing comes back at us?"

"Think of it as information amnesty," Winchester laughed, in referencing Vietnam headlines. Ever the rebel himself, Winchester reveled in his role. He loved kids, especially kids that rebelled against the system, especially one that was screwed up, like his.

This guy is like a big teenager, Bam thought. But why did he need them? "Who gets to hear the tape?" he asked, knowing nothing was safe from Sally.

"Not your mother, Bam," Winchester laughed. "Only the school board and I hear the tape."

Bam and Clyde eyed each other with growing confidence, each nodding. They were both visibly relieved. "Okay, we're in," Bam said.

"Good, let's roll. I'm going to refer to Bam as #1 and Clyde as #2." Winchester pressed the switch on the recorder, then cited the date and place of the meeting. "Let's talk about drugs first. Do either of you use drugs or alcohol? How about you, Number One?"

Bam shook his head. "No drugs, sir. Just beer and liquor. Mostly beer."

"Have you had any problems getting beer or booze?" Winchester asked.

"It was hard to get before I turned fourteen."

Winchester nodded, not terribly surprised. No one ever had a problem getting liquor in South Louisiana.

"How about you, Number Two. Do you use drugs?"

"Certainly, sir," Clyde responded in his most serious, articulate tone. Bam shook his head with concern. He knew anyone in Bumkin would recognize Clyde's voice.

"What kind?" Winchester shot back, appreciative of the honesty.

"Mostly marijuana. Lots of speed. Tried some acid once, but it was expensive."

"How often?" Winchester's confrontation with reality had suddenly become more real than he had contemplated.

"Whenever I can."

"When was the last time you had a joint?"

"Math class this morning. All those little numbers and symbols are pretty awesome when you're high."

Winchester put both hands on his head in an immediate reaction. "What?" his voice boomed through the room. "At school! This morning? Are you kidding me? Are you stoned now?"

"No sir, "Clyde retorted. "But I grabbed a joint on our way out, just in case," he said, fumbling in his shirt pocket. He plucked out a rolled joint and offered it up to his elder. "Want a drag? It might settle us all down?"

Winchester focused on the expertly rolled marijuana joint. The recorder hummed along, catching the audio shock of Winchester.

"Oh my God!" Winchester exclaimed. Bam couldn't tell whether it was genuine or for the benefit of the old farts at the school board. Winchester stood up, holding his finger to his lips as he walked over and scrutinized the joint. "Number Two, do you always take a joint to class with you?"

"Sure. Wouldn't you?"

It was an unexpected, poignant question. Winchester turned off the recorder and stretched his right hand out to Clyde with the curiosity of a child. "Can I take a look at that?"

Clyde looked over at Bam, shrugged, and handed the joint over to Winchester, who pulled his glasses from his coat pocket for closer inspection. "Hmm," he murmured, looking up over his glasses. Who rolled this?"

"I did, sir," Clyde said with pride.

"Really good job," Winchester acknowledged like a schoolroom teacher approving homework. "I haven't seen one rolled that clean since graduate school in California. What's it cost you these days?"

Clyde received the compliment with a grin and took back the joint, placing it carefully back into his shirt pocket. "The quality of the paper makes all the difference. A bag is about ten. What did it cost in the old days?"

"About the same," Winchester said casually, proving his mettle to two young bucks. "But it was a hell of a lot harder to come by and it was a weekend kind of thing. Production is just now getting more efficient and cheaper, you know. In my college days it was like getting drunk once a month over a weekend, not like going to class! And sure as hell not in high school." He punched the recorder back. "This will wake the board up."

"Number Two, no one says anything to you about your drug habit?"

"No, sir. Not really."

"Why the hell not?"

"Maybe they're stoned too? There are lots of stoned people in class."

Winchester's face turned scarlet at the thought of his teachers being so negligent under his leadership. How could it happen? Bam couldn't help but laugh out loud. Winchester took off his glasses and rubbed his forehead as he digested the conversation. "Unbelievable, ... unfucking believable" he muttered to himself. Bam wondered whether that part of the tape would be edited.

Bam spoke up, feeling the need to assist. "Dr. Winchester, the teachers aren't stoned, they're just overwhelmed and disorganized."

"I dunno man, they look stoned to me," Clyde intervened.

"Why do you think that is, Number One," the Superintendent asked, ignoring Clyde's dig at his teachers.

"Because," said Bam matter-of-factly, "it's too much. There is no order in the classroom. No one is in charge." He tensed in his chair, worried about his criticism getting back to Greely, then decided to continue. "No one gets disciplined for anything, much less smoking some weed. Most of the black kids are disruptive and intimidating, at least to white people. And they get away with it! Teachers can't discipline them, so they don't discipline anyone. So, no one does anything. So, we can get away with anything. Two years ago, any white kid who didn't show up with his homework would have been bounced out of school and sent to boot camp. Now there is no homework."

It was an incriminating response the Superintendent was glad to capture on tape. Nonetheless, Winchester was shocked and felt a need to defend his teachers. "C'mon, we both know there are plenty of good teachers out there."

"Don't you understand?" Bam's voice unleashed a frustration that bordered on anger. "It doesn't matter how good the teacher is. Everyone is physically scared. There are no rules. You threw us all together thinking you are in charge because you say you are, but no one is in charge. It's a fucking play school, Dr. Winchester. Good students don't stand a chance, no matter what color they are." His words slapped Winchester back into his chair. His eyes closed as the implications rolled over him.

The tape recorder made a clicking sound in the silence of the room. Bam concluded that Sally would ultimately learn about the tape from one of the school board members. It was too explosive and there weren't that many students who *could* be on the tape. Then she would badger Winchester into letting her listen to it. She would be proud of him for standing up for his beliefs, right after she decked him. But then again, she would never admit to having heard it, he consoled himself, because Winchester had assured him it was confidential, and she couldn't violate his guarantee to the boys. Southerners were complicated but predictable in their own way.

Winchester quietly took off his glasses yet again, placing them on the yellow legal pad where he had been jotting down notes. A cold shiver of reality ran down his back. He had never viewed integration from a real student's perspective. Now he understood.

It's not about racism, it's about controlling the rate of change which any organization, any community, could manage. The kids adapt faster than we can … and they blame it on the factors we create. We threw them into the future without a structure from the past to hold onto. We detached them from the tether of teacher authority and now they are freelancing way ahead of us. Younger kids are exploiting the void through drugs and sex. Things we used to do in college. What's next? Violence?

"Are you really going to play this to the school board?" Bam asked abruptly.

"You bet your ass, Number One," Winchester promised into the recorder. "Why do you ask?"

Clyde jumped in. "This is Number Two speaking," he said with farcical authority, "because whoever listens is going to think we're a couple of teenage honkies with a hard-on for black kids, who hate teachers, and are generally pissed off at the world, and it just ain't true." He paused for the moment of reflection. "Fact is, I'm happy. I'm stoned, but I'm happy."

"Number Two, could you handle school without being stoned?"

"No way. It's way too scary."

"Scary?"

"It really is. It's like going to a foreign country, gangs with guns and knives, probably teachers too, for that matter. It was never that way. It's easier to buzz out."

"Wait a minute, fellas," Winchester interrupted. "You and I know that half of the pickup trucks at the Bumkin High School parking lot are filled with rifles and shotguns. That's always been true. So, what's the difference?"

Bam spoke up. "The rednecks hunt with guns. It's part of their culture. Blacks and gang members use handguns and knives for self-protection. It's part of their culture. Guess which one ends up at school?"

Bet the Judge never saw that one coming, Winchester thought. "Are you fellas prejudiced?" he asked, his glasses back on again, his eyes sparkling with delight at the discussion.

"Only against violent idiots," Bam responded.

"Didn't used to be, but I'm learning," confided Clyde with a voice of honesty.

Winchester stared up at the ceiling, contemplating more questions. This was incredible. The shock effect was invaluable. It was just what he needed to jack up the geriatric crowd on his school board. It was so explosive that down deep he already knew it would be difficult to contain. "So, tell me about sex," he said.

Whoa! Now I'm in really deep shit if Sally gets a hold of this! Bam thought. Sex never happened in Bumkin, only pregnancy. "Gee, Dr. Winchester, we figured you knew about those things."

Clyde laughed. "I like it with females, how about you?"

The boys went quiet. Bam pointed to the recorder. Winchester nodded and turned it off.

"C'mon fellas. My generation couldn't get laid until we were in college. You guys are ahead of your time. You gotta talk to us."

"Wow, no wonder you guys are so strung out," Clyde said.

"It's all out there," Bam mused. Things have changed a lot, quickly. It's all wrapped up together. You know, more drugs, more sex, more violence."

Escapism, Winchester thought. "Tell me, fellas, there must be some good changes. Something at school that has improved since integration?' He was searching for a rainbow.

"Looser chicks," Bam jested. "The black girls are a lot savvier. They've taught the white chicks a lot about controlling men with sex."

"Better drugs," Clyde added thoughtfully. "And cheaper too."

Chapter Twenty
Free Money

It had taken some time, but it was worth it. Oh, was it worth it! A little over three months after Sally Callahan's attack on Ethan White, the *Bumkin Record* headline read like Hezekial himself had written it: **"Mount Zion Receives Grant to Fight Racism."** A header in lower case letters announced Hezekial's leadership in obtaining a $150,000 grant to educate the population on racial tension and the process of integration. Hezekial laughed out loud, relishing the moment.

Of course, everyone knew there wasn't any damn process for integration. He had to create one as an excuse to help his new best friend in Boston. Suddenly Hezekial was an acknowledged expert on a process that never existed. If white girl Sally Callahan would write her books on black history, then Hezekial would write the book on integration. My, my, my, he chuckled. How times have changed!

Hezekial placed his bare feet up on his wooden desk, re-reading the article out loud to himself. "The Reverend Allen said that he opposed and abhorred the fact that it appears that the school board had already favored certain students with admission policies. Allen said he was concerned that the establishment was already creating educational inequities that would subvert the national effort to integrate."

Hezekial knew his words would create a storm across the tracks, forming dust devils in the fertile soil of malcontent. And yet, it was the only way. Bam Callahan happened to be the most obvious example of lingering, inequitable, white influence in the process of integration. Of course, the fact that his fate would justify Mr. White's position was a grand benefit.

The article went on to cite the obligatory congratulations from Gil Winchester, the school board, the mayor, and various councilmen. There was no comment from First Baptist, but that was good. It gave Reverend Hudson time to make his play. The headline would scare the hell out of the redneck deacons that ran "First Bubba." Hezekial knew he had become their biggest fear; a nigger with a microphone, a bible, and $150,000 in free cash money! He laughed out loud with enjoyment.

Hezekial checked the small slips of paper that Maggie had organized for him with loving care, writing down each of the recorded messages he received after she returned from her day's work across the tracks. Even Beverly Dillard had left a message, congratulating him. "Said to tell you she understands," Maggie's double underlined message stated in her neat, orderly script. "She wants to come to one of your sermons in a show of solidarity." Hezekial grimaced at the use of a word recently made famous by a Polish Union half a world away. Leave it to Beverly to be fashionable.

Beverly was clearly a woman in need of a cause, Hezekial mused. Perhaps, better stated, a mouth in need of a message. Hezekial and Mount Zion were now visible "charities" for her to affiliate. How else could she get headlines? He knew that she resented Sally Callahan, whose loyalty she could never buy and whose intellect she could never have. For the first time in her life, Beverly had to understand minorities without owning one. As if a white woman like her could ever truly understand.

After a hundred years of waiting, black women deserved the social recognition that the Great Society had ushered in. Even Hezekial admitted to the irresponsibility of black men. Besides, he wanted to champion all the women for himself. But, in the complex chess game of life in which he was now a player, Hezekial knew that he needed Beverly also. She had unwittingly become God's chosen pawn in a Divine Plan. Beverly had become the equivalent of a biblical Egyptian queen who aided the slaves, anxious to side with a just cause for her personal recognition, but ignorant of the havoc she would bring to her own people. Beverly was to be used, not abused, he thought.

And then there was Maggie. A spy for his cause with the goodness of an innocent and the curiosity of a child. She was swimming rebelliously against the currents of change, not unlike young Callahan, venting her personal disdain against the establishment, too innocent to recognize the opportunity in front of her. The singular disadvantage of young girls in love was an inability to see the big picture. God's picture. But it hardly outweighed the advantages. His groin hurt just thinking about her firm breasts and slim hips. Sex like that could make the devil himself believe in God.

~~~~

At First Baptist Church, the phone had been ringing off the hook since the *Bumkin Record* made its weekly delivery. Reverend Carl Hudson's secretary, Sadie Hoffman, usually carried double duty as a church secretary while she arranged flowers for the altar. But even that sacred duty had gone unattended since Hezekial had made the headlines.

Few people in the church knew she had been raised Catholic; even fewer knew she had an Irish temper that could make a sailor blush. She marveled at the politics and hypocrisy of the big church. The Baptist congregation needed a pope and a six-pack to get their stuff together. Actually, they already had their six-pack hidden away. The good news was that the Baptists offered more comic drama daily than the Catholic church could deliver in a millennium.

After all, the Southern Baptists still had energy; their church wasn't but a hundred years or so old. In fairness to the Baptists, a hundred-year-old organization was no church. A support group, maybe, but not a church. St. Anthony's had nuns older than that.

But the differences were more than the result of the ages. The TV thing had really changed things. Jimmy Swaggart was broadcasting salvation to the world like McDonald's was serving up hamburgers. Who wanted to be saved by a guy with white shoes and big hair? His clan even looked Baptist. Catholics never looked "catholic." And here they were clamoring about black people. At
~~~~

least Catholics and blacks got to have fun on their way to Hell. These Baptist people didn't even have a good hangover to show for their sins.

Stifling her frustrations, Sadie looked down at a long list of unanswered phone calls. Always a drama. Who would have known so many people would get pissed off because Reverend Hezekial got a grant? These people needed to get a life here on earth. Wasn't Reverend Hezekial one of their own? Mount Zion was a "mission" supported by the First Baptist congregation. She sent checks from First Baptist to support Mount Zion Baptist Church for its regularly scheduled financial crisis. Now Hezekial got them $150,000 in free government money and everyone hates them.

Sadie privately thanked God that the Catholic Church had spent a millennium getting their system down pat. They had been running a private white school for forty years and nobody cared.

Sadie copied her final lists together as she cleaned her desk. Reverend Hudson had asked that she keep a poll of all the messages in order while he returned calls from Bubba and his henchmen. So far, it was Rednecks 36, Christians 14. She walked into the pastor's office to find Reverend Carl laid out on his couch. It was usually a place of peaceful relaxation reserved for distressed wives and distraught children in need of spiritual guidance. Not today. The phone was stuck to his ear, the receiver held tightly in his right hand, his left arm covering his eyes in a sign of surrender. Sadie could hear Bubba Tremblay's voice railing through the receiver.

"This here is an assault on our rights! Our guv'ment is funding civil action against the very people what pay the taxes to support the dam guv'ment! This is anarchy! Now they done funded a fed'rul grant to a black chu'ch, *our* black chu'ch, without even asking us! Hell, it's a travesty to the separation of chu'ch and state!" Bubba stopped to catch his breath as he wheezed out cigarette smoke.

Reverend Carl didn't give him a chance for a second wind. "Bubba, I know this offends you, but we need to let it settle down. We need to think this through."

"We can't let it settle down, Carl. How can private cit'zens compete in a world where the guv'ment is prejudiced agin' its own majority? How you gonna compete against chu'ches that get fed'rul grants to support particular people?

The boys and me gotta keep comin' up with money just to keep the institutions we love from bein' destroyed. They want us to change our way of life!"

Bubba was clearly taking Hezekial's grant as a personal assault. Carl had enough political instincts to know that the right wing of his ministry was dangerously close to spinning out of control, just as Hezekial had predicted. Bubba's position in the community required him to fight back. He didn't have any choice.

Unfortunately, white males over fifty like Bubba were responsible for seventy-five percent of the contributions to his church. Hezekial had been right in his political calculus. Carl had to respond accordingly.

Bubba and his clan were slow and obstinate but over time they would ultimately get swept into the mainstream by force of nature if not by natural desire. But now, like all people drowning in a sea of change, Bubba was fighting back floodwaters. They all just needed more time to drain the swamp. Sally had been right.

"Bubba, I want to sleep on this," Carl announced, trying to sound commanding. "There needs to be a coherent response from the congregation." That means there are voices other than yours, thought Carl.

"And what are you going to do about funding Mount Zion in the meantime?" Bubba demanded.

"What do you mean?"

"I mean we can't be funding a black chu'ch who's going to tell us how to integrate!" Bubba fumed. "What if I don't want to integrate?" his voice rose an octave in acknowledgement of the obvious. "What the hell does Hezekial know about integration anyway? Ain't like there are a bunch of white people going to *his* chu'ch. If there were, we wouldn't be sending him money all the time! This is bullshit Carl! You think the deacons are going to keep funding some renegade church? Hezekial's been bought off by the guv'ment! He can't con us like he did that damn, Yankee-nigger bureaucrat, 'specially while we are keepin' the bank from foreclosing on that raggedy-ass chu'ch of his. We need to cut him off, let him hang!"

Carl avoided pointing out the political sensitivity of that statement. He had often wondered if Bubba's ancestors were lurking in the background of the infamous lynching near Pollock only thirty years prior. "So, Bubba, what exactly do you want me to do?" he asked with the calm exasperation of a middle-aged man-of-the-cloth.

"Call the note! Let him explain that to the newspaper. Shut Hezekial up! He should be payin' our money back for bailin' his black ass out every time he got an overdraft at the Bumkin Bank & Trust!"

"Bubba, it isn't our note. It's the bank's note." Carl knew it was a meaningless response in a Southern town where egos were a crop, money was married to the land, and local institutions were just a back door address to the local gentry.

"To hell with that, Carl. The bank is lending my money. It's the same money that built Hezekial's chu'ch. The guv'ment cain't intervene in our position. It's our chu'ch! We done paid for it!"

Suddenly Bubba's voice calmed, dropping from an outraged scream to a low articulation, seething with the intimidation reserved only for owners of plantations and the towns they owned. "And while you're thinking about how to handle this situation, Carl, you remember who raised your money for the new teen center last year. Remember who has been there at every turn for you. You're the wrong color for a guv'ment grant, Carl, and it's payback time."

Carl could now see himself dangling from that same tree limb in Bubba's history, and suddenly found an epiphany buried deep inside Bubba's own conflicted world.

"You know, Bubba," he spoke in a soothing voice, "from an education perspective, this could be a good turn of events…" The preacher could hear the rapid breathing inside of Bubba's barrel chest slowly moderate over the phone.

"Huh?"

Hooked him, thought Carl. "Do you really want to pull the plug on Hezekial at the bank, Bubba? Mount Zion's affiliation with the government is the best advertising your new school can get. How many white parents want Hezekial telling them how to integrate their children?" He let the thought hang delicately in the ether of the telephone lines. Then, for a moment, he thought he heard Bubba licking his chops.

Bubba sat at his great granddaddy's desk, suddenly envisioning a wave of parents storming the doors of his school, clamoring to get in before all the new desks were taken up by someone else's child, doubling tuition. Bubba would be a hero. Hezekial would prove him right. And everyone would know it.

"So, your thinkin' that we just let the nigger hang hisself. We don't have to worry with him 'cause he's our best salesman." Bubba could take the high road. His picture would be in the news as "Bumkinian of the Year" announcing a new expansion to make more room for more white kids to get properly educated. Politicians would line up to have their picture taken with Bubba, the sage of education. The Citizens Council would name him President.

"You might be on to something, Carl," Bubba conceded slowly, his voice now calmer, the beat of his heart now barely audible. "Maybe we just ought to sleep on this a bit." And with that final statement, Bubba's raspy voice was replaced by the solace of the dial tone that comforted Carl's ear. He had bought some time.

Carl looked up at Sadie as he handed her the phone with a disgusted look. He was exhausted and he could feel a migraine starting. He needed to get some relief. Well versed in the signs of Carl's migraines, Sadie hovered over him, fussing with water and his pills. She waited patiently as he took his medicine, handing him a hot washcloth to place over his eyes.

Carl gratefully accepted the washcloth and settled in for a short moment of peace while Sadie took her seat to watch over him while she sorted out his messages. Besides, they both knew she couldn't leave for the weekend until she knew where Bubba wound up.

These Baptists were like working a three-ring circus, Sadie figured. She had the best of all worlds: go to church with the Catholics and go to work for the Baptists. Low-cost salvation and high-priced entertainment all rolled into one. Watching Baptists behind the scenes was better than the Women's World Wide Wrasslin' match that had come to town. 'Course, she still hoped Bubba would get his ass kicked one day. No priest would ever put up with that son-of-a-bitch. But then, the Catholic Church didn't need his money.

Sadie noticed Carl stealing a glimpse of her shapely legs from his horizontal view. Obviously, he was feeling better. She accepted that the demands of the cloth were difficult, especially during tense times, and preachers were always easy targets and powerful influences, filled with empathy for the people around them. She didn't think he had ever violated his calling or his marriage, but neither was he dead. He was a preacher, not a saint.

"That was some fancy footwork with Bubba, Preacher," Sadie complimented him warmly. Carl flushed, as she bent over to check for fever.

"What do you think?" he asked, in order to divert his mind from her attention.

"Well, I only heard half the conversation, but I can imagine what Bubba was saying. He's probably threatening to cut his support for the annual fund drive."

Carl chuckled at her prescience as he sat up. "And how would a good Catholic girl respond to that?" Carl asked with genuine curiosity.

"I'd tell him to fuck off, Reverend. He's a snake." The words flowed eloquently, innocently off her luscious lips. Like a velvet brick. Carl shook his head and immediately laid back down, his face contorted, searching for an appropriate response. No wonder Catholic girls went to confession.

Sally picked up the conversation before he could respond. She handed over twenty-six slips of paper and related messages. "Know what I really think, Reverend?"

"I'm sure you will tell me, Sadie."

"I think you should call Mrs. Sally Callahan."

"What makes you say that?"

"Well, you know, I talk regularly to Maggie over at Mount Zion—we're constantly trying to keep the church checking account straight over there." There was a pregnant pause in the conversation as Sadie sought to avoid elaboration on what she really knew about Hezekial's expenses. Then she continued, unabated, "Anyway, Maggie and I have become good friends, and Maggie let it slip that this grant money Hezekial got is aimed at that ruckus between Mrs. Sally and the black attorney from Boston who she embarrassed at that Rotary speech. Hezekial is getting paid by the powers-that-be in Yankeeland to use that boy of Mrs. Sally's as an example. Looks to me like Sally and Bubba have common objectives to take on Hezekial, but only she knows how to talk to Hezekial in a way that he would understand.

"On top of that, everyone in town knows Hezekial is blowin' the feds for money, and everyone hates the feds, because, well, they're the feds."

Only a female could view it so dispassionately in such a passionate context, Carl thought. Maybe that was the real appeal of Catholic girls: they were mercenaries. They were trained to buy forgiveness through dispensations without fear of reprisal. This was just business to Sadie.

"Sally really hates Bubba," Carl acknowledged. "Well, she doesn't *hate* him," he restated himself as an afterthought. "She just hates his ignorance, his coarseness, his prejudice, his arrogance and everything he stands for. That's all."

"Amen, Reverend," Sadie exclaimed, her voice like honey flowing over hot coals. "We all love to hate Bubba. He's the devil whose money helps us all do God's work," she explained in her sweet manner, as if talking to a child. "Sometimes, Reverend Carl, you've got to dance with the Devil to do God's work."

Chapter Twenty-One
Ez Money

The bright, fair days of October had given way to the Indian Summer of Thanksgiving, which had given way to the blustery, on-again off-again weather of early December in the Deep South. It was an impatient month, partial to hot tantrums that were bad for hunting and drizzly cold that was bad for football, but life at EZ plodded along with indifference. The florescent lights burned no brighter, the dirty, sullied front of the building was no cleaner, and the price of Thunderbird wine remained below its sixty-nine cents a quart. Still, something was different at EZ Mart. Bam could sense it. It was subtle, even spooky.

Bam watched the line of plaid flannel shirts and Levi blue jeans fall in line to cash checks for minimum wages during harvest. Gloved hands hugged warm coffee cups while they waited in line, stomping mud off their boots to increase circulation and shake off the inescapable chill of lingering humidity. Business was good. Poverty knows no season.

Bam threw an empty coffee cup in the trash can and returned to an innocuous steel desk, itself now cold to the touch. It dominated the sole ugly office in the back of EZ, and like everything else at EZ, human and otherwise, it was there because it was cheap and utilitarian. Bam sat at the desk and finished his calculations. He jotted down the totals on a pad of paper, tore off the top sheet and slipped it into a worn pouch made of the finest fake leather with "Bumkin Bank & Trust" stamped on its side. He zipped shut a record Friday night deposit of $4,000 into the old bag and rubbed his eyes. His legs still ached from standing eight hours on unforgiving cement floors.

Bam sat back, musing about the last four-thousand-dollar night he had closed out. It was on the Fourth of July, he remembered, at the end of a 10-hour shift. The same revenues just weren't possible during bad weather in the middle of December, especially with a losing football team at Bumkin High School.

He unzipped the bag and pulled out the wrinkled deposit sheet, trying to make sense of the information. Then he saw it: $3,400 in food stamps. Over eighty percent of the total revenues in one night. He sighed with exasperation and looked up at the wall calendar. It was the first week of the month.

"Shit," he muttered involuntarily into the empty room. It wasn't supposed to work this way. It couldn't work this way. The increases were too large. Tim was selling between eight and ten thousand a month. Almost a hundred thousand dollars per year for a high-school student in Bumkin, Louisiana. It was only a matter of time before someone would catch on. It was too much money in too small a town, and he sure as hell wasn't paying taxes on it.

Bam wasn't involved but it was still his idea. He would be guilty by association if the scheme were discovered. He wondered if the boss knew about it. Did the boss even want to know about it? Probably not on both cases. EZ was doing well on the scam, but he couldn't ignore it forever.

Bam dropped the money into the floor safe and put the lock in place. He pulled a tattered rug over the brass lock and went to confront Timmy. He stopped abruptly when he saw him standing outside the main door with Foster. They swatted at a cloud of gnats and moths that swirled around seeking warmth in the cold of the night, irritating an already animated discussion. Bam saw them exchange identical brown paper bags. Foster held the rolled package in a threatening manner and shook it in Timmy's face angrily.

Bam remained in the shadow until Timmy returned inside. His hoarse voice cracked through the cold air inside EZ. "Mother Fucker! I hate that asshole!"

"Who in particular?" Bam asked quizzically, moving from behind the doorframe.

Timmy was startled to be questioned in the middle of his private temper tantrum. "Foster, who else?" Timmy shot back.

"So, what's up with Foster and you?"

"He's a lying sonofabitch! Other than that, nothing that concerns you, Bam. Leave it alone."

Bam pulled a small slip of scratch paper from his shirt pocket and laid it on the counter in front of Timmy. "Looks to me like it does," he said with authority. "Food stamps are eighty percent of the deposit tonight. And on top of that, we had a $4,000 night! There ain't no way in hell this store is producing that much revenue, with or without food stamps."

Timmy didn't look at the numbers, he already knew them. "Hey, as far as anyone knows, EZ has a surge in growth." His voice was calm, but his face burned with a red blush in the dark of the store. "Long as EZ makes money and everyone gets their share, nobody knows - and nobody cares, do they, Bam?" Tim asked in a veiled threat.

"Not my problem, dude. I'm not signing off on this deposit." Bam waited to see if his hook had set.

Timmy gave in. "What's the problem?"

"It's the stamps, Tim. No one takes in that percentage of food stamps. It doesn't match without liquor sales that are illegal, and too many stamps are showing up in your deposits for the shift. It means you are selling liquor for stamps or you're laundering money. Or both. The boss, or the bank, or the government will figure it out."

"It's not as bad as you think." Tim dug into his jacket pocket, produced the bound paper bag he had taken from Foster, and casually threw it on the counter toward Bam. "Check it out."

Bam opened the bag and grabbed it by the bottom to turn it upside down above the counter. Six stacks of neatly bound one-hundred-dollar bills flopped onto the counter, each two inches thick. Bam couldn't withhold his surprise as he looked back at Tim. He had seen money before, handled it every day, but not like this. This was different somehow. Powerful, sinister, beautiful. Not like the stuff you handled for other people. This was real, raw money just waiting to be claimed. He couldn't turn away from it. Then, like an afterthought floating in the air, a white card floated out of the bag, landing face up on the worn counter. Bam picked it up and read it out loud, trying to hold his shock: "Imperial Knights of the Ku Klux Klan, Protectors of the White Race."

Timmy snatched the card from Bam and stuffed it into his blue jeans before he could finish reading. Then he rewrapped the cash silently with careful attention.

Bam was stupefied. The KKK was somehow attached to the money, not to mention the Bumkin Police Department, and the drugs. Before Bam could ask the obvious, Timmy said coolly, "You're smart, Bam, figure it out. Foster needs stamps to launder money from The Spot, niggers need drugs, and the KKK needs cash to regenerate. We buy drugs from the Klan for cash, sell them for stamps at a premium, and exchange the stamps for cash from The Spot. Everyone wins."

"You accumulate stamps during the first half of the month, then replace them with cash from The Spot at the end of the month," Bam said. "But when there's a good month, you have too many to cash out quickly, so you swap them into the cash register."

"Right you are," Tim said. "Just the way you taught us. That idiot Foster missed his delivery, and you counted the stamps before I could replace them with his cash. "By the time the bag gets deposited tomorrow, the stamps will be replaced with cash so no one will ever know the difference. It's real EZ money that ends up clean," he chuckled. "Go ahead, Bam, take a couple of hundred for yourself."

Bam needed to buy time and clear his head. He walked around the corner to the freezer. "How about a beer?" he asked casually.

"Sure," Timmy responded, equally cavalier in his response.

Bam returned with two long-neck Buds, wrenching the cap off both with a spew of foam. He guzzled half the bottle and sat it down on the counter.

"I know this is a dumb question, but how does the KKK get away with it?

"Man, you are so naïve," Timmy laughed as he sat on a nearby stool. "Do you think any drug deals go down in a small town without the Sheriff taking his cut, without planters growing their share? How do you think The Spot has been selling pussy in front of the whole damn world ever since we were in grade school? That's what Sheriffs do, Bam, they protect their citizens. Where do you think I've been buying my grass from, some hippie joint far, far away? Think of the cash they take in, Bam! They've been around for a hundred years. They own the system, Bam. They protect the people who they serve, which doesn't mean taxpayer. They don't want it to change. Don't matter whether it's drugs today or slaves a hundred years ago. It's still their system, their land, and their cash. But now you showed us all how to use food stamps to make money off of the government.

Bam squelched a sudden awkward pride he got from Timmy's compliments. It had really worked, way beyond his expectation. "What's the 'take'?" he asked.

"I've been swapping stamps for drugs at thirty percent higher prices and my man Lester is gainfully employed like never before. He keeps me in more stamps than I can fund, so I needed more cash from Foster."

"Slick," Bam admitted. "The increase in stamps doesn't show up on EZ's books unless you miss the exchange. Foster must be collecting his cash from The Spot when the weekend business is good, the same time EZ is collecting more stamps which helps hide the scam. Then Foster launders their undeclared money through the bank under a different Tremblay account."

"The bank loves us," Timmy commented. "They just know why."

"Is Foster a part of the Klan also?" Bam queried in disbelief.

"I don't know," Timmy snapped angrily, suspicious of the question. "And you know what? You and I don't want to know. It's all the same, this is how life is, Bam. Get used to it. Call it the Masons, the Daughters of the Confederacy, the DeMolay or the KKK, it's just another group of old Southerners pulling strings for their own agenda. They're all part of the same woodwork, and they are all that's left to this crummy little town with two red lights and a broke-dick railroad station. What the hell, Bam, who else is pulling for white people these days?" It was a feeble attempt at a reasonable lie.

Bam had his answer. "Does Lester know?"

"Know what?" Timmy shot back.

"That he's working for the Klan?"

"Give me a break, Bam. Lester don't know and don't care. Lester gets a stay-out-of-jail-free card, lots of babes, lots of drugs, and a monopoly for selling food stamps. He's always stoned and will probably die from syphilis before he's twenty."

Tim ceremoniously crushed his empty beer can with his right hand to make his point. "I couldn't have done it without you."

Bam listened to Tim's hollow arguments, as he nervously paced the floor with dilated pupils and frantic movement. He was in over his head and trying hard to stay in control. He had become an important cog in a well-oiled machine. A machine that would run over him.

Tim came closer. "So, take some of this action, Bam. Everyone will feel better. We know you deserve it."

"Thanks, but I'll pass."

Tim fell into an intimidating silence, his drug-induced paranoia becoming more visceral. "So, what's the problem?" he shouted at Bam, like an auctioneer who had missed his last pricing call. He had to know what it would take.

"We're cool, but it's just not my style," Bam said simply. "But don't worry, I know how to keep a secret."

"What do you want?" the older boy persisted.

"First, I want another beer," Bam said. Temptation made him thirsty. "Second, I want you to swap the night shift with me tomorrow night so I can get into Angela's pants, and third, as the guy who figured this out, I'm curious. I want to know how you get the drugs from the farm to the school?"

Tim recoiled at Bam's question. He had little doubt that he really was curious. Now he understood why Foster wanted Bam compromised. How else do you stop curiosity?

Tim knew Foster wasn't going to let it go. It had gotten too big and Bam knew too much. To make a bad matter worse, Foster didn't like Bam, and Bam's disgust for Foster was all too evident. Tim had to confirm a lock on Bam or Foster would take it into his own hands.

Tim slapped Bam on the back and led the way out the door without an answer. "Okay," he said, throwing another beer to Bam, "I'll handle the shift for you tomorrow so you can play with Angela." He held out three hundred-dollar bills. "And here's some money for a hotel room and a good time. Just pretend you like Foster and don't say anything stupid. Got it?"

"Sure. You want me to act like I'm on the take."

"Absolutely," Timmy laughed.

"I can do that. Where is he?"

"Watching us from across the street," Tim responded without moving.

Bam took the money and stayed in place as Timmy slid behind the steering wheel of his new fire-engine red Camaro. He paused and walked over to the driver's window, bending down to look inside. He slid two bills back into Tim's shirt pocket, holding one for later. "Thanks for the hotel, but you don't know Angela like I do. She's into nature," he winked. "Where are you headed?"

"To The Spot to get laid," Timmy smiled. "It's a perk of the job. Are we cool, Bam? Don't screw this up."

Bam detected a hint of concern over the roar of the engine.

Chapter Twenty-Two
Street Fight

Bam gazed out over the school grounds with Mike and Clyde, perched on the third-floor classroom window during lunch recess. Tensions at the school ran high in the choked hallways of Bumkin High since the bomb blast and the death of Quinine. A tense pall of rumors and suspicion hung in the air, strangling the school with apprehension. The boys hid away on the top floor to look down at girls in low-cut blouses and tight skirts with keen interest as they munched on chips and Dr. Pepper.

"I'm hungry and I'm pissed, cher," Mike announced in his Cajun accent. "Someone has been stealing my lunch bag in shop class, eating my candy bars for three days in a row."

Clyde passed him the Frito bag in apparent sympathy. "Who done it?" he asked.

"Tyrone, that little black dude that sits next to me. He knows I keep my bag stashed with chocolate."

"Watcha gonna do 'bout it?"

"I got a plan to make him watch what he eats," Mike growled.

"Check out Barbara," Bam interjected, pointing to the shapely figure below them.

"You should try that, cher," Mike observed.

"Never happen," Bam said. "She likes girls."

"You could be a lesbian too," the Cajun volunteered.

"Better than being a Pentecostal," Clyde added.

"My fragile teenage convictions on the sanctity of Pentecostal girls and heterosexuals done got confused," Mike feigned. "Is there such thing as a lesbian Pentecostal?"

"Hey! Look at that!" Bam interrupted their jousting and pointed toward the street entrance to the school forty feet below him. A battered, black 1960 Thunderbird pulled up at the curb, unnoticed by throngs of teenagers milling around during recess. The Thunderbird was filled with black passengers too old to be students. The melancholy stir of the campus continued uninterrupted as all four doors to the Thunderbird opened in unison.

Bam's heart jumped. He couldn't believe what he was seeing.

Six muscular, young black men jumped out of the car, running at a dead heat toward the nearest white male student they could find. The first strike caught Paul Simpson square on the jaw. Bam thought he could hear the quarterback's jawbone crack three stories away. The second assailant punched Mike Kiting in the gut. The stringy basketball player bent over only to be hit behind the head and kicked by his attacker as he fell to the ground. The momentary shock of the attack wore off quickly as a flood of white students ran to the scene, yelling obscenities and swinging at the attackers.

Bam could feel the vibrations from waves of students running down staircases and pouring out of school doors onto the campus beneath him as the fight spread, not knowing its cause, only that it was black against white, expected, and overdue.

Bam, Mike, and Clyde watched the scene unfold, transfixed by the spontaneous violence. The mob grew in numbers to a hundred or more quickly. Figures grappled and boxed with each other in the mayhem, wrestling in the dirt and gravel amid the occasional splatter of blood. The screams of teenage girls filled the air from the sidelines as they fled the fracas.

Principal Greely and his football coaches appeared out of nowhere, running onto the school grounds blowing whistles as they pulled students off students, catching an occasional errant fist in the process. Greely motioned his teachers to surround the perimeter of the gang fight, effectively blocking new students from entering the fight, containing the scene to the existing combatants, who were clearly starting to tire from frantic exertion. Fourteen teachers watched fearfully as they held the line, nervously watching for knives or guns to appear, welcoming the unexpected sound of advancing police sirens.

The assailants quickly broke out of the riot, running behind the gym in a well-timed exit. The rest of the crowd froze and quickly began to dissipate. The Thunderbird was now half a block away, turning the corner slowly, waiting patiently for five black forms to jump in.

The Thunderbird fled unnoticed by the raging riot they had initiated or the police cars beginning to careen around the corner behind them. It was a cleverly planned maneuver that left the boys seething with anger as they watched the Thunderbird cruise north across the tracks.

Two police cars pulled up along the front of the high school with six of Bumkin's finest, Billy clubs and handguns drawn, oblivious to what they had missed. The scene of the crime was already abandoned, its shadow just a scene for a dozen dirty student soldiers stretched out on concrete benches, with teachers figuring out what to do with them. Half had headed for home or ran in fear, seeking distance from the police. The remainder stayed huddled inside the protection of the old school building, pretending to resume classes like they had before violence was more than a rumor.

The final afternoon bell rang like the end to a boxing match, and the school yard gradually returned to a placid landscape of grass and big oak trees. Bam could still feel his heart pounding as he looked down at the parked police cars and then at the wall clock: only twelve minutes had lapsed.

"Wow," Clyde exclaimed, his pulse still racing. "Can you believe how fast the cops got here?"

Bam said nothing. There was no chance Bumkin cops were that efficient. Someone had advance notice, he conjectured with a growing knot of anxiety forming in his gut. He said nothing. There was no sense making his buddies as paranoid as he was becoming.

"Who were the dudes in the black car? What the fuck was Lester doing?" Clyde asked.

"Don't know, cher, but we need to report it. This was deliberate."

"Lester?" asked Bam, confused.

"That was Lester's wheels," Clyde said, pointing to where the Thunderbird had disappeared. "What a bummer. He's my favorite source."

Greely's voice crackled over the loudspeakers with a scratchy quality, breathless and angry. "All students are to stay seated in their current location. The school is now under lockdown. A policeman will come to your room shortly. You are to depart the building and go home immediately after you visit with the policeman. We will vacate from the first floor up." Click.

The boys looked at each other, each silently wondering what to do. They were in the last room, on the last floor. It was going to be a long wait. Bam wondered what they should say to Greely. Surely someone else had seen them too. But only he knew that there was a connection between the police and Lester. If Clyde and Mike helped to identify Lester, it could put them at risk for things they didn't know.

Bam took in a deep breath to clear his mind and look normal. He contemplated the incendiary information that had befallen them and turned to his friends. "Fellas, let's plead ignorant with the police and talk to Sally before we tell anyone anything."

"I'm in," said Clyde. "I don't like talking to pigs."

Mike nodded with agreement and began digging into his knapsack. "Me, I got things to do anyway." He delicately extracted a box of Ex-Lax and two Hershey bars, laying them out neatly side by side on his desk, then opened a small pocketknife with an ivory handle and held it up for his friends to see. "Granddaddy gave this to me," he said with pride.

Clyde walked over to Mike's desk and looked over his shoulder curiously. "Ex-Lax?" he laughed. "I always knew you were full of shit."

"Screw you, cher," Mike retorted, gently unwrapping the Hershey bars and the laxative. They looked virtually the same. "My momma, she always tell me this stuff taste just like chocolate," he said with a smile. "So, I gonna find me a chocolate thief." Mike gently scraped the blocks of Ex-Lax with his knife. Then he folded the Hershey foil neatly around the reshaped Ex-Lax and slipped it expertly back into the thin paper sleeve of the 'Hershey Chocolate Bar' wrapper. He handed it to Clyde and Bam for inspection and received their approval. No one could tell the difference.

Chapter Twenty-Three
Different Shades Of Gray

Sally sat down at her typewriter and flicked the power switch to "on" much later than her normal morning regimen. She had been up late comforting friends of all colors and genders about the gang fight. It was unnerving, she thought as she sat in contemplation with a cup of tea. The electricity humming through her keyboard waited anxiously for her familiar fingertips.

Two yellow legal pads lay to her side, one filled with the firsthand facts Bam and Clyde had given her about the school riot. She was thankful Bam was out of harm's way when it happened, and she wasn't about to let him get involved if she could help it. It was yet another of their secrets.

The second pad neatly listed the relevant facts and questions required to get answers about Meadow. It listed all she knew and all she thought she knew to build a good article for the paper. The story had more heft than a local article, with all the makings of a good novel, if she could ever ferret out all the facts. She didn't know Meadow, but she had known Quinine, and he was too cautious a soul to let this happen. Something was terribly wrong.

Sally considered asking the Sheriff personally about Meadow. She didn't think he could bluff her; they had been friends far too long. Then she remembered Meadow shaking from fear as Foster entered the police station, with Bubba's profile sitting menacingly across the street. Talking to the Sheriff would certainly leak to Foster and Bubba and wouldn't be fair to Meadow. She remembered his recent denial to Trigger about drugs. The Sheriff always knew more than everyone else in town, but that didn't mean he would own up to it. Sally had no way of knowing if any of the recent events were actually connected.

Sally had to dig up a source that could help her while she stayed in the background. That could only mean a preacher. Surely a teenage girl held in custody was due a preacher. The only remaining question was, which one?

Meadow's skin color and her undocumented kinship to Lee Esther argued calling Reverend Hezekial Allen. Of course, Hezekial wasn't on anyone's hit parade in Bumkin these days and that could present a few barriers. If Hezekial emerged as advisor to Meadow, it could well seal the girl's fate with a white jury. Then again, he would certainly create a lot of public visibility, which could be required for a fair trial.

That left Reverend Hudson as the only other possible champion for Meadow. He was the exact opposite of Hezekial. Unfortunately, he was regarded as a front man for Bubba Tremblay, although Sally regarded him as a man of personal integrity who did his best to manage Bubba. His patronizing attitude toward Bubba was a political balancing act that was transparent to informed observers. Bubba was intellectually no match for Carl, that was certain. But there was also no doubt that First Baptist relied on money from the Tremblay family and all their ass-kissing buddies whose livelihood could be impacted by the Tremblays.

Carl Hudson and Bubba Tremblay were both born again, full-bore Southern Baptists; "the mouth and the money" of First Baptist Church. They had been born eight million dollars apart but otherwise were closely associated. Money and religion always had a way of finding each other, Sally thought, not necessarily for the best of purposes or outcomes.

Snowball's claim about Bubba and Meadow was a potential bomb for First Baptist Church and of great concern to Sally. It placed both Meadow and Bubba in an unforgiving position. She knew it was true, but it would be virtually impossible to prove. Even if it could be done, it would produce a devastating backlash at local banks, schools, and churches. The Tremblay name carried remarkable economic influence and power which ultimately benefited Bumkin.

Meadow's history was dangerous, but Sally knew the Judge would expunge any record of her claims. But, if her claim was wrapped up in Quinine's death, that would be an entirely different story.

Sally also knew that everyone in Bumkin, black and white, would embrace the honesty of Snowball's accusations over Bubba's denials. Lawrence had no reason to lie and would never lie to her anyway, especially when he was drunk or hungover. That left her as the only one who had the credibility to verify Snowball's facts. Those revelations would create a tectonic shift of the existing fault lines.

Sally had to be careful; a choice between Bubba's honor and Meadow's life was no choice at all. At the end of the day, she would need the buy-in from both of the preachers in town to give Meadow a fair shake. Bubba wouldn't play fair once it all started to leak out. Neither would she under the circumstances.

At the bottom of her yellow pad, "*Tell Maggie*" was jotted down in bold strokes and underlined. Sally had to let Maggie know about her sister. That certainly meant confronting Lee Esther and unearthing more of the truth. Truth, she smiled to herself. Whose truth? History had a way of making everyone a liar. It was never black or white.

The ring of the phone startled her. She picked it up unconsciously, still deep in thought. "Hello." Sally's Southern drawl welcomed the diversion.

"Mrs. Sally, this is Sadie down at First Baptist. Reverend Carl would like to speak with you."

Sally hesitated for a moment, then remembered that's Sadie's office was out of earshot of the Minister she served. "Sadie, I needed to talk to Carl anyway, what is this about?" she asked in a hushed tone.

"To tell you the honest truth, Mrs. Sally, I told Reverend Carl he should call you. He's stuck in the mud with all this ruckus between Bubba Tremblay and Reverend Hezekial, the church, and the money. Mostly the money, Mrs. Sally. These Baptists love money more than the Pope! I just thought all this bible totin' testosterone needed an experienced woman to sort things out." Sadie's rapid-fire summary made Sally smile. The gumbo of life in Louisiana never ceased to amaze her.

"Put him on," Sally commanded. "And thank you for your confidence, Sadie."

Moments later, Reverend Carl Hudson's voice came on the line. "Hello, Sally, how are you?"

"Good so far, Reverend, but the day is still young," she quipped, pulling her glasses off and letting them hang around her neck. "To what do I owe this pleasure?"

"Well, Sally, I guess I'm a little over my head on these integration issues and I could use some help. I thought I had a good understanding with Reverend Allen at Mount Zion, but he has been particularly aggressive since he received his grant to further integration. As I am sure you know, we have supported Mount Zion financially all these years, so it is a very sensitive matter."

Sally knew, everyone knew, about the money First Baptist provided to Mount Zion. She also knew Bubba made sure everyone knew. "Supported, Carl, or enslaved the black church to Bubba's money?" Sally asked bluntly.

Carl bit his tongue and glared at the phone. He knew this was why people sought Sally out, to cut to the chase. "Well, I guess it depends on one's perspective, doesn't it, Sally?" Carl was too diplomatic to deny her inquisition.

Sally continued, "Hezekial has received a grant, which is an obvious political endorsement of some form, Carl. Every grant has a constituency, and one might presume that he is now motivated to mobilize his congregation for notoriety and more grants."

"Well, that fits into the current wisdom," Carl acknowledged. "I guess I was hoping that Hezekial's funding could produce more thoughtful deliberation and less rhetoric, Sally." He appreciated her objectivity and elected to ignore that Sally had stirred the pot with Ethan White, which indirectly delivered the infamous grant to Hezekial.

"Sally, my congregation was tense before the school fights. That riot just threw gasoline onto smoldering embers. With a parish population that is sixty percent black, we could have a real wildfire on our hands. This riot was an eyeopener. We can't afford another one." Carl paused. "And this movement of politics and broadcasting within religious circles looks like the beginning of a bad trend to me. Churches aren't supposed to be run that way. Religion and politics are dangerous bedfellows."

"History says you are right, Reverend," Sally said, with her thoughts on the school riot. She hadn't mentioned her conversation with Bam and his friends to anyone yet. So far, the identity of the mysterious crew that incited the riot hadn't bubbled to the surface. Bam was the last person who should have witnessed it, but he always found a way to be in the middle of things. She also knew he felt guilty as hell about his role in precipitating it, which might not be all bad.

"Well, as fate would have it, Reverend, I have need to visit with both you and Hezekial on an urgent matter anyway. Maybe we can get focused on some common good. Why don't I call Hezekial and invite him to visit with us at my house around four o'clock tomorrow?"

It wasn't what Carl had in mind, but how could he refuse? "Okay, Sally. What's on your mind?"

"I will tell you tomorrow Reverend, but I promise you it's important and you won't be disappointed. I will look forward to seeing you then."

Sally next called Mount Zion. The phone rang three times before Hezekial Allen's deep voice answered. "Reverend Allen, this is Dr. Callahan." Sally couldn't resist using her official title with Hezekial. She was still the expert, and they both knew it. Or maybe that was her own prejudice?

"Why yes, of course, Mrs. Sally, how are you?" Hezekial's congenial voice greeted her while avoiding her title.

"Hezekial, I would like to ask you and Reverend Hudson to join me tomorrow for tea, my house at four o'clock if you are available. I know it is short notice, but I have a critical need to talk to both of you and from what I hear, you both could probably use a neutral place to talk to each other."

Hezekial didn't blink. He could never be accused of not meeting with white folk. Besides, the mountain was definitely coming to Mohammad; it was just having a hard time crossing the tracks.

"It would be my pleasure, Mrs. Sally, and I sincerely thank you for the invitation. I will see you tomorrow."

Hezekial was placing the appointment on his desk calendar when Maggie walked in with his morning coffee. She slid out of her shoes and closed the blinds after placing the mug on his desk. Then she locked the door and straddled him in his chair, holding his big frame as they kissed. "I told Mrs. Beverly that you would drop me off at work late this morning, after a little choir practice," she whispered into his ear with a devilish smile.

Chapter Twenty-Four
Preacher Sermons

The following afternoon Sally waited impatiently in front of a hot teapot on her kitchen table. She had told Lee Esther that the two preachers were coming over to discuss integration and sent her out on errands. She needed to make sure that Lee Esther wasn't stuck with her ear to the door while Sally and the preachers talked about Maggie and Meadow. Sally also knew Maggie would be making her appearance for tea about the same time as the meeting. If her timing was good, she would be able to talk to Maggie about her history while both Reverends were present.

The polite knock on the door was five minutes early. She looked up to see both Reverend Carl Hudson and Reverend Hezekial Allen both peering through the wrought iron door. They looked like two opposing schoolboys requesting entry back into a classroom.

In the driveway, a spotless, vintage gold Cadillac, its new wax coat gleaming in the sunlight, stood parked next to a sky-blue Ford station wagon, with the popular new faux wood exterior. Cars for a promoter and a family man, Sally observed. She reached out to shake Hezekial's hand, taking his black fedora with a matching aqua band in a gesture of Southern hospitality.

"Good afternoon, gentlemen," Sally exuded graciousness, always happy to welcome her guests. "It's good to see you both. And Hezekial, I can really see you today! I love that tie." She motioned the preachers to follow her through the rustic home with the musty smell of antiquities and unending shelves of books and manuscripts. It was a home of living history and the written word that offered a big pine kitchen table for guests.

The two men saw their teacups set neatly across from each other on plaid tablemats. Sally pulled up her wooden rocking chair and took a seat at the head of the table. She sat on her favorite pillow so her diminutive height wouldn't be at a visible disadvantage to her guests, each of whom took his position on opposing benches without speaking.

"Well, Gentlemen," Sally began, "I have some things of my own to say today. I know you fellas have things you want to discuss also, so let's just get started, okay? Carl, as the elder statesman, why don't you get us started, then we'll let Hezekial follow."

Both men nodded their consent. Carl Hudson cleared his throat as if he were going to launch into a new sermon. "Sally, as you know, the entire town—black and white—is tensed up like a fiddler's bow. It's the court ruling. It's Quinine's death. It's the private school. And, now it's a mob fight at the public school. Our children are afraid to go to school! It's tragic. This is not the town we all know and love. This is the time when the churches on both sides of the tracks must work together." He straightened his back and established a strong eye contact with Hezekial, continuing in his soft voice.

"Hezekial and I have had private discussions about this matter. These conflicts are opportunities that stand to define our churches in a new era. Now Hezekial has drawn a line in the sand that, if the truth be known, enriches both churches at great expense. Contributions are up at First Baptist and I have no doubt that they are up at Mount Zion, all because there is great conflict in the air. We benefit in the short run, but unless we find common ground, we will both destroy our community in the long run."

Sally put her hand on Carl's as a sign that his time was up. "Before we hear what Hezekial has to say on this matter, I want to say that you won't destroy the town, you will just create a lot more Catholics." They all laughed as Sally broke the tension of the moment. "Okay Hezekial, it's your turn."

Sally and Carl sipped their tea for a long moment as Hezekial sat with his hands compressed and his eyes closed, calling upon the Holy Spirit to guide him. His eyes opened quickly, white orbs against a large black face that stared deep into Carl Hudson. "What black people see in this conflict is a way to get redeemed. We have been wronged! We know well that God does not lead us into the Promised Land without sacrifice or conflict. We have been wandering in the desert of poverty for generations. We have had no great providers like Bubba Tremblay who can pay his messengers while he creates greater conflict and barriers for black people. We have to take action ourselves. Now our time for redemption has finally come. We have the power to fight back the enemies of freedom, the protagonists of repression. First Baptist is associated with a racist school whether it likes it or not! Its hands are stained with the blood of oppression!"

Sally quietly put her hand calmly on Hezekial's arm and stared into his eyes. "Cool it, Reverend, we're not here to get converted. Get to the point—without the emotion," she said sternly.

Startled by the discreet tongue-lashing, Hezekial deflated from political activist to local preacher. "Okay, Mrs. Sally. Let's face it. This is about money. Churches must have crusades to justify their existence, to mobilize the armies of Christ and raise the consciousness of their people. Integration has given us a voice! It has given us a crusade! It has given us energy! It has freed us from the bonds of banality. We as leaders must translate this rare opportunity into hard money to improve our lot in life or our opportunity will be lost."

Sally nodded attentively. Hezekial could only talk in sermon mode, but if you wanted a sermon, you wanted to hear it from Hezekial. "Thank you for your honesty, Reverend, and your brevity."

"Your turn, Carl." Sally pushed a plate of ginger snaps over to Hezekial to munch on. Better to fill Hezekial's mouth while Carl responded.

Carl thought momentarily about his rebuttal. He maintained his normal soft voice, unwilling to let Hezekial affect his demeanor. "No. This is not about money, Hezekial. This is about philosophy and religion. It is about the very essence of what we do. It is about how we guide people to live together."

"I agree it's about living together as long as your people keep the money," Hezekial shot back sarcastically.

Sally squelched an urge to laugh. Carl ignored the interjection and continued. "Hezekial, you brought Bubba's name into this and referenced me as a messenger. I represent the church, not Bubba Tremblay. You know that.

I represent a consensus. You and Mrs. Sally know I don't agree with many of Bubba's positions or tactics but those are outside my purview. Bubba has a right to his beliefs just as you and Sally have a right to your own. Besides, the very people you are denouncing have provided financial help to Mount Zion for decades. You have never turned down our financial support knowing that Bubba and his family are major contributors. So, what I see here is Mount Zion playing all sides against the middle."

Sally raised her eyebrows at the unusually blunt statement for Carl, who was a diplomat at heart. But Sally knew it wasn't simply about Hezekial playing both sides against the middle. It was about Carl feeling stuck in the middle. "Hezekial…" she said calmly, prodding his response.

Hezekial was getting animated and fidgety. His oratorical skills were not meant for captive meetings. Nor was he used to having a rebuttal to his sermons. Congregations never argued back. Besides, he was worth more money than Carl would ever guess. He never took a vow of poverty, only a vow of faith. Hezekial knew a thing or two about money. What was this white boy really saying? What did he really want? Surely, he didn't expect Hezekial to turn down the money from First Baptist or grant money from the government? He was black, but he wasn't stupid. Mount Zion's rise to prominence was Carl's problem, not his.

Hezekial took a deep breath. "Brother Carl," his voice oozed out in soothing waves that were almost melodic to Sally, a massage for the ears. Hezekial was a cultural megaphone, an echo of history produced from generations of sweat and toil. " I will wager that your church has never turned down a contribution from Bubba Tremblay or his cronies," Hezekial challenged Carl. "Why would you expect me to? If these contributions were never from the heart, they now stand to become a lever of hypocrisy. I am now threatened because I am making progress for my people that First Baptist never thought possible. Tell me, Reverend, does First Baptist want to pull funding for a poor black church in the middle of integration and racial riots? The world will see your charity for what it is! All because we are getting heard and getting organized. We now are getting money from new sources. We are having influence, and First Baptist has less control. We are no longer just an extension of Bubba's plantation."

Hezekial cleared his voice and paused for effect. "Now Reverend, let's be candid." His deep voice was now lofty and concerned "This issue is between the Old South and the New South. The mighty and the impoverished. The haves and the have nots. Integration has given us a foothold with court evidence of our suffering, and a stand upon which we can now speak as a people with voting power to our representatives. And speak we have!" His voice suddenly boomed, his hands were clenched in double fists, raised high into the air to make his point. "There is no turning back for us."

Carl's face flushed as he fought for the words to defend his position. "We will not be held hostage by our own charity, Hezekial, or the politics of racism."

"You are held hostage by your own truth! These are the same floodwaters you have held back for a century. Your problem is that Mount Zion's truth threatens to splinter your congregation and divert your own flow of funds. That is not our problem. Truth is self-evident, Reverend. It is what it is. It can only be accepted or reputed, but it cannot be neglected or destroyed. First Baptist will have to accept the New South or splinter into two churches, a church of the past and a church of the future. You either have to shift your position of leadership toward redneck fundamentalism that breeds prejudice and hides behind your literal interpretation of the bible or embrace us as equals."

Sally silently poured more tea for the men at each side of her. A century of racial frustration flowed out of Hezekial's oratorical mastery. If only she trusted him to be worthy of his rhetoric. It always boiled down to money, religion, and race. The historian in Sally knew it had always been so but she had naively hoped that the clarity of black and white neighborhood issues would keep them free from the color of money. That would never happen. The purity of substance had long since been blurred by politics and greed. The only thing missing in this saga was illicit sex. She was sure it was in here somewhere.

Clearly his congregation trusted Hezekial to represent the black cause. Who else was there? Black ministers were imbued with the same absolute power as white Sheriffs in the pecking order of Southern life and largely shared the same institutionalized corruption. Avignon Parish might be even more dysfunctional with an honest Sheriff, and Mount Zion would have long since capsized if Hezekial didn't benefit from his position. Right now, Hezekial was an educated man, seated among educated people at her table fighting for his corner of the universe. This was far different than a Mount Zion congregation where the eloquence of his rhetoric was unequaled, and his decisions unchallenged. In the opposing corner was "First Bubba," a wealthy caste of plantation characters and the last generation of wannabes trying to hold onto their position amid a social upheaval.

Sally could imagine the frustration of strait-laced Reverend Carl as he attempted to respond to Hezekial's passionate eloquence with logic and wisdom. Carl would never possess the silver tongue that Hezekial wielded so well. He managed his church from a position of corporate authority and white economic dominance, held together by a thin swatch of puritan ethic glue. First Baptist only served white people who relied on the support of the landed gentry as a cornerstone of Southern culture. Ironically, whether by design or circumstance, Sally knew there was no chance that Mount Zion or First Baptist would be racially integrated in her lifetime.

Carl's face was getting redder by the moment. "First of all, Hezekial," his voice caustic, "I don't see any difference between redneck fundamentalism and black fundamentalism. You call upon a biblical mandate for your cause just as Bubba does for his. Both of your interpretations are contrived and incendiary. Now, I grant you that there is a fault line in the congregation of First Baptist Church that comes from that same biblical nonsense. But believe me, Hezekial, if that fault line splits our church, everyone will suffer the consequences. Only our congregation can rid this community of Bubba's brand of prejudice and ignorance, and it isn't easy. You cannot do that for us. Bubba and people like him are ingrained into our system. Ultimately, they have to die off. But for people like Sally and me to keep them at bay, they would still be riding around in sheets and burning crosses in your front yard. And if you think you will personally benefit from the demise of First Baptist," Carl said with finality, his expression far more serious, "you might think again. We both know about the financial problems and accounting irregularities at Mount Zion. The federal government may turn the other eye for the moment, but the politicians will not be nearly as tolerant about your indiscretions. There are also those who might suggest that you have been involved with women that could topple your house of cards," Carl said with daggers blazing in his eyes.

"Women!" Hezekial exclaimed. "What women?" He ignored the slam on his accounting practices. He had never considered that the government would want to know where their money was going. That's why it was called a grant, wasn't it?

"Women other than your wife," Carl countered with a sour expression. "Surely you understand that you are putting my church and me in the most difficult of positions. If I don't fund your church, we will be viewed as prejudiced, but if I press your cause within my church, I am condoning activity we cannot tolerate."

"This is part of the black man's myth that the white hypocrites perpetuate! Black men are never honorable and always promiscuous in the white man's world. This is little more than character assassination. I have always been faithful to my calling."

Sally's female instincts sensed that Hezekial had always been a peacock strutting around a henhouse full of admirers. Poor Carl probably couldn't get laid if his life depended on it.

Hezekial continued, his outrage palpable. "If there are those who would throw stones at me, let them be named, Reverend!"

Undetected, Maggie walked into the foyer, the images of her passionate tryst with Hezekial still on her mind. The vivid memory had filled her mind all day like a recurring song she couldn't stop singing. She was in love. Hormones flooded her young body with emotion. She burst through the door, surprised to find her lover in the warm comfort of Sally's home.

"Oh, Hezzy!" the girlish voice squealed from the front door. All eyes turned to see Maggie running through the doorway, her shapely figure silhouetted by a big-paned window as she wrapped her arms around Hezekial, leaning over to kiss him on the cheek, her face aglow, her arms folding over him with obvious familiarity.

Sally glanced at the clock on the wall. Right on time. Not what she had planned, but her timing was perfect.

Hezekial stood, shocked, and cleared his throat, awkwardly pulling Maggie's arms off as he tried to regain his composure.

Maggie stepped back, quickly correcting herself as she stared up at her lover with a hint of recrimination. "Reverend Hezekial," she said sharply. "It's so good to see you."

Hezekial cleared his throat again. "How nice to see you, Sister Magnolia!"

Sally instantly understood. Maggie's voice had a different quality now. She was no longer a teenager.

"Well, hello, Maggie," Sally interrupted with the knowing voice of a mother as she gave her a hug. "Why don't you come sit by me. Obviously, you know Reverend Hezekial *quite well.* Do you know Reverend Hudson?"

"Oh, yes ma'am," she responded, her eyes still fixed on Hezekial as he fumbled about, distancing himself sheepishly as Maggie invaded his personal space. Carl looked at Sally in silent condemnation.

Sally returned Carl's glare with a telling nod. Reverend Carl cocked an eyebrow in response and thanked God for His divine intervention. Then he regained control over the conversation in the most gentlemanly manner he could. "I rest my case."

Sally knew it was time for her to break in. Hezekial knew he was busted. There was no way for Hezekial to refuse her now. She placed a cup in front of Maggie and poured her tea. Silence filled the void that had been a vociferous conversation.

"Maggie, I'm so glad you showed up. I invited you all here to discuss a remarkable story that involves us all."

Reverend Carl raised his hand in protest. The former high school wrestler had Hezekial pinned down and he intended to walk away with a win. "Sally, I think we should finish the business we started. Perhaps we should ask Maggie to give us a moment alone," he said in his most ministerial voice.

"Oh, I am sure that won't be necessary, Reverend. If we had to finish the gory details to make our point, we'd be just another group of Yankees. We Southerners know divine intervention when we see it, don't we Hezekial?" She paused with a damning look.

Sally continued before Carl could object. "Carl, I have no doubt that the Holy Spirit has spoken to Hezekial's heart directly about your concerns, in a way never before possible," she said, a steely irony in her voice, laced with her best Southern manners. "And I know in my heart that Hezekial is going to help us to overcome *both* of our concerns. Aren't you, Hezekial?"

Hezekial nodded with enthusiasm. "How can I serve?" he asked with renewed humility. Sally looked at Carl, who returned a begrudging nod.

"Now, where were we before Sister Maggie joined us?" Sally mused. "Oh yes, Hezekial, I recall you were just saying how you would go out of your way to reconcile the accounting and congregational concerns between First Baptist and Mount Zion quietly and confidentially. You don't want our young people to be impacted by the actions of any irresponsible adults that could misconstrue your relationship with the Mount Zion congregation, the federal government grant administrators, or possibly even your relationship with Sister Maggie," Sally said, drilling her point home while looking sternly at Maggie. Hezekial stared into his teacup to avoid Sally's verbal guillotine.

Sally smiled and turned toward Carl unexpectedly. "And, Reverend Hudson, I am sure you agree that we all want to preserve Hezekial's stature as a beacon of integrity so he can continue to pursue government grants that can help our community. I'll bet Hezekial will help us present a common front on our negotiations with all these damn Yankee government agencies converging on us. We certainly would want to avoid any controversy for him and Mount Zion during this *very* sensitive time. Wouldn't you agree, Carl?"

Carl simmered. Intellectually he understood that nailing Hezekial to the proverbial cross was less important than directing his energy, especially for the town, but he still didn't like it.

"Am I missing anything, gentlemen? Anything at all?" Sally asked Hezekial, her voice calm and serious.

Hezekial responded with uncharacteristic timidity. "No ma'am, Mrs. Sally, not at all. I am sure that we all understand each other."

"So, gentlemen, do we have a deal?" Hezekial closed his eyes in silent prayer and quietly nodded his concurrence. Carl studied the situation and slowly nodded in accordance with the unwritten rules of the South. Sally would make sure that Hezekial got in line or Sally would let the world know his latest mistress was an underage parishioner. Carl had won; he just couldn't say he had won.

"Amen!" Sally exclaimed in her best evangelical voice as the two men shook on it. "Surely we know that God works in mysterious ways. And now, gentlemen, and you too, Maggie, listen up. We all have far more important issues to discuss which affect us all. But if you stay here, you are bound by a blood oath to God Almighty that our secrets remain in this room. Raise your hands and agree. Now." Everyone complied and welcomed the respite.

"I visited the girl who was accused of shooting Quinine this past weekend at the town jail," Sally began anew, intentionally shocking her audience. Each shifted forward to listen intently. "I am convinced of three things. First, she cannot receive a fair trial in Bumkin. Second, she is Maggie's twin sister." All heads turned to Maggie, who sat in shocked silence, her eyes wide. "Her name is Meadow." Sally hesitated. "And third, she and Maggie are the illegitimate daughters of Bubba Tremblay."

Carl, Hezekial and Maggie were immobilized. "What?" they chorused, unable to contain their shock.

"Oh my God!" Carl exclaimed, suddenly aghast. "How could you say that? I can't believe that! How is it possible?"

Hezekial's voice rose again from the ashes, suddenly restored. "Of course it's possible! It's just another case of white men taking advantage of black women!"

"Oh, for Heaven's sake, gentlemen, get a grip. Men and women of different races have been cohabitating for all of history. Quit arguing over different shades of gray so you don't have to deal with civilization's corruption and inequity." Sally scolded the preachers. "And quit acting so damned pious, both of you!" Silence shackled the small group. Sally reached over the table and took Maggie's hand. "Maggie, did you know you had a twin sister?"

Maggie couldn't believe it. Everyone presumed she had some white blood in her, but Tremblay blood. How could that be? She caught her breath. "Yes, ma'am, Mrs. Sally, I knew, but I was told she was dead. "Can I meet her, Mrs. Sally?" her voice choked with emotion, her eyes filled with tears, as Sally reached for her. Maggie was once again a teenager.

"That is why I wanted you here," Sally said, gently patting Maggie's hand. "These gentlemen are now your spiritual advisors, Maggie… in the very least," Sally cocked an eyebrow and shot a hard look at Hezekial. "They are under a binding oath to protect your privacy." She drew a breath and spoke to the preachers. "This is a family matter involving a minor. It had damn well better remain confidential. I am now talking to you solely in your ministerial capacity as Maggie's spiritual advisors, gentlemen. Don't forget it. Nothing goes beyond this table."

Both reverends nodded obediently, now overcome with curiosity. Sally told them the story about her talk with Snowball and her visit with Meadow. Finally, Sally moved her hand toward Maggie's neck and pulled at her necklace, holding the odd-shaped pendant in her hand. "Maggie, this was handed down to you from Roberta, wasn't it?"

"Yes, ma'am."

"Your sister has a similar bracelet that is also very important to her. I want you to compare the two when you visit her, but don't tell anyone."

"Yes, ma'am," Maggie said obediently.

Sally looked defiantly at both preachers, pausing for effect, then summed up the meeting. "You gentlemen must drop your differences. Now. This is not a request. This community needs both of you. We all do. You will collaborate with me to protect Maggie and Meadow in a manner that keeps the city from blowing apart. This is the only way to protect yourselves, your congregations, and this town until we can get to the bottom of this mess."

"Somehow, I don't know how, these revelations are mixed up with the recent school riot. History has lit a fuse on our own little powder keg and all Hell will break loose if we don't find a way to stop it. That won't happen with Meadow in jail and subject to Southern Justice. If she doesn't get a fair trial, I will get the whole story into the press and I don't have to tell you where that leads for your churches and the town. Now, you fellas go save some souls until I call on you, but be ready to act when I need you. We all have a lot to deal with this week. And God bless you all."

Chapter Twenty-Five
The Mission

Lucery Butts hesitated as she looked up the phone number of the *Bumkin Record*. The mission she had received from the muffled, anonymous voice on the secret KKK line was very clear.

The Wizard was so important he couldn't tell her his name, but he did ask her to quit calling him Mr. Wizard. Mizery dialed the number to the newspaper, looking around for the notes she had lost in her flustered state of mind.

Levi Epstein pulled the phone to his shoulder as he typed up his notes on his manual typewriter. He was reviewing the unauthorized draft transcript of a conversation between the Superintendent of Education, Bam Callahan and Clyde Dillard once again. Faye Betty Bordelon, cousin to Trigger's secretary, was the best stringer he had. She always turned up good stuff. He never really knew how she got it and he probably didn't want to know, but it was the best $100.00 a month he spent for content.

The phone rang next to him. He looked under the mass of papers and pizza boxes, until he finally located it. "Epstein," he answered matter-of-factly.

"Mr. Levi, this is Mrs. Lucery Butts, the Senior Administrative Assistant to the Principal at Bumkin High." Levi smiled to himself as he heard Lucery recite her new title.

"Well hello, Lucery, what can I do for you?" he asked.

"Mr. Levi, I thought I should mention something to you, confidentially, of course. I wouldn't want this to get past our own discussion right here, today," she nervously rambled on.

Levi rolled his eyes and studied the intricate old tin sheet molding in the ceiling tiles above him. "That's why you called a newspaper, here, today," he mimicked her, then responded seriously. "We are talking in confidence, Lucery. Right here, today." he said in his blunt reporter's voice.

Lucery's heart was beating fast. She measured her words in her most articulate Southern drawl, as a woman of her status must. "Mr. Levi, I have been noticing that a lot of these nig—that is, these young black people what got to go to school here, they've been flashing thousands of dollars in food stamps lately. Now, Mr. Levi, I know that's how these people live, but this seems very unusual to me. When I saw that picture in the paper with Quinine's dead feet hangin' out of the car and all those food stamps on the ground, it just made me wonder if there weren't something goin' on, you know? I personally think it must be some of that marijuana money, Mr. Levi."

Levi hadn't made the connection between the food stamps, marijuana money, and Quinine's dead feet, but he had to hand it to Mizery, it conjured up a Southern image worth thinking about. He also knew damn well that Mizery Lutz couldn't have put those pieces together by herself. With the other stories he had heard, there seemed to be a "run" on food stamps in town. How was that possible?

The unedited transcript of the Superintendent with two students he knew well left no doubt that drugs were making their way into the school system faster than anyone had ever imagined since integration had begun. Somehow, it all made some kind of weird sense—maybe. He just didn't know how. Levi pulled a notepad from the bottom of a stack. "That's very observant of you, Lucery," he said in a patronizing manner. "Any idea who is wrapped up in this?"

Lucery fumbled for a moment, thinking hard to come up with the right response. Mr. Wizard had told her to be short, and not to talk too long to the reporter so he didn't have time to ask questions. "Well, Mr. Levi, they all look alike, you know, but maybe I could work on getting you some names of those people, that may be wrapped up in this mess."

"Have you told this to the Sheriff, Lucery?"

"Oh, my no, Mr. Levi, I couldn't get in the middle of something like that! That's why I called you, 'cause I wouldn't want the school board or Mr. Greely to be embarrassed. We've had enough issues lately with the riot and all."

Levi sensed he had gotten all he could get out of Lucery. Her mention of the school board was out of character, so he made a note and decided to wrap it up. "Well, Lucery, I will look into this," he promised, "and I will keep it just between us, here today," he couldn't resist. "You tell Principal Greely I said hello and I know he's in good hands with you as his Senior Administrative Assistant."

Lucery smiled with the recognition she so richly deserved. She fluttered the air with a newspaper to fan herself. "Thank you kindly, Mr. Levi," she said as she hung up the phone. Her mission was half complete. Being a spy wasn't all that difficult; Lucery kind of liked it.

Levi placed the phone down on the receiver, looked at his watch and walked over to his tin coffee pot. He returned to his desk with a hot cup of coffee and picked up the transcript of Bam and Clyde. "Another six minutes," he muttered to himself with a brief look at his watch, then returned to the page where he had left off.

Eight minutes later the phone rang. Levi looked at his watch to confirm the time as if destiny itself was calling. "Epstein" he said into the phone.

"It's Franklin, Levi," the brusque voice informed him.

"Well, Sheriff, what a surprise," Levi exaggerated. The tone of his voice met with silence on the other end of the phone. They both knew they had both just talked to Lucery. "What can I do for you, Sheriff?" Levi's tone was light-hearted.

"I read about this transcript of a conversation between Trigger Winchester and that Callahan kid in the newspaper," the Sheriff said matter-of-factly. "I also heard that he said in there that there are drugs in this town. That kid is a pain-in-the-ass. I will be needing a copy of that transcript."

It wasn't at all the question that Levi had expected, and he considered his reply carefully. "Now, Sheriff, even if I knew that was true, I probably couldn't do anything about it … unless maybe you could tell me why Quinine was naked with a bushel of food stamps when he was killed."

"Everyone has food stamps in this town. What's different about that?" Levi caught an edge in the Sheriff's normally calm demeanor.

"Yeah, but dead police and live hookers generally don't carry bags of stamps with them, especially on a hot date."

"Must have belonged to the hooker, Levi. How the hell would I know where they came from?"

"'Cause you're a Southern Sheriff in a small Southern community, Franklin. What you don't know, you get to make up 'cause nobody is going to question you anyway. I always thought that being Sheriff was better than being a preacher 'cause you get to keep the tithe. Now, Franklin, who the hell would bring food stamps to a murder?" Levi asked as he wrote the question on his tablet.

The Sheriff's ire rose as he ignored the reporter's insolence. "And why would the *Bumkin Record* give a rat's ass, Levi?"

"'Cause I'm a Jewish publisher trying to eke out a living in a small Southern town of Christians and I get to tell people whatever you make up so I can sell advertising. It's good for the economy. News is kinda like drugs, Franklin," Levi hypothesized, "people buy it 'cause they need it, not 'cause they want it. But it has to feel good. By the way, Franklin, are there drugs in this town?"

"Hell no, there ain't no drugs in this town! You can write that down, Levi! And stick to the Garden of the Month Club," the Sheriff commanded. The dial tone suddenly buzzed in Levi's ear. Levi looked at the receiver, shocked at the response. That wasn't very Southern, he thought.

Levi knew it was just a matter of time before the Sheriff got his hands on a copy of the transcript. But even a day or two would give him time to get some more headlines out and put the Sheriff on the defensive. How did the Sheriff know it was Bam anyway? The article hadn't actually disclosed his name.

He pondered the conversation. Education wasn't the Sheriff's beat, especially at the school board level. Why didn't he want to know more about a black market in food stamps? Why didn't he ask what new information Levi had learned about the race riot? It was clear to Levi that Mizery had called them both. But this defied Mizery's capacity, despite her new title. Who would be giving her instructions to pit him and the Sheriff against each other? He had lived down South long enough to know a setup, especially when he was the settee.

Levi drained the remainder of his coffee and decided it was time to personally visit Bam Callahan. He was the only common thread that came up in his last two phone calls, not to mention the transcript he held in his hand.

Across town, Mizery locked up her desk drawer and removed herself from her new executive assistant padded chair. Her day's work was done. The thought of Mr. Wizard calling her back excited her. She wished Herman had robes and a hat like that. She picked up the notes from her conversation with Mr. Wizard and tore them into little pieces before putting them in her trash can. All the evidence had to be destroyed. The neat, scripted notes reminded her to tell the newspaper about Bam and the transcript and the Sheriff about the food stamps at school.

Suddenly she raised her hands to her face in abject horror and plumped back into her chair. She got it backwards! Her heart raced. Crestfallen, she picked up her new Cosmopolitan Magazine to fan herself. She inhaled deeply as she considered her demise and gradually calmed down. After all, there was no reason for Mr. Wizard to ever know, was there?

Chapter Twenty-Six
High Visibility

Bam's knuckles turned white as he clamped his fists around the leather strap. He gritted his teeth, searching for something else to grab onto in the tight confines of the small Cessna 150 passenger seat. Like a kite in a March thunderstorm, the plane shuddered with each gust of wind. It hadn't occurred to Bam until he was 5,000 feet above the ground that Clyde was only a year older than him. They had totaled three cars between them in the last two years and now he was in a plane Clyde was piloting. He had to be a better pilot than he was driver.

So far, they were both still alive. Bam had to admit that he had never seen his friend this calm or focused. He had made Clyde promise he wasn't stoned before they took off. Bam looked around the lush green earth beneath him, gradually getting his bearings. "So, where's the farm?" he yelled at Clyde over the noise of rotors and rushing wind.

Clyde pointed to a clump of trees on the horizon. He leaned his head toward Bam while keeping his eye on the controls in front of him. "That's the bayou directly beneath us!"

Bam looked down at the bayou, a ribbon of water that looked silken with the reflection of the sun's rays, winding a path toward the clump of trees ahead of them.

My plot's carved out of the trees, a little under an acre. It was a lot of work. Nobody in his right mind would want to be a farmer. I planted it four months ago. It should look greener than the surrounding foliage and it's much taller than soybeans. I used Granddaddy's tractor to clear out the land and plow the rows, so it would look just like a small crop, inset deep inside the tree line. I imagine the plants will be about four foot or so by now. Weather has been good this year. I ought to have a good harvest coming." Clyde smiled.

Bam nodded. He had never thought of marijuana in agricultural terms. He could understand why Clyde wanted to scout his crop before he visited it in person. An acre of marijuana was hard to hide and would certainly attract attention. But an acre inside of the Tremblays' vast land holdings would be virtually invisible. All they had to do now was find the forest. Bam had never seen an acre of marijuana, much less from an airplane, but he loved new adventures.

The single-engine plane crossed over miles of green soybean sprouts and freshly plowed soil. Flat land of rich alluvial soil from the Mississippi River and Red River stretched into a cloudless, blue sky. Bam watched the shadow of the plane rippling over plowed rows as Clyde dove to a lower elevation to approach an island of trees surrounded by miles of plowed ground. The bayou made a half-moon bend around a grove that was covered by oak and willow trees that fed on its waters.

"All of this is Granddaddy's farm," Clyde explained with pride. "That over there is the original family cabin. He never plows this part of the farm since it's next to the cabin. Says he likes to hide out there from the rest of the world."

Bam looked down at a small cabin on a lone dirt road between the bayou and a large meadow, a thin trail of smoke spewing out of the chimney. A huge magnolia cast its shadow in front of the cabin. It was easy to understand the pride in Clyde's voice. Landscape like that was every Southerner's dream.

Clyde leveled the plane to within a few hundred feet of the canopy that lay beneath them. Bam choked back the Coca-Cola he had downed before taking off, tensing as the plane seemed to drop into a freefall, then leveled out just above the tree line.

The farmer's cultivation ended at the forest's edge, like a razor had cut a line between two warring forces. Clyde leaned over to Bam again. "Should be around here somewhere," he shouted, looking about in all directions. "Hey, there it is! It's on my side of the plane." The excitement in his voice overcame the noisy hum of the engine in the cockpit.

Bam looked down at a clear-cut square of vegetation, fit like a light-green postage stamp inset into the middle of a big, dark-green envelope. It was neatly sectioned off in the middle of the forest by a thin strip of dirt road that accessed it on all sides. Sheltered by the tall trees surrounding it, the site was only visible to the trained eye.

Clyde grinned as he inspected his crop from afar, bringing the plane around full circle. Bam looked quietly out the other side of the plane, finally starting to enjoy the ride. "Gee," Clyde boasted, "Looks like I have great production. I wonder how long that stand will last me."

Bam yanked on Clyde's shirtsleeve to get his attention as he stared out the other window. Clyde turned around to see Bam pointing on the far side of the plane. "Don't worry about it, buddy, I think there's a lot more where that came from. Look over there," he said as he pointed toward the ground on his side of the plane.

Clyde focused his eyes on the landscape beneath the other side of the plane as he gently maneuvered it clockwise, in a descending circle. Beneath them, a series of identical, large "postage stamp" crops came into view, neatly planted snug against large stands of big oaks and cottonwood trees. Bam figured each was at least ten acres. The telltale sign of precise, engineered crop rows broke out of the random, thick blanket of green canopies. Bam counted eight sections immediately on the horizon, each cut deeper into miles of untouched forest, insulated from trespassers by fence lines that marked the inner boundaries of Tremblay property.

"Shit," Clyde stammered, not believing his eyes as he grabbed the controls to maintain altitude. The crop that was in view was easily fifty times the size of Clyde's entrepreneurial effort, probably more.

A sparkle of light from the ground suddenly caught the corner of Bam's eye. He turned, holding his hands up to shield his eyes from the glare. The cabin that Clyde had pointed out to him came back into focus, with a lone figure standing on the porch. The glint could only be from binoculars, unless it was a gun scope reflecting the sunlight. Then he watched a bright red Camaro depart hurriedly, dragging a cloud of dust behind it at high speed. It was Timmy. Bam turned to Clyde, pointing at the speeding car. Clyde was still at a loss for words. He nodded silently as he brought the nose of the plane back into a heading for the Bumkin landing strip.

After thirty minutes of silence, the Cessna landed on the single asphalt strip from which it had risen just an hour and a half earlier. Bam had been thinking through the implications of their observations and hoping that Clyde was not doing the same until they were safely on the ground.

Bam crawled out of the plane, glad to be on the ground, and looked at his older schoolmate with a questioning glance. "What are you thinking?" he asked.

"I think Granddaddy has a problem he don't know about. And I can't say anything about it 'cause I'm not supposed to know either."

"Well, buddy, you got it half right. But I gotta tell you, there ain't no way in hell your granddaddy don't know about 50 acres of grass growin' on his farm. Anyone could tell that stand of weed was well tended. It took more than one tractor to clear and plow that ground."

Clyde stopped and turned to face Bam fully. Bam wondered if he was headed toward a fist fight with his friend, who was too tenderhearted and intellectual to be a good fighter. He planted his feet and stared back at Clyde.

"You think Granddaddy is growin' dope, don't you?"

"No shit, Sherlock! We both *know* he's growin' dope." Bam watched his friend's anger running through his veins, trying to figure out who to be mad at.

"Dammit!" Clyde yelled at the sky while kicking the ground. The boys got in Clyde's truck and rode in silence, awkwardly wondering what the other would do or say about the day's journey. Bam finally broke the silence. "Okay, bro', we both know that was Timmy's car at your granddaddy's cabin. People don't just carry binoculars around for no reason."

It don't matter anyway," Clyde lamented. "There just ain't no good answer to any of this."

Chapter Twenty-Seven
Visitation Rights

Maggie, Hezekial, and Sadie walked serenely behind Danny down the dark hallway to Meadow's cell. Danny fussed over a huge ring of keys that advertised the importance of his position as he tried to keep his eyes off Sadie. She was a striking woman beyond the reach of Danny, or anyone he knew. She walked elegantly in a crimson suit with matching red heals that made her a particularly stately distraction.

Hezekial could only empathize with the disadvantaged, young deputy. He loved pretty women in high heels. Of course, he loved pretty women without the heels also.

Maggie stood in Sadie's shadow, fighting her nerves to stay calm. She stifled a giggle as Danny dropped his keys. Sadie bent down to pick them up, her tight skirt held together at the knees. She handed them back to Danny with a sweet smile and big eyes, picking out a single key. "This one, Tiger," she said with a wink. Danny managed to open the door and ushered the preacher and his female assistants into the cell. Maggie had her hair in a bun and wore a Sunday hat under strict instructions from Sally to obscure her profile.

Hezekial had laughed out loud when Sally voiced her concern that Danny would recognize the twins. "Since when do we not all look alike to a white police officer? We've got natural camouflage, Mrs. Sally, don't worry," he assured her.

Sally conceded the point, but instructed Sadie to dress in her brightest, best outfit as a diversion. Besides, she wanted Danny to remember Sadie for future purposes. Hezekial happily supported her strategy. It had been easier than she anticipated to get the Reverend and his "charity assistants" access to Meadow. Nonetheless, she briefed Reverend Carl without going into specifics, in case something went wrong and a white cavalry was needed. She forgot to tell Carl that Sadie was representing First Baptist Church to grease the wheels with the Sheriff and Bubba.

"The Sheriff said I could give you folks 30 minutes," Danny said in his most diplomatic voice. "You just yell, and I'll come let you out." Hezekial thanked him as he held the cell door for the women to pass through. They pulled the door shut behind them.

Sally, Carl, and Hezekial had argued about who should visit Meadow. It was, on the surface, a counseling session, but just as importantly, a fact-gathering mission. Neither Sally nor Reverend Carl had any illusions that Hezekial or Maggie could be objective about Meadow's innocence, but everyone agreed that Reverend Carl or Sally's presence would create too much unwanted interest. The whole town would soon be asking questions. No, it had to be led by Hezekial.

Sally felt Meadow would have an easier time talking to a black preacher with her twin sister, but First Baptist had to feel represented. So, Sally volunteered Sadie as an independent observer. She was, in fact, a very spiritual person directly affiliated with First Baptist, and a keen observer. Hezekial readily agreed to Sadie's inclusion. A good-looking white woman following him around was great for his image.

Hezekial preferred to move quickly with a spontaneous, church-sponsored visit that was part of his regular schedule to meet local prisoners. It was always better to ask forgiveness than permission with white folks. His pulse quickened as the cool, damp air of the cell block met his nostrils. Something about jail visits triggered the darkest fears that sent goose bumps up a black man's spine. Maggie visibly shuddered also as she entered the room.

Hezekial closed his eyes and willed himself back to his favorite psalms. He was certainly not above showmanship, but his ethos was no act. This was the Valley of Death for his black people. Jails were the epitome of symbolism of the white man's control over the black man's life, and that of his church congregation. He had counseled many a black person inside these same dingy walls. Most were taken away to a darker life at Angola, the infamous Louisiana State Penitentiary.

God's love arrested his nerves, but the fears of a black man still flooded over him. Long ago he had promised his God that he would fight back, but he had also promised himself that he would escape the fate of his kinsmen. Only a black preacher could do both in Louisiana with any measure of success.

Hezekial's love of money and God were not incompatible in his world, where survival was still more primal than not. His environment was still a jungle, just a different type of jungle than his ancestors had been born into.

Hezekial searched deep for the calmness that his faith gave him in times like this. He welcomed the cleansing sense of spiritual renewal that these surroundings solicited from his soul. Money and power meant nothing in a jail cell.

Hezekial stopped so he blocked any view from the outer hall as held his bible in his hands. Maggie and Meadow were transfixed, each staring into a mirror as Maggie slowly took off her hat. Their emotional intensity filled the small cell. Sadie stood by Hezekial, quiet and nervous.

A tear streamed from Meadow's eye as she walked forward to embrace her twin. Maggie hugged her back, trying to stifle her own tears. Hezekial knew that Meadow had never known a family. He could only guess how it would feel to find your twin sister while you faced a lynch mob. He strode over to the two young women holding each other, groping for inadequate words. "Sisters, we are all part of God's miracle today," he said in his best preacher's voice. Sadie immediately pointed at the bracelet and the necklace, remembering Sally's strict instructions. Hezekial nodded, taking Meadow's hand in his right palm, his bible held close to his chest in his left hand. "Allow us to look at these emblems of your youth while you talk and we all say a prayer of thanksgiving."

Sadie moved toward the girls with a finger to her lips to ensure silence. She gently lifted Maggie's necklace over her head as Meadow's eyes questioned her movement. Maggie nodded at Meadow with assurance, squeezing her hand for security as Sadie took her wrist to remove her bracelet. Meadow hesitated, then handed a trembling wrist to Sadie, who uncoupled her bracelet.

Sadie and Hezekial quietly walked over to a far corner of the cell as the girls sat down on the bed. Sadie placed the two pendants on Hezekial's bible cover and noticed his eyes focusing on her chest. She smiled nicely and tapped a perfect red fingernail on the bible to refocus his attention. Men were men, no matter the color or religion.

Hezekial and Sadie inspected the two pendants They had promised Sally they would do this first, although neither knew why, or what they were looking for. Sally had explained that the only tangible connection to the history of the twins lay in the two pieces of jewelry that both girls had held onto. Somehow, a deep sense of purpose for the pendants was instilled into them at an early age. Sally's sense of history told her they had to be studied and salvaged before the police finally took them.

Hezekial looked closely, turning them over in his hand. Both were abstract in design, and neither seemed symbolic or complete on its own. They were clearly hand-made from the same source of thick, high-quality silver. They were made to weather the test of time. They bore the shape of misaligned 'V's and, like the girls, seemed to be mirror images, identical but different.

Hezekial laid them over each other, shifting positions, looking for writing or numbers and seeing nothing. Finally, he placed them directly above one another. As all the 'V's converged, Sadie's and Hezekial's eyes locked in silent shock. Sadie quickly pulled the two symbols tightly together, the combination screaming out a harsh message: KKK

"Motherfucker!" Sadie's whisper ricocheted in the small cell. Hezekial's eyes widened in fear and quickly closed as he put his hand over Sadie's lips. He slid the jewelry in his coat pocket for safekeeping and began reciting the 23rd Psalm. Who could have guessed? Only Sally Callahan.

Chapter Twenty-Eight
Sign Language

It was late on Saturday night. Clyde stood on the bumper of his truck, holding onto the tailgate to steady himself. The truck was parked directly underneath the big Bumkin sign on the edge of town. He leaned forward and gave Mike the "go" signal. Mike scurried up his big frame, grabbing Clyde's hands to steady himself. He walked up Clyde's backside and planted tennis shoes firmly on both shoulders, scaling the billboard sign with his hands. The two of them were just tall enough. Mike gradually stood at full height, tenuously balanced on Clyde's shoulders, and grabbed the edge of the big billboard sign to stabilize himself.

Fortunately, the City Fathers had been too cheap to rent sign space, so they elected to put up their own sign, smaller and lower to the ground. It stood barely fifteen feet high, supported by four creosote poles. "Welcome to Bumkin!" was printed at the top in bold, red letters against a white background. Below that, the mantra of the Chamber of Commerce proclaimed Bumkin to be "The Best Spot Top Side of God's Green Earth."

Rat stood on the ground next to Clyde, stirring the white paint with a stick. Two new paintbrushes were stuffed into his back blue-jean pocket. Bam leaned against the truck door, reading a copy of the *Bumkin Record* to his buddies by the fluorescent light of the sign.

"The newest headline reads 'School Board Transcripts Say Pot Active in Schools.'"

"Who would have thought?" Clyde asked philosophically as he and Mike concentrated on balancing themselves. The crew giggled in response. Clyde and Mike were both stoned; it made the plan all the better.

"Hey, listen up, this is important stuff!" Bam cleared his throat. Rat passed the small can of white paint and one of the new brushes to Clyde who, handed it gingerly up to Mike. Bam started over in his best reading voice: "The *Bumkin Record* has reviewed transcripts of tape recordings between Superintendent Winchester and two unidentified students from Bumkin High School. The tapes present shocking evidence that students get stoned in class, have ready access to marijuana and other drugs, and are sexually active."

"Well, at least they didn't quote us by name," Clyde said.

"You idiots!" Mike shouted as he painted over the big 'S' with white paint. "The whole damn parish knows it was you guys. What were you thinking?"

"This was supposed to be confidential," Bam complained. "That sonofabitch Winchester sold us out." He looked up briefly from the newspaper article to judge the paint job with admiration. "Very good work, Mike, but I still think you need to replace the small 'p' with a large 'P,' or it just won't look professional." Mike nodded and requested the red paintbrush. Rat looked up approvingly and stirred the red paint.

"Hurry up, fellas. I'm getting tired." Clyde shifted himself to grab the posts that supported the sign. "What else does the paper say?"

Bam began to read again. "The tapes were secretly produced and transcribed by Superintendent Winchester who presented the results to the Board of Directors last month in a closed-door meeting. The Superintendent had hoped to spur the Board into action by taping real-life experiences from actual students. The transcripts indicate that two male students from Bumkin High, a sophomore and a junior, were interviewed in the Superintendent's offices. In the meeting, the Superintendent was actually offered a marijuana cigarette by one of the students." Bam stopped, interrupted by Mike and Rat's laughter.

Mike looked down at Clyde with renewed admiration. "You really did that, cher?"

Bam spoke up on Clyde's behalf. "I was there. Winchester even told him his wrap on the joint was one of the best he'd ever seen." Bam picked up where he had left off. "The transcript went on to describe the views of teenagers in the school system who now have ready access to drugs and sex. Superintendent Winchester and School Board members refused to return calls by reporters." Bam stopped. "Sally ain't going to be happy."

"I thought she wanted us to meet with Winchester?" Clyde said.

"Sure she did, since she didn't know the whole truth." Bam dreaded the thought of his next confrontation with Sally. It wasn't supposed to happen this way.

"I don't think they'll ask more questions 'cause they don't want any more answers," Mike volunteered. "Besides, the School Board is pissed at Winchester 'cause he asked questions in the first place."

"It's a good thought but they are going to take it out on someone," Bam lamented.

All four boys were back on the ground now. Rat had replaced the tops on the paint cans and wrapped the paintbrushes with newspaper. For a kid who never completed his homework, Bam was impressed at how meticulously Rat worked. The boys backed away from the sign to get a full view, looking up at their handiwork in red and white stained blue jeans and T-shirts.

"Really nice work, guys," Bam complimented his buddies, putting his arm around Rat's shoulders, the only place there wasn't sticky wet paint. They slapped each other on the back and climbed into the cab. "Don't get my truck messed up," Clyde screamed. Rat immediately jumped into the back bed of the truck and lay down, looking up at his handiwork. High above them, the sign now read:

Welcome to Bumkin!
The Best Pot Top Side of God's Green Earth

Truer words were never said, if only they knew, Bam thought. He had promised Clyde that he wouldn't tell anyone about the Tremblay crop. But Bam also knew their prank would deliver a special meaning for Clyde's grandfather, Bubba Tremblay. Even Clyde didn't know the full extent of the message, but Timmy certainly would.

Bam pulled the truck door shut and sat up in the front passenger seat with Clyde, who was looking at his watch. "Well, boys it's about time," he announced. "Floyd ought to be hiding in his alley by now. Who has the 'weed'?"

Mike handed over a cellophane bag of finely ground green flakes. Bam opened the bag and leaned across the seat to share a sniff with Clyde.

"Smells like bad shit to me!" Clyde boasted. Mike nodded as he resealed the bag. Rat handed a bag of corn chips through the back window of the truck as Clyde revved up the big engine and pulled back onto the road.

"Cigarettes, Rat!" Bam yelled to the back of the truck. Rat passed around several hand-wrapped tobacco cigarettes. Bam punched in the truck lighter. Clyde pulled onto the blacktop and headed into town. The lighter sprung with a click as they entered the city limits, four blocks from the black-and-white Bumkin Police car that sat in a narrow alley between Randall's Floor Furnishing and Becky's Floral Shoppe. The boys all lit up in unison, blowing smoke out of the truck windows barely opened. The red tips of their cigarettes acted like beacons in the darkness, screaming for attention.

Floyd Ducote watched the passing traffic in the solitude of the balmy night, ever vigilant, ready to chase down another speeding visitor to Bumkin's main streets. The alley was an ideal space to catch cars headed south on the main highway. Plus, he was on the edge of town where he could catch a little sleep without worry about the mayor or the city council members running up on him unexpected.

Clyde Mallard's big green truck rolled up just four blocks away, cruising at just over 10 miles per hour down the main drag, weaving slightly. Mallard was constantly on probation for speeding tickets. He and his pot-head friends had to be getting stoned while they cruised through town. Floyd sat up in his seat, adjusted his cap, and leaned over the steering wheel, squinting for a closer view of the truck as it approached. He watched, like a bobcat waiting to pounce on unsuspecting prey, as the oversized tires slowly passed in front of him.

The windows of the truck rolled down slowly, almost in unison, releasing wafts of white smoke out of the cab like a chimney. Floyd could see the teenagers sucking on joints and laughing as plain as day. He had 'em. Floyd turned his key and flipped on his siren, shooting out of the alley like a bullet with his foot to the accelerator, the big police car careening onto the highway with the element of surprise and the squeal of smoking rubber. The chase was on.

The big truck seemed to jerk, then sped up for a short distance. Floyd goosed his siren to let the teenagers know there wasn't any getting away from Bumkin justice. Clyde gradually, too gradually, slowed the big truck to a crawl and pulled over next to a line of empty parking meters in front of Poche's Hardware Store. Floyd jumped out of his car, his gun unholstered and pointed at his adversaries. "You boys get out of the truck. Hands in the air. Now!" he yelled. Floyd was on the case.

He could see chaos and shouting inside the truck, the boys all fumbling about as if they were confused. Rat sat up in the back of the truck, momentarily scaring the policeman. Clyde, Mike, and Bam rubbed their eyes red as they piled out of the truck, their heads held down in shame.

Clyde frantically threw up his big hands into the night sky. "What is this about? I wasn't speeding! You can't stop me for nothin!"

"Move away from the car, boys, I got you red-handed!" Floyd yelled in a menacing voice.

Clyde gave the stub of his cigarette to Rat, who was still sitting up in the back of the truck. Rat held it above his head, then dropped it down his throat with great panache and a wide grin.

"What's that?" Floyd looked angrily at Rat. "I'm gonna haul your ass to jail and pump your stomach!"

Rat said nothing and with a single gulp, swallowed the stub.

Floyd ran to the truck, pushing Clyde aside. "Don't move!" he warned in his toughest voice. His hands reached deep under the seat, sweeping for drugs he knew had to be there. And then he found it. He slowly pulled out a cellophane bag and held it high in his hands for all to see. Clyde looked at Mike, horrified at the turn of events, his hands covering his face in shock. "Man, I told you to get rid of that shit!"

It was too late. Floyd had found the bag, its contents neatly rolled up and bound with a rubber band, waiting to be smoked by teenagers getting high on a Friday night.

Bam shook his head in dismay. "Looks like he's got us, fellas. I told you that we shouldn't be messing with this shit when we were in town."

Clyde was near tears. "C'mon Floyd, give us a break," he pleaded. "We didn't do no harm. My dad will kill me for smoking this shit!"

Floyd kept the gun pointed low in his right hand, the voice on his walkie-talkie crackling to life in his left. A Bumkin Police car turned the corner, screeching to a halt in front of Clyde's truck, sirens blaring.

Foster Landeaux pushed the car door open forcefully, slowly pulling himself out of the police car with a grunt. He pulled his belt up and tucked his crisp, ironed shirt into dark khaki pants, surveying the scene of the crime. He watched the teenagers in grim silence, directing an exaggerated sneer at Bam that was meant for all to see.

"We got trouble with these little farts?' he asked Floyd.

Rat finally spoke up, his voice choking. "Foster, help us out here, man. This is really bad shit, man. We don't need any trouble."

"Too late, boys," Foster announced proudly. "It's all over. You quiet down or I'll bury your ass in jail right now." He beamed as Floyd silently handed over the bag of contraband, dutifully reciting the events that led to his capture of the juvenile delinquents. Foster took the rubber band off of the bag, nodding as Floyd embellished his story about the chase down Main Street.

"Looks to me like we got us some real potheads here, Floyd." Foster spat out his tobacco chew and dug into the cellophane bag, pinching off some of the contents to test its veracity, just like in the movies. He looked up as the contents hit his tongue. He immediately knew he had been had. The scarlet hue of his face rose from his open collar and gold chains to the top of his big military haircut head. Then it hit him.

"Shit! Goddamn motherfuckers! Shit!" Foster stomped his feet and jumped up and down on the pavement like a giant four-year-old. He squatted down, putting his hands behind his head and tucking his head between his knees to seek relief. "I need water!" he gasped, his hand at his throat. Then it became a scream. "I need fuckin' water! Now! Water!" Foster ran to his car and threw open the door. He shot a middle finger at the boys. "You'll pay for this!" he yelled, and then sped off in his car through the stoplight, tires screeching. Floyd stood like a statue in the street, staring at the taillights of his boss receding into the night. The sirens went silent as Foster sped away in search of water. Floyd didn't know what to do.

Mike picked up the bag as the boys broke out in laughter, finally breaking the silence. "Cher," he said sincerely, "we tried to tell you this was bad shit." They all burst into laughter again. "We really didn't think you would call Foster for backup."

Floyd closed his eyes and asked, "What's in the bag?"

"Dog shit, tons of cayenne pepper, tobasco and parsley," Bam confessed quietly, trying to keep a straight face.

Floyd took off his cap and slapped his knee with it in anger. Red-faced and humiliated, he stalked back to his police car and left.

"Man, I ain't ever seen a cop get that mad without getting a ticket!" Clyde said.

"You ain't seen mad yet," Mike announced with a smile. "Wait till you see Tyrone."

Bam looked at him quizzically. "Tyrone, the little black dude?"

"Yeah, he's in the hospital. Mom was on duty when he got checked in last night with a really bad case of diarrhea. Think I'll get you to drop me off at the hospital so I can pay him a visit."

"Guess he liked his Ex-Lax candy a little too much," Clyde said.

"Not his, cher. My candy," Mike corrected him.

"Tyrone may be white by now," Bam laughed.

"Why do you want to see him?"

"So I can give him a shit-eating grin," Mike responded.

"Mike," Clyde slapped his buddy on the back as they loaded into the big truck, "it occurs to me that you and Foster finally got something' in common."

Chapter Twenty-Nine
Golden Nuggets

Bubba placed the most recent copy of the *Bumkin Record* face up on the old cypress table and pushed it in front of Timmy. He placed a small shot glass of Southern Comfort with a single cube of ice on top of the front-page picture, offering a toast as he pointed to the headline in large black print: "*Welcome to Bumkin - Best Pot Topside of God's Green Earth?*"

It was a comfortable, seedy room that held its secrets close. Bubba could hear the patrons of the Golden Nugget milling around in front of the shabby bar, waiting for the card game to begin. He had the back room cleared so he would not be interrupted at his unofficial office in the back of the bar. Bubba leaned back in his favorite bar chair, he flared his nostrils and sucked in the sweet aroma of bourbon and fried chicken.

"Hot damn! Flossie is at the grill!" he yelled out to no one in particular. Food got dispensed to the bar, the poker game, and to the owner's living quarters, or whoever occupied them at the time, from a central kitchen that touched the nose of everyone in the old, ragged building. Scantily clad barmaids moved back and forth, lugging beer for the good ol' boys as they gathered for the game.

The austere light exposed shadows of names carved deeply into the earthen hues of the old oak table, worn from decades of card games and bar fights that gave the room its authentic, nostalgic feeling. The heavy, cypress floorboards had long since succumbed to the moisture of the bayou that flowed beneath them, producing a warped, crooked room with a charm that seemed cobbled together by its own history.

Bubba and Timmy sat directly across from each other. Dinah, the most recent inhabitant of the Golden Nugget Bar, stood shyly immediately behind Bubba's seat, her delicate hands softly resting on his big shoulders.

Bubba leaned his head back, nuzzling into Dinah's chest. He claimed ownership of her with big hands that reached behind his chair. Grabbing her buttocks, he explored the lean body while he looked up at the ceiling and searched for words to describe his mood.

"Ah don't think that we ever agreed to let this sort of thing happen, did we, Timmy?" he asked. "My own grandchillin' flying over my crops and now some kids are telling the whole fuckin' world that there is marijuana to be had here in my town. That's bad advertising, Tim. That's bad for our business, bad for my family. Even though the town don't know, I think those kids have figured out that it's my marijuana their smoking. Tim, what do you think we should do about all this?" A menacing tone suddenly crept into his voice.

Timmy's hands still shook from the amphetamines and adrenalin that filled his bloodstream. He had just returned from a ZZ Top concert, happy to escort Dinah and her friends at Bubba's insistence. His eyes were bloodshot from Valium, his head fuzzy. The ice rattled against the edge of his glass as his hand quivered, producing a distinct clicking sound that bounced off the wooden table. Tim looked up at his supplier, a man old enough to be his grandfather and sinister enough to be his killer.

A voice suddenly came from behind the bar at the other side of the room as a silhouette rummaged for liquor. "Somethin' needs to happen fast or I'm going to kill Bam Callahan myself and Dad won't mind if I do," Foster Landeaux said matter-of-factly as he came out from under the shadows.

Bubba suddenly opened his eyes and stroked Dinah as she stroked his thinning hair. "Well, I don't know that you should bother your dad for that sort of thing," Bubba returned, with a grunt.

"Why not? The Sheriff does what I ask him."

"You're still smarting from that shit those kids fed you, ain't you, Foster?" Bubba laughed heartily. "I imagine I'd be pissed too, but I'd have never let it happen. Those kids can fuck with you, but they ain't gonna fuck with me." His eyes narrowed as they always did when he was thinking business. It was all just business to Bubba… his business. "Besides, dickhead, your father lets you get away with what you don't tell him, not what you do tell him. There's a big damn difference, Foster. You see, boy, unlike yourself, your daddy still has some vestige of morals left." His head turned as he stared at Foster across the bar, bushy red eyebrows rising up and down as he talked with an unusual air of authority. "I don't need to be calling David Tremblay again to cover your ass on another 'incident,' shall we say? That law degree of his ain't cheap."

Foster shut up immediately. Bubba paused momentarily, holding the conversation in abeyance as he made a production of reaching for his drink. He took a long sip with his right hand while he slid his left arm around Dinah's slim waist and pulled her to him. She sat on his knee like a blow-up doll while he pulled the straps off of her shoulders with unexpected tenderness. Dinah giggled, letting the flimsy t-shirt fall to the edge of her breasts where it hung momentarily, then fitfully fell to her waist.

Timmy was mesmerized by the show. Foster ignored it with indifference.

Dinah leaned back into Bubba, arching her back and pushing her chest out for all to admire. Now fully exposed and instantly available on Bubba's lap, her nipples hard and swollen, her hands caressed his face behind her as he rubbed her flesh.

"Why don't you pay some attention to Timmy here?" Bubba asked as he pushed her forward and grabbed his shot glass. Dinah sat up, vulnerable and half naked in front of Timmy, her tongue caressing red lips as she pushed her butt against Bubba's crotch in a practiced bordello pose.

Timmy leered, unable to take his eyes off her. On the other side of the bar, Foster popped a Budweiser tab with seeming disgust. Bubba finally took the last of the bourbon in a single gulp and slowly continued the conversation as Dinah rubbed against him. "This here is power, Timmy. I get what I want, when I want it, how I want it. Tell him, darlin." He stuck Dinah's hand down his pants and smiled at Timmy as Dinah chortled, "Anytime, all the time, Bubba. You know that."

"You need to learn from this, Timmy. This is what we work for, take risk for, make payroll for." He pointed at Foster. "Now Foster here has got no respect for authority. Course, I know how different he and Franklin are," he jibed. "Unlike Foster, his daddy is just a good front man who lets me do my thing. As long as we stay low key, ol' Franklin lets us keep things orderly so he don't get his hands dirty and can claim there ain't no drugs in his town. That's the deal, and I hold to it 'cause Franklin wouldn't knowingly sell out for money or drugs or anythin' so obvious. Ol' Franklin, he don't have a lot of vices like me an' Foster. He just likes pussy a little too much, if that's possible. Hell, even that Callahan kid figured out the Sheriff was bangin' that neighbor of his. That's why Judge Jim is going to let him off the hook. I was hopin' he would ship him out of town to a new school. But rest assured, ol' Franklin would sell his soul to protect his onliest son." He looked at Foster, who was now a shrunken figure behind the bar. "Down deep in his soul, Franklin knows there is something wrong with Foster. He and I both know Foster ain't like his dad, but we'll just keep that our little secret, won't we Foster? As long as you do your job." Bubba talked to Foster without acknowledging his presence, just as he would have his best slave if he could own one.

Dinah shook her head in mock horror as Bubba traded glares with Foster in the shadows. "Tough luck," he lamented to no one in particular. Bubba grabbed the bottle and poured another shot glass of bourbon, sipping it with obvious delight. "So, Foster, unless you want your daddy to know all your secrets, you better hold on to your gun and your temper. That is, unless I tell you otherwise. Killing a white kid like Bam Callahan ain't as easy as killing a nigger cop."

Foster froze, deathly still, silenced by his master as Bubba turned his attention back to Timmy.

"Now, Timmy, tell me what kind of damn country do we live in that requires us to constantly protect the public from the guv'ment? We gotta keep people like Foster on payroll just to clean up a mess every now and then." Bubba tilted his head toward Foster and shook it with a face of dismay. "It's a damn shame people cain't just have fun, chase women, and make money all the time, just like you an' me. That's what America is about goddammit! Course, there's a price true Americans like us gotta pay. The good things in life don't come for free, Timmy-boy," his raspy voice filled the empty room.

"Take a look here at these beautiful tits." Bubba cupped both big hands around Dinah's breasts as she returned her attention to him. She closed her eyes and feigned pleasure as she squirmed her hips in response to her captured audience. "Things like this ain't free. No sireee, ain't nuthin' free no more, Timmy, and Lord knows good things are expensive! I pay for Dinah's services myself, 'cause Dinah here has got a right to make a living, jus' as long as she don't hurt no one, ain't that right, honey?" Dinah giggled on cue, while Bubba ran a finger along a slight scar from a plastic surgeon's silicon insertion.

"An' me, I got my rights too," Bubba explained. "I got the right to educate people no matter what the fuckers in Washington say. I got the right to grow crops that people smoke, just like those assholes that grow tobacco up North. The only difference is they done got the whole damn country addicted to cigarette taxes, not to mention they done bought and paid for Congress."

"So now we got to get our own lobbyin' group to protect ourselves from our own damn guv'ment! Imagine that! It's so bad we have had to reinvent the KKK so we don't lose more ground. I want you to come join me at the Citizen's Council meeting. Us regular people gotta pay politicians so we can do what is good for everyone. Just like the cigarette lobby or just like the niggers that deliver a bloc of Democrat votes anytime for a price. Just like the revolutionaries had a right to grow their own tea, we have a right to grow marijuana, Tim. 'Cause it's the only cash crop what makes any sense anymore. Growing marijuana ain't no different from the Kennedys running illegal whiskey during prohibition. And look where it got them! So you see, Timmy, protectin' my redneck rights takes money and organization."

Bubba slapped Dinah on the rump as he leaned back in his chair. The show was over. "It's all part of the responsibility of bein' American. Ain't no different if your name is Kennedy or your name is Tremblay. You gotta give people what they want 'cause they gonna get it somewhere else if you don't. No matter if it's women or drugs, it's all the same. And these days, anyone can get anything! The world's done gone damn near crazy! The guv'ment done reduced my cotton subsidies to the point that I can't make a normal livin' on the farm. We don't have any choice! "They've done allowed South America to start destroying the sugarcane market with imports. So now some Columbian son-of-a-bitch prints money by shipping in cocaine instead of coffee to pay off the same damn politicians that done sold out our subsidies. Well, two can play that game, son. So now, Timmy, we are getting involved, as they say. We are getting reorganized and sophisticated and we gonna use our own drug money to deliver our own votes, have our own lobbyists, to protect us white people." Bubba's voice grew boisterous as he pointed a big finger at himself to stress that Bubba was taking charge of Bubba's world. His eyes raged with anger, his teeth grit as he thought about the corruption in Washington that had threatened his way of life.

"Everyone wants to be boss today on our nickel, Timmy-boy. Niggers, politicians, even women!" He paused for a deep breath and swigged his last sip of bourbon, his big head turning redder by the moment. "Why in God's name would women want to be burnin' their bras and trying to be men? Hell, they own fifty percent of the wealth and a hundred percent of the pussy in the world! What else do they want?" He broke into loud laughter and looked to Dinah for confirmation, who nodded agreement.

His voice calmed back into the balm of grandfatherly advice. "Anyway, Tim, so as to preserve our way of life, son, to keep your distributors in drugs, keep me satisfied with hookers, my school in students, and my church in contributions, we just can't fuck up again. The Tremblays have a deal with the Sheriff that has worked for generations. We got to stay out of sight and control our destiny. It's just as simple as that."

"Take for example that little ruckus at the high school we staged. We gotta keep the niggers and the whites at each other's throat so no one is concerned about 'the growing drug problem.'" He used two fingers on each hand to form quotation marks in the air. "We gotta do what we got to do, Timmy-boy. This here is a real war. A war for the American way of life! "That plan of yours for tradin' drugs for food stamps was pure damn poetical genius. We done tripled our sales and we are makin' more money than ever. But it's got to stay between you an' me or we gonna attract more attention from the Feds than we care to see until we have our whole plan in place to deal with them. But we will."

Bubba pushed Dinah aside, then pulled his chair next to Timmy, draping a massive arm over his slumping shoulders, his face within inches of the teenager, the smell of Southern Comfort on his breath. "You got it, Tim? Do you understand me here, boy?" His voice acquired a steely tone, his face contorted to make his point as he whispered in Timmy's face. "I can't have some punk teenager puttin' up billboard signs on major highways in my town, drawin' attention to my marijuana crops. In my own fuckin' town, Timmy! It ain't nobody's goddamn business what I grow. Hell, Levi Epstein even called the Sheriff about drugs and foods stamps in this here town. So ah'm just starting to feel a little stressed out, as you young guys say. And when I get stressed, you gonna get stressed." Bubba's massive forefinger jabbed sharply at Timmy's chest to make his point.

"This shit runs downhill real fast, Timmy boy. If you want me to keep buying those nigger food stamps that are makin' you rich and keep you supplied with inventories that keep you in business and keep policemen like Foster here coverin' your ass, you better get everythin' quieted down at that EZ Mart, real fast. 'Cause in a war, there are casualties," Bubba said menacingly, staring into Timmy's eyes. "Casualties on all sides," Bubba repeated.

Timmy sat silent. He gathered his nerves and looked over at Foster as his brain registered the threat. "Why Quinine?" he asked, his throat parched with fear.

Foster shrugged in the background. Bubba sat still for a moment, his eyes flaming with emotion. "Let's just say Quinine fell in love with his work. It's easy to do." Bubba smiled at his own humor.

Bubba stood up slowly, looking down at Timmy for a long moment from his full six-foot-four height, his starched khakis hanging loosely on his big frame like the plantation manager he was. Bubba patted Timmy on the head the way a coach might pat his best football player.

Bubba pulled two crisp hundred dollar bills out of his money clip, handing it to Dinah on his way out the door. "Lil' gal, why don't you take Timmy here home tonight and screw his brains out so maybe he'll be thinking clearer tomorrow when he gets back to bid'ness." He silently turned to leave and put his left hand out, palm up, as he approached the door. Foster immediately placed a brown paper bag wrapped with rubber bands in his upturned palm. Bubba tossed it gently into the air and held it for a moment in silence, mentally weighing it. Satisfied, he headed out the door. "Keep an eye on him," he told Foster, "and keep countin' my money right."

Dinah downed a shot of whiskey then walked dutifully over to Timmy, taking his cold hand in hers as they followed Bubba out to watch the poker game.

In the dark shadows of the foyer to the women's restroom adjoining the kitchen, Flossie finally opened her eyes and let out a long, slow breath. She was frantic, trying to forget what she had heard, wishing she could have closed her ears. Her heart was pounding. She had frozen in her tracks as soon as Bubba entered the room, making sure she didn't call attention to herself. Her dark color and small profile were absorbed into the cubbyhole shadows and dark wood of the old building.

Flossie slid quickly through the back door of the kitchen to check on her fried chicken. Then she had to call Mrs. Sally.

Chapter Thirty
Collaboration

The call had come as no real surprise to Bam. It was only a matter of time. In some ways it was a relief. The flight over Bubba's property with Clyde had scared Bam, but the sight of Timmy's car speeding away from the old cabin had connected some of the dots. It was one thing to be a small-town dealer exchanging weed for food stamps with local cops. It was quite something else to be Bubba Tremblay's front man for distributing illegal drugs.

Bubba the planter, Bubba the deacon of First Baptist Church, and Bubba the segregationist educator, was into illegal crops of hookers and marijuana. Bam didn't know enough, but he damn sure knew that he knew too much. He needed someone he could confide in other than Sally, so he quickly agreed to visit with Levi Epstein after school. Bam had been brought up by a journalist and had a natural respect for the fourth estate. It was more trustworthy than any other Louisiana institution he could think of, even though it wasn't terribly effective.

Sally had always said that real journalists were surprisingly rare. Few elected to investigate the fertile ground of sin and corruption that was always present in Louisiana life. Maybe Epstein was different. Trusting Winchester had been a mistake. The leak of the transcripts had thrown him back into the spotlight after the infamous trash can bomb. Was the mistake in telling the truth or trusting the system? It really didn't matter. He was screwed. It was already affecting him and Sally.

Instead of creating pressure on the school board, the tapes had put every teacher at Bumkin High under attack by outraged parents, shocked by a drug problem they wanted to ignore, courtesy of Bam and Clyde. Then came the riot at school. Fortunately, he and the boys had kept quiet about Lester's incitement of the riot at the command of Sally, but down deep he knew it couldn't be contained forever. Nor did he think it should be.

Bam pushed on the old brass doorknob and entered the *Bumkin Record*. It was a dark, gloomy room permeated by the smell of ink and paper, lit only by the glow of outdoor light that seeped over the door transom. The front-glass windows of the old building had been boarded when the small newspaper offices became easy targets for wannabe civil-rights rebels and racists looking for headlines in the early sixties. Rough cypress wood now replaced the old glass windows, giving it an abandoned, foreboding appearance. Bricks and bottles gradually turned into twenty-two caliber bullets from small drug gangs that cost the newspaper a small fortune in plate-glass windows. Now the Main Street front of the *Bumkin Record* was a scarred badge of courage for a local Southern weekly paper.

Norma Billadeau looked up from her manual typewriter, her headset firmly in place on top of black, curly hair as she converted dictated tape into printed words for the next paper. She acknowledged Bam's arrival with a curt nod, silently pointing to the door to the pressroom where Epstein's office was nestled behind large barrels of ink.

The smell of newsprint and chemicals stung Bam's nostrils and gave him a momentary headache.

Bam found Levi Epstein pouring himself a cup of coffee in his cramped office. He quickly pulled the door closed to shut off the deafening noise of the press. Gratefully, the little office was much quieter than Bam expected. Levi noticed Bam's surprise. "It was cheaper to add insulation than to move my office. How about some coffee, Bam?"

Bam eyed the thick, black syrup pouring out of the ancient tin coffeepot and quickly shook his head. "No thanks, Mr. Epstein." Bam carefully removed an abused dictionary and a messy stack of papers off the single chair available for a guest and sat down facing the journalist.

An awkward moment passed as Levi scrutinized the teenager over his eighth cup of coffee for the day. Each hoped the other would start a conversation that both wanted to have but neither knew how to begin. The reporter, being a reporter, finally decided to jump in. "Bam, you know I cover the school board. I was wondering whether you might know anything about these taped conversations with Superintendent Winchester that were supposedly leaked by 'clerical error?'" Epstein's face gave away his disbelief. He hesitated for a moment and drank more coffee, watching Bam's reaction. "It took some guts to talk about those things," he offered. It was a patronizing start, but it was also true. How else do you get a sixteen-year-old to talk?

Bam sat motionless. "And what if I do?"

Epstein shoved his reading glasses to rest on his high forehead. "Well, it would depend on the circumstances, Bam. Let's say, hypothetically of course, that those tapes were made in confidence and released by accident or otherwise, without the knowledge of the people who were involved. That might mean that someone at the school board violated the trust of students who they enlisted to help. If so, the public needs to know."

"What good is that to the people that made the tapes?" Bam asked pointedly.

"You tell me," the reporter shot back coolly with a grin. He liked the kid's directness and even found it refreshing. "Regardless of the source, I can assure you that anything you tell me is confidential unless you tell me otherwise."

"The tapes speak for themselves," Bam said, "but you can assume that the conversation was supposed to be confidential. And I can probably assume that it was leaked to you intentionally."

"Okay, Bam, let's talk candidly. We both know this is a hell of lot more than a leak about two students. The Sheriff called me about the interview between you and Winchester, but he really called me to say that there weren't any drugs in our fair town, despite what the tapes said. Seems to me that it was a pretty transparent effort to protect that hooligan son of his who everyone knows is dealing drugs."

"Ain't just him, Mr. Epstein." Bam said matter-of-factly.

"Who then?"

"Bubba Tremblay," Bam blurted out without meaning to.

"What? Bubba Tremblay?" the reporter spilled his coffee in his excitement. Bam didn't flinch while Epstein frantically moved his papers and grabbed a stack of napkins, trying to stop the brown liquid that was trickling down the desk.

"Okay, Bam," the reporter said as he sat back down, no longer the avuncular figure who had everything under control. "Let's agree on ground rules. I am a reporter; I can't give away my sources. You and I can talk, and nothing goes past me. I tell you what I know, you tell me what you know." His hands waved back and forth in the air to make his point. "I never reveal anything by name or reference, unless you agree."

"That's what the last guy said," Bam responded miserably.

"I'm not an educator or a politician," the now anxious Epstein said. This kid was barely old enough to drive and already more cynical than himself. But he was still a kid. Levi had to protect him as both an informed source and an innocent bystander. "And if you haven't noticed, Bam, I'm not from around here. I'm not related to the Tremblays and I owe them nothing. So, what's the problem with talking openly?"

Bam thought a minute, regaining his concentration once more. "It's complicated, Mr. Epstein. I have this deal with Dean Ableton at the college. It's gonna get me out of high school early. Greely doesn't like it, but Winchester backed me up. If anything upsets the apple cart, all my existing college credits could get wiped out and I end up back in high school for another two years."

Epstein frowned. "Are you talking about Dean Ableton?"

"Yes, sir."

Epstein paused deliberately with a sobering look. "You may have worse problems than you know, Bam." Epstein again scrutinized the young teen who had very adult problems and looked at him quizzically, waiting.

Epstein knew Bam needed the truth. He figured it was better to hear it now from a credible source than to get an unexpected surprise. "Dean Ableton had a heart attack this morning. He died at Cabrini Hospital around noon."

Bam stared at the reporter while his eyes grew moist. The rhythmic sound of the press got louder, its drone filling up the room. Bam felt sick. He heard his father's voice in the back of his mind. Take a deep breath. Slow down. Think. He inhaled through his nose and let out a slow breath, clenching his teeth to regain control over his body.

His decision was easy now. He needed help. "Okay," Bam spoke up slowly. "What I say doesn't go past us, right? Not to Sally, not to the Sheriff, not to Greely, not to anybody."

Epstein silently held up his right hand like he was taking an oath, then extended it to Bam. Bam shook it, first with hesitation, then with a firm grasp. He had to trust someone.

Hours later Epstein laughed as Bam told of his singular explosive success with the Sheriff's trash can and sat transfixed as he described Clyde's flight over Bubba's marijuana fields and his conversations with Timmy. He described the bag of cash, the unexpected demand for food stamp exchanges at EZ Mart, and the KKK card that fell out with the phone number. He recalled the front-page picture of Quinine's feet and Maggie pointing out the stack of food stamps next to him, scattered over the grass.

Epstein held no love for Bubba Tremblay. But his disdain for racists and hypocrites knew no limits. Of course, that was personal. This was different. He had never considered the possibility of Bubba as a criminal enterprise. Among other things, he had never visualized Bubba as that focused. Shrewd maybe, powerful, definitely; but not focused. Maybe there was some form of redneck, Darwinian survival of the fittest at work here. Maybe rednecks were just born knowing how to make money in the mud of the Mississippi delta.

For years the town had buzzed about Bubba Tremblay making his crops pay while other farmers faced tragedy. Now he understood Bubba's magic. Marijuana was the new tobacco and the new alcohol, all rolled into one. And food stamps were the new subsidy, thanks to Bam. Still, Bam had not established a real direct link between illegal crops and Bubba. The illegal acreage that appeared to be on Bubba's farmland could have been a sharecropper for all anyone knew. The collage of information pointed to a web of activity that not even Bam could make up. His reporter instincts told him there was something to it.

Then there was Bubba's school and First Bubba Baptist Church. Everyone knew it cost him a small fortune to organize and build the school, and the financial support for the church wasn't cheap. It was all relative, of course, given the size of the Tremblay family holdings. The pathway to heaven was always paved with a fair amount of gold for the wealthy, but Bubba had invested big bucks to institutionalize himself, even during lean times, and apparently for good reason. It was all about protection.

The Tremblay family facade was like one of those tall colonial columns that supported an old, decaying plantation home: nostalgic, impressive, but no longer practical. The family influence and respect were tied to the support of an old structure that was increasingly irrelevant to a new generation. Bubba Tremblay had to have money and respect, at any price. So, he made illegal profits and bought his own institutions: the bank, the church, the school, the oil company. All Bubba needed now was a political party. It was a brilliant strategy, too brilliant for Bubba. It had all the fingerprints of Judge Jim.

"Wait a minute," Levi said, interrupting Bam. He opened a file drawer and dug out a small red brochure, which he laid on the desk in front of Bam. "Ever run across these people?"

"Who are they?" Bam asked.

"They call themselves the Citizen's Council. I believe they are an evolved arm of the Ku Klux Klan. They want to legitimize the Klan's policies through political participation rather than a vigilante process. They want to extend their influence, like the good old days," Levi said sarcastically.

"Kind of like Ku Klux Lite," Bam muttered.

Levi chuckled. "Not a bad analogy. They certainly have watered themselves down so they can appeal to a larger population. But don't kid yourself - these are the same hard-core people who burned crosses while they hid under sheets. I've been seeing these rallies out in the countryside, little towns like Oakgreen and Mansura, with all these signs popping up all over the place. The local arm of the Citizen's Council seems to be centered around Bubba's School. Bubba is pushing membership in this thing pretty hard."

"Why?"

"The same reasons they burned a cross in your front yard, Bam. Intimidation. Power."

Bam's mind transported him back to a night etched into his childhood memories, his sister shaking him violently to wake him, his older brother throwing him on his shoulder to escape the hot glow of flames from a large cross in their front yard. He could still feel the wet grass and the cold air shocking his senses while half a dozen white, sheeted figures ran from a twelve-foot burning cross. Its flames had reached high into cottonwood trees and power lines as they squealed away in trucks. The Callahans' house was spared, but the warning was clear. Sally's affiliation with the black community was not acceptable to the KKK. Bam had retained a deep, hidden fear of the Klan.

"I just presumed that sort of thing didn't happen anymore," he said, his voice shaky.

Epstein stared across his desk in silence at the innocence of youth.

Bam cleared his throat, realizing how naïve he must have sounded. "Oh. So, these Citizen Council guys are against integration?"

"No, Bam. These guys are against changes in their power base. They are used to dominating their world because of their land, their religion, their money, and their color. You don't have to be a different color to piss them off, Bam, you can just be a white Jew like me."

The statement startled Bam. He had never thought of integration without color. Nor did he know that Epstein was a Jew. It was a lot easier to pick a Yankee out of a local crowd than it was to spot a Southern Jew dressed in blue jeans.

The brochure was a full color glossy tri-fold with the Citizen's Council logo encircling the State of Louisiana profile. Bam had seen the signs before along state highways but presumed they represented a state-sanctioned agency. A phone number was printed on the back in big, bold letters: "Call the Citizen's Council Free-of-Charge at 1-800-469-4483."

Bam shook his head. "Don't know anything about this," he said, handing the brochure back to Epstein. Then, suddenly, he jerked it back.

"What's wrong?" Levi asked.

Bam took Levi's pen from him and pulled the reporter's yellow pad from across the desk. He lifted the black AT&T phone onto the desk, so its big white numbers and letters for each hole of the heavy mechanical dialer were facing him.

Then he carefully wrote down the letters that corresponded to the phone number on the Citizen's Council brochure: 1-800-IMWHITE.

Bam looked up. "I have seen this number before, Mr. Epstein. It was at the bottom of a bag full of cash and food stamps."

"I'm white?" Levi questioned. "And food stamps." It was the second oddball conversation about food stamps in one day. Suddenly, it came back to him. He opened his desk drawer and pulled out the small white card he had found on the ground at Quinine's shooting. His eyes lit up and his pulse jumped at the sight of the same phone number. It had been a long time since he was on the trail of something bigger than himself.

It was early evening before Levi set his glasses down on his yellow legal pad. It was filled with twenty-two pages of the reporter's hand-written notes from his discussion with Bam. His eyes hurt from strain and his head pounded from too much caffeine. He looked down at reams of scribble, lines, and arrows that attempted to tie his thoughts and observations together on the notepad. The longer he waited, the harder it would be to decipher his own notes, he knew.

He paused for a moment to get his bearings, worried momentarily about a leak. He would be extra careful with the typed notes; they could well become part of a trial or federal investigation. This was no longer just a story. It was an investigation into criminal activity. One leak to anyone in town and all of his leads would hunker down and vanish, especially if they got a call from Bubba Tremblay or one of his henchmen. And who were Bubba's henchmen? The better question was, who wasn't? Bubba owned the town and the cops that went with it. Apparently, he, or someone close to him, owned Lucery Lutz too, the secretary to the principal of the public school that his school was challenging. His influence was everywhere.

Levi pulled up his old typewriter and began to type up his scratchy notes. The trail was complicated, swirling faster and faster with new information. It was at hurricane status. It just hadn't hit land yet.

Chapter Thirty-One
Angela

The moon hung low in the horizon, partially covered by the low-hanging canopy of the big oak tree. The silhouette looked like black lace covering the face of an ivory ball. "It looks like a big billiard ball," Angela said.

"Yeah, it kinda does," Bam acknowledged. He shifted his weight against the tree bark that was cutting into his back. They lay naked on the soft moss and algae that filled the crook of the giant oak limb, floating just six feet above the ground. Angela rested on her back, her head on his chest. The tree only worked for them when it was dry, but the limb was big enough for two and it had a resiliency that they both enjoyed. It was their favorite place.

Bam leaned over to yank a beer from a six-pack hanging next to Angela's satin bra and panties, hung from an adjacent branch.

"Nice bra," he said, pulling the tab on the beer.

"Thanks, I've grown some more you know."

"You know, the guys and I were betting on that in class yesterday. They look great."

She slapped his leg. "You're bad."

"So how is Judge Jim doing?"

"He's fine. He asks about you occasionally."

"I'm trying to avoid Judge Jim," Bam responded honestly.

"I know, I know. You don't want to get caught screwing the Judge's daughter."

"I especially don't want to get caught by Judge Jim screwing his daughter."

"Well, he'd be less of a problem than Mom would. Dad knows I'm much too much like him. He has to know. Everyone knows," she giggled with a little girl's admission, acknowledging the passion of womanhood.

Every teacher and student at school knew of Angela's exploits. The Judge had to know. "Okay, Angela, if Judge Jim knows so much, why doesn't he confront you about seeing guys like me?"

"Because of Jim Jr. and Stanley," she replied quite logically. Hers was a family of contradictions. Jim Jr. was a star football player in his senior year. He had been in more than one brawl and the recurring gossip of rough play and abuse among cheerleaders and girlfriends were ignored due to his father's position. Like many of the sons of wealthy Southerners in power, Jim Jr. was tolerated, not liked, because he was the favored child, a spitting image of his father, handsome and athletic.

Then there was Stanley, the younger brother, by far the superior intellect and the better liked. A gentle soul with a sharp wit and a slight build whose effeminate mannerisms betrayed his sexual preferences at an early age. Bam said nothing and tried to play dumb.

"We were all supposed to turn out like Jim Jr." Angela explained. "Athletic and aggressive, just like Daddy. So when Stanley came along it threw Mom and Dad and First Baptist Church a curve. There aren't any gay people at First Baptist because it would be a sin, so everyone just plays along. But Mom couldn't let go of it. Stanley's sexuality pitted her against her own beliefs and church doctrine. Here she was in the center of the church with a queer kid who was starting to deal with being homosexual. She spent all her time praying for God to remake Stanley into a real man."

She sipped from Bam's beer and snuggled closer. "I never figured out whether she blamed Daddy or herself, but she started to retract into a hard-core religious shell, kind of like God had punished her. That just put more pressure on Stanley to rebel, and more pressure on Daddy to prove he wasn't the cause of Stanley's preference in men, and on me to prove that I didn't like girls. Well no," she reconsidered thoughtfully, "actually, thank God, I only had to prove that I really liked men."

"You mean, you felt you had to prove that you weren't a lesbian?" Bam questioned in disbelief.

"Yes, that's it. And you know what, Bam?" she winked at him with large blue eyes. "Stanly and I became real close. We both really love men."

"Good news," Bam laughed, tipping his beer in salute.

She grabbed his hand and placed it on her breast. "Yeah, but it kind of backfired. I'm just kind of perpetually horny now. So, I guess we're just an all-American family. One macho man, one queer, and one really horny chick."

"All the more reason for me to avoid Judge Jim."

"Maybe, but he really likes you. He just thinks you need to grow up."

"Sounds like he's been talking to Sally too much."

"They're big buddies, you know. I mean, *real* buddies, from way back. In fact, I think they may have been buddies like you and me are buddies."

Bam looked up, astonished at the thought. "You mean like, naked-in-the-old-oak tree-under-the-moonlight kind of buddies?"

"Could be."

"Naw. I can't imagine that," Bam said. But as it settled in, it didn't surprise him. His mother's affection for Judge Jim was unmistakable. The Southern world was one continuous loop of friendships and extended-family trees, linked by genes that transcended generations. "Well, maybe," Bam said on second thought. "I'm pretty sure Sally was never a prude."

"They go back a long way, Bam," Angela explained. "Dad wasn't always a judge and Sally wasn't always a professor. They were probably the only two kids who went to college from Bumkin in their day. They had a lot in common and I bet they had big oak trees back then too. Women plan these things, you know. But I still don't know why Dad married my mom."

"Why do you say that?"

"Well, Dad's a pretty cool guy and she's so…"

"So Baptist?" Bam interjected. He was trying to be nice. He watched Angela's expression in the moonlight.

"That's as good a description as any, I suppose. She's just cold. I don't think they do it anymore. Well, at least not with each other. He screws around a lot. She got hurt and went into her own world."

"Well, if she isn't screwing around, she's definitely not Baptist," Bam laughed.

"Here's the deal. She's a devoted Christian who loves the church for inner purposes and he's a devoted Baptist who visits the church for exterior purposes."

"Sounds about right."

"You know the old joke, don't you, Bam? Why don't Baptists make love standing up?—'Cause someone might think they're dancing." Angela giggled and took another swallow of his beer. "That church is a perpetual soap opera. I have to fight some of those old men off me in the choir loft every Sunday."

Bam leaned back. This was different from their normal discussions. He loved the shallowness of their relationship and didn't want it to become complicated. "So, who are you planning to marry this month?" he asked. It was a game they played.

"Edgar," she responded without hesitation.

"Edgar?" Bam feigned surprise. "Edgar Bandes? Of all people, Angela! Why Edgar?"

"What do you mean, 'why Edgar?' Isn't it obvious?"

"Not to me, Angela. He's a nice guy but he's definitely a lightweight."

"Of course he is. But he's a rich lightweight. That's perfect for me. Edgar will always be rich. He will never be smart, and he will always need someone to tell him what to do with all that money."

"Guess I never thought about it that way. But you would get bored with Edgar."

"Not true. Edgar would get bored, not me."

"Why in the world do you think you would bore him?" he was still incredulous at the thought of Angela matching herself to Edgar, the ultimate spoiled child of landed gentry.

"Come now, Bam, you know I don't bore men. You're missing the point." She turned on her belly to face him. She leaned over Bam to make her point, putting her arms around him and kissing his neck in a sensual manner. "You see, Bam, I'll be flitting around with my lovers in our plane. Edger won't care. He'll be out farming, which really is boring. Not me. I'm much too horny to get bored," she said in her sexiest voice.

"I get it now." Moss and layers of oak leaves muffled his laughter in the night. It was true. She was insatiable. Some day she could probably write a good book about her exploits. They were indeed a weird family. A jock, a gay and a nymphomaniac, all from the same blue blood family. And a great friend. He smiled as he stroked her hair. He always enjoyed her company and her body, not necessarily in that order. She loved screwing in the big tree. It had first happened in a spontaneous moment when they decided to climb the tree one night. Then they became buddies.

"I can't imagine an old, Baptist codger chasing you in the choir loft," Bam spoke into the darkness.

She toyed with his short ponytail. "You know, Bam, those good Baptist boys are no different from the girls, they were so stifled growing up in their church."

"That's not a fair comparison, Angela. You happen to be a beautiful, smart girl with a great body."

"Is that what you tell all your girlfriends when they're naked in our tree?" she teased.

There was something she wasn't telling him. "Never shared our tree, Angela, but it's time to fess up. Who's the lucky guy?"

Silence. Then an impish smile. "How did you know?"

"You are way too occupied with Baptist men. Something is going on."

"Well, now that you mention it … I can't tell you."

"You can't tell me? You can't tell me while we're naked in our big tree together? I'm hurt."

"Silly boy. Don't be. Go ahead and guess. He's a man."

"You mean he's a man or he's older than you?'

"He's both."

"And he's suppressed?"

"Yes. He's suppressed. Well, he used to be suppressed," she giggled.

Bam smiled and considered the possibilities for a moment. "Let's see, he goes to First Baptist so he must be a deacon," he deduced.

"I am impressed, Mr. Callahan."

"Probably married."

"What makes you say that?" she asked, surprised.

"Because you are always trying to get something over on your mom, and you wouldn't settle for a lowly choir director or youth director to make your point. It's your rebellious nature. And let's face it, Angela, who else is there in town? It isn't like there is anyone who has turned you down." It was a nice way of saying that her reputation was quickly preceding her in the small geography of Bumkin.

She curled her bottom lip and bit it in a pouting gesture. "You mean you don't think I've been faithful to you, lover?" she whispered.

He smiled and kissed her on the forehead, "I am sure that you have been as faithful to me as I have been to you," he said with a serious tone. "So, who knows about your affair with the married church deacon?"

"Oh, everyone. And no one. It's so much fun."

"Must be a Tremblay," Bam continued thinking out loud. "Maybe David Tremblay?" It was a calculated guess. The Tremblays owned the church; therefore, there were an inordinate number of Tremblay deacons. David was Bubba's only son. He was single, educated, and dapper. He was the lawyer for the family and word was he was the polar opposite of Bubba.

"No," Angela sighed. "I tried David. He's the treasurer for the church, you know. I thought it would be fun to become a part of his expense account. But I couldn't get him interested. Besides, he's not married, and I wanted a married man. Just for the experience, you understand. So, David kind of suggested his cousin Martin instead."

Bam was stunned. "David Tremblay turned you down? And sent you to Martin? What kind of man could turn you down?"

"Thanks for the compliment, but it was kind of good to know that there was a man alive who could think with his right head. David even confided that he already had someone in his life. Besides, he is a little proper and persnickety for me. All the little old ladies at church love him 'cause he dresses so perfectly and he makes scads of money investing in deals for them."

"Angela, if he sent you to his married cousin to get laid, he's either a liar or gay, or both."

"Well, that's a little harsh isn't it? But, you know, I hadn't ever thought of him as gay." Her face reflected a momentary epiphany. "His answer did come a little quick, and I don't ever remember seeing him with a female other than those old biddies he invests for. You know, he does kind of remind me a lot of Stanley. Oh well. I guess everyone needs a man." She shifted her weight and latched her legs around Bam, with an alluring smile. "I just love wrapping my legs around a big limb" she cooed as she kissed him passionately.

Chapter Thirty-Two
Deliverance

Hezekial stooped down to smile his biggest smile through the bulletproof glass cage. Danny was caught by surprise. Then he remembered it was Sunday.

Maggie and Sadie sat priggishly in the jailhouse waiting room chairs directly behind Hezekial. Maggie looked striking in a white dress that contrasted with her coffee au lait legs. Sadie sat adjacent to her in a black silk dress, her long white legs pulling Danny quickly under her influence, red hair casually draped over bare, flawless shoulders. Both women wore stylish church hats with netting draped over their faces, their gloved hands atop the King James Bibles sitting in their laps.

Danny stood up to look closer at his guests through his caged world. For a fleeting moment, he noticed something familiar about Maggie, but the hat and the netting made her look different than he remembered. Besides he couldn't take is eyes off of Sadie.

Hezekial moved in front of the glass cage, his big body blocking the view in a polyester suit of burnt orange.

"What can I do for you, Reverend?" Danny asked.

"Officer Dan, God has sent us to witness to the wicked and to comfort the poor on His day of rest!"

Danny nodded. He wasn't wicked, but one out of two wasn't bad.

"Can I hear an Amen!" the Reverend asked the room, his arms outspread.

"Amen!" the girls shouted. Hezekial looked down at Danny as if he were on Mount Calvary itself, waiting for his chorus.

"Amen," Danny stuttered quietly. He had heard about these people but had never seen any of them up close. He looked around nervously to make sure no one had heard him.

"God Bless you, Brother Dan!" Hezekial's voice bore directly into Danny's soul. "We need to speak to that condemned, young black woman, Officer Dan, to bring her into the bosom of salvation!"

Danny nodded. He liked bosoms. "Amen," he stammered again without provocation. "But Reverend, there's no one here but me until after the Sheriff gets his nap. Can you wait?"

"God waits for no man! God has schedules, just like you and me, Officer Daniel. Time and souls are precious!" His deep voice echoed against the concrete walls.

"Reverend," Sadie said, "I think Officer Dan is just concerned that there are too many of us here to visit that poor girl all at once. Isn't that right, Officer Dan?" Danny nodded, attentive to Sadie's every word. "Why don't I just sit here and minister to Officer Danny while you and Sister Maggie visit the prisoner? That way Officer Dan can keep an eye on me while you offer salvation to that poor girl," Sadie cooed.

"Why thank you, Sister, what a beautiful Christian gesture," the Reverend replied. "I will say a prayer for all of the prisoners in the hall while Maggie steps in to visit that poor young woman. I won't even go into her cell. We won't need but ten minutes, Officer Daniel."

The door creaked open behind Danny. Snowball made a well-timed entrance into Danny's cubicle, his red suspenders pulled neatly over his bleached white tee shirt, a steaming plate of red beans and rice in hand. He placed it on Danny's desk and looked up at the visitors with a smile and a wink. "Mornin', Rev'rund," he said softly. "I can let you in while Danny eats lunch."

"God's work will be done before you finish," Hezekial assured Danny. He placed his hand expectantly on the cold handle of the steel door like he was parting the waves of the Red Sea. Snowball turned the handle as Danny succumbed, semiconsciously pressing the button to release the lock. The door popped ajar as he raised a fork of red beans and rice.

"You got ten minutes, Reverend, so I can eat my lunch and visit with your - uh, sister here," Danny declared authoritatively.

Snowball pulled an enormous brass key ring off the wall. "You go 'head an' eat Danny, I'll let Sistuh Maggie in while the Rev'rund prays for the prisoners," Snowball volunteered conveniently. He welcomed the Reverend with a handshake, then stepped aside to let Maggie in.

Snowball pushed open the heavy door to Meadow's austere cell, keeping his back to Danny in the small, dark confines of the hallway. Hezekial's favorite sermon about delivery by the Hand of God boomed through the hallway as Danny returned his attention to red beans and rice and Sadie.

Hezekial was barely finished with the 23rd Psalm when Snowball announced loudly to the preacher that his time was up. Danny nodded approval, then looked down the hallway to make sure that everything was okay. Snowball stood quietly with broom in hand, sweeping the floor, with Hezekial behind him, blocking part of his view. But Danny could see that Maggie was emerging from the prisoner's cell, her pristine white suit and stylish hat standing out brightly in the gloom. She walked closely behind Snowball and Hezekial in the crowded hallway.

Sister Sadie stood up in the foyer and walked over to Danny's window as the entourage passed out the door into the lobby. She bent over gracefully to talk to Danny through the hole in the glass. "Officer Dan, could I see your big gun?"

Danny's view of the lobby was filled with bare shoulders and busty cleavage. He swallowed hard. "Yes, ma'am, uh sure, just for a moment, ma'am." Danny smiled. "Do you like guns?"

"Well, a girl has to protect herself these days and I just wanted to see what kind of gun you have. I'm thinking I could use some help in selecting one," she explained in her best stranded-maiden voice.

Danny pulled his pistol out of his holster, with great pride and showmanship, carefully removing the bullets, and handed the barrel through the glass aperture into Sadie's outstretched hands. She caressed it gently, feeling it all over.

"It's so big and hard, Officer Dan," she visibly shivered in recognition of the manly weapon in her hands. Danny's mind went more blank than ever before.

"Well now, Sister Sadie, that there is a standard-issue gun just for us law enforcement people. It's probably a little b-big for you," he said with a slight stutter.

"But I like my guns big, Officer Dan," she said with a wink.

Snowball shut the door to the hallway behind Maggie and tapped Danny on the shoulder. He hung up the big key ring. "All done, Mr. Danny," deflecting his attention as Maggie walked into the sunlight.

Danny mindlessly nodded at Snowball while Sister Sadie slowly placed the gun back into the Deputy's hands with a brief caressing motion.

"You know what they say, Officer Dan. Size doesn't matter as long as you've got the right gun. Thanks for letting me hold your pistol." She followed Maggie out the door quickly.

The good Reverend held the doors open for the women in a display of Southern manners. Hezekial then settled himself into the driver seat of his Cadillac and let out a big heave.

Danny walked over to the window near his desk and pulled up the blind to catch a final, rare glimpse of femininity that had just graced his jail. The smell of perfume and bath oils graced air that otherwise filled with nicotine and sweat. He looked salaciously at the redhead one last time, catching another glimpse of Maggie through the back window of the Caddy just as she took off her hat and netting. Somehow, she seemed a little different.

Snowball appeared out of nowhere again, delivering a hot cup of coffee and the Sunday newspaper to Danny as he took his empty plate. Roy sat on Snowball's shoulder, sniffing the coffee with interest, a vanilla wafer held tightly in his little "hands."

"Roy don't drink coffee none, does he?" the deputy asked.

"No, suh" said Snowball. "He only drinks green tea with a speck of orange."

"Didn't know you liked pretty girls, Danny," Snowball chided the deputy.

Danny looked at Snowball, slightly embarrassed. "I shore do, Snowball, but, unfortunately, Mrs. Danny don't like 'em none at all," he lamented. Whadaya know 'bout that redhead, Snowball?"

"Nuthin' much. Jus' a good Christian woman doin' God's work."

Chapter Thirty-Three
Escape

Meadow placed her hat on the car seat and burst into tears as the big sedan sped off. She sobbed uncontrollably, laying down on the back seat while Hezekial drove toward his private garage at Mount Zion Baptist Church. Fourteen days in a parish jail had made her weak and gaunt, no match for the healthy features of her sister who had traded places with her. She was panicked that the deputy would recognize the switch but not surprised when he didn't. He was just another man to be manipulated by his lunch, a preacher, and a smart redhead.

Meadow didn't understand why the sister she had never known would risk everything to help her, but at least she was out. Now she had to think. She had to get more distance behind her and Bumkin.

Hezekial could hardly stay on the road as he saw Sadie strip down to a red bra and panties in his front seat without hesitation as she pulled on a bright red dress. He looked up to heaven and praised God for women without inhibitions. Sadie handed Hezekial the black dress and her hat in a brown bag that he was to burn in the open barrel full of sycamore leaves waiting at his church. No white cop would trace her there, and there weren't any black cops left alive in town.

Sadie jumped out of the car as it came to rest, pulling her straps over her shoulders and pulling her dress down. She had to get to Sally's house for tea to satisfy her alibi. She reached across the seat and grasped Meadow's frail hands, looking at her intently. "You just sit still for a few days, and it will be okay, honey," she promised. Then she looked at Hezekial who was uncharacteristically silent. "And you quit looking at my ass!" she said, half in jest. She slammed the door and got behind the wheel of her grandmother's car that she had borrowed for the day. The tires squealed as she headed for Sally's house.

Chapter Thirty-Four
Ez Payoff

It was the end of a quiet Sunday night. Bam let his workers off early and finished the weekly report at EZ after a ten-hour shift. The rest of the world had enjoyed the sunshine and clean air that early spring rain produced in the Deep South. He recounted $5,340 in food stamps for the weekend deposit and bound them neatly with rubber bands into five packets of $1000 and one of $340. The total deposit was a little over $8000. That meant that about 70% of EZ's revenues from weekend trade were from food stamps.

Anyone who knew anything about the convenience store business would see through it instantly. Timmy's greed, or maybe his boss' greed, was getting way past good sense in hiding an otherwise simple scheme. Or, alternatively, his food-stamp-for-drugs volume had increased so much that Timmy had no choice. What else could you do with food stamps besides deposit them?

Sooner or later, someone would notice that the inventory turnover couldn't match the food stamp trade. And when they did, there would be a problem, depending on who caught it. Then Bam would be viewed as part of the problem.

The margins at EZ were also increasing. The owners had to know something was up but had no motivation to find out as long as profits were increasing. Another 10% in profits was a tidy sum in a small town. Drugs were the only growth market within the poverty-stricken confines of Bumkin. Ignorance was indeed bliss.

"Cat got your tongue?" Tim's voice shocked Bam out of his concentration. He turned around to see Tim standing in the doorway with a cold longneck Budweiser. Past him, in the EZ parking lot, Bam could see the lone outline of Foster Landeaux in his police car.

Bam took the beer and returned to his work. "Just getting the weekend bookkeeping done. Looks like we got one hell of a lot of food stamps this weekend. I thought Foster would be swapping cash for stamps, like you said."

"He said he's a little short on cash this week. Besides, who cares?"

"Don't worry about me, big boy. Worry about the dudes at the bank."

"You mean Bubba's Bank?" Tim brushed the concern aside with youthful arrogance. "Not a problem."

Bam zipped the contents of the deposit into the old leather bank bag and tossed it to Tim. "Since you're already headed out with a police escort, why don't you drop the deposit off at the bank?"

"Good idea," Tim said, finishing off his beer. He pulled a thick white envelope out of his coat pocket, placing it in front of Bam. "That's for you. Straight from the head guy. He wants you to have something for all your trouble."

Bam picked up the envelope and clasped it between his hands. He could feel the outline of a thick stack of cash through the paper. Easily a thousand dollars. He sliced the envelope open with his pocketknife to look inside, feathering it with his thumb. "It's been no trouble at all," Bam said curtly, handing it back.

Tim glared back at Bam, his face angry and distorted. "It has to be," he asserted, nodding towards the police car outside. "Those guys are going to make it big trouble for both of us."

Bam ignored him. "That's 'cause they're not smart enough to know that I need to stay clean so I can cover your ass when the shit hits the fan."

"They don't care about me or you, Bam, or anyone else for that matter. They just need to know that you're on their side and you're going to keep quiet."

"Why wouldn't I?" Bam asked. "I'm trying to get into college so I can get out of town."

"It's headlines, Bam, headlines. Not just what you say to people, it's what you do. No one likes headlines."

"Oh yeah. Well, there is that. Bet the "pot" sign really pissed Bubba off," he acknowledged with false concern. "Okay, I try to be a good boy but sometimes I just can't help myself, like when your buddies sent Lester to start the riot at the school. Levi Epstein has already called me to identify Lester. Did you know they are talking?"

The contrived statement hit Timmy like a bomb. Lines of fear creased his face, turning into a display of red-faced anger in the shadows. "How does he know?" he demanded with newfound seriousness.

"Got me," Bam lied calmly.

"Why would he call you?"

"Because he knows that Clyde, Mike and I were the only students on the top floor, the last ones allowed out to be interviewed. They know we saw it all, we just didn't tell them. Someone else must have seen Lester also."

Timmy's jaw locked. "Lester doesn't know what he's messing with, Bam. Neither do you. You need to call him off."

"Me? I can't call anyone off. I'm a high school student keeping my mouth shut so I can get out of town. If I got involved, it would draw more attention to both of us. I'm just the messenger here, bud. This is your roadshow. Tell your new best friend out there to leave me alone and I'll try to keep quiet and keep you updated. In the meantime, you should tell Lester that he needs to move away for a while."

Timmy fell silent. He knew that wasn't possible. Foster already had his orders; he wouldn't let Lester leave. Tim changed the subject. "Take the cash and stay out of our way, Bam. Messengers get shot, you know."

Timmy's voice was vacant and unemotional. This was a different Tim. Long gone was the laid-back high school senior whose only care in the world was who he was going to take to prom. Before him stood a seasoned drug dealer acting under orders out of fear.

Bam looked through the envelope of bills again with an appreciative whistle. He pulled the bills out of the envelope and stuffed them into Tim's shirt pocket, then neatly buttoned the flannel pocket. He stuffed the empty envelope full of napkins and placed it into his own back pocket. "If I showed up with that kind of cash at home Sally would make headlines like you and your buddies ain't ever dreamed of. 'Little lady history professor kills drug dealing son, puts ransom up for accomplices.'" Tim's eyes widened at Bam's humor.

"Keep the money, Tim. Tell your buddy out there that I took it, if it makes him feel better. He'll see the envelope in my back pocket. I'm out of here. Thanks for the beer, dude. Make sure the deposit ends up at the right spot tonight, eh?" he said in a lackadaisical tone that Tim didn't like.

Tim stood alone as Bam walked out the glass doors of EZ and gave Foster a thumbs-up sign with a big, false smile. Foster could confirm the bribe to the boss and the pressure would lighten up on Tim, at least for the moment. But Bam knew that Lester had a big problem.

Bam got in his car and took the envelope out of his pocket, extracting the single crisp $100 bill he had left in it. It was the second bill he had captured. He turned the envelope over, looking at it closely in the darkness. The return address read in small print, Citizens Council, Rt. 2, Bumkin, LA, the address of Bubba's school. He could see Foster watching him in his rear-view mirror. His perspective of Foster had changed remarkably in a short time, from an older drug thug to the psychotic enforcer of a major criminal enterprise.

Bam pulled the first Ben Franklin he had pocketed from underneath his car seat, placed it into the envelope with the new bill, and threw the envelope into the glove compartment. He would deliver the envelope to Epstein tomorrow, let Epstein know about his fabricated story of Lester talking to him and ask Epstein to call Lester. He hoped Lester could indeed be lured into talking to Epstein to trade some form of protection for confirmed information. However bad a pill it was to swallow, it beat the hell out of his alternative.

Bam felt a slight pang of guilt for setting up Lester, but he dismissed it quickly with the memory of the school riot, which was the only leverage he had to deflect Foster from himself and Sally. Lester was savvy enough to know that he had to make a decision. Presumably, he would have enough sense to bail out of town under cover of darkness or call Epstein to make a deal with the police of some sort. He suddenly realized there was no chance of finding any real police outside of Bubba's reach. That only left Epstein and the Judge.

Chapter Thirty-Five
Jail Bait

D oc Hines shut the door to his small office at the Bumkin City Jail. It was actually a closet that had been cleared for him to use on his weekly visits to the jail. It was cramped but it was all he needed for quick examinations of inmates as required by arcane Louisiana public health laws. It was easy money, and it broke the monotony of his local practice.

The Doc had seen three of four prisoners. The last, and the most notorious, was Quinine's killer, whom he was anxious to meet. The quiet mulatto was in surprisingly good health given her lifestyle. He hadn't expected her to be so finished and educated, but she was articulate, intelligent, and seemingly highly motivated. That notwithstanding, there was a surprise that he had to disclose to the Sheriff. This certainly would not be a typical weekly meeting.

The Doc walked through the Sheriff's open door and leaned against the doorway, LSU mug in hand. He waited casually and listened to the conversation, drinking his coffee.

Reverend Carl Hudson stood in the opposite side of the doorway, bidding the Doc "hello" with a soft slap on the back. Reverend Carl generally followed behind Doc with spiritual healing for inmates. Carl focused on helping the disadvantaged as much as he could every Monday morning.

Sheriff Franklin sat relaxed behind a disorganized stack of forms and paperwork as he and Foster went over a weekly list of tasks and schedules. The Sheriff's uniform was perfectly starched as always.

Danny sat on the couch in his Bumkin Police Dept. cap, coffee mug in one hand, biscuit in the other. Foster had made sure Floyd was on patrol to avoid any embarrassing comments about the attempted marijuana arrest with him and Foster.

The Sheriff checked off his last item and finally turned to the good doctor. "Well, what's up, Doc? We got any sick patients today?"

"No, not really, Franklin. Just one more patient than you might think."

"What the hell does that mean?" the Sheriff looked up curiously at his old friend.

"It means, Franklin, that I'm betting your number one inmate is pregnant. And fairly recently, I would guess." Four shocked faces turned toward the doctor as denial swept over the room in various forms.

The Sheriff spit out coffee over his desk. "Oh shit!" He wiped his mouth with his shirtsleeve and grabbed a napkin off his desk. He took a deep breath and stared at the doctor in silence. Foster sat motionless, stunned to silence.

Reverend Carl stood frozen, watching closely the unexpected turn of events, particularly the reaction of Foster. Even in shock, the Sheriff's Hollywood good looks contrasted with those of his son, who suddenly looked slightly scared.

"Are you sure, Doc?" Franklin asked, regaining control of his voice.

"You betcha," Doc Hines responded casually. He couldn't help but enjoy the moment. The coroner's business was usually confirming death; to find life in one of the dark, lonely jail cells had given him unexpected pleasure. He sipped his coffee and waited for his friend to respond.

"Dammit! The newspaper is going to have a field day with this," the Sheriff responded. "Here she is up for murder with a potential death sentence. We'll have everyone from Sixty Minutes to Jesse Jackson coming to town."

"One thing you all might want to consider is that she may not even know she's pregnant yet," Doc said. "Have there been any changes in her diet. Any special requests?"

"She shore don't drink coffee anymore. That's for shore," Danny said. I'm tellin' you, that gal used to love Snowball's coffee. Not no more. Maybe now that makes some sense."

Something about that last bit of information jolted Reverend Carl. His suspicions were aroused but he couldn't discuss what he couldn't confirm.

Foster spoke up, uneasy with the conversation. "Any way to find out who the father is?"

"Locating people is police work, nothing doctors know much about. The good Reverend would probably get better results on that issue than any of us," Doc Hines said. "She could share that information, but that doesn't mean you'll get the right answer. You might want to be careful what you ask for."

Foster sat in stony silence, unusually absorbed in his thoughts, Reverend Carl noticed. "Any way to know whether the father is white or black?" Foster asked hesitantly.

"I'll let you know in a little over eight months, Foster," Doc Hines smiled over his coffee cup.

"Do you think the prisoner knows who the father really is?" Foster persisted.

"Probably."

"You mean a whore like that can tell?" Foster asked, visibly defensive.

Carl's trained ear caught Foster's tone and questions. He remained expressionless, listening closely as a preacher always must.

"Women generally know, Foster," Doc said. "But it all depends on the circumstances. I figure this has happened recently, so it is probably pretty traceable for her. How long has she been in jail?"

"Less than a month."

"Any known conjugal visits?"

"Of course not," the Sheriff interjected.

"You could have a problem," the Doc said earnestly.

Franklin nodded as the blood drained from his face. Danny signaled Snowball for another biscuit while his boss looked around. Snowball silently entered the room like a black ghost with suspenders, barefoot, with a hot tin coffeepot in hand.

The white men in the room all offered up their cups, one by one, each staring at Snowball as he fulfilled his self-assigned task of refilling mugs and dispensing fluffy biscuits. Snowball looked around as a quiet pall seemed to follow him. He shrugged, then walked out as quietly as he came.

"You don't think it's possible?" the Sheriff voiced the obvious question after Snowball left the room.

"I wouldn't jump to any conclusion, Franklin," the Doc said. "You simply never know… but I guess we do know Snowball has always been quite a lady's man."

Reverend Carl walked down the long hall to Meadow's cell after the briefing, falling behind Snowball in his customary fashion to visit and counsel prisoners. Snowball slowly opened the cell door for him. Reverend Carl noticed Snowball flickering a suspiciously big smile as he followed the preacher into the cell.

Reverend Carl returned the smile and then nodded solemnly, holding onto his bible and contemplating what inspiration he could deliver to a young, presumably pregnant, black prostitute facing murder charges, a woman he had never met. Or had he? He knew of the kinship between Meadow and Maggie that Sally had ferreted out, but that information was still buried deep within the confidences that only a man of cloth had to bear.

"Hello, Meadow," he said in his most upbeat preacher's voice, extending his hand to accept the frail hand of the young girl in front of him.

"Hello, Reverend Carl!" Maggie squealed. "What are you doing here?"

Carl froze and looked hard at the prisoner. "Maggie?" he asked, shocked at her presence. He put on his glasses as the truth he had suspected hit him now with the impact of the Holy Spirit. "Oh shit!" he mumbled in a muted voice. He shook his head briskly as if to ward off evil spirits and slowly took a seat on the hard prison bed, freshly made with clean linens and military precision by Snowball.

"So that's why you would only drink the tea. You've always been allergic to the coffee, haven't you?" the preacher said in a hushed voice as she nodded happily. "Maggie, I can only guess how you got in here, but I must ask you something before you tell me where Meadow is. Who got examined by Doc Hines this morning? You or Meadow?"

"I saw Doc Hines today," Maggie responded politely.

"Had you ever met him before?"

"No, sir."

"And he examined you?"

"Yes, sir," she said, wondering if the preacher was getting that old-people's disease a little early.

"Maggie, you're pregnant."

"Oh, shit!" Maggie and Snowball exclaimed in chorus. The preacher had forgotten that Snowball was behind him. Maggie fell back onto the bed upon hearing the news while the Reverend searched Snowball's face for answers.

While Carl was counselling Maggie, Foster slid into an old booth opposite Bubba in the back of the local Dairy Queen. It was Bubba's favorite "afternoon office" when it was empty of customers and the manager had time to make a giant double chocolate malt for him.

"Meadow is pregnant," Foster announced abruptly without a preamble, attempting to bury the glee that he felt at Bubba's expense, beneath a surface of defiant arrogance. He enjoyed delivering the dagger into Bubba's heart if, in fact, Bubba had a heart.

"Oh shit!" Bubba was visibly shaken, his voice raspy.

"The Doc just told us."

Bubba grit his teeth stoically, stifling the emotion that attempted to swell up in him. He looked at the big LSU football calendar on the wall with a full portrait of Coach Dietzel and his national champion team. He hadn't considered this. A child. Their child. He wondered what coach Dietzel would do?

"Whose is it?" he asked disingenuously.

"It really doesn't matter," Foster said coldly. "It's still your grandchild." He slowly turned the knife with controlled pleasure. "I don't know what you would call your child who is also your grandchild."

The statement hung in the air with no reaction from Bubba. Foster decided to go for the final stab. "Of course, if it's Quinine's, it will be your black grandchild."

Bubba jolted sharply, uncontrollably, scowling with hatred. He pulled his massive fist back, ready to strike the deputy as his other hand grabbed Foster by the collar, then remembered they were in a public place. Bubba noticed the deputy's hand dropping reflexively to his pistol. The big man let go of the deputy, barely able to control his urge to smash his face. Bubba plopped back down in the booth and took a deep breath to regain control of himself. He contemplated the conversation, then turned calmly to Foster, a different personality now resuming control.

"You've known the whole time," he accused the deputy, his eyes ablaze with revenge. "A million hookers to recruit out of New Orleans and you went to Leesville instead to find this one. You set me up, you son-of-a-bitch." His eyes drilled fear into Foster who hid behind his regulation sunshades with the slightest hint of a smile.

"Get a grip, Bubba." Foster deflected the accusation, meekly at first. Then, remembering his well-prepared script, he went on the offensive. "I looked all over for the right recruit. We both agreed she was perfect for the job. How the hell would I know you would fall in love with her? Something changed after you took her to the cabin. What the hell did you tell her?"

"It was the bracelet." Bubba seethed, unwilling or unable to say more.

Foster kept up the offensive. "You've been screwing her mercilessly for six months. It isn't like you couldn't have stopped," he said in a staccato, unsympathetic monotone. "Besides, all you had to do was let her leave with Quinine like we planned. None of this would have happened if you hadn't followed them in a blind rage. What the hell were you thinking?"

Bubba's face turned mischievous, almost friendly, as if fond memories descended on him. "I couldn't help myself. She had no business leaving with that nigger. She knew she had to make a choice. She is perfect, we both are, together. She played Quinine like a fiddle; I couldn't have done it better myself. Then the bitch double-crossed me with the demand for more money."

"Yeah, that's when I knew she had to be your kid," Foster observed wryly.

Bubba ignored him. "You should have killed her. It's the only way I can ever get rid of her."

"You told me not to. Besides, there would have been no one to blame for Quinine. It was the only way."

"Where is the deed to the property?" Bubba demanded.

"Still in the lockbox at your Bank. I can't locate the key. No trace of it in his belongings or at his apartment. She hid it somewhere before you showed up."

"Find it!"

"You don't get it, do you? She's as crazy as you are. She's not talking to anyone. She figures you have to get her out and now she knows that she has a twin somewhere nearby that is due part of the estate. She's out for revenge, not just money. I figure you got less than a month until the probate lawyers show up for Quinine's estate."

Bubba turned white. "Why would that matter?"

"If I were the lawyer for a nigger whore in jail, I would claim Quinine as her common-law husband. That would leave her twin as the only remaining heir."

"We have to shut them up."

"One is in jail for murder and the other doesn't know she's a twin, yet," Foster responded, trying to deter the conversation.

"You better make sure it stays that way, 'cause right now we've got to deal with Lester. He's got too big for his britches."

Foster shook his head with disgust and left the booth, walking out the door with his usual swagger and attitude. He was tired of worrying about Bubba's lovers. He had to start making time for his own.

Chapter Thirty-Six
Ben Franklins

Levi Epstein looked at the envelope with two $100 dollar bills in it as Bam recounted the previous night's discussion with Timmy. "It must have been pretty hard to walk away from all that money."

"Not really, Mr. Levi," Bam said. "Dad always taught me that it was just money; it was either yours or it wasn't. He said that if you ever thought of it differently, it would control you forever, so I guess I never did."

"Your father had a great reputation, Bam."

Bam nodded appreciatively. "Have you talked to Lester yet?"

"No," Epstein shook his balding head. "I haven't been able to find him."

"I'm off from EZ Mart on Friday. He should be pretty easy to track down on a Friday night."

"Think he'll talk?" the reporter asked.

"I don't know, but I should warn him. I set him up. They think he's already talking to you. That's going to piss everyone off."

Epstein's eyes widened as the implications hit him. "Can't say I blame you for trying, Bam, but it could get dangerous, especially for Lester."

Bam nodded. "No doubt."

"Okay, you locate Lester and I'll go to the Citizen's Council Assembly at Bubba's school this weekend. There's a big shindig out there Saturday night."

"Nothin' personal Mr. Epstein, but you really think they'll let you in?"

"I hadn't planned on asking permission," the reporter chuckled. "Believe it or not, there was a time when I went to places where I didn't belong in search of a good story, Bam. In the meantime, I presume you know that we are going to have to report all of this to the authorities sometime soon."

"What authorities can we trust?"

"It's a valid question. I'll have to think about that. In the meantime, you have to be careful. I don't want to be explaining this to Sally. Lester may not be the only one Bubba wants out of town."

"I'll catch up with you later, Mr. Epstein," Bam said, dismissing the adult's concerns as teenagers often do. He left and began the walk home before dark set in, more worried than he had let on.

Levi pulled a particularly old and crumpled card from his Rolodex file and read "Rick Bledsoe—FBI" out loud to himself, then dialed the number.

"Hello, Rick? Rick Bledsoe? It's Levi Epstein. Yep, been a long time. Everyone's fine. Not much, you know nothing much ever changes down here. I do need to call in a favor that might be of interest. Think you could check out some currency for me? I may be on to something. I've got two Ben Franklins that might lead to one hell of a drug bust with a little lab work. And one other thing. You might want to check out Bumkin Bank. There's something going on."

Chapter Thirty-Seven
The Black Cat

The boys rocked lazily on the front porch. Twilight had passed and darkness brought a mellow breeze over the bayous. A semi-tropical rain fell from puffy clouds. Bam liked night-time showers best. The sound brought a sultry sense of familiarity he associated with home.

"He really said he'd do it?" Clyde asked.

"I'm telling you straight," Bam answered for the fourth time. "Dennis has been trying to take us across the tracks for months."

"Why?"

"I don't know. Maybe he wants to show off his whitey friends. Everything has changed since integration, you know."

"Cool." Clyde crossed his big tennis shoes and relaxed as he thought about their imminent adventure. "So, tell me again why we're doing this?"

"We need to find Lester, get him to fess up about starting the riot, let him know word is out."

"Why?"

"So we can prove it wasn't really a racial riot."

"Why?"

"So we can find out who paid him."

"We know who paid him," Clyde said decisively.

"Who?"

"My grandfather. Who else would pay a drug dealer to start a riot at a public school?"

"Okay. Why?"

"So he could get more students enrolled into his honky school," Clyde responded, enraged by Bubba's actions.

"Okay, you go tell the world that Bubba Tremblay started a racial riot and see who listens. His honky school doesn't need attention and he sure as hell don't need the money."

"Okay, Bam. So, you tell me who's going to listen to a spade pimp decked out in purple satin tell people he got paid to start a riot while a juke box is blaring on his shoulder?"

"The readers of the *Bumkin Record*. That great icon of journalism," Bam said sarcastically.

"I'm sure that will comfort Lester. If he has any sense, he'll lie. Pimps lie, you know, no matter their color."

"True enough, but local folks will believe Epstein, especially if it's about rich people doing bad stuff."

Clyde conceded the point with a silent nod. "Why do you think that is?" he asked philosophically.

"Because there are a lot more miserable, poor readers than happy, rich readers in our fair parish," Bam responded.

The orange GTO with the big wing spoiler hovering over the trunk whipped around the corner. A handsome, well dressed black man exited the sports car and walked up to greet Bam and Clyde. Dennis Johnson carried a boxer's physique and a Hollywood square jaw. He moved with the stealth of a cat in a blue suit and crème colored v-neck shirt that made him look like Sidney Portier. Dennis had worked his way up the management chain of Dixie Dandy. Everyone knew Dennis would go places.

"You little white dudes got nuthin' better to do than rock on the porch like old Southern folks? Must be a honky thing. Black folks stay inside, watch the tube, and eat fried chicken," he mocked his culture.

"And watermelon," Bam added. He held his hand up and got a high five from Dennis. "Thanks for coming bro'. Clyde and I need to find Lester. We need you there while we talk to him. Can you help us out?"

Dennis looked shocked. "What's the story, Bam? You buyin' or sellin'?"

"Neither, Dennis, you know that."

"I buy and sell," Clyde volunteered.

Dennis smiled and looked at Clyde "That shit you sold to me last month was bad stuff. I could have smoked better weed from my mama's vegetable garden. I want a refund. I had to buy my girl a whole fifth of tequila to get laid."

"You just losin' your touch," Clyde said. "But I've got some good stuff for the ride tonight."

"Tell me the whole story first."

"Lester needs to fess up about starting the riot at school, Dennis."

"He ain't gonna do that, Bam, you know that."

Bam jumped to the offensive. "I watched it all in real time, but how do you know he did it?"

"Everyone on my side of the tracks knows. It's old news."

"So it shouldn't be a surprise that Epstein is talking to him. At least Timmy thinks he's talkin' to the newspaper on our side of the tracks."

Bam's comment got Dennis' attention. "Whoa, that ain't cool. If Timmy knows, Foster knows; if Foster knows, Bubba knows. If Bubba knows, shit could happen real fast. So how does Timmy know Lester is talking to Epstein?"

"I might have told him," Bam said.

"Why'd you go and do that, Bam?" Dennis asked as an accusation.

"The town needs to know. He'll either leave town or deny it. Either way I want to know why he did it."

"That's a dangerous question, Bam. No one is gonna find out why anything happens in this town. It's all rigged. Why does it matter anyway?"

"C'mon, Dennis. You live here too. It can't happen again."

"And who made you the race police?" Dennis asked.

Bam looked at Clyde with a sigh. "Let me explain what no one else can know, Dennis. Clyde and I are responsible for the bomb at the Sheriff's house. We were just playing around, but Bubba used it to play up the race riot and distract from his drugs business. Another bomb threat allows the cops to justify anything."

Dennis looked at Bam with a new respect. "You really did that?" he asked, looking at Clyde, who nodded in verification.

Dennis looked at Clyde. Ain't Bubba Tremblay your grandpa?"

Clyde nodded. "Guilty."

"Damn, you white boys sure can create a mess. What does Mrs. Sally say about this?"

"I can't get her involved. Besides, Sally can't help Lester. He's ultimately a police matter."

Dennis sat on the porch step to think through the situation. "If Foster thinks Lester is talking, he could be another dead nigger like Quinine—shot in the back while he's banging his chick, mindin' his own business. Shit! That man still had a hard on! That ain't right! But that's how I want to go. You boys remember that. No matter how I go, I just want you to arrange an extension on my casket that is bigger than Quinine's so I can go down in history."

"Got it, Dennis," Bam laughed. "But tell me about Foster."

"Foster just likes to kill black people if he can find a reason to get away with it. He's a nigger-Nazi, part of a machine. He's like a hit man for Bubba. This ain't like a missing white boy where people care, Bam. It ain't like that at all. Nobody cares about Lester. Foster will drop him like he did Quinine and enjoy doing it."

"So I guess we should let Lester know?" Clyde said.

Dennis thought for a moment. "I guess we have to, now. Okay, honky, let's do it. We can catch Lester at the Black Cat tonight. Are you sure your white ass is ready for this action?"

Bam and Clyde nodded naively, pulled on their jackets, and headed toward Dennis' car. "Say, dude, where're the women?" Clyde asked. "I've never seen it empty."

Dennis looked at his watch. "It's only nine o'clock, white boy. We'll pick up some squeeze at The Cat, then we got time for another round before midnight. We don't do that dating thing like you white boys, spending money all night on one chick who's gonna bleed you, then go home to momma so she don't have to give you nothin'." Dennis shook his head. "Hang 'round, honky, you might learn somethin'."

The dual mufflers roared from an oversized engine as oversized tires kicked up gravel and the boys were pushed back into velvet-lined seats. Clyde crawled to the front and lit the joints he had promised Dennis while Bam stared out the window and let himself get lost in the ride.

The big car caroused like a predator among the narrow streets … of what? Bam wondered. "Across the Tracks"—the only name he knew for this place. Not a location, a confinement. A barricade. A new subdivision would have been named "North Bumkin" but that would have meant it had its own identity. No, "Across the Tracks" was the name of a place where white people weren't, not where the black people were. A place neither wanted to be.

The streets got bumpy, and the faint smell of sewage crept into Bam's nostrils. They pulled onto a one-lane asphalt street peppered with potholes. The small yards were filled with old cars and broken trailers. Little flower gardens peeped out of the broken landscape, the only sign that life could persevere. There were no sidewalks in front of the shotgun homes. The rickety shanties stood like a precarious stack of dominoes ready to fall. Bam could hear the wail of a crying baby in the otherwise eerie stillness of the night.

Dennis eyeballed a parking spot on a street lined with cars bumper to bumper. He backed the big car into a slot that could facilitate a quick departure, making sure no one could block him in. The joint hung from his lips as he backed half of his car onto a small yard latticed with ruts left by the last patrons of The Black Cat Bar.

Dennis turned off the car and looked at the boys seriously. "If I tell you to haul yo' white ass, you better get to this car before I do or you gonna be left behind. Got it?"

The boys nodded attentively. "Why don't you leave the car windows open so I can dive in?" asked Clyde.

"'Cause they'll steal the car before they shoot us," Dennis said as he slammed the door shut and locked it.

"Makes sense," Clyde said with a sick smile. He hadn't smoked nearly enough for this venture. They were directly across the street from the side entrance to the legendary bar. Its famous pink neon sign blinked the outline of a cat against a black background, its tail flared and its back arched, ready for a fight.

Bam took in the view. The Cat was part of the folklore of his life, a forbidden hangout never meant for white boys. He had never dreamed of getting inside, especially on a Saturday night.

"Keep your heat hid," Dennis commanded.

"My heat?" Clyde echoed.

"Your heat, man. Your bang. Your gun, you punk-ass white boy."

"Wow, man, I didn't know we would need a gun," Clyde moaned.

Dennis looked up to heaven and spread his hands wide. "Me 'n a couple of chicken-shit white boys here at The Cat with no guns. Help us, Lord, we know not what we be doin'." Clyde finished with an "Amen."

Dennis looked back at the boys. "Stay behind me and look cool. You gotta <u>act</u> like you own the place. You do that Southern thing and start apologizing and you'll get us all shot." He turned to Bam. "Lester will be on the other side of the bar hanging with his girls when we walk in."

"I'm cool, I'm cool," Bam said nervously.

"Me too," added Clyde. "Say, you think there's a dress code?" he asked, looking down at his tennis shoes.

Dennis shook his head and motioned Clyde to shut up. He pulled his shoulders back, striking a handsome pose as the patched screen door to the Black Cat opened. A dim light beckoned through the silhouettes of a milling crowd in a room filled with thick smoke and the music of the Supremes. The boys walked in behind Dennis, scared to death.

Scores of friendly voices greeted Dennis in the patois of the black culture. Then silence slammed down on them while everyone in The Cat gawked at the two white boys. They weren't cool; they didn't own the place.

Dennis pointed to a round table surrounded by plain chairs. The wooden floor inclined toward the center of the room from decades of dancing and moist air. The room was similar to The Golden Nugget, Bam thought as he attempted to look around nonchalantly.

Low hanging ceiling fans circled lazily with a constant mechanical whirr. The blue hue of the jukebox permeated the room with a glow that bounced off the low ceiling and clouds of swirling cigarette smoke caught the motion of fast bodies and slow fans. Lifetimes of untold stories begged to be told by weather-worn walls patched with uneven planks that let in the outside air.

The local crowd slowly resumed their activity as the white boys carefully sat on instruction of Dennis. Clyde gave his best smile and waved at the crowd, like an explorer in a foreign land.

So this is what it feels like to be the minority on the wrong side of the tracks, thought Bam as the stares pierced him. He was submersed into the very heart of the culture that lived next to him that he had never really seen, like being transported to a foreign country five miles from home. It didn't take an iron curtain to divide the town, just a railroad track.

Clyde leaned over to him. "This is really weird, man, really weird. How about I tell a joke and you sing?"

"You first," Bam said tersely. "And it better be a damn good joke."

Dennis stared at two ebony men, bulging with sweaty muscles. "Watchu lookin' at? You ain't never seen no white boys before? They be cool or I wouldn't be bringin' them. We just passin' through so be cool," he demanded. Bam couldn't decide whether it was a statement or a threat. Dennis looked at the bartender and waved his hand. "Bring us some beer, Ray, and take yo' hand off o' that gun befo' I wrap it 'round yo' neck."

Ray stood still, thought about his intentions, then nodded slightly as he moved away from the bar. "You better finish yo' business 'fore Pappy gets here," Ray yelled at Dennis. "He ain't gonna like it none."

Dennis looked back at the bartender. "Since when do Pappy tell me what to do?" He took out a thick roll of money with great fanfare and put it on the bar for all to see. Employed patrons were hard to find at The Cat; it was time to show some appreciation to Dennis, the customer. "Where's Lester?" he demanded.

Clyde tugged at Bam's shirt. "Who's Pappy?"

Bam shrugged Clyde off, still focused on Ray the bartender, poised to haul ass if the hidden gun appeared.

"Pappy sounds like a bad dude," Clyde said out loud to no one in particular.

Ray pointed to the far wall behind Dennis, and Bam heard the jingle of chains behind him. He turned to see Lester in his purple splendor, laden with gold chains that weighed as much as he did. Two slim, buxom girls in skin-tight shirts stood on either side of the drug dealer.

"They must be twins," Clyde joked. "I can't tell them apart."

"That's news, honky," Bam said cynically.

"We should watch out for Pappy," Clyde said again.

Lester motioned to Bam. "What you doin' here, Whitey? You better get yo' white ass home before Pappy gets here."

"See, I told ya," Clyde said, turning toward Bam.

Dennis brought the beer over to the table and sat down, directing Lester to do the same with a single pointed finger. "You better sit down here and listen to what Bam's got to say," Dennis interjected. The boys eagerly grabbed their beer, only to have Dennis pull them back and hand them over to the girls, smiling at Bam and Clyde apologetically. "Ladies first," he said in his most patronizing voice.

The girls smiled and quickly sat next to Dennis. They had seen his full money clip.

"Do either of you ladies know Pappy?" Clyde asked as he and Bam took their seats.

Lester looked at Bam and Clyde with a renewed interest, begrudgingly electing to sit between them. "What's the word, Thunderbird? You a long way from EZ." Not to be outdone by Dennis, he plopped a roll of Ben Franklins on the table and signaled the bartender with the flick of his wrist. Suddenly two more beers appeared on the table.

The milling crowd returned to normal, ignoring the two honkies under guard of Dennis and Lester. They were a good topic of conversation, but they seemed harmless enough and they were clearly outnumbered. Best to leave the honkies alone until Pappy got back.

The din in The Cat increased with Al Green's "Heard It on the Grapevine" blaring from the jukebox. They really were just like a bunch of white people, Bam suddenly realized, they were just black. He took a deep breath. Then he turned to Lester.

"Who paid you to start the riot, Lester?" Bam blurted out. He wanted to get it all out on the table, quickly. No need to overstay his welcome, if you could call it that.

"Don't know what you talkin' 'bout, white boy," Lester sneered. "Shit, I shouldn't even be talking to yo' white ass, especially in The Cat." He rolled his eyes and looked up at the ceiling. "What is the world coming to?" He spread his hands wide as if questioning God. "Black people get sent to fight in Vietnam and white boys get sent to question me at The Cat?"

"Save it for those other white boys you work for, Lester. We saw you. And I came to deliver bad news, Lester. Timmy and Foster think you been talkin' to the newspaper so I may be the only white boy you *can* talk to."

Lester got rattled, quickly. His startled look told Bam he had hit the mark.

Dennis confronted Lester with a stern look. "Lester, why you do this shit, man? Here you are, man, you got babes, you got drugs, you got cash. Now, why you wanna start a fuckin' riot and mess with everyone?" Dennis asked earnestly. "So some white man can make more money off us? That ain't cool. You need to be out hittin' on women like this here pretty lady, not startin' up some racist fight like this. Keep this up and we'll all be hunting you down."

Lester tried to clear his head. He had been smoking his stash all day. Dennis commanded everyone's attention and the conversation was too loud. He didn't need his customers to know he was a hired hand for The Man.

"They needed the heat off of the drugs," he explained to Dennis in a low voice with the hint of an apology. "It was bad for business. That crazy shit with the city sign made them panic. Too many headlines, too much attention. Then the bomb thing happened, and The Man didn't know who was responsible. He was worried about it spreading over to him, so he wanted a school riot to focus on the integration thing. Besides, I need them and they need me. I buy their weed and they buy my stamps. We got a good thing."

"My dad collects stamps," volunteered Clyde.

Dennis looked hard at his white friend. "Clyde, you a fool sometimes, you know that? We talkin' food stamps, man."

"Got it," Clyde said, somewhat deflated.

"And I ain't been talkin' to no reporter," Lester protested to press his innocence. "I ain't no fool. Epstein been trying to call me, but I never returned his call."

Bam leaned closer to the dealer. He had him on the ropes. "I know that, but Foster doesn't, and you know what? He doesn't care, Lester. Someone must have told Foster you were talking to Epstein. You will have a hard time convincing him otherwise, so you need a plan, Lester. You need to get out of town and away from Bubba."

Lester was getting agitated, but he caught on quickly, and his indignation was evident. "Why you done that, motherfucker? Why you told Foster that?"

"I didn't. I told Timmy because Clyde and I saw you and your boys start the damn riot, Lester. That's what happens when you do stupid shit for no reason."

"Foster gone' kill me, man," Lester said glumly, his high voice suddenly concerned. He looked at Dennis, as fear gradually crept into his bloodshot gaze. "Timmy told me he'd shut me off—put someone else into bizness if I didn't deliver a school riot." His chains clanked as he took a joint from Clyde's shirt pocket and lit up a reefer.

Clyde shrugged and lit up one for himself and the girls. He felt more confident when he was stoned, and he sure as hell wanted to be stoned when Pappy showed up.

Dennis raised five fingers to catch the watchful eye of Ray the bartender for more beer. Clyde stood to pay for the beer. He shook Ray's hand profusely. "Excuse me one moment, sir," he said, holding up a finger with perfect manners as he dispensed the beer to the table. Then he grabbed the large mug and downed it in one long gulp. He handed the mug back to Ray with a $5 tip and asked for another round, which he downed in five seconds. The crowd took notice and Ray went to get more beer.

Bam looked at Lester with concern. "I got nothing else for you, Lester."

"I thought you want to help me, man!"

"I am, Lester, I'm telling you to call Epstein and leave town. Bubba will force everyone to lay low if the newspaper confirms you were paid to start the riot. You can buy time, come back when it blows over. It's your ass, man. If you really think they need you more than you need them, you will find out soon," Bam said contentiously.

Lester sat up, tilting his head up as he blew circles of reefer smoke into the thick air. "What other nigger is Bubba gonna use, Bam? They gotta use me, and I get the stamps." There was now a hint of stoned arrogance in Lester's voice. He was beginning to enjoy the notoriety of it all. "In this game, if I leave,

I lose. Someone else will take up the slack while I'm gone and then I'd have to reclaim my ground. It could get ugly."

"It's already ugly, Lester," Bam said with finality. He had accomplished what he came for. The only thing left to do was get out.

The side screen door of The Cat clapped against its wooden frame and the background noise of the crowd quickly came to a halt. Aretha Franklin was the sole voice in The Cat.

Pappy was a wiry black man in his late thirties. He strode in like a peacock in a black and yellow Hawaiian shirt with large pink flowers. He headed straight for the bar to pick up the cash in the register before the normal Saturday night fracas broke out and someone stole the cash, the register, or both. Pappy was looking at Ray as he crossed the room. Ray nodded toward Dennis and his table of white boys. Pappy came to a dead stop in the middle of the dance floor.

"Rabbits!" he yelled. "Rabbits! What the hell are a bunch of rabbits doin' in my bar? Who the fuck let rabbits into my bar?"

The beer and marijuana had started to penetrate Clyde's brain. He turned to Bam. "What's a rabbit?"

"You are," Bam responded. "And I'll bet that's Pappy."

"Fuck him!" Clyde said nonchalantly, chugging another high-speed beer in record time. Bam closed his eyes and wished the scene away.

"What did you say, rabbit? What did you say?" Pappy demanded.

Dennis leaned over to Bam as he rose out of his seat. "I'm gonna get my heat from the car and pull up to the side door. You jump in when I pull up. Five minutes." He kissed the neck of the girl next to him with charismatic ease and stood up to exit the door between him and Pappy.

"Hey, man!" Pappy yelled at Dennis. "Why you bring these rabbits into my place?"

Dennis coolly responded in black dialect, "Dey be my friends and deys mindin' their bizness. Back off now, Pappy." Dennis warned, his voice suddenly forceful.

"No fuckin' way, man, this is my place, and I don't let rabbits in here. Why you leav'n dese rabbits behind?"

"I'm going to get my heat, so they better still be here when I get back or I'm gonna blow your black ass away." Bam was suddenly sober enough to feel his adrenalin kick in. He caught the hand signal that Pappy gave to Ray and watched Ray move slowly to the end of the bar.

Lester looked at the boys, like a cat watching panicky mice. "What you rabbits gonna do now?" His hands were splayed behind his head as he leaned back in his chair.

It was time for a diversion. Bam stood up quickly and jammed the table forward against Lester, pushing the drug dealer onto his back, beer soaking his purple outfit. Bam snatched a $100 bill from Lester's stack on the table and stuffed it in his blue jeans while Lester thrashed around on the floor, tangled up in his gold chains. Lester cursed and yelled as he held the reefer high, making sure to keep it away from layers of hair spray that could easily start a bonfire.

Clyde clambered to his feet, tucked his shirttail in his pants and ran his hands through his hair, like a preacher about to address a congregation. The calm demeanor of the big white boy seemed to appease the crowd.

Pappy didn't care about Clyde's imposing size. "You want some action, rabbit?" he yelled.

"No sir," said Clyde coolly in a drunken and drugged stupor. "I want a beer." He grabbed the last full beer mug on the table, wavering slightly. "And I am not a rabbit, my dear sir," he slurred.

"You ain't' a fuckin' rabbit?" Pappy sneered in disbelief, wary as Clyde held the mug in front of him. "Then what the fuck are you?"

"I immensely prefer honky, thank you very much," Clyde sputtered back. And if I am a honky, you sir, are a spade," he announced to Pappy and the world with articulate conviction. Clyde toasted his adversary in a spectacle of showmanship and chugged his sixth beer incomprehensibly fast as he watched Dennis slip out the side door through the bottom of his mug.

Behind the bar, Ray had figured this wasn't an ordinary bar fight and didn't want to be responsible for two dead teenage rabbits. He nervously dialed zero on the dial phone and told the operator to call Danny. The operator knew the drill and was quickly on the line with Danny. "Time to get to The Cat, Danny. Sounds like you better send help fast."

On the other end, Danny nodded in affirmation. "Well, they had a good three-week run. Thanks, I'll talk to ya later." He placed the phone on its cradle and flipped on the CB radio on his desk. "Danny to Foster, get to The Cat immediately," he said. Normally he would have called Quinine but that was no longer possible. He thought about going himself but decided against it, as there would be no one to man the station. Foster's voice sprang over the airwaves as if he knew what Danny was thinking.

"Roger that, Danny. Stay there. I'll handle it."

Back at The Cat, Pappy glared at Clyde from the middle of the scuffed floor. The crowd hugged the walls, surrounding Clyde. If he hadn't been a rabbit, he would have had Pappy's admiration for world-class beer drinking.

"What?" Pappy yelled at the top of his lungs. You call me a spade in my own crib? You-rabbit-motherfucker? I ain't no fuckin spade!"

Pappy's muscular right fist shot out with the speed of a street fighter just as the sound of the police siren filled the air, breaking his concentration. Clyde stumbled back and held up the beer mug for protection. Pappy's hand cracked loudly on the mug.

"Ow!" Clyde yelled sympathetically. "Man, Pappy, I'm really sorry."

The mug flew out of Clyde's hand and hit a patron of a nearby card game in the shoulder. He fell forward momentarily and came up swinging at the man standing behind him. The bar exploded as the fight began to converge on Clyde and Bam. Bam grabbed Clyde's shirtsleeve and pulled him toward the door with a crowd of footsteps closing in behind them.

Pappy was on his knees in the middle of his bar, holding his wrist and bellowing in pain. Clyde looked at Bam. "He's the only black dude I ever knew to get mugged!" he yelled, with a goofy laugh that only belonged to him. Pappy failed to see the humor. He was bent over, holding a broken wrist. "I'll kill yo' rabbit ass," he promised.

Outside the door, Dennis pulled the GTO to the curb with a screech, horn blaring. The trunk was wide open and the side door slightly ajar as everyone poured out of The Cat. Bam dove into the trunk of the GTO with Clyde's weight crushing him on top. The acrid odor of burnt rubber permeated the trunk as Dennis accelerated around the corner. The loud exhaust sent vibrations throughout his body. He could hear the police siren closing in at the bar. For one frightening moment, he thought he heard the sound of a gunshot.

The GTO sped toward the white side of town, taking flight over the hump in the tracks with a bounce.

Chapter Thirty-Eight
School Yard

Four miles east of the Black Cat Bar Levi Epstein pressed down on the clutch of his old Rambler, gliding to a halt on the shoulder of the road next to Bubba's School. The school building was lit up like a Christmas tree against the pitch darkness of flat cotton fields. The parking lot was packed with an odd mix of Cadillacs and four-wheel drive trucks.

Levi spotted Foster standing guard outside the main entrance, gun holstered, arms folded, and a large "Welcome Citizens Council" banner suspended above his head. He watched closely as Foster grabbed his radio, spoke into it, and then ran to his squad car. The police car skidded out of the parking lot onto the main road with the screech of rubber and the wail of his siren. Unfazed, Levi watched Foster speed off a safe distance before beginning the walk toward the school.

Levi saw a packed room of adults seated before clean-shaven speakers. Younger, clean-cut men stood at rapt attention in starched white shirts and sport coats that clashed against a classroom of farmers in khakis and their wives pant suits.

Levi watched at a distance. He recognized several of the vehicles. Then it hit him. There were maybe twice as many vehicles than there were guests. He looked around for the missing drivers as he walked toward the back of the school to snoop around.

He heard the rumbling of pickup trucks nearby but couldn't see the source in the pitch darkness. Levi cautiously followed the sound of movement, stumbling through wet, sticky sod, wishing he had thought to bring boots and a flashlight.

Epstein emerged at the end of the crop row gasping for air. He squinted to adjust his eyes to the darkness. Gradually, he could make out a well-dressed parking attendant parking trucks behind the school. The trucks lined up at a large shed where they fell into a short queue while four men unloaded bales from the trucks methodically.

As he walked carefully to the back of the trucks, he was hit by the smell of fresh-cut marijuana, a smell he knew well from his college days.

Chapter Thirty-Nine
Fallout

Bam woke late Sunday morning, sore and bruised from the trunk of a fast sports car and two hundred pounds of Clyde jammed against him. He winced from the swelling, gingerly rubbing a knot on his forehead from Clyde's elbow. He crawled out of bed and followed his nose down the hallway, sniffing the thick smell of his favorite coffee.

Sally never drank coffee, but she did like its smell. The thick brew was ready for male consumption, its aroma the best alarm clock on a Sunday morning. She sat peacefully in her rocking chair reading the Sunday paper, waiting for Bam to come in search of coffee.

"Mornin' Mom," Bam said with a hoarse voice. "Anything new in the paper?"

"Nothin' much, son. There was a bad blowout at The Cat last night. Looks like Foster Landeaux shot the drug dealer that started the ruckus."

Chapter Forty
The Crews

Hezekial looked over his congregation and counted two full pews of red shirts huddled together. They were increasingly well organized, he observed. He admired their chutzpah. Attending Lester's funeral en masse was politically shrewd. Bereavement in the black community was an intense communal event. Funerals were a cultural ventilation system for pent-up frustrations and depression from inequity. Attendance was an important statement that relied as much on neighborhoods as on families. It was so important that burial insurance was one of the few credit-worthy businesses for blacks.

The community would remember kindly the attendance of the Crews gang members during this time of loss, and their recruiting of new members would reflect their sensitivity. Hezekial had never associated Lester, with his fetish for purple satin and his passive nature, as a member of the Crews, a far more physical bunch. But then again, he had never imagined that gangs seeded by Los Angeles Latinos would ever proliferate in a rural Southern community where blacks and rednecks were in constant conflict with each other.

They were certainly "gangs" in the perception of public safety, Hezekial reflected, but he knew they were also entrepreneurs exploiting their environment, and their brethren. They met a demand no different than the pawnshops and loan sharks who made a living from the commerce of poverty.

But the drug trade was far more profitable, and it required far more organization than mere moneychangers. The Crews delivered protection just like New York mobsters. Black-on-black crime was increasing daily. Integration pitted blacks against whites and created new fissures within Hezekial's community. Everyone was scrambling to maintain their position in an unknown, once-in-a-lifetime transition. The integrated world was definitely a work in process.

The Crews were more of a company, an employer, and a source of security than a gang, at least in Southern terms. Objectively, they resembled a black KKK, but were younger and more savvy marketers. They even had a public relations policy, although they didn't call it such. The Crews had become a source of competitive pride for the downtrodden, a kind of "Robin Hood" on the wrong side of the tracks.

Hezekial didn't believe the KKK ever helped white people as much as they hurt black people. But the Crews seemed to have learned the benefit of being more protective of their own community - for their own purposes, of course, because drugs, not racial justice, was their core product.

Now the leadership of the Crews stood in front of Hezekial, blocking his entrance into his own office with an onerous silence.

Hezekial had no fear inside his arena. "Hello, brothers," he said politely. "It was good to have you at the funeral. We will all miss our Brother Lester."

A muscular Hispanic took a small step forward to identify himself as the leader. He eyeballed Hezekial's green suit, pink shirt and abstract tie, his thick forearms crossed over his chest. "We gone' miss him more than you are, Reverend. Tell us what you're gonna do about Lester?"

Hezekial refused to let the conversation be controlled by intimidation. He, too, had grown up in the 'Hood.' He had no patience for insolence, no fear of a good fight. If the Crews' young leader had any political savvy at all, he would know better than to screw with Hezekial. Hezekial extended his hand. "My name is Reverend Hezekial. And yours is…?"

"Tyrone," the youth seethed, unimpressed at the effort the preacher was making to communicate.

Hezekial judged him to be twenty years old at best with a west coast accent. He knew all of the boys, and they were but boys, standing behind

Tyrone. He smiled at them and elected not to identify them by name to cause any embarrassment. Hezekial waited, staring at their leader with his hand extended, his smile wide.

Finally, the youth blinked, shaking the preacher's hand in a quick motion. "That deputy killed Quinine. And then he killed Lester. What you gonna do to protect your flock, Rev? Pray for us while we get killed every time the motherfucker decides to come across the tracks? You think we gone' let white boys come over and start a fight at The Cat so the pigs can kill my man Lester?"

"I will absolutely pray for guidance as I pray for Brother Lester, his killers and you, Brother Tyrone. Clearly, God has called upon you to communicate your concerns to me. What is it that you want me to do?" Hezekial asked.

"I want you to tell that honky pig that the next time he shows himself across the tracks, he's a dead man."

"Brother Tyrone, I am touched by your conviction. But you cannot gain comfort by avenging the loss of a friend. He will still be a lost friend."

Tyrone stepped forward again, within inches of Hezekial. "My friends are right here, right now, Rev. This ain't about no lost friends. This is about money, Rev. Lester was my main man, my biggest supplier. I got a business to run. I got overhead to cover." His message delivered; he motioned his small army to follow him with a slight nod of the head.

Hezekial contemplated his response as they departed. "The church also has overhead, Brother Tyrone. The blessing of God comes with sacrifice." Tyrone stopped and slowly turned around, his new high top tennis shoes with green neon threads leaving tracks in the soft grass. He pulled two crisp $100 bills from his pocket and handed them to Hezekial with a black business card that read:

Tyrone, The Man. ph. 346-CREW

Hezekial was visibly impressed. He had never seen a gang member with a business card. "Blessed are the givers! Brother Tyrone, I will seek answers … for both of our flocks," he pronounced coolly to his newest parishioner.

Hezekial sat down at his desk and looked up the phone number of Tremblay & Lee. He contemplated his objectives and decided quickly on his approach. He had no choice but to call Judge Jim. He didn't need another casualty on his side of the tracks.

Judge Jim answered the phone himself, as he frequently did in the morning. "Judge," he announced blandly to his caller.

"Judge, this is Brother Hezekial at Mount Zion Church."

Judge Jim looked up from the papers on his desk and rubbed his forehead in contemplation of a new problem about to fall on his lap. "Hello, Reverend, how's the flock today?"

"Judge, I feel I should report something of concern, and I will ask that you pass it on confidentially to the Sheriff."

"I'm listening," Judge Jim responded intently. Calls from concerned preachers, especially black preachers, were an increasing demand on Judge Jim's time since the integration order. It was now his true civic duty to deal with the fallout inside the racially explosive environment.

"I am concerned over the welfare of Deputy Foster Landeaux. The leader of the Crews gang has essentially delivered a threat to his life," Hezekial announced.

Judge Jim considered this in light of current information. "I presume that this is a response to the shooting the other night at The Cat?"

Hezekial shut his eyes, shook his head in silence, and made a conscious effort to control his temper. Sometimes the white man was just another dumb-ass redneck in a judge's robe.

"No, Judge. It is not the effect of a singular killing in a honky-tonk across the tracks. It's the response of a hundred years of being black and poor. It's the response of being desolate and living in violence. It's the response of a territorial accumulation of power by highly organized gangs who now traffic in drugs. It's the response of having two black men killed by the same deputy in the last six months under suspect conditions."

He continued before the Judge could respond. "You see, Judge, it's a response to living on the wrong side of the tracks. The shootout at The Cat is not a cause, it is an effect. It is like striking a match to the bonfire of racism." The preacher's voiced peaked in a crescendo that produced a silence on the phone.

Judge Jim shook his head. Hezekial was the smartest nigger he had ever heard. Must be how he got all that free money from the government. The Judge knew better than to try to beat Hezekial at his own rhetoric.

"Okay, Hezekial," Judge Jim responded in his most soothing tone. "I accept your assessment. Whatever the reason, it certainly sounds like a dangerous situation and I will pass the message on appropriately. I had no idea that the Crews were that organized, or that violent."

Hezekial started up again. "White people have political machines that take money from the public largess and kill with the pen of legislation and warfare, Judge. Poor people of color have gangs who take money from their own race and kill enemies with impunity to protect their territory. We each have our own perfected ways to kill our brothers."

"I see," said Judge Jim, privately humbled. Wonder where he learned to come up with all this good bullshit on the spur of the moment? the Judge asked himself. It was time to change the subject. "This is actually a very timely discussion, Hezekial. I was about to call you anyway. We have another incident in our community which requires your unique position and special talents." Judge Jim had his own reserve of bullshit when he needed to schmooze his constituency. "Of course, it must be held in extreme confidence."

"Of course, Your Honor," Hezekial's voice predictably softened. He had never before been approached by Judge Jim for his services. "What can I do to assist our community?"

"It's about the girl in jail, Hezekial. The girl who shot Quinine. I believe her name is Meadow. Doc Hines found out yesterday that she's pregnant."

"Oh shit!" Hezekial burst out. "Who else knows this?"

Judge Jim looked into the phone, shocked by Hezekial's expletive. "No one on your side of the tracks."

"We must keep it that way, Judge."

"Yes, Hezekial, I know full well it could have huge implications."

"More than you know, Sir," Hezekial answered honestly.

"The Sheriff and I thought it would be best for you to tell the prisoner."

Hezekial tried to contain his panic. "I am certainly the man for the job. You must allow me to meet privately in her cell."

"Consider it done. Danny will let you in."

Hezekial needed to shift the focus to another subject. "There is one last thing to discuss, Your Honor."

"What is that, Hezekial?"

"The shooting the other night took place after two white boys visited The Black Cat."

Judge Jim knew where this was going, but he had to play along. "What? Who the hell was crazy enough to do that?"

"I am told it was the Callahan boy and a friend."

"What was Bam Callahan doing at The Cat?"

"You will have to ask him yourself, Your Honor."

"Who else knows this, Hezekial?"

"No one on your side of the tracks."

"We have to keep it that way," the Judge parroted.

"We must rely on each other's silence, for the sake of everyone, Judge," Hezekial pleaded.

"Agreed," the Judge responded firmly and placed the phone on the receiver absentmindedly. He rustled through papers on his desk and picked up a weekend police report that identified Bam Callahan and Bubba's grandson at a brawl on the wrong side of the tracks before the shooting death of drug dealer Lester Williams at The Black Cat Bar. He would have to tell Bubba. Hezekial got the easier conversation, he thought.

Chapter Forty-One
Bad Gris-Gris

David Tremblay always took his international calls in his private library on Saturday morning, after normal business hours. Phone connections were poor for Angola and his business there wasn't for others to hear. It was a small room made of intricately laminated shelves that housed his favorite books, centered around a sixteenth century Rococo desk. Unlike his father, David had read every volume of his extensive collection. His lifelong embarrassment over his father's crass ignorance had driven him to acquire an expansive knowledge of the world by an early age. He waited eagerly for the voice to answer the ringtone late afternoon Angola time.

"Hello, it's me," he said.

Dead silence portended the worst. "It's a dry hole," the voice across the Atlantic said in a melancholy tone. "There is no salvation."

"I see. Have we made the announcement yet?"

"No."

"Good. Keep drilling," David instructed.

"What?" the voice asked, incredulous.

"I said, keep drilling."

"Why? I don't even have enough pipe."

"Then act like you are drilling. I need time. Don't stop until I call you."

"I understand …, I believe" the voice responded hesitantly. "When will I hear from you?"

"Soon," David said with cold precision. He put down the phone and threw his head over the back of his seat, deep in thought. He had about a week, ten days at best.

David stood and straightened his tie to make sure his corporate persona revealed no cracks. He had to remain a striking image of the New South, wealthy, worldly, young, and dapper, a man always in demand. He felt better when he dressed the part.

David walked through the door into an anteroom where he was surprised to find Kipper waiting.

"Well, Kip, you should be on the golf course. What brings you here?"

Kipper was the only real operating officer for the Bumkin Bank &Trust, the go-to guy constantly stuck between Bubba, the redneck Chairman, and David, the dapper President, and son of Bubba. "I need to visit briefly, cher, may we?" Kipper asked.

"I'm a little preoccupied this morning, Kip. Is there a pressing issue?"

"Not exactly, David," the Cajun explained quickly. "Profits are generally up and loan quality is good at the bank. But I need to remind you that the $40 million balloon note is due for Dynasty next week. I have to advise our bank syndicate that payment will be made by the following week under the loan agreement."

"Of course," David said, "we should be putting the new well into production quite soon. Anything else?"

"Yes, there is," Kipper said delicately. "The farm's account balances have grown significantly, with big cash deposits. You now have about $25 million cash on hand."

"What's the problem?" David asked, irritated.

"Harvest season is well over," Kipper said hesitantly, a slight hint of concern in his voice.

"Dad held onto inventories for better pricing this year. Looks like he called it right, once again. Based on low sugar prices, I would expect that balances will rise as prices go up."

"David, Bumkin Bank is only an $80 million bank. I need you to move some deposits elsewhere."

"Need I remind you that this is my bank, Kipper?" David's voice was indignant, defensive.

"I do understand that, cher. And so do the regulators. You are drawing attention to the bank, and to yourself. We have too much cash to easily explain."

"Do I have to explain our success to the government? I thought that was what taxes are for, Kip. We will have to address this matter next week." Kip didn't move. He studied his boss with a combination of concern and curiosity. He noticed lines under David's eyes that were new for a young man not known for work ethic. "What do I tell the regulators?"

"Tell them it's an aberration that will resolve itself over the next two weeks. I have to go now," he said, closing the library doors behind him.

Kipper had long since stopped questioning David's flippant volatility, or his ephemeral motives. He could only hope that David was a lot smarter than him. A whole hell of a lot smarter, for everyone's sake.

Across town, Sally gave Bam a letter addressed to both of them from Greely. It was as succinct as it was ruthless. It informed the reader that the high school had no knowledge of, nor would it honor, any relationship between the college Bam had been attending on an unauthorized basis for the last two years. Sally read it to Bam in her own reassuring way.

"This is a crock," she said in her Southern drawl. "He can't put the genie back in the bottle, even with the Dean laid to rest. Too many people knew about it. Don't worry, son, we'll sort this out."

Bam nodded. He never questioned his mother's ability, but this time he wasn't so sure. The loss of two years of college credit was bad enough, but the threat of starting over was overwhelming. He considered the unthinkable of simply dropping out of school. He didn't fit in anyway. There was just no going back for him.

"If I were black, they would promote me through the system," he spoke to no one in particular, staring into his coffee cup. He needed advice. He needed to talk to Buster. It was time to get drunk.

Sally was about to respond when the phone rang. She answered and handed the receiver over to Bam. "It's Angela," she said as she began stroking his head the way sympathetic mothers do to console difficult teenage sons. She was happy Angela would break the sullenness that had fallen over the kitchen. Angela always made Bam smile.

"Hello," said Bam, putting on his best face. "What's up?" he asked.

"Can you talk?" Angela's voice whispered.

Bam looked casually up at Sally as she refilled her teacup by the stove, making sure she was a safe distance from the phone.

"Sure."

"I'm pregnant, Bam. I have morning sickness. We need to talk right away."

Bam's ears filled with the static of an overloaded brain. He blinked several times. He took a long swallow of hot coffee. His face flushed with heat as the information and the coffee hit home.

"Well, okay," he finally stammered, clearing his throat. "Let's talk tonight." His voice was clear and crisp, as adrenaline began pumping into his arteries. "I'll pick you up around seven. That'll be great," he said, delivering the pretense of happiness into a dead phone for Sally's benefit.

Great! Just fucking great! He had become a high school dropout and the father to an illegitimate baby of Judge Jim's daughter, all in one morning! Now it was really time to get drunk. Bam dialed the rotary for Buster's number.

"Hullo," the deep voice answered.

"Buster, it's Bam. I gotta talk. How about I meet you in an hour at EZ?" This was a prearranged code for the L&M bar on the other side of town. Buster would assume Sally was close by.

"Okay, little buddy, but we're starting a little early, aren't we?"

"It's been a bad day, Buster."

"Hell, Bam, it ain't but 8:30 in the morning. How bad could it be?"

"You don't even want to know. See you there," Bam said. He hung up the phone and turned to Sally.

"I'm going to visit Buster, okay, Mom?"

"Make it back before dinner. We'll talk about this school stuff later," she assured him. "And by the way, Bam," Sally winked, "the L&M doesn't open until 10:00."

Bam managed a troubled smile as looked back at his mother.

"Thanks, Mom. I just need to unload."

"Please stay out of trouble. The day is still young."

Bam turned his mustang into the gravel driveway behind the L&M Bar & Lounge at 9:00 AM. It was a dive landmark near the edge of town. The simple, one-room red-brick building sat on a corner lot surrounded by fifteen ramshackle motel rooms that wrapped around the back of the bar. The rooms were in a constant state of disrepair, serving a limited market for migrant workers and one-night affairs that utilized the bar as a discreet meeting place on short notice.

Bam walked confidently through the back door of the bar, as was customary for under-age locals. Burma, the bar maid opened up an hour early for friends on Saturdays while she was stocking the bar.

"Hi, Burma" Bam attempted a smile.

Burma was petite, sexy, and cute, always dressed in her standard outfit of a man's white Brooks Brothers shirt with exposed cleavage and tight-black stretch pants filled by strong hips that accentuated a slim waist, all of which produced enough tips to live on comfortably in Bumkin.

Burma's affection for men, and men's affection for Burma, had created a safe harbor against bad gris-gris for over fifteen years. L&M patrons were her friends and confessors, her neighbors and lovers, an interlocking crowd of recurring drama that could only be shared with Southern Comfort in the close confines of the L&M.

"Cher, baby, what you having today"?

"How about a Bloody Mary?"

"You got it, cher. What brought you here so early?"

"Need a place to think, Burma. Buster here yet?"

"No, cher, just Martin Tremblay at the bar, you know him don't' you? He was asleep in his car when I got here. Looks like he got bad gris-gris going on today."

"So, tell me, Burma, I've been hearing about gris-gris all of my life. What is it, really?"

"Gris-gris, cher? Oh, you know, it's the other side of voodoo. It's what makes things happen, mostly when bad stuff happens all at once and there ain't shit you can do about it. It floats in the air until it washes away. Gris-Gris just accumulates, sometimes it works for you, sometimes not, and some people just carry gris-gris with them all the time."

Voodoo still penetrated the consciousness of Creoles in Louisiana. Even if it wasn't real, it was as good an explanation as he had heard of his current condition. "How do you get rid of it, Burma?"

"Gris-gris never goes away, cher. It just rubs off."

Bam nodded thoughtfully and walked around the simple bar, taking a stool next to an older man, one of the many Tremblay cousins in town. He leaned against the bar quietly in the dark. The L&M was always dark. It was both an occupational necessity for patrons and an economic necessity to save on the light bill.

Burma emerged from the back room with a Bloody Mary for Bam and another margarita for Martin. She slid four Bayer aspirin on a napkin to Martin as she collected the dirty glasses from the last four margaritas.

"You boys are depressed," Burma announced. "This one is on the house." She returned to stocking the bar on a step ladder methodically while Bam and Martin admired her profile.

Bam thought about the good times with Angela while he pondered the future. He chuckled to himself about the havoc Angela was wreaking among the Baptists, and about … Martin! She was banging Martin! Martin Tremblay, the same Martin Tremblay sitting next to him on a bar stool at the L&M on Saturday morning.

Bam's heart began pounding. He turned his head slowly to look at Martin, sucking on his fifth margarita. He looked like hell, like a married man who had slept in his car all night. Sonofabitch! There was a God.

"Aren't you Mr. Martin Tremblay?" Bam asked innocently.

"Yep," the body said with a flash of life.

"Didn't you go to school with my brother, Bo? Bo Callahan?

"Yep."

"How are you, sir?"

"Call me Martin. I'm really drunk. You must be Bam. How are you?" he slurred. "How's that brother of yours? Haven't seen ol' Bo running the streets for quite a while."

"Bo is wherever the women are," Bam answered honestly. "He's a machine."

Martin grunted with appreciation. "Good answer. Bo got laid more than the whole male graduating class combined." He looked at Bam with drunken sympathy. "I'll bet that's a hard act to follow."

"You have no idea, Martin."

"He's a legend," Martin concluded with an appreciative nod. "Did he ever marry?"

"Not more than three or four times that I remember," Bam offered with detached humor, then waited patiently.

"Believe me, Bam, once is enough. I'll never do it again."

"Good advice. Did something happen?"

Martin pushed his seat closer to Bam and put his arm around his new friend as he attempted to articulate the appropriate response to the complex issue of marriage. It was buried somewhere beneath five of Burma's margaritas. Finally, it arrived. "Bam, it ain't that wives are all that bad, it's that mistresses are just that damn good."

It was an unusually profound statement for the L&M, especially in the daylight hours. Bam noticed Burma nodding thoughtfully in agreement.

"Dat makes sense, cher," she agreed, as she stacked glasses.

"Got caught?" Bam asked innocently.

"Worse. Got pregnant."

"Whoa! Man, I'm sorry to hear that, Martin. Which one?" Bam drilled to gain his freedom with as much sympathy as he could muster.

"The mistress, not the wife." Martin's eyes filled with tears and his voice cracked with regret. "Her dad will put me in jail. I'm in deep shit." He motioned Burma for his next margarita. Martin's eyes searched for empathy in a sea of melancholy. "And what about you, Bam? What brings you to paradise this early in the morning?"

Bam restrained a grin. "Just came to scrape off some bad gris-gris." He raised two fingers for beer just as Buster's massive frame filled the back door of the bar.

"Bam, what the hell is going on?" Buster asked as he walked into the bar.

"We're just here to help a brother through his moment of need, Buster." Bam smiled, slapping his buddy on the shoulder. "Pull up a seat, I'm buying."

Buster pulled off his baseball cap and looked confused for a moment, then took the stool next to Bam. He assessed the situation while Burma brought over two longneck Budweisers.

Chapter Forty-Two
Big Talk A Comin'

Judge Jim Keys stretched back, reclining in his favorite red leather chair, and stared at the ceiling. He pulled his thick, black glasses over a tussle of hair and began to rub his temples in harmony.

He looked down at his messages, delivered by the answering service through his secretary while he was in court. In the last three hours he had received urgent calls from the FBI; Kipper, who was both his banker and his client; Bubba, his de facto boss; Carl, his white preacher; Hezekial, the local black preacher, and Levi, the local newspaper publisher.

He looked through the messages. Only one name missing. He punched the button on his phone that rang through to his secretary. "Get Sally on the line."

"Mornin' Mrs. Sally."

Sally recognized Jim's voice instantly and couldn't help but smile. She occasionally wondered how different her life might have been had she elected to be a Southern belle instead of a Southern scholar. She blinked that thought away; she would never know and didn't want to.

"Good morning, Judge. To what do I owe this pleasure?"

"You know the story, Sally. Anytime something is going on in town I have to call you to find out. It must be time for a Big Talk."

She knew it was not unusual for Judge Jim to call her about local events but they both knew there was far more involved this time around. Sally already had her response prepared for this calculated moment.

"Who else is coming?" she asked innocently.

"Who else needs to come?"

"Last time we did this, Jim, it was an intimate meeting of just you and me and city hall."

"It's called corroboration, Sally. Us legal types got to have corroboration to know that justice gets done. That's how those KKK guys got put away last time, or don't you remember?"

"I remember. I still had to pay for their damages to my house and Bam still has nightmares about them."

"That was legal justice, Sally, not Southern justice. You know that."

"Didn't help me any that their houses got burned down, Judge."

"Of course it did. That's what Southern justice is about. Those yahoos gave everyone a bad name. If they hadn't been run off, you and the town would have never been rid of them. They wouldn't listen to authority. There was only one way to end it."

Unfortunately, she knew he was right. "This isn't like the last time around, Jim. There is a lot more involved, and a lot more serious. I don't know if even the Plantation Master himself can stuff this one back into the Bumkin box." She knew Jim always responded better to a challenge.

The "Big Talk" had always been Jim's preferred way of dispensing local justice in unruly situations that might affect the whole town. Get everyone in the same room and shout it out. By and large, it was a good system. It kept things off the record before it got out of hand, but sometimes it required unconventional methods so the town could live peacefully after the crisis passed.

"Well now, Sally. That just means we need to talk sooner than later, don't you think?"

"Okay, Jim, but you better have plenty of hot tea available."

"I always do, Sally," he chuckled. Alone in his office, he momentarily let his mind take him back to a gentler time long ago and a young teenage girl who had just discovered her love for tea. "Sounds like it's going to be one hell of a 'Big Talk,' huh, Sally?"

"Could have been shorter if you had called earlier, Jim."

"You know me, Sally. Sometimes it just takes me a while to catch on. I don't pretend to know all that is happening right now, but I know you do."

"And you know I have to protect the innocents, Judge. We're off the record and out of the line of fire or it doesn't happen. I'm talking real amnesty here."

"Amnesty? Amnesty for whom? For what?" the Judge was caught by surprise.

"Anyone I bring to your little party."

"Would that include young Bam?"

"Most certainly, among others."

"What has he done now?" Judge Jim inquired with a concerned voice.

"Nothin' you didn't do in your younger days," she laughed into the phone.

"Sally, you know that I cannot openly support or knowingly provide legal cover to anyone who knowingly breaks the law."

"Don't bullshit me, Jim, you already have." Sally's quick retort was unusually tough and to the point. This is hardball, Jim… this time around people we know have been killed by people we know, Jim. The facts tell me it's a cover-up." She waited for her bomb to explode on the other end of the phone.

"Murder? A cover-up?!" Judge Jim bellowed. He hated that word. Everything was a damn cover-up in Louisiana. It was supposed to be a cover-up. It had to be a cover-up. Reality was too damn ugly. "Damn it, Sally, that kind of information is supposed to get reported to authorities."

"That's why you called me, Judge," Sally said sweetly. "What's it gonna be, Big Guy?"

He put down the phone momentarily, gripping it in his fist while he caught his breath. She was a maddening woman. She never played the game until she had a winning hand.

"Okay. It's a deal. 1 p.m. Friday. You and yours are cleared for discussion, but only to the degree that no one benefited from illegal activity and were acting in the best interest of the law."

"Since when have I ever benefited from working with you, Judge?" Sally teased. "And it needs to be on Tuesday, same time, Judge."

"What? Why?" he asked, angered to renegotiate his appointed schedule.

"Press time for the *Bumkin Record* is Monday night. You will need a full week to work your magic before the next edition."

"That must mean Epstein isn't invited?"

"No, Judge, it just means you will have one week to sort this mess out in the best interest of the town, which may not be in the best interests of your clients and partners. Better clear your docket. You have a lot to do, but I have faith in you, Jim. Always have. Always will," she choked. See you at the Big Talk."

Sally hung up before the Judge could ask another question and sipped her tea in contemplation of events yet to unfold.

The Judge reached for his bottle of Southern Comfort. Where the hell was this going? What had she dug up? It worried him. A researcher like Sally could dig up plenty of dirt on Bubba and his son due to the sheer span of his holdings, the Judge pondered. He hated being cornered, especially by Sally Callahan.

Chapter Forty-Three
Cover-Up

The first week posing as Maggie had been particularly difficult for Meadow. She was forced to take over Maggie's domestic work for Beverly, for her own safety. Beverly picked up "Maggie" at the appointed time and immediately began complaining. Meadow did her best to remain silent during these tirades, fighting back the urge to say, "Listen to me, bitch…"

One wrong step would blow her cover and put her back in jail. White women couldn't tell the difference in black women any more than white men could, which made her blackness her best hideout.

Beverly complained about everything as she rode around in her new Lincoln. What right did she have to complain about anything? It made Meadow miss her life at The Spot. But Meadow slowly began to notice that Beverly paid close attention to the leers she got from men, both black and white. Perhaps she had even fooled herself into thinking they were looking at her. Or maybe it was sufficient satisfaction in Beverly's world that she "owned" a hot chick who made men pay attention. Beverly craved respect and envy.

Meadow altered her strategy quietly in the back seat of Beverly's big car. There would be a high cost to deceiving Beverly if she got caught, but Meadow had a lifetime of practice manipulating pimps. It was time to use it.

Meadow cleared her throat loudly to get attention and focused on producing her sister's softer voice. "Ms. Beverly," she meekly interrupted Beverly's incessant complaining, "It don't do no good to yell at me. If I knew what to do to become like you, I would just love that, … but I am just a nigger girl, I don't know no better." She hung her head in dismay. "I just never been educated like you have been, Ms. Beverly, I never been trained."

Beverly actually went silent, which was fine with Meadow. And the next day, when Meadow was behind schedule, Beverly was noticeably more congenial than usual. She turned the Cadillac down Main Street, pulling the big car up in front of the local clothes store for the upscale women of Avignon Parish. "Follow me," Beverly commanded as she got out of the car.

The store owner watched, unbelieving, as Beverly opened the door for her black maid and magnanimously instructed the clerk to produce a suitable wardrobe for the young black woman who would be going places with her. Meadow feigned shock, even generating a tearful hug and a teenage shriek of excitement for Beverly beneath the sly smile of a woman once again in charge of her own destiny.

Chapter Forty-Four
Showtime

The big conference room was centered around a massive mahogany lion's claw table which dated back to the late 1700s. The Judge had acquired it in return for legal fees a family couldn't afford.

Sally reviewed the attendance list she requested from Judge Jim's secretary. She sipped her tea at one end of the long table, well opposite the Judge's seat. It was going to be one hell of a Big Talk. She always enjoyed a good intellectual battle of wits with the Judge, but this one was very different. The next two hours would ensure that inhabitants of Bumkin wouldn't lack in gossip for years to come. She was relieved to confirm that everyone on the list was covered by the Judge's amnesty agreement. It wasn't that she didn't trust the Judge, she just didn't trust lawyers.

The Judge's big frame suddenly filled the doorway. He entered the room with his famous smile. He wore his favorite suspenders, his thick glasses stuck on his forehead, keeping fashionably long hair out of his eyes. The Judge dropped a thick pad on the table and immediately walked over to hug Sally in the best of Old Southern tradition. They lingered momentarily with small talk about neighbors, friends, and old lovers, as Southerners do.

"Got quite a crowd out there," he said, nodding toward the reception room.

"Ought to be a hum-dinger, Judge. I'm ready. Are you?"

"Sure am." Judge Jim opened the door and signaled his receptionist to let the visitors in.

Sadie, Hezekial, Bam, Clyde, Levi, and Carl paraded in quietly. The Judge noted that Flossie stayed behind in the waiting room, shutting the door after everyone had entered the room. They took their seats around the table, a comical crowd with an irreverent air about them. Reverend Hezekial carried his worn, leather-bound bible, the beacon of his faith and the source of his authority. Sadie sat next to him, facing Bam, Clyde, and Levi. With her conservative dress and hair pinned back, she looked every bit the virgin secretary for First Baptist Church, hardly the vamp who had made her way into the heart of the Bumkin Police Station. Next to Sadie, erect in his chair, sat Reverend Hudson. Clyde sat close to Sally, hands interlocked and eyes twinkling with anticipation.

Sadie smiled at Hezekial and patted his arm in friendly affection. She loved teasing the philandering reverend.

Levi hunched over the table, reporter's pad out, short legs barely reaching the floor. He, Sally and Bam had talked before the meeting, so he knew more than the others. He planned to stay quiet and take copious notes, as reporters always should.

Judge Jim had greeted each participant at the door, making sure to snare a hug from Sadie. After everyone was seated, he took his seat at the head of the table with a politician's chuckle. "My, my, we have quite the distinguished crowd here today. I am sure there is good reason for this eclectic congregation. Where should we start, Mrs. Sally?"

Sally took command of the group as if the classroom bell had just been sounded. Her professorial voice shocked the Judge. "We are here to cut through a lot of crap, Judge. Today is serious business." Everyone turned toward Sally. The two reverends looked at each other and shifted uneasily. Maybe they should have opened with a prayer.

"We are all here under an agreement of amnesty granted by you, Judge, so long as no one here intentionally broke the law or benefited from breaking the law. We are here to prove that an innocent woman who was in jail because you allowed her to be, while our city fathers covered up the murder of a public servant who just happened to be black."

Judge Jim closed his eyes and grit his teeth. This meeting was a big mistake. He knew he had been had, but then, he had naively agreed to be had. She had brought her own army. This was not a meeting; it was a trap at best, a lynching at worst.

"Those are very serious charges, Sally," the Judge recovered coolly. "But I am most curious why you said that we have an innocent woman in jail. Is that because she is no longer innocent?"

"No. That is because she is no longer in jail, Judge."

Judge Jim leaned forward, half in shock. "Are we talking about Meadow, Sally? The woman still in custody?" Judge Jim maintained his calmest voice, but he could already feel the answer about to slap him in the face.

"Wrong girl, Judge." The girl in your jail is Maggie, Meadow's twin sister. And I'm betting you already knew she had a twin sister."

"Maggie is Meadow's twin?" Judge Jim feigned, placing his hands on the table to steady himself without giving away the past. "I saw Maggie with Beverly Durham just today at lunch. Less than an hour ago."

"That was Meadow," Sally said with certainty. "She dresses up pretty good on Beverly's nickel, don't you think, Judge?"

Judge Jim ignored giggles around the table. "How do you know this, Sally?" His tone implied an accusation.

"'A,' because I am a history professor and I know the genealogy of Roberta, Maggie and Meadow's mother and their biological father. And 'B,' because it doesn't take a history professor to identify twins when you've known the family for a lifetime. They are identical, Judge, though they are individually very different. And finally, I know that when two identical young women end up with matching pieces of historic jewelry, it is very meaningful. Try this on."

Sally walked around the table and laid out the disparate pendant and bracelet pieces of "Vs" that Hezekial had collected from Meadow and Maggie. She gradually pulled them together so that "KKK" was spelled out in shocking detail. The crowd around the table stood up to watch the silver initials coalesce, gasping at the singular message.

"Damn!" Reverend Hudson muttered, then quickly apologized.

Judge Jim inspected the objects closely, dumbfounded. Even he had been unaware of the symbolism in front of him that tied together the destiny of two young children and the actions of a client. And perhaps even his own.

"Okay, Mrs. Sally," Judge Jim emphasized the "Mrs." as he always did when Sally frustrated him. You're on to something, but I first want to know how Meadow is out driving Beverly around while Maggie is in jail?"

Hezekial started to explain, but Sally immediately put her hand up to silence him. The Judge glared at Sally for an explanation. "What Reverend Hezekial was about to say," she explained, "is that he, Sadie, Maggie, and other concerned friends and relatives doing God's work at the jail delivered the Good Word to all the inmates about two weeks ago. Somehow or another, Maggie and Meadow must have switched places. After all, they are identical, Judge. It was impossible for anyone to know."

"Of course," the Judge responded cynically. "And I know you called this meeting as soon as you found out about the "unexpected switch," he concluded, his voice full of sarcasm.

"Obviously," Sally responded sweetly.

"How, exactly, did you figure this out, Mrs. Sally?" Judge Jim pressed.

"Just a SWAG, Your Honor. It began with a picture in Levi's newspaper and a visit I paid to the prisoner when I went to pick up Snowball on a Saturday morning. There was no doubt in my mind she and Maggie were sisters."

"So now we have a suspected murderess driving around with a local socialite," Judge Jim said to no one in particular.

"Don't worry, Judge, Meadow has been in worse company, she can handle it," Sally offered up as the crowd chuckled.

"And, of course, all of you understand that Maggie is now in deep trouble for helping Meadow escape," Judge Jim said sternly.

"That may be true, Judge, but it might be hard to find a jury of Maggie's peers in a town that is fifty percent black, to convict a young, innocent, pregnant black woman for helping her young, innocent, twin sister escape the death penalty in order to protect your client's corrupt ass. Especially with a newspaper that has a lot more facts." Levi sat in smug silence.

Judge Jim went to a cupboard to search a small drawer for aspirin to combat a sudden headache. He poured a glass of water from a crystal pitcher.

His face had begun to turn red. "Maggie's pregnant?" Judge Jim asked with an inquisitive look, attempting a diversion. "She's not even eighteen yet, is she? Who is the father?"

Hezekial froze instantly. Levi quietly picked up the pen he had been playing with and noted on his pad the fact that Judge Jim knew the age of an obscure young mulatto girl.

Reverend Carl immediately began to voice his opinion about the pregnancy. "I think we know who…"

Once again Sally raised an open palm and slowly bent her fingers into to a tight fist held up for all to see. The preacher stuttered, then shut up. "As Reverend Carl was saying," Sally's voice took over the room again, "it is quite possible that Snowball and Maggie may have been fraternizing in the jail. We have no way of knowing, of course, but it certainly would be a serious liability to the city." Hezekial pulled out a silk handkerchief and mopped his forehead.

"Anyway," Sally continued breezily, "you, Judge, now have an innocent, black, pregnant woman in your jail and a former black hooker dressed up like Cher Bono driving around with the Wicked Witch of the North in your town. But, we both know several unanswered questions yet remain, don't we, Judge? Why would someone want to frame Meadow? How did these twin girls get separated eighteen years ago? And, most important of all, who is *their* father?"

Judge Jim stared deeply into the diminutive historian's eyes for several seconds. She was too good. He knew her too well. She knew him too well. She already knew the answers, or she wouldn't be asking the questions.

"I think we both know the answers, Sally," he confessed in a somber tone, unwilling to be further upstaged.

Sally's voice grew sharper, her eyes narrow and steely. "I think we do, Judge. Almost eighteen years ago, you handled the transfer of the cabin property from Bubba Tremblay to Roberta Williams shortly after she gave birth to twins, but the property transferred back to the original owner upon Roberta's death. Three years before that event, you were just a young lawyer in town when things started to blossom for you. That was about the same time Sheriff Landeaux was "elected," for lack of a better term, and according to the land records, about six months before five thousand acres of supposedly 'worthless' swampland in the Atchafalaya basin was sold from Avignon Parish to Dynasty Oil Company in a sweetheart deal for less than $50 an acre. That land built Dynasty Oil Company."

Sally continued with the story. "Fifteen years later, you took David Tremblay into a new law firm formed specifically to represent the Tremblay family's interests. The SEC records confirm that the Tremblay family is still the majority shareholder of Dynasty, but somehow the Sheriff of both Avoyelles and Evangeline Parishes managed to become millionaires when the company went public." She paused. "And so did you, Judge. And as Dynasty's lawyer, you engineered for the Sheriffs to receive a long-term lease on a hundred acres of land in the middle of nowhere for a pittance which was to be used as a 'nature recreation resort,' located where The Spot sits today."

Silence befell the room. Judge Jim stood, his jaw set. He looked flustered by the deluge of embarrassing information as he began to pace the room. He knew now that the meeting had never been for him to judge the people and circumstances around him. It was for them to judge him. He was standing in front of a jury. Sally had always been a few steps ahead of him. That was what he always loved about her.

Judge Jim began to speak almost in a trance. "There was only one known, illegitimate girl when I found out Roberta was pregnant from Bubba, Sally. I knew the infant was threatened when I heard that Roberta was giving birth, so I drove to the cabin where Bubba and Roberta had shacked up for years. Bubba was there holding the baby and he was surprised to see me. The Sheriff was driving off when I came up. Years later I learned there had been another child, but she never surfaced, and I never asked. The Sheriff must have taken Meadow while Roberta was knocked out. I came in before he could return to take Magnolia also. They didn't expect me to ever see Magnolia, but I had no way to verify that there was another child." His voice was defensive.

"Did you even try?" Sally asked, her voice resonating, a tone below accusatory.

"Honestly, no. No, I didn't, Sally. I didn't want to know because there was nothing to be done about it. It was all I could do to make arrangements for Maggie. I worked out a deal for Maggie to live with Lee Esther so Roberta could reside at the cabin as long as she lived. She loved it there and agreed to keep quiet to protect the Tremblay's interests—and the town's. Meadow's interests were lost in the moment. And there were other forces at work," he said glumly.

"Forces like Dynasty Oil which began stealing oil from Quinine before it went public. How much stock did you get in Dynasty by engineering that coup, Judge? More importantly, how much did Quinine get?" Sally's voice was stronger now, relentless in its pursuit. "How much oil money found its way into the KKK to intimidate black people? How many young women like Meadow got enslaved as whores?" Gasps filled the room with each accusation.

"My part was all legal, Sally," Judge Jim argued. "I have no interest in The Spot, or Dynasty. Those were Bubba's affiliates," he said, avoiding the KKK and choosing his words carefully.

"Your role may have been legal, Judge, but it was far from right! You hid behind the law when it was convenient, and you gave the option to your clients to ignore it when it wasn't," Sally scoffed at him, her voice choking with emotion.

"My job has always been to protect the town," Judge Jim exclaimed defensively, his own sorrow starting to surface. He was not accustomed to defending his own actions. "The stock in Dynasty was given to the Sheriffs to ensure protection of the Dynasty basin property from outsiders."

"And to keep landowners like Quinine under control," Sally added without flinching. "What about the school and the marijuana?"

The Judge changed the subject. "I don't do drugs. You know me better than that, Sally," he said, huffing with indignation that she would even think such a thing. "What the hell are you talking about?"

"Twenty acres of marijuana," Bam spoke up. He didn't like the way the Judge seemed to talk down to Sally. Besides, he had a few surprises of his own.

"More," volunteered Epstein without looking up. He was writing furiously on his yellow pad. "There's much more."

"That's a haul." Clyde said with enthusiasm. "Where does it go?"

"It ends up at Bubba's school," Epstein continued, putting down his pen. "Then it gets redistributed by members of the Citizens' Council who make contributions to support the KKK lobby effort." The two reverends looked at each other in shock as Epstein began to tell about his trek through the cotton fields during the last meeting of the Citizens' Council. Fifteen minutes later, everyone in the room sat in stunned silence, staring at each other as they searched for the right questions.

Sally poured her third cup of tea, looking around the table with a cocked eyebrow and stern face. "So, here's what I get out of all this," she said, her voice reverting to her academic demeanor as she began to summarize history, her particular gift.

"Eighteen years ago, Bubba Tremblay sired illegitimate twins by Roberta at about the same time he was given the reigns to the Tremblay fortune from his father, the 'General,' a self-proclaimed general in the KKK, the Grand Wizard. It's unclear whether his son or grandson followed directly in his footsteps, although Bubba certainly remained loyal to the cause if he could use it to make a buck."

"I think you can safely assume Bubba didn't have the right skills to ever lead the KKK," the Judge offered in defense of his client.

Sally continued. "One of Roberta's twins was kidnapped for disposition, and the other got lucky, presumably because of the Judge's intervention, and grew up as Lee Esther's daughter. We all know her as Maggie. Meadow, the missing twin, ended up in an orphanage in North Louisiana, which was the equivalent of Outer Mongolia back then. Meadow ultimately became a prostitute at The Spot, a possible coincidence that is very hard to imagine. My money says there was some sort of sick plan involved."

Sally sipped some tea and continued. "The Spot was given political protection by the Tremblay family as a payoff for the Sheriffs of two parishes, in return for the de facto enforcement of their claim on cheap oil land that was illegally leased to Dynasty Oil, largely at the expense of taxpayers and poor sharecroppers like Quinine. Given what we know now, it appears Bubba became obsessed with Quinine's inheritance, and Quinine's father met with a suspicious demise, which was ignored by the Sheriff.

"Everyone made out like bandits on Dynasty stock over the last twenty years while the KKK got transformed into a lobbying machine for white supremacists backed by the Citizens' Council. The Spot turned out to be a great tool for gaining leverage on other politicians through a free flow of young women.

"Maggie and Meadow were never aware of each other. But we can guess what evolved between Meadow and Bubba when she showed up at The Spot. He had to have identified her by the pendant she kept."

Sally now sat back in her chair as she continued. "It was a brilliant plan, far beyond the capacity of Bubba Tremblay," she said, glaring at the Judge. "But years later, the oil in the basin began to play out. Dynasty had harvested its profits and moved into the big plays offshore under David Tremblay. Now Bubba needed a new scam for revenues, and marijuana became his new payday. He called on his old partners in the KKK who were more than willing to help.

"The KKK had put on a new face and become a lot savvier politically. They created a nonprofit entity dubbed the Citizens' Council to seize upon the friction of forced integration and rally the troops. Their core constituency of Southern farmers presented a rich source of anti-government sentiment and agricultural production that gave Bubba a soap box for center stage, and a political organization to support his politics. He compared marijuana to tobacco which enjoyed huge subsidies and began to spread cash around to buy influence under the shroud of the Citizens' Council. So, everybody won, just like the oil play. But, so far, we've only counted money, not bodies."

The Judge sat at the opposite end of the long table; eyes closed as if in pain, as Sally continued. "Quinine, as we all know, was the bag man for Sheriff Landeaux. Ironically, he was also a black second cousin to Bubba, who the Tremblay family oppressed through the Sheriff. Megalomaniac Bubba got some sort of perverse power by controlling the destiny of his black cousin and kept him on the force. Quinine made regular pickups for the Sheriff at The Spot and somehow connected with Meadow. If she's telling the truth, Bubba shot Quinine when they tried to elope and set her up for the blame. Flossie overheard a conversation between Bubba and Foster that incriminates both of them in the death of Quinine."

"Whoa! Stop right there!" Judge Jim yelled, suddenly standing up with nervous energy and pacing the room again. "I've heard enough to know we have to get depositions and call a grand jury. We can't even be discussing this anymore, especially while we have a damn reporter and a bunch of kids in the room."

Sally walked up to him. "That's why Flossie is still outside, Judge. Or would you rather me invite her in for all to hear?" Her head barely reached his shoulders, her finger pointing to him as if scolding a student. "Call your grand jury but be prepared to indict yourself and the rest of us that are caught up in your damn mess. You've dispensed Southern justice all of your life. You know better than any of us what happens if this gets out. This time you are going to make it right for people other than your clients and yourself or there will be hell to pay and your lifetime of work in this town will be meaningless."

A deathly long silence filled the room. Judge Jim turned his tired eyes slowly to Levi Epstein. "What are you going to report?"

Sally held up the omniscient hand once again. "Right now, he's got a bunch of speculation. No proof and no comments from me or Flossie. That can change very quickly. It's up to you, Jim." Her voice held an edge the Judge had never heard before, like a machete cutting through cane.

Judge Jim knew a statement from Sally would be as strong as any physical evidence. It might not convict Bubba, but it would start a brawl that would end everything, including his own career and retirement fund, maybe even his license to practice law. Sally broke the silence. "If the *Bumkin Record* reports on this before next week's press time, I'll call Epstein a damn liar and I'll call his competition with the real story. Epstein is like all of us, Judge; he needs the town to survive more than he needs a juicy headline, or he won't have a newspaper to print. So, I expect we are going to have all of this behind us by press time next week, don't you, Judge?" The historian smiled as she calmly delivered a lethal threat to her friend while she poured a cup of steaming tea.

Judge Jim slowly eased back into his chair, nodding slowly. "I will need some help, but as usual, I suppose you are right, Mrs. Sally." He looked at the reporter. "You will hold off the story in the meantime?"

"There is no story. Yet," Epstein confirmed.

"Aren't you journalists supposed to be people of conviction?" Reverend Carl asked in a holier-than-thou voice. His outrage was building over the entire turn of events.

"You're confusing me with gentile journalists. I'm a Jewish publisher in a small Southern town filled with hypocritical evangelical Christians. Give me advertising and I give you articles, on demand, Reverend." Then Epstein added, "Suck it up, Carl. Your church has more to lose than any institution or individual in here because of Bubba Tremblay and his Judge."

Judge Jim winced at the conversation. "I guess that answers all but two questions for me, Sally," he said in a dejected manner. He didn't need Epstein changing his mind. "First, why were Clyde and Bam at The Cat the night the drug dealer was killed?"

Sally sighed and turned to her son and his cohort. It was the surprises she hated most. "That's news to me. Spill it, young man."

Bam knew his time had come to fess up. He told the whole story, starting with the first marijuana trade he had negotiated between Timmy and Lester for food stamps and how the idea had caught on, developing a life of its own. Suddenly, Lester was a major drug distributor in the black community, supported by Timmy, both making more money than they knew was possible, Bam explained.

"Then we saw Lester start the riot at school and it didn't make any sense. I told Timmy that Mr. Epstein was trying to reach Lester, knowing he would tell Foster. Clyde and I got Dennis to take us to The Cat to warn Lester, hoping he would call Mr. Epstein. He told me then that Bubba made him start the riot as a diversion. Bubba was afraid the town was getting too focused on the drug trade because of the school board tapes Clyde and I made with Dr. Winchester, and the front-page article about the sign. Everything got upside down at The Cat and Dennis got us out quickly. But all we did was provide cover for Foster to kill Lester," Bam said sadly.

The Judge looked at Hezekial, who nodded in confirmation of Bam's story. "You could have been killed!" Sally yelled at her son; her emotional control suddenly broken as her maternal instincts echoed in the office. She stopped suddenly to take a deep breath, allowing the Southern belle to revert back to the steel magnolia. "Bam, I'm proud of you for trying to warn Lester, but that was the dumbest damn thing I've ever heard of."

"Not as dumb as a bank board member who doesn't know that his bank is laundering money from illegal food stamps," Bam responded angrily with an undisguised jab at the Judge.

"What do you mean?" Sally asked, unsure of his outburst.

"The Judge may not have been peddling drugs, but he should have known that there was something funny going on at the bank. His law partner is the President of the Bank and he's a board member. He just didn't want to know. Just like he didn't want to know why Lester was killed." All eyes turned back to the Judge.

Judge Jim looked at Sally with a soft gaze. "He's good at research, learned from the best," he said, shaking his head with humility. "You are right, Bam. There were two issues I ignored because it was easier to ignore them than to address them."

"What's the other one?" Sally asked.

"Who pulled the trigger on Quinine?"

"That's easy, Jim," Sally responded. "The same person who will attempt to kill Maggie."

"Why Maggie?"

"Because the whole town thinks she's Meadow, who witnessed Quinine's murder, and happens to be pregnant with the bloodlines of a black Tremblay."

Judge Jim looked around the table, wanting to bring the meeting to a quick conclusion while he had some negotiating room. "I will handle this in the best way possible, but I need everyone to keep quiet and give me time. Are there any other surprises I don't know about?"

Hezekial slid an envelope across the table to the Judge unexpectedly. "You may wish to look at this, Your Honor. It's a copy of Quinine's will, along with the contents of his lock box at your bank ... including his marriage certificate to Meadow."

Sally picked up her notepad and headed toward the door, motioning the others to follow. She left the Judge alone at the conference table. "See you in a week," she said firmly as she pulled the door shut.

The Judge contemplated his options in sulking silence. What else did Sally know? Did it even matter? The only good news was that she wasn't interested in seeing any of the dirt surface any more than he was. He knew that targeting Bubba's transgressions was relatively easy for a professional of Sally's caliber but surfacing the Judge's role was potentially far more damning to him and the Tremblays. She knew he couldn't wipe the slate clean without delivering Southern justice.

Chapter Forty-Five
Personal Contact

K ipper Duron answered the surprise front doorbell of his modest home in his favorite LSU sweatshirt. It was a weekday night and visitors were rare when kids were in school.

A business card was thrust in front of him that read "Joe Damon—Special Agent, Federal Bureau of Investigation." Kipper looked guardedly at his guest as he took the card and read it in the light of his small foyer. The sounds of young children and a loud television emanated from a back room along with the heavy smell of chicken and andouille gumbo.

"What can I do for you, Agent Damon?" Kipper asked, clearly jolted by the visit. The agent's marine haircut and gray hair left little doubt that he was as seasoned and fit as he looked.

Damon straightened his narrow tie and stood tall in a suit so starched it could have stood alone. "I would like to speak to you alone, Mr. Duron."

Kipper opened the door and led him into a small dining room. The men took seats across from each other at the dinner table.

"Again, what can I do for you?" Kipper was still shaken by the unexpected visit.

"Mr. Duron, I will be blunt. The FBI is investigating a money-laundering operation. I think we both know that your bank has experienced significant deposit increases during the last several years. I would like your cooperation in analyzing the source of that liquidity."

"Obviously, Mr. Damon," Kipper said, "you must already know that the liquidity of this little country bank comes from a relatively few, large accounts which are all controlled by the same family. A lot of their holdings come from oil income."

The slightest of smiles came over Agent Damon's face. "Yes, we do. And we have no reason to believe at this time that you or your employees are knowingly involved in any illicit activity … yet. You are a bank officer and even if you weren't aware of any illicit activity, you can still be held responsible for it. So, if you want to cover yourself, we will require your personal cooperation. If not, we can certainly get the information through other…"

Kipper shut him off quickly. "That won't be necessary, Agent Damon. I will help any way I can. I have nothing to hide. But I also don't know what you're looking for." Kipper showed the honest face he had inherited from his mother. "What information do you need?"

"Mr. Duron, I want to know a lot of things. But I especially want to know how a single cane farmer consistently makes more money than everyone else combined in this whole, damn piss-ant town, with less acreage in production every year. I also want to know why your bank now receives over 30% of the food stamp deposits in the whole parish—and growing."

Kipper could not answer either question. He wanted to know too. "Can I speak to my counsel, Judge Keys?"

"You mean the counsel for the bank? Certainly, until he has to get his own attorney."

<div align="center">~~~~</div>

Just a few miles away, resident FBI agent Tommy Joe Theriot knocked on the door of a small, well-manicured mansion belonging to one David Tremblay III. The water in Bayou Boeuf moved lazily off a weir beneath huge moss-draped oak trees. Theriot's backup, Agent Van der Hove, stood next to him.

Van der Hove was young and spunky, a petit woman with naturally blond hair and a beautiful tan that was foreign to the Cajun culture. She was also tense and nervous, and always playing with her newfangled camera. Theriot wondered how you could be an FBI undercover agent in Louisiana with blond hair and a name like Van der Hove? She was definitely from another country, he thought. Some damn place like California.

"You ready, cher?" he asked calmly.

"You bet."

Tommy Joe had staked out the location for the past several days in expectation of receiving the search warrant in his shirt pocket. He looked over the big GM truck parked beside the flashy red Maserati in the garage. He knew the Maserati belonged to Tremblay; the truck belonged to Foster Landeaux. They were right on time.

The truck arrived every other day about dusk, just after the maid left. Theriot usually liked to present search warrants in the evening while everyone was relaxed and unprepared, but their schedule was predictable, and he didn't want to miss any action.

This was his watch, his country, his people. He unsnapped his gun holster and nodded at agent Van der Hove. "Showtime, cher," he said, pressing the doorbell for three successive rings.

A distinguished, indignant male voice yelled that he didn't want to be interrupted.

Theriot yelled back to the door, "This is the FBI. Open the door. We need to speak to Mr. David Tremblay."

Silence followed, then the door opened, restricted by a gold chain that held taunt to the frame. The tall, distinguished man behind the door was barely visible but for an Italian silk pajama top draped over a muscular bare chest. "What can I do for you?" he asked.

"Mr. David Tremblay? I have a search warrant for the premises. Please open the door."

"That's impossible!" David shouted. A rush of cool air flowed out of the door opening with a familiar sweet smell.

Agent Theriot was reminded of his days in the narcotics division, watching kids get addicted so pushers could afford their Maseratis. Kids like his young Philippe, safe at home, the apple of his eye. Theriot could feel his Cajun blood begin to boil. "Let me in now!"

"I'm not dressed," David responded, stalling for time while he collected his thoughts. Theriot was having none of it.

"Sure, I'll wait," Agent Theriot said calmly. He held up the warrant so David cold see it. "You're a lawyer - just let me slide the warrant through the door." His demand dictated a response. David grumbled an indignant approval and stretched his fingers through the opening, curious to receive the warrant.

Theriot seized the moment, first pulling the door shut on David's fingers, then kicking the door in with the full force of his 260-pound body. The chain snapped easily as the door slammed into the side of the lawyer's head, dropping him to the floor while he grabbed his fingers and whimpered in pain. Theriot was instantly on top of him, gun drawn. Agent Van der Hove tried to hide her shock as their new prisoner screamed and writhed on the floor. This wasn't in any handbook she had seen but it was time to go with the flow. She drew her gun instantly and held it high in the air as she had been trained to back up Agent Theriot.

"I'll sue you," David's voice reached a high note as the gash on his head spewed blood onto a thick Persian rug beneath him.

Theriot smiled. "I think you must have slipped, cher. Let me help you up. Nasty cut you got there," Theriot said as he pulled out his cuffs to put on his new prisoner.

Theriot froze. He heard sounds coming from the open door to a large bedroom. He pointed the gun at the hall entrance as Foster Landeaux rushed out. "David, what's going on?" Foster asked.

Agent Van der Hove held her gun steady with her right hand, deftly pulling her new camera up with her left hand. "The real question is what's going on with you, big boy?" she asked. "Smile for the camera." She captured the image in front of her with a flash that blinded Foster momentarily.

Foster blinked in disbelief. He stood alone, naked but for nylon underwear and stockings, a leather choker and a whip held menacingly in his right hand. His lipstick was smeared, but his eyeliner was perfect.

Chapter Forty-Six
New Impressions

"Maggie" twirled in front of a full-length mirror at Gerald's Boutique on Main Street. She looked stunning in her new designer dress, a tight, short, white knit number with matching shoes. Her new clothes made her the poster child for Beverly's charity which, of course, was the purpose of the exercise.

Meadow was quickly becoming a masterpiece of cultural benevolence for her mistress. Even her dialect was changing as she adapted to the patterns of the local elite, following Beverly around dutifully between bible classes at First Baptist, Garden Club meetings at the Bailey Hotel and then, of course, tea with the rich and famous of Bumkin. Staying in character as Maggie was no different than acting out roles with her more physical customers.

Meadow enjoyed playing to Beverly's ego. She acted shamed by the legacy of her race, acknowledging her obligation to help diffuse the racial tension for her community.

"I am no longer a black person," Meadow, a.k.a. Maggie, told Beverly with smooth sincerity. "I am becoming a white person in a black body, thanks to you." Beverly beamed at her creation and opened her checkbook to pay for most anything Maggie needed to complete her transformation. Beverly wondered what Reverends Hezekial and Hudson would have to say about her transformation. Surely, if it could be done with Maggie, it could be done with an entire school of ignorant, poor, little nigger girls, Beverly thought.

"Maggie" pressed Beverly to visit the Tremblays at their home as sort of a "coming out" party. They walked hand-in-hand over the fine polished oak floors of the Tremblay mansion. It was kept in immaculate condition by lesser beings who scurried around meekly. The black maid who led them into the main room eyeballed Meadow with suspicion, startled that she would suck up to Beverly of all people.

Mrs. Lilly Tremblay walked down a large winding staircase to greet them by a luxurious couch, under a French chandelier suspended from the twenty-foot ceiling. Meadow quaffed her reaction for fear of exposing her vulnerability to the social vultures who circled around her. Still, it was spectacularly exciting.

Lilly was a squat woman with a kind face, an elegant version of the once-tiny debutante who married Bubba twenty-three years prior. She had aged well. She walked gracefully toward Beverly and Maggie, earnestly going out of her way to compliment Maggie on her new outfit. Lilly clasped Maggie's hand and welcomed her into her home, even as she privately admitted to herself that there had never been a black woman in her home who was not a maid.

The women took their seats in front of a tray of tea and sugar cookies. Meadow didn't like tea and requested coffee instead, earning a curious look from Beverly, who vaguely remembered the girl's coffee allergy.

Meadow saw the maid shaking her head in disgust as she walked back to retrieve coffee. "White" prejudice was civil compared to black prejudice; Meadow knew. Her only protection was the height of the social ladder she had climbed in record time.

Beverly opened the formal introduction of the afternoon with a smile. "Lilly, I wanted you to personally meet Maggie. Maggie has become a dear friend of mine," Beverly said, her voice oozing with empathetic honey. "We both know how difficult it is to find, shall we say, 'compatible' women in the black culture. I want to assure you that Maggie is not like that. Maggie is a mulatto.

"And Maggie has made a real effort to improve herself above other less desirable people in her class, if you know what I mean. If you just could have seen the mess she was in when we first met, you wouldn't believe how well she has done! Of course, Tom and I have supported Maggie's, shall we say, 'transformation.'" Beverly giggled, leaning back against the soft, Italian silk cushion, while holding her napkin to her mouth in a genteel way.

"Maggie and I thought it was time for her to meet you and Bubba because we all know that we just have to learn to live together. Maggie is particularly concerned about the prosecution of the black girl involved in that terrible Quinine incident. Since we are all activists in our fair town, I knew that you would be coming across Maggie sometime and I wanted you two to be friends."

Lilly Tremblay smiled graciously, trying her best to understand her guests. She wasn't sure what this was all about. It was always hard to figure out the motivations of people like Beverly, born to play a perennial second fiddle. Beverly had no chance of rising beyond her own station in life if she remained in Bumkin. Maybe she identified with this mulatto person? So why not let Beverly have her fun and get some accolades for educating black people?

Lilly eyeballed "Maggie" behind a plastic smile. There was a canny quality about her that seemed familiar, camouflaged by the subdued colors and expensive fabric, at Beverly's expense.

"Well," she finally spoke, after finishing her tea. "This is quite a surprise. You know, I don't think that these floors have ever seen a black woman in high heels!" It was all she could think to say.

"Maggie" smiled and laughed, as if to acknowledge how special they all were. Then she feigned humbling herself before the powers-that-be to her tactical advantage. "Mrs. Beverly has been most patient teaching me how to walk properly for this occasion."

Lilly smiled back and patted her hand. "You're doing great."

"Is it true that you are married to Mr. Bubba Tremblay?" Meadow asked behind her guise.

"Why yes, it is, Maggie. Bubba and I have been married since I graduated from NSU, back when it was an all-girls' school up in Natchitoches. My daddy introduced Bubba to me as the man of my dreams and you know, he was absolutely right."

Meadow jerked the line to set the hook. "He is such a great man. I know that his new school required a lot of guts to build. Few men could take such a bold stance. Someday I would like to teach there myself."

Lilly instantly imagined the media hype of a charming mulatto teaching at Bubba's school for white people. What a coup! It was a sign from God. "Oh, how wonderful, Maggie. Do you think you are qualified to teach?" she asked, not that it really mattered.

"Well, Mrs. Tremblay, I have made application to get into LSU and I know that they would help me through a work training program," she lied. "Do you think it would be inappropriate for me to ask Mr. Tremblay for a recommendation to get into college?"

Lilly shivered with expectation. She could already see the headlines: "Tremblay Charity Gives Poor Black Woman Scholarship to Teach at Bubba's School." "Dear," Lilly gushed, "I will personally help you. Let's go talk to Bubba right now. Why don't I see if he's in his office?"

"How wonderful!" Beverly cheered, clapping in rapture. There had to be an award from the Rotary Club in this somewhere.

"Ms. Lilly," Meadow put her hand on Lilly before she got up, leaning over close to her host in a hushed voice. "If you don't mind, I would like to discuss this matter with a man of Mr. Tremblay's stature alone, business like, you know. I do not want to impose on you. It is important for people like me to learn to stand on their own and set an example for the less fortunate people so that we can earn his respect," Meadow said, reeling in her fish.

Lilly Tremblay nodded her complete understanding, with tears in her eyes. "I am sure Mr. Tremblay will see you for a few moments, Maggie. Just one minute," she said, and walked into her husband's office. Bubba would love this.

Moments later the big oak doors to Bubba's office swung open and Lilly motioned for Maggie to come forth. Meadow looked nervously back at Beverly who smiled and patted her hand, beaming as if her own daughter was headed to her first communion.

Lilly walked across the marble floor and sat by Meadow, her heals echoing in the big room. "Mr. Tremblay has altered his schedule to meet with you a few moments, dear," Lilly said warmly. "Don't be scared, he's just a big teddy bear. He's at his desk. Take a seat in the office and wait till he finishes on the phone while Beverly and I visit."

Bubba sat in a red leather chair facing the window looking out over a large, well-tended pond surrounded by cut-flower gardens and weeping-willow trees. His back was to Meadow, with his stocking feet propped up on the windowsill as he barked orders into the phone. His big hand waved behind him, signaling "Maggie" to approach him while he carried on his conversation uninterrupted.

Meadow winked at the women she left behind and deftly flipped the big, brass lock quietly behind her. She pulled out the bobby pins in her hair, shaking her hair down from under a dressy hat that she threw onto a nearby chair, directly in front of Bubba. She walked behind him and ran her hands beneath the collar of the starched khaki shirt and over the big shoulders she well knew.

Bubba looked up behind him, startled, his eyes wide and quizzical. He knew the face but couldn't believe the vision. Something was wrong. How the hell could this be? Meadow put her finger up to her lips as Bubba stuttered in his conversation. The other voice on the phone kept talking.

Meadow pulled up her skirt ever so slowly, revealing black silk stockings and a garter belt he had given her, framed against red silk panties and creamy skin. Bubba went silent. He smiled and ran his hand under her dress, fumbling with the phone and holding his breath as Meadow unzipped his pants and kneeled between his legs, quickly assuming a familiar position with aggressive passion. Bubba squeezed the phone and bit his lip with full force in ecstasy, groping her breast with his free hand as he finally shut off the conversation he had already forgotten.

"How?" he whispered as he fell under Meadow's spell. "How did you get in here?" It was too much for Bubba to grasp, not that he cared. He pressed her head down and enjoyed the moment as Meadow willingly went down on him for more.

Moments later she stood over him. He was spent, his head spinning. Meadow straightened herself up and pulled her hair back into its original bun. She bent over him, looking into Bubba's helpless eyes; the prey had become the predator. Slowly, Meadow raised her skirt over shapely thighs for him to see, sliding her panties off with a wiggle and wink. She held them up in silence like a dark angel, and then stuffed them into his big shirt pocket as he gazed at her with helpless eyes, the phone still hanging in his hand.

Meadow grabbed her hat, placing it meticulously on her head with a smile before she left him aroused yet again. Stopping momentarily, she looked back over her shoulder and caught her breath. Bubba had pulled the panties out and was looking at them curiously. He read the message written by a black market as mouthed it to himself:

THE CABIN
6 TOMORROW

Meadow pulled the door open and walked out to the big hallway in a stately manner with visible new pride as she met Mrs. Lilly Tremblay and Beverly.

"How was your talk?" Bubba's wife queried.

"Oh, my Lord, Mrs. Lilly, it was a mouth full," she sighed in her best Southern drawl.

Chapter Forty-Seven
Reactions

J udge Jim sat alone in his office, massaging his head with one hand as he downed another shot of Southern Comfort in the other, his habit in times of stress. His list was scribbled out in front of him. Since the meeting yesterday, he knew he had to be proactive, and he had very little time to get results. Judges rarely understood how to take action. Their job was to diagnose the sins of society, not engage or capture them.

This wasn't just a political or legal issue to be negotiated over whiskey and beer. It was, in fact, a criminal cover up. Covering up a racial murder that opened wide the racial wounds of Bumkin couldn't be handled in a congenial manner. Fortunately, even Sally understood that justice would only be served outside the legal system. Otherwise, it would not get done or it would decimate the town, and the Judge with it.

He had several fateful calls to make. Down deep he knew this was no less reprehensible than what he had already allowed, no, even enabled, other people to do. He dialed the first call.

"God Bless you today, Mount Zion Church," Reverend Hezekial's effusive voice bubbled over the line. "How may I help you?"

"Reverend, this is Judge Jim," the Judge said gruffly, trying not to slur.

"Hello, Judge." There was hesitation in Hezekial's voice. He remained unsure of his legal exposure after the meeting in Judge Jim's chambers, even after Sally made the Judge reassure them that they all had "Local Amnesty," subject only to their total silence. She had even managed to protect him from disclosure that he was the father of Maggie's child. Throwing Snowball's name out as the lucky man was brilliant; it diverted everyone from him while it created an obligation to Sally which Hezekial knew he would be long in paying. "What can I do for you, Judge?" Hezekial asked, mustering some of his normal cheer.

"We need to talk about the Crews, that gang you told me about that had reason to threaten Deputy Foster."

Hezekial found it an odd request in the wake of the larger issues. "Why yes, Your Honor, I'm pleased to know that you are concerned about their presence. What can I tell you about them?"

"I would like you to communicate with them confidentially."

"About what?"

Judge Jim downed a large swig of whiskey. He answered Hezekial's question cryptically and the phone grew silent. Hezekial suddenly understood. God delivered justice in many forms. Who was he to intervene?

After his call to Hezekial, Judge Jim dialed another number and waited for the connection.

"Winchester," a voice answered.

"Gil, this is Judge Keys in Bumkin. How are you?"

Gil looked into the phone suspiciously. "Well, I'm fine, Judge. What's up?" he asked guardedly.

"Gil, I'm calling to make a recommendation which I believe would help you and the entire Bumkin community."

"Okay, Judge, shoot." Gil couldn't wait to hear what the Judge had to offer.

"Seems like young Bam Callahan was doing some college work ahead of schedule and he got upside-down with your principal at Bumkin High, who is now holding him hostage to make him return to high school. Now, why the hell anyone would want that kid back in his school is beyond me. Anyway, I think the kid should be allowed to move on to college so he doesn't get himself and the whole damn town into trouble. I want Callahan out of town before he and the principal shoot each other, or the kid blows the school up." And before he can tell anyone what he knows, the Judge thought to himself.

"I hope Bam is a better shot than Greely," Winchester responded. He knew something bad had to have happened for Judge Jim to interject himself into the situation. He decided to play ball.

"Judge, let's agree that I won't ask about your sudden interest in young Bam or your bullshit concern about 'my' principal. You can assume, off the record, of course, that I think Greely is one generation removed from Cro-Magnon Man as an educator. The real problem remains that we have to create transcripts for high-school courses that Bam never attended because he has been in college on an unofficial arrangement with the Dean, before the Dean died."

Judge Jim was prepared for that. "Gil, let's assume that I could find those missing transcripts. What happens next?"

"Say what? You found the transcripts, Judge?" Gil asked, incredulous at the thought.

"Yeah, Gil. I just woke up and found them on my doorstep this morning. Damnedest thing I've ever seen. Tripped right over them."

Gil thought intently about the Judge's meaning, unable to figure it out in short order.

"Alright, Judge, I'll play with your rules. Bam would have to take the ACT test two years early. If he did okay on the test, we could get him into college on a GED. He wouldn't have to finish high school, but the college would have to let him in again, which I could probably arrange. If we were smart, we could get him out of town before the fall semester started."

"Sounds like a deal, Gil," Judge Jim said with finality. "What say we agree to make it happen?"

"Hold on, Judge," Gil demanded. "I'm not finished. You haven't told me what I get out of this deal."

"Why would you deserve anything, Gil? I thought this was your mission in life, to help educate kids." The Judge wasn't used to negotiating his position.

"That is my passion, Judge. And I'm losing my number one lightning rod for educating the Bumkin community about drugs, sex, and rock 'n roll because you want him out of your hair. Having Sally and her son in the middle of things has put the school board and the town at risk and in the headlines, with drugs on the front page. Your Bumkin Police Department can't find their ass with both hands, so Bam is an invaluable tool for me. That kid has pissed off more people in one month than you or I could afford to piss off in a year."

"You want the kid gone for exactly the reason I want him here; he obviously knows too much. He's a pain in the ass for you and the good Baptists at First Bubba, but not for me, Judge. I love reading about that new welcome sign in your town newspaper. I want the *Bumkin Record* to print a fold out of Bam giving the system the finger. Bam can stay stuck in Bumkin's face for another two years for all I care."

"Humph," Judge Jim growled over phone. "Okay, Gil, what do you want?"

"What I have always wanted from the Bumkin judicial system - a major drug bust, for real. If you can't get the names of the pushers in town, I can sure as hell provide them to you … or you can call Bam for their phone numbers. I'm talking twenty-five to thirty people to shock the shit out of everyone and give me a fighting chance to take back my school. I either get my school back or you get to live with Bam for another couple of years. And by the way, I *will* agree to not ask you or him what this is all about."

"Okay, Gil, you have a deal," Judge Jim said. Another complexity, but a diversion might not be bad idea.

"When? And when do I get Bam's transcripts?"

"Soon. On both counts," Judge Jim answered calmly. "Stand by for a few days. I will call." He hung up the phone quietly, totally exasperated.

The Judge took a set of keys from a hidden compartment underneath his desk drawer. He walked over to his office door and locked it to ensure his privacy, then he opened the giant, ornate armoire which graced the back corner of his office. It wasn't just the gold leaf trim or the elegance of its design that defined it; rather, it was what it had protected for a hundred years that mattered.

The Judge unlocked the door, then pulled the wooden handle hidden in the base which released a fake interior wall, revealing a hidden space. Inside a white phone sat in front of a beveled mirror with and emerald green satin cloak and the hood of the Grand Dragon of the Ku Klux Klan neatly folded over a wooden hanger.

The Judge dialed numbers on the phone and waited for a voice to answer. "Franklin, we have a problem. It's time for a drug bust. A major bust."

~~~~

Across the street Kipper opened the seizure notice from the FBI. The notice read:

By Order of the 5th District Federal Court, all assets of Dynasty Oil are to be frozen and placed under a trustee to be named by the court, effective immediately.

Kipper knew he and David were going to have a lot of mad creditors calling him. "Why Dynasty?" he asked the agent.

"Misappropriation of funds. All those widows and orphans David Tremblay sold interests to thought their money was going into producing oil wells in Nigeria to replace depleted deposits in the basin. Tremblay forgot to tell them he was subsidizing his oil speculation with marijuana production. Impressive earnings, but illegal activity. Worked well until he hit a major dry hole in Nigeria."

Kipper couldn't believe what he was hearing. "What about the bank?" he asked in a panicked voice.

"The money stays on deposit but it can't be used for lending. The board needs to find a new owner for the bank immediately. As a practical matter, it's your only chance of preventing a run on the bank and keeping it in operation. The Bureau knows it has a case against the bank, but we have no desire to hurt the community, as long as the bank changes hands quickly. We only want Dynasty."

Kipper knew that "the board" meant Bubba and David Tremblay. "How long do we have?"

"One week," Agent Damon said, his monotone void of sympathy.
~~~~

Chapter Forty-Eight
Payback

Meadow drove Beverly's sedan slowly up the gravel road, mesmerized by her surroundings. Childhood images began to resurface. The magnolia tree's heavy limbs spread out fifty feet to embrace the meadow she had been named after. Tears welled in her eyes as she fought off the swell of anger. She jammed on the brakes and slammed her hand against the steering wheel in rage. "That bastard!" she screamed. The lost life she could never recover seemed to rise around her, consuming her with pent-up hatred for the man who had abandoned her, then deceived her in the worst conceivable way.

Meadow saw a flicker of moonlight from the police car windshield, hidden in a cluster of the pine trees. Foster was keeping a lone vigil over the cabin rendezvous as he agreed.

Meadow let the big car come to a halt at the cabin porch. She got out and looked around, then lit a cigarette, signaling Foster she was going inside.

For a fleeting moment she considered life's cruelty. If only Quinine had been a real man, a man who protected her, not simply a white man's messenger. But he had accepted her abuse by whitey as easily as he had accepted his own.

Meadow stared at the cabin door and at Bubba's truck. Somehow, she had always known it was him. Even while he was just a random customer, somehow, she knew who he really was. He was merciless. He paid for her favors generously with stolen money and deception. It had to be him. They were too much alike.

She didn't deny that their relationship carried an animal arousal, however disgusting and immoral. Was sexual attraction to a father you didn't know immoral? What did she care? She wanted control of him as much as he wanted control of her. Was it revenge or lust? She needed to be wanted and he needed her to want him. She loved him and hated herself. Or did she love herself and hate him? Once again, it didn't really matter. It had boiled down to survival and she would always be a survivor.

She threw her purse over her shoulder with a flare as she walked up the wooden stairs to the front door of the cabin, where history began.

The haze from the bayou had just begun to roll over the meadow like a silent white wave. Meadow pushed the hinged door open, instantly feeling the warmth of the crackling fire. She moved slowly, looking cautiously around the open room.

A wicked smile crossed her face, her heart pumping furiously with expectation as she crossed the threshold. She jumped with fright from the force of the door slamming shut against its frame. Bubba stood behind her leering, ready to strike.

Meadow raised her hands to her face in fear as two giant arms surrounded her, groping and pushing her toward the table behind her. Bubba pulled at her clothes like a rampaging bear, tearing the straps off her shoulders as he pinned her face down on the table. Her purse fell open onto the floor with a hard thud.

"Needed some more, huh, bitch? Couldn't stay away from me, could you?" he yelled, his face red with rage. The coarse tone dropped as he buried his face into the nape of her neck. Meadow's experience quickly overcame her impulses. She arched her back, pushing her chest out as she caressed him. She pulled his head closer to her..

"I want to talk-" her voice cracked.

"Shore you do," he bellowed. What the hell did you think you were doin' bringing your black ass into my home, in front of my wife?"

He forced her face into the table, ripping her shirt and pulling her bra down violently. Meadow obediently bent over the table and spread her legs.

"You little whore, wait till I'm finished with you," Bubba slapped her down and yanked her skirt over naked buttocks as he fumbled with his belt.

Meadow could see the shadow of the gun handle flicker on the fireplace in front of her. It came down quickly, just before she heard the soft thud of the handle sink into Bubba's skull. His body slumped, pining her against the table. His eyes rolled into his head as she pushed him onto the floor.

She turned to see Foster holstering his gun behind her. She slid off the table and pulled her skirt down, staring angrily at Foster. She walked toward him and slugged him in the face, rocking him back on his feet. "Took you long enough, asshole!" she screamed. "You leave me to rot in a fucking prison, then you're late to keep me from being raped."

"Since when did you mind?" he replied coolly, feeling his lip gently for a trickle of blood.

"I mind! I ain't your queer buddy, you know."

"Back off, bitch. If you hadn't shot Quinine, neither one of us would be here."

"What was I supposed to do, smart guy; go on a honeymoon after Bubba blows the whole plan, like some schoolboy? You think I was going to turn over the deed to this asshole so I could stay trapped in this fucking cabin like my mother? History ain't repeating itself this time around, big boy." Meadow spat out her fury at Foster and then turned to Bubba, lying unconscious on the floor.

"I'm sorry it turned out this way," Foster apologized meekly. "The only way I could protect you from him was in jail. Hey, it worked out better than I would have thought, but..."

"But what?"

"But David's in jail," Foster said, searching for sympathy.

"What happened?" Meadow asked, now concerned with the unexpected change in events.

"The Feds caught on to Dynasty. They've seized the company's cash for laundering drug money. Bubba's drug money." Foster looked down at Bubba with disgust. "Not even he knows yet." She could see the impact on Foster. He was fighting hard to hold back tears.

"The FBI let me off the hook because of Dad. He wants me to squeeze information out of Bubba and David. I'll never see him again." Foster began to cry. Meadow leaned over and gave him an unexpected hug.

The big face on the floor beneath them opened his red eyes and looked up groggily, groaning in pain. "What about David?" Bubba asked, almost involuntarily.

Meadow kneeled down, a sinister sympathy on her face. "Your special boy, my half-brother, is queer as a three-dollar bill, Daddy-dearest. Your deputy here has been porkin' him for years. What do you got to say to that?"

A sheath of consciousness reclaimed Bubba, his temples pulsing as he attempted to engage the conversation. His eyes widened with the gradual recognition of his circumstances.

"You dumb bitches," Bubba managed a laugh at his own choice of words. "You think I don't know? What the hell was I gonna do, let the whole town know? Make David Queen-for-a-Day at the town fair?"

Foster stared at him in shock. "You knew and you still blackmailed me for being gay to do your dirty work?" he asked, his temper rising.

"Dirty work you liked, you sadistic fag. You never walked away." Bubba spat out blood as he attempted to sit up.

Meadow shook her head and looked up at the ceiling. "Man, you just never know what shit life is gonna throw atcha'. Like findin' out that your biggest customer is actually your father and a pimp for your queer half brother's boyfriend. What a fucked up world," she exhorted, her voice becoming steely cold.

"So, Pops, you knew about Fostie here and you kept his secret so he could service David and manage your whores, like me. And what better way to keep your hookers in line, huh, Big Daddy?" she asked, mocking him. "Until us 'girls' started talkin'. Then I pieced it all together. You never needed the property deed to steal Quinine's oil revenues and you didn't even want it in your name while you were growing marijuana on it. But when Dynasty stock began to move, you got greedy. You could swap the land for more stock, pocket ten million and still keep the oil and the crop. You're a greedy bastard."

"And you aren't?"

"Like father, like daughter, Pops." She looked back at Foster matter-of-factly. "Okay Fostie, where's the money?"

"Where's the deed?" he demanded.

"You first, I was the one you left in jail."

Foster pulled a large envelope out of his jacket. "$300,000 cash and all the food stamps you can eat. Been pretty easy pickings since I took over Quinine's run." He plucked out half of the contents of the envelope and placed it in in a neat stack on the table. "Shame we couldn't have kept it going longer. But it won't do me any good without David," he sighed.

"Half of $10 million in land and oil might make it easier to live without David," Meadow said.

"Did you get the will into the bank box?" Foster asked.

"Even better. The Preacher is delivering a copy of it and the marriage certificate to the Judge."

A brief smile of appreciation flashed over Foster's face. She was indeed her father's daughter. "Okay, what about him?" He pointed at Bubba, the hatred in his voice palpable. "You son-of-a-bitch! You blackmailed me into handling your problems and you used David to wash your money." Foster's hand unsnapped the holster on his gun as his emotions spiraled, his face growing redder as he stared down at Bubba.

Bubba pointed up at Foster from the floor with a shaky finger. "Now look here, Foster, just kill this bitch and I'll get David out of jail for you. How about that? Just kill her like you did that other nigger and you and David can walk into the sunset together with a bundle of money."

Meadow looked down at Bubba with a sneer, "You never quit, do you?"

She slid her hand around Foster as if looking for security, then yanked his gun from his holster. Before Foster could stop her, she raised her knee up and stomped Bubba in the chest with a spiked heel, forcing the air out of his lungs and his head back onto the floor.

Foster looked at her appreciatively. "Thanks, Meadow," he said softly. "I was about to go out of control again. I would have killed him."

"Can't let that happen, Fostie. You can't let this dick get to you. After all, I had to kill Quinine for this prick. After I got a signed will and the deed, it should have never happened." She looked down at Bubba, "Couldn't let it go, could you, Pops? Why did you need another 300 acres so bad?"

Beads of sweat rolled off of Bubba's forehead. He had to keep talking. "Because he wouldn't sell it to me. Everyone knew it was the best oil production in the state. It was like a trophy he didn't deserve."

"His name was Quincy. And he was my husband, Bubba." She laughed with hollow humor. "You had long since taken his life away, just like you took mine. But he is the last nigger you ever gonna own. Time to beg for mercy, you son-of-a-bitch."

"Wait, you dumb bitch, you're a felon on the run, you can't even own the damn property in this state!" he screamed. "Let me help you."

"No chance." She fired the thirty-seven-caliber round into his chest without hesitation. Bubba's body jerked from the impact as blood splattered the floor and wall.

Foster jumped at the sound of the discharge. He hadn't expected her to kill Bubba. But then, he hadn't expected her to kill Quinine either. As if on cue, his radio crackled to life as the sound reverberated in the small confines of the cabin.

It was Danny. "Foster! What's your status?"

Foster pulled the mike up to his mouth, wiping the sweat off his face as Bubba's blood pooled into crevasses on the uneven wooden planks.

"Foster here. All okay, Danny. What's up?" he asked, in a surprisingly cheerful tone.

"I just got an emergency call from The Cat. They got a real ruckus goin' down. They need you there right away."

Foster nodded to Meadow. Taking his gun from her and holstering it, he grabbed his envelope and slid it between his back and his holster. He needed a good fight to clear his mind. It would be his last, official duty before he left Bumkin for good. He spoke to Meadow. "I'll meet you in the morning as planned," he said, and ran out the door.

Meadow picked up her purse and headed back to Beverly's car. She thumbed through the stacks of hundred-dollar bills and food stamps in her envelope. Satisfied it was all there, she peeled off her gloves and stuffed them into the envelope. Then she changed into an old dress as she watched Foster's red and white lights race out of the driveway in a cloud of dust, sirens blaring.

He was a queer killer, she thought, but he was very honest. And she intended to be honest with him. She would sign over a split of the oil and land while they both went underground. She wanted to retain his services for the future, just in case. Meadow thoughtfully checked her purse to make sure her gun was still inside it. She still needed it.

Chapter Forty-Nine
Bad Call

Foster drove his police car with the intensity of a hunted man, the pedal stomped fully to the floor in a high-speed plunge toward The Cat. He had to maintain the perception of being on patrol so he wouldn't be tied to Bubba's death. He had left no evidence at the cabin. He kept only his cash and his revenge.

He began to weep uncontrollably as memories of David boiled through him. His lover of ten years was certainly going to prison. They would both be left to a miserable existence. Now his father and the entire world would know he was gay. Everything he had worked for, his only links to a normal life, had evaporated. Any chance of him and David ever being accepted as a couple was gone forever.

He fought to get a hold of himself, wiping his eyes as his professional training slipped into place. Bubba's death was unplanned but overdue. It was time to put it all behind him. He had work to do.

Any trace of the murder would fall on Meadow. She had pulled the trigger on both Quinine and Bubba for no good reason. She had made sure he watched her both times, like an audience to an execution. She was killing for revenge.

The hundred fifty grand in his back pocket was little comfort given his loss, but it was good for a new start until the big payoff came with the oil property. He had pilfered money from Bubba for years to build a decent retirement stash. He had planned to travel the world with David, living off of oil revenues, but that was not to be.

Foster grit his teeth and gathered a second wind. Now he got to stop a bunch of black gang members from tearing up a bar and killing themselves. He relished the moment, the excitement, the power. Maybe he was more of a kindred spirit to Meadow than he knew. He smiled with a calmness that overcame him when he resumed his control over life and death.

Foster wheeled the big Ford onto the sidewalk with an abrupt shudder, leaving the sirens blaring as the lights flashed under The Cat's neon sign. The faint smell of scorched rubber sifted into the humid night air, mixed with sewage and sweet honeysuckle in bloom. He threw the car door open and stood to face the front door of The Black Cat Saloon. Normally, there would be a crowd standing outside, waiting patiently for the fight inside to stop so they could return to their favorite watering hole. It usually took nothing more than Foster's grand entrance to clear the bar and get everyone settled down. It was oddly peaceful tonight.

Foster checked his watch, unholstered his pistol and pulled his billy club from beneath the driver's seat. He grasped the club with one hand and his ivory-handled Colt 45 with the other. He needed to vent some frustration, and this was a great time to do it. It was his right. He was the law in this town. This would be a fitting statement before leaving to find a new life.

Foster momentarily envied blacks, they had nothing to hide. Better to be recognized in a black body than hiding out as a gay man in plain sight in a white body.

Now he got to fight back, to feed his anger. He swaggered toward the door of The Cat, his billy club moving in a menacing circle. Foster stopped short of the door momentarily to peer through a broken window. Three black men playing cards sat at a dimly lit table. There were only a few cars, he noticed, and no visible signs of violence. It was quiet, too quiet. He grabbed the walkie-talkie on his belt.

"Unit 1. Danny, I'm in." He waited for the normal high-pitched response but got nothing. "This is Unit 1, Danny, I'm at The Cat. All quiet." Static crackled in the silence. Must be a radio problem, Foster thought.

Across town Danny Guillory poured his first cup of coffee for the night watch. The switch on his radio was off. Snowball had taped a neat sign on the receiver that said it was being tested and couldn't be turned on till morning hours. It seemed a little odd, but Danny was never inclined to ask questions.

Foster pushed the door in with his foot, knowing his silhouette would be highlighted by the streetlights behind him. It was his standard grand entrance into The Cat. The door creaked open slowly, revealing the same docile card game. The black card players ignored the white cop. They were all dressed in red, Foster noticed. A slim, busty woman stood behind one of the players in a satin red dress with a plunging neckline. She was too classy to be a barmaid. Her black skin and long black hair shone against the shiny cloth. She watched Foster serenely, shaking her head sadly as if she were in a dream while she sipped crème de cocoa from a glass.

A large plastic sheet was spread out on the floor like construction had been underway, Foster noticed. He froze. Something was wrong, very wrong.

The leader spoke up. "So, the big dude done come to visit us po' black folks again. He done come to deliver whitey justice to da Cat," Tyrone said loudly, calmly, never looking up from his cards.

Foster snarled, holding his pistol up, cocked and loaded. What the hell was going on?

The thunder of the door swinging against him answered his question before he could respond. He threw his arm up in defense, only to hear a sickening crack of bone as the edge of the door cut into his arm with unexpected force. His gun landed with a metallic thud, skidding over the floor as he stepped backward to regain his footing.

Two red-shirted black men emerged from behind the door. Two others came from outside. They were all young and muscular, unarmed street fighters. They moved with blinding speed, capturing him in a head lock, cursing and hitting Foster with their bare fists. Like locusts swarming a tree, they toppled him quickly, then forced him to the ground.

The struggle was over in seconds, too short to qualify as a real fight. They stood over him with a deadly silence. He quickly understood that judgment was being rendered as he gasped for air on the floor. He wheezed involuntarily, coughing violently while he cursed his smoking habit. He tried in vain to wipe the blood from his eyes. It had all happened so quickly.

An army boot stomped on the nape of his neck, forcing his face into the musty bar floor, thick with grime from eons of patrons past. He felt strong arms tying his hands and feet as the four fighters now lifted him off the ground and dropped him onto the plastic sheet.

"Well, Well. What we got here?" Tyrone asked euphemistically. "Look to me like we got a P-I-G, pig. This is the same PIG that killed my man Quinine and my man Lester," he said coldly, identifying Foster to a small congregation of Crews members.

Foster's head shifted back and forth. It was a setup. He was getting frantic. Where was his back-up car?

"Dey ain't comin', Pig. You done been set up by the Big Whitey. Ain't nobody wants your white ass around no more," Tyrone said as he bent down to pick up Foster's gun, making sure the chamber was loaded. He cocked it and pointed it at Foster's head.

Foster looked up at his black master. He tried to talk but gagged on his own blood. He shifted his body on his belly, steadying himself with arched feet as he got a breath, his eyes closed. "Don't. I'll pay you." His voice was raspy and scared.

"I don't need money, PIG."

"Everyone needs money." Foster shot back, his voice solemn.

The gun slowly lowered with a chuckle. "Guess I can't argue that, Pig. How much?"

"A hundred fifty thousand."

"Whooeee! You a rich PIG! Where's all that money?"

"Promise you won't kill me first." Foster demanded into the floor. He arched his back to look up at his captor.

"Damn, this pig can talk some talk, can't he?" the handsome Crews leader asked his men. They nodded in obedient agreement as their leader pondered his next move. He squatted down to look closely at Foster, now drenched in sweat, dirt and blood. "Okay Pig, I won't kill you. But you better have the money. Then we gonna talk." Tyrone nodded to one of his men who pulled a switchblade from his boot and cut Foster's bonds.

Foster's grimy body rose from the floor. The plastic crackled beneath his feet as he shuffled about. His eyes were swollen and red, blood dripped down his naval cavity into his throat, and his nose was broken, detached from its bone structure. Finally, he pulled his shirt up and clumsily felt for the envelope of money, handing it over to the Crews Leader like a peace offering.

"Cut dat man loose, he be telling the truth." Tyrone looked up at his men with a grin. "Dat's why dey call dem PIGS. Pride, Integrity and Guts. You men need to think on your feet under pressure like this PIG," Tyrone preached to his men.

Foster felt surprisingly relieved even though he knew he would never see the money again. There was more cash in his safe deposit box. He would just leave. He had no reason to stay. He struggled to gain his composure so he could make a quick but graceful exit.

"Well PIG, ah guess you done held up to yo' part of the bargain, so I ain't gonna kill you," Tyrone said casually. "No, siree, I am a man of my word. Mondo there behind you, he gonna kill you," he said with a sudden sneer.

The billy club slammed into the back of Foster's head before his emotions could register with his brain. The break in his skull sounded like a firecracker, followed by the nauseating soft thump of his face hitting the floor. A crimson pool of blood slowly spewed out of his ears and nose and began to collect on the clear plastic cover. His eyes remained glossed and wide open, frozen in the shock of sudden death.

Tyrone walked around the circumference of the plastic sheet, kicking its edges over to keep spattered blood off the wooden floors. He didn't want this incident to become a part of the cherished history of The Black Cat. Too much black blood had been spilled here to dishonor The Cat with the blood of a corrupt whitey. He looked up at Mondo, a black behemoth holding Foster's club over his shoulder.

"Break it," Tyrone commanded simply.

On command, Mondo slowly took the thick club in both hands and held it out in front of him. He brought it down as he raised his right knee in one single motion, snapping the club in half like a toothpick. Mondo held both pieces at his side, waiting for further instructions.

"Clean up the car and The Cat. Leave the pieces of the club in the front seat of the cop car as a message for whitey. Dump this pig in the bayou for gator meat and burn all his clothes and yours—everyone's clothes," Tyrone commanded. He peeled forty one-hundred dollar bills out of the envelope he was holding. He handed half over to Mondo, and folded half into his pants pocket. "And get some new threads for you and the boys. I'm tired of you looking like sloppy-ass niggers. Get everyone a good suit and tie. We got a funeral to attend."

Mondo smiled with obedience, but Tyrone caught him gaping at the envelope that still bulged with cash, and temptation.

"Dis shit here wasn't for any money, Mondo. Dis here was a policy matter," Tyrone explained. "You got that? You know what policy is, man? Policy is what you do when you gettin' big, man, when you gonna take over this little town! Policy is when you too big for mere money to matter. We done established that the Crews gonna protect its people on our terms. Now, you will deliver the rest of dis here money to Preacher Hezekial with instructions to spread it around to every church member who attended Lester and Quinine's funeral. You understand that? Every dollar!" Tyrone's voice boomed.

Mondo nodded. He didn't understand, but there was no doubt he needed to nod and obey. Tyrone dismissed him with a wave of the hand and walked back to his card game. "Rub my neck, baby," he commanded. The babe wrapped a shapely leg over his shoulder, massaging his neck as he gently rubbed a strong thigh covered with fishnet stockings. Tyrone leaned his head back into her satin skirt, pleased with the day's work.

Killing criminals could sure make you uptight.

Chapter Fifty
Details, Details

izery Lutz looked around the dark office for any sign of life. The afternoon bell had rung, the students were long gone. Greely had left early, disgusted with another day in purgatory. Satisfied she was alone, Lucery pulled out the bottom drawer on the old steel desk until it stopped with a metallic clank, then she fingered the alphabetical files until she found the "C" file that was particularly thick and unmarked. She slowly extracted a new Cosmopolitan magazine with the thrill of raw sin she hadn't felt for decades.

She put the magazine face down on her desk while she set the latch on the door. She pulled the window shades down, allowing barely enough light to see, then she turned on her desk lamp, slipped out of her shoes, and began to rub her feet together in girlish anticipation.

Lucery patted the back of her hair and straightened her full skirt emblazoned with pink camellias in a primly manner. Brother Hudson had already warned her congregation about Cosmopolitan Magazines. Any magazine without men in it must be pornographic, she knew. But she was in a difficult position. Her authority as First Assistant to the Principal meant that she had to protect young children from communists. Someone had to read this devilish stuff so they could warn parents and administrators. She turned the Cosmo pages as if they contained a mystic spell. She had made Herman buy it in an out-of-the-way convenience store in Evangeline Parish, where all of the Catholics lived. No one in her bible group had ever been able to find a copy. It was surprising how much Herman knew about it, now that she thought about it.

The buxom blond on the front cover was fully clothed, her short dress with the revealing neckline exposed perfect, white skin and lean, taut legs. At least she's white, Lucery thought. But she didn't have anything Lucery didn't have to offer. She eyed the image carefully with a smug smile and ran a finger down her own deep collar that covered size 42D breasts. What was so special about her? That wasn't no cleavage. Lucery had cleavage—lots of cleavage. The girl on the cover was just one of those hippie-bitch Yankee girls covered with too much makeup.

Lucery located her glossy Maybelline Raving Red lipstick and applied it subconsciously, pursing her lips as she pored over the magazine. Southern men wouldn't be attracted to a skinny rail like that one, she thought. She momentarily considered becoming a blond but decided it wouldn't be proper. All those teenage males at school would be all over her. It would disrupt the school.

Lucery gasped as she read the headline of the top article: 47 ways to have sex! Who were they kidding? Kids will believe anything these days. She shook her head in disbelief and immediately turned to page 69 to debunk the rest of the story. She was on position number eight when the telephone ringer made her yelp. She looked around to see if she had been caught, immediately stashing the Cosmopolitan back into its hidden file. Flustered, she answered the phone on its fourth ring, primping her hair to calm herself.

"Bumkin High," she answered.

"May I speak to Ms. Lucery Lutz, the Senior Assistant to the Principle?" a powerful, muffled voice asked.

Lucery instantly recognized the voice of the Grand Wizard and panicked for a fleeting moment. She picked up the magazine and began fanning herself to lower her blood pressure, she pulled her glasses off and let them fall to her chest. She was repentant; The Grand Wizard had caught her reading Cosmo.

"Lucery," the voice repeated ominously, the Knights of the KKK have need of your services," the voice boomed.

"Oh, My God! Mr. Wizard, I didn't know if I would ever hear back from you. I was just sitting here doing research for my bible class. How can I help?" she asked.

"Are you prepared to do what it takes for our cause?"

"Well, yes, of course, I am," she stammered with sudden conviction.

"You are aware of Bam Callahan, are you not?"

"Yes, I am. Can I help you get rid of him?" she queried without hesitation.

"Uh, well, yes. In a manner of speaking," the Wizard stumbled, not quite sure where Lucery was headed.

"Well, sir, I'm not particularly good at hurting people," Lucery explained, "but I got these cousins in Lone Pine that would be real good ..."

The voice quickly interrupted her, "That won't be necessary," he said. "I want you to fix his transcripts so he can be sent away to college," the voice interjected.

"What on earth for?" she complained, shocked. She looked around the office to make sure her voice hadn't spilled over into the outer halls.

"To remove a distraction from our cause. Your time is far more valuable dedicated to the cause," the Wizard explained patiently. "This is the only way to vanquish him, Sister Lucery, and only you can do it. You know that our battle is never fought in the open. Sometimes we must all make small sacrifices to achieve larger ends."

There was silence as Lucery contemplated what she must do.

"Well," she conceded with a sigh," I know what to do, if you're sure this is the only way."

Knowing he was on the threshold of success, the voice probed for a response. "This must be done immediately. Your services are deeply appreciated, Lucery. Perhaps there is something the Klan can do for you in return?" he pressed.

Lucery put her glasses back on the bridge of her nose and picked up the Cosmo. "Perhaps there is, Mr. Wizard, perhaps there is," she said thoughtfully.

Chapter Fifty-One
Protests

A week later, Ethan White looked closely at the AP photograph in disbelief, rereading the subscript while he waited for Reverend Hezekial Allen to answer the phone. White read the Associated Press footnote while he waited. Sure enough, the printed image had been distributed nationally, with credit to the *Bumkin Record*. The raging bonfire with the large burning cross left no imagination to its root cause, but it made no sense. Why would they do this? How could this be?

"Mount Zion," Hezekial's soothing voice came over the phone. He sat in his familiar position, barefoot at his desk; the same newsprint photocopy was laid out in front of him, a thousand miles south. It was right next to a story about race riots in Boston that had been precipitated by stringent bussing requirements.

"Reverend, this is Ethan White," the lawyer said matter-of-factly. He wanted to get straight to the point. "I am in bad need of clarification. Since when has the KKK begun burning Cosmopolitan Magazines to protest white women?

Hezekial was unperturbed. He raised his eyes toward the ceiling as he tried to deal with his Yankee brother's naiveté. "It's called marketing, Brother Ethan."

"Marketing?" Ethan inquired, surprised at the answer.

"Of course," Hezekial said in a knowing tone. "We live in a world of two household incomes now. White men alone cannot support the Klan. Today it takes the participation of women also."

"But they are protesting against white women here, Hezekial," Ethan contended in his most lawyerly voice.

"No, Brother Ethan," Hezekial corrected him, "they are protesting against sexually-appealing black and white models used as cover girls for all of those things which threaten redneck women. Direct your attention, sir, to the crowd in the picture."

Inside his Boston high-rise office, Ethan White looked closer at the picture, forcing himself to use his hated bifocals. The small crowd in the background gradually came into focus. It was mostly frumpy, heavy-set women in long skirts. "I'll be damned," he said to himself, nodding silently.

Hezekial smiled as he leaned back in his chair. "Not many Cosmo models in that crowd, are there Brother Ethan? Ever been to a redneck bible study?" he asked euphemistically. "This is a way for the KKK to mobilize the women in their ranks. It is apparent that their hatred is not limited to black women, it includes beautiful women in general. Of course, you and I know it's really a rally for anyone that doesn't look like everyone at the rally."

Ethan White sat up in his chair in thoughtful recognition of his lack of understanding of his enemy. "Come see me about your next grant, Hezekial," he offered.

"It would be my honor, Brother Ethan. By the way, I need to inform you about our approach to the growing level of gang violence. We are making unexpected progress in ministering to these young men in a way that benefits the entire community," his voice had a reassuring quality to it.

Hezekial pulled open his desk drawer and admired the stacks of $100 bills freshly delivered from the Crews messenger along with a surprisingly well-written personal note from Tyrone.

"I'm surprised to hear that, Hezekial, how did that come about?" Ethan questioned.

"God works in mysterious ways, Brother Ethan."

Chapter Fifty-Two
Clean Escape

Levi Epstein called Deputy Danny before putting final touches on the weekly press run.

"Any word on Foster, Danny?" Levi inquired.

"Found his police car today," Danny replied, clearly depressed.

"Where was it?" the reporter asked.

"Suddenly appeared in the exact spot where we found Quinine's car, Mr. Epstein."

"Any prints?"

"Nuthin at all. Clean as a whistle. Been washed and waxed, even the oil was changed with some of that expensive Pennzoil brand. Best damn detailing job I ever seen. I know he's dead, Mr. Epstein, and I know that black gang done it."

"How so?" Epstein asked.

"'Cause we found his billy club broke clean in half, not cut, broke in two and placed neat on the driver's seat just waitin' for us, but mostly 'cause there ain't no white folk that can detail a car that clean."

Levi held the phone on his shoulder while he took notes, smiling at the simple truth of Danny's assessment. "How can you prove it?" he asked bluntly.

"Impossible without a body, Mr. Levi," Danny acknowledged.

"Are you bringing in the FBI?"

"They say it ain't their dance. They all tied up on the David Tremblay scandal with Dynasty."

"How's Bubba?"

"Hanging in there. Doc cain't figure out why he didn't die but they think he might pull through. Apparently, the bullet missed the heart by a fraction of an inch and just sailed through his backside. He's probably ornery enough to live but he lost lots of blood. Going to be stayin' at the hospital for quite a while no matter what. The world is shore going to shit, Mr. Levi. At least we were able to confirm that Maggie ain't Meadow, so she could go home. Now we just got to find Meadow."

"Got a trail?" Levi asked.

"We think Meadow done high-tailed it on the evening Greyhound to Houston after she shot Bubba. I found Ms. Beverly's car there at the terminal. Shore wasn't as clean as Foster's car. Mud in it, some blood, Probably Bubba's. Oil needed changing. Not like Foster's car. That was the best damn detailing job I ever did see. Ain't no tellin' how long it took them boys to clean Foster's car."

"I got it about the detailing, Danny," Levi said softly as he hung up.

Chapter Fifty-Three
Busted

"Need help up here!" Bam yelled at Timmy. The line was getting ahead of Bam in the early-evening surge for beer, booze, and cigarettes. Twelve people were stacked up in front of Bam, another eight were mulling about in the store, looking to buy or steal something. It was prime time for shoplifting. Bam needed help.

Timmy moved quickly behind the counter space to assist Bam, bagging bottles and cans as fast as Bam could ring up sales. He still went through the actions of a lowly salesclerk although his real job had become that of a growing drug dealer, he had begun to consider himself a food stamp trader. The demand for his services had increased to a level that he would soon depart EZ Mart and open his own convenience store on the other side of the tracks, with some help from Bubba.

The untimely departure of Foster had left an unexpected vacuum within Bubba's gang that had benefited Timmy. The Sheriff remained preoccupied in a fictitious investigation of Quinine and Bubba, so Timmy had free run at the moment to do as he wished.

Of course, there was still the issue of Bam. The new store would put distance between the risk of him talking and Timmy's all-around safety. He had half expected Bubba to deal with the Bam issue himself, but there was too much going on and the loss of Foster left him without a henchman to do his dirty work.

"Been back to The Cat lately, dude?" a familiar voice queried.

Bam and Timmy looked up to see Dennis Johnson purchasing two fifths of cheap wine, little more than flavored alcohol. Bam laughed to deflect the question, not wanting to admit anything in front of Timmy. The town was still recoiling from two recent cop killings, and the attempt on Bubba's life, although there was still no explanation.

Bam, leaned toward Dennis to change the subject as Timmy joined. "So what's the story on Foster? Word is his last stop was The Cat." Bam asked in a low voice. Dennis thought for a moment, keenly aware of the history between Foster and Timmy. He had even bought some decent weed from Timmy in the past. "Word in the hood is he ain't comin' back, and the next cop better be black." Dennis said in a serious tone.

"What about bizness?" Timmy interjected coolly.

"Bizness is going to be handled by the Crews. There won't be any lone players left across the Tracks. They're tired of the middleman," Dennis stated emphatically, especially white middlemen. Timmy nodded. He knew he would have to make a deal with Tyrone, but that was okay. The Crews needed him to buy back the stamps which had become a lucrative business.

Bam noticed a big van pulling up to The Mart alongside a strange police car. He immediately gave Dennis a high five and motioned that he should leave. Sheriff Franklin Landeaux was walking into The Mart with a seriousness that spelled trouble, just as Dennis walked out of the opposing door.

Bam turned his attention back to a bustling line of customers but he noticed that the van seemed to be vibrating, shaking, as if there was activity inside it. He could see heads moving behind the driver, and arms waving out the windows. He thought he heard the howl of a dog and Clyde's characteristic laugh somewhere in the background. Across the street, the patrons and girls in training at the Golden Nugget gathered on the street corner, beers in hand, as if they were watching a parade.

The Sheriff nodded a curt hello to Bam and immediately requested a private meeting with Timmy. Bam nodded, keeping his head down as he took over the register. The Sheriff and Timmy talked quietly in the corner of the store. Bam fervently tried to reduce the growing chaos of the crowd building up inside EZ. The only good news was that the Sheriff's presence resulted in a sudden exodus of the younger patrons, reducing the chaos to some semblance of order.

Timmy glumly walked back to the register, motioning Bam that he needed to talk. He handed his keys and his wallet over to Bam, his face flush from the tension of the moment. "I'm getting busted Bam, along with half the town," he whispered. "Hold on to these for me and take my car home tonight," he asked politely.

"Sure," Bam said, sympathetically. He slid them into his pocket and watched as Timmy followed the Sheriff to the back of the store to read him his rights without interruption. Suddenly he noticed Clyde's big arms poking out of the van, waving at him. Next to him Clyde's smiling head became visible and beside him Spot, his Dalmatian howling at the nervous activity surrounding the van. Clyde beckoned at Bam to come see him.

By now the crowd inside the store had dissipated, or fled, depending on their personal circumstances while the Sheriff was cuffing Timmy. Bam locked the register and walked over to the cooler. He pulled a six-pack of Bud out and handed one to each of four patrons left standing in line, then asked them to wait while he checked out the action outside. Bam wasn't going to miss local history in the making. The door was barely opened when Bam could hear Clyde's voice; "Hey Bam! Bring me some olives!"

Bam smiled and retrieved a large jar of Clyde's favorite green olives off the shelf. He walked up to the paddy wagon and handed it over to the big, outstretched arm.

"Thanks, man, I'm starving. Hey, the gang's all in here," Clyde exclaimed, "even Spot!" We've been riding around for hours picking up everyone."

"You okay?" Bam inquired.

"Oh sure. It's been kinda fun. They searched the house and I had just made some brownies. I fed them to Spot and told them he had eaten the evidence, so they let him come too." Clyde unscrewed the top of the olive jar and fed one to Spot.

Bam laughed at the sight. "Spot likes olives?" he asked.

"Only when he's stoned. He's got the munchies," Clyde explained as Spot licked his chops.

Franklin came out of the store, leading Timmy into the van with Clyde, Spot and half the senior class of Bumkin High. Timmy stuck his head out the van window as they drove off, "Make sure you take care of my car!" he yelled.

~~~~

Kipper was tired from an exhaustive day of paperwork and analysis. He had convinced the board that they had no choice but to sell the bank and sold the feds on the benefits of letting the bank survive if new ownership took over. His head was still spinning. It had all happened at lightning speed. The rest of his day had been dedicated to collecting information for all the investigations that were underway. His secretary stopped by his office on her way home, turning off the lights in the bank as she made her final report for the day.

"Headed home?" he asked.

"Finally," she said, exasperated. She was still nervous about her job, despite Kipper's soothing confidence. "You should do the same."

"Got a way to go yet," he confided.

She handed over a plain white envelope with two sheets of paper in it. "I located this in a deposit box under the name of one deceased Quincy Tremblay Jackson," she said.

"Quinine?" Kipper asked.

"Yes," said Maude. "It's a last will and testament, fairly recent and very simple. He didn't have much, but then, maybe he had a lot. There is also a marriage certificate to Meadow Williams, signed by Rev. Hezekial Allen."

Kipper put down his pen and looked up at his secretary. "Is it in there?"

She nodded silently. "The deed is in the box, must have been there for forty years or so. Quinine willed the deed to 300 acres of oil producing property to his last surviving heir. Since Quinine had no kids and his only wife is a felon, Judge Jim said he would only confirm Maggie Williams as the last heir to Tremblay Williams blood line. Since felons abdicate their rights to inheritance in Louisiana, Maggie is the only known surviving cousin to Quinine. With
~~~~

David and Meadow convicted, Maggie is also the only direct heir of Bubba Tremblay who isn't in jail. I saw her just yesterday with Beverly Dunham."

"Wow," Kipper said in his understated manner. He could only speculate about the implications. "Maggie not only is a wealthy woman in her own right, but she will have a claim on Bubba's estate if he dies, or when he dies," he corrected himself. "I'm sure Beverly will be relieved to know that she was in better company than she realized."

"Want to know the best part?"

"There's more?"

"The will is notarized. It was witnessed by Officer Foster Landeaux. It's as good as gold.

The bank is going to have a new major depositor. She ain't white, and she ain't a 'he.'"

Chapter Fifty-Four
Exit Strategies

Meadow stepped off the bus in Oakdale, Louisiana, at midnight. The bus driver had cautioned her in a hushed voice that it was not a town where any young lady should be walking alone at night. Oakdale was a town of "red bones" a separate clan of rednecks that were particularly violent and particularly redneck. They tended to roam around in the darkness until they went deer or duck hunting before dawn.

Meadow thanked him sweetly for his concern. She smiled as she recalled satisfied customers from Oakdale during her time at The Spot. Red bones were certainly crude, but they made energetic lovers. They reminded her of uncared-for animals. She hadn't found them any more reprehensible than other males she had entertained. She grabbed her bags and walked across the two-lane highway to the Honeybee Inn, a garish motel constructed of horizontal wood planks painted in alternate black and yellow stripes. A neon bumblebee identified the front door in the late fog. The manager eyed Meadow suspiciously as she entered. Single, black women usually meant trouble, and he was in no mood to be turning away a mad husband or jilted boyfriend.

Meadow didn't waste any time putting the $100 bill on the counter, and he didn't waste any time taking it. "How many nights?" he asked hoarsely with the voice of a chain smoker and the smell of whiskey.

"One," she replied sweetly, "but only if you don't tell anyone I'm here."

"Where are you from?" he asked, curious.

"Nowhere if you want to keep the change." Even in his drunken haze, he knew it was double his normal rate, which meant he had $50 more to play bingo at the Moose lodge this month.

"Who would I tell, even if I knew who you were?" he joked.

"A man neither of us wants to see," she retorted in a stony voice.

He took the hint and carefully chose a room key that would ensure she stayed well out of sight. He never told anyone when blacks stayed at the motel anyway, it was bad for business.

Meadow slid the key in her pocket and walked over to the garbage dumpster in the parking lot. She heaved her new leather luggage case into the garbage with both hands, along with all of the expensive finery Beverly had purchased for her. "Fuck you, bitch," she said angrily.

Meadow clutched the remaining canvas duffel bag as she opened the door to her room. It was cleaner than she expected with a plaid blanket laid neatly at the base of the bed. She sat on the cheap mattress to measure its comfort. She was an expert on beds. As far as cheap beds went, this one wasn't as bad as many she had visited. She found herself exhausted, glad to have finished the first phase of her plan. She had twenty-four hours to rest up. Tomorrow would be a hell of a day.

Chapter Fifty-Five
Parting Shots

It had taken three days before anyone was allowed to visit Bubba. Judge Jim sat by his bed at Tremblay Memorial Hospital in Bumkin. He was dressed in his finest white shirt and vested suit, complete with a new Yves St. Laurent blue and red striped tie that gave him a new "corporate look," his wife said he deserved. He read over legal papers judiciously while waiting quietly for Bubba to stir. He had regained consciousness but was understandably weak from a near-death experience at the hand of his abused daughter, and her gun. Bubba recognized his visitor and tried to sit up, grabbing his chest in pain as he attempted to do so.

"Where is she?" Bubba demanded.

"Don't know," Judge Jim said.

"Where's Foster?"

"Gone. Probably dead. Never made it back from The Cat on his last official call. We can't find him. Course, he may not want to be found, but I suspect he's dead."

"Dead?" Bubba's eyes widened. "Did she set him up?"

"Someone did," Judge Jim replied honestly, without any visible emotion.

"Where is David?"

"He's in jail Bubba, and lucky he wasn't lynched by a gaggle of old women who he took to the cleaners. If it's any comfort, he says he doesn't mind jail.

He'll be in a low-security confinement for a long time. Lots of men, you know … that sort of thing," the Judge tried to obscure the obvious, shaking his head with sympathy. "Dynasty has filed for bankruptcy."

"What about the bank?" Bubba asked.

"The bank is going to be sold before the feds file a claim of money laundering and throw it into receivership. I offset your cash accounts at the bank against your debt. Even paid the school off and funneled some money into a trust account so the feds can't get their hands on it. The feds seized everything as ill-gotten gains. I struck a deal with them to take the proceeds from the sale of bank stock and let you off the hook on criminal claims, so you could keep your land," he replied in a comforting voice.

Bubba grabbed his chest where he was shot. He felt old and out of control, caught in a dream not of his making. "Who are we selling to?" he rasped dolefully.

"Me," Judge Jim said with a faint smile. "And at a very low price, I might add. You're also transferring the cabin and forty acres to Maggie, although it appears that Maggie stands to inherit Quinine's claim to the oil land and possibly more of your estate. She may even elect to go after past damages for stolen oil, but that's for a later discussion." He handed over a folder of papers to Bubba as he pulled a gold pen from his inside pocket. "Sign here, now."

Bubba didn't totally comprehend his new reality through the narcotic haze. His eyes still took on the cold fury that Judge Jim had seen many times before. "Why would I sign for you?" he demanded.

The Judge had never dared to return the stare in the past, but times were different now. "Because my silence is quite valuable. As an added benefit, all traces of the Citizens Council have been expunged along with two hundred acres of marijuana which will be burned off of Quinine's property before the feds can cause you any more problems. You're on your own going forward. And, oh, by the way, if anything suspicious ever happens to Maggie or me, a sealed letter will make its way to the FBI and the press that would leave you wide open for murder charges that are now pinned on Meadow. I doubt seriously whether those government agencies you bitch about, the ones that guarantee all your crop loans, would have much sympathy for you."

Bubba sat motionless, fuming and in pain.

Judge Jim stood up, hovering over the hospital bed impatiently. He extended the pen and nodded at the papers with a knowing smile. "Jail or farming?" he asked succinctly, "which do you prefer?"

Bubba took the pen and scribbled his name haphazardly as the Judge slowly turned the pages. He gently took the papers from Bubba, folded them, and placed one set of originals into an envelope that he licked and sealed, placing it on the nightstand labelled "Private and Confidential." He put the other set in his coat pocket.

"I wouldn't leave those papers around for just anyone to see," he told Bubba as he lay helpless.

"Don't take it personally," Judge Jim said. "We both woke up on the wrong side of the system one day, Bubba. I delivered Southern justice because I could, in a place where only locals can prevail, and I was wrong doing it," he admitted shamefully.

"You fucked me, you son of a bitch," Bubba wheezed, coughing involuntarily as he attempted to deliver a meaningful threat.

Judge Jim walked to the door, turning as he pulled it open. He stopped for a moment and looked back at Bubba for the last time. "Yes, I did. I had to, thanks to Sally Callahan, but don't think I didn't enjoy it." He departed with a lawyer's smile as the door clicked shut softly behind him. He had a new board of directors to convene at the bank.

"You'll pay for this," Bubba shouted.

"Not today," the judge retorted.

Chapter Fifty-Six
Workout

On the other side of town, Bam stood with the keys to Timmy's Camaro swinging from his finger. He had to admit, she was a beauty. Inside and out, she was as clean as the day he had bought the fire engine red sports coup. Timmy came out of his home, approaching Bam, and said, "Wow, Bam, you shouldn't have."

And you shouldn't have either, Timmy," Bam said with a menacing smile. "I told you not to get me involved in your drug business and I meant it. I had to clean up after you. Here are your keys." Timmy looked at Bam with confusion as he walked away and got into the waiting car that Clyde was driving. Timmy was to follow Clyde out to the site where they had been assigned community service for the drug bust. Bam had chosen to assist in order to earn some merit points with the Judge.

"Hold on, guys," Timmy said as he went to the trunk of the Camaro to unload his inventory. "This won't take but a minute."

Bam was safely in Clyde's car before the eruption came. Clyde looked at Bam for confirmation as Timmy was practically crawling into the empty Camaro trunk. "You cleaned out his whole stash?" Clyde asked.

"Yup," Bam confirmed. "Full of grass and hard drugs that he forgot to tell me about while I was doing him a favor. Burned it all up in the Sheriff's new trash barrel while he was locked up. I just don't like being used."

"I hear ya, bro." You probably did him a favor," Clyde bellowed over Timmy's ranting and raging outside. "Time to go."

Hours later, Clyde and Bam leaned back against a large oak tree as they passed around a thermos of a new drink called Gatorade. They were covered with soot and grime from the smoke, their eyes red and their heads fuzzy from the smell of marijuana fumes. Dark smoke bellowed into the air fouling the clear sky. The boys had been on bush-hogs all day, cutting marijuana and pushing it into piles soaked with diesel. They were watching Timmy chop his way through the brush of the nearby woods in search of more illegal crops.

"I'm surprised Judge Jim allowed Timmy to work out some of his fines," Bam observed. "The Judge ain't fooling me," Clyde said. "This ain't about community service. He knew Tim and I were the most qualified people in town to clear this crop and the Judge didn't want anyone to know."

"Guess that explains why he told us to keep this quiet," Bam observed.

"What a terrible waste," Clyde lamented as the fires rose to engulf the new cuts. "Good thing I kept a few bales in the barn for posterity. So, what are you doing tonight?" Clyde asked.

"First, I'm going to take a major bath, so I don't smell like a walking joint when I see Sally. Then, I'm going to lay low and rest up for the ACT test tomorrow. All of a sudden the school has worked out my curriculum problems," he snapped his fingers, "Just like that."

"Wow, how did that happen?" Clyde asked.

"Mom calls its Southern Justice. I don't have a clue and I don't care," Bam said cynically. "I don't have to go back to high school, but the hitch is, I have to pass the ACT test and I only have one shot."

Clyde could sense a tentative attitude. "So? Ride that train out of here, brother. When are you going to learn to quit? You don't have to fight every battle. Your ticket just got punched. Take it! When's the test?" Clyde asked.

"Tomorrow morning. You don't get it, Clyde. I'm a lousy tester. I'm worried. This is one big multiple-choice test. I always get uptight and over think the answers. I need tests where good quality bullshit counts. I'm already nervous. If I screw this up, I'm dead meat." Bam said. "It's like overtime on a goal line stand. Everybody's worn out and I've got to make a touchdown." He was getting depressed just thinking about six hours of testing the next day.

Clyde pulled a joint out of his pocket and lit it up. "Don't be depressed, Bam. Just suck it up," he laughed at his own joke as he inhaled the weed.

Early the next morning the familiar blue Trans Am drove up promptly at 7:00 AM at Bam's house. Bam was waiting fitfully outside. The March air was still nippy. Buster was fiddling with his new tape deck stereo from the insurance money that had paid for Buster's last two sports cars. None were his fault this year, but they sent him a termination notice anyway. Bad luck was uninsurable.

Buster wished he still had his old Challenger; it was more of a babe magnet. But right now, he was genuinely more worried about his best bud, Bam, the younger brother he never had. It was an irony to Buster that Bam had always had such difficulty taking tests. It made no sense. Bam knew his stuff—that was why he was such a pain the ass to everyone. He just over thought things and the pressure on him was too great. He looked like hell. Even before he got in Buster knew Bam hadn't slept. He was an insomniac even when he didn't have tests. But Buster had thought this one through; he had a plan. Now, if only he didn't get another ticket on the way, he had departed early so he could drive slow.

Bam pulled the door open hurriedly and climbed into the small car. "Where are the babes?" he asked rhetorically. His rides with Buster were a constant search for female passengers.

"Couldn't find a morning shift," Buster said. "I thought we did pretty good last night."

"Yeah, but I need another cup of coffee on the way in. Did I tell you I'm worried about this testing bullshit?" Bam started up for the umpteenth time. "Did I tell you that if I mess up, I'm condemned to live a life of abject poverty in Bumkin. I will probably be banned by my family as a high-school dropout. Maybe I could become mayor one day and make $12,000 a year. How do you think I would be as a middle-aged, Southern mayor on skid row?"

Bam always asked and answered his own questions when his mind moved into hyper-drive. Buster drove quietly into the EZ parking lot, checking his watch to make sure the store was open. It was 7:00 AM. Testing started at 8:30 AM. He left Bam in the car, "Just stay put, little buddy, I'll be right back."

"Bring coffee and a loaded gun," Bam said. "Say, ya think I can sue the town for cruel and unusual punishment if I shoot myself?"

Five minutes later Buster returned with two small brown paper bags, the top of each was twisted around the bottle inside. He re-entered the driver's seat with a big smile. Bam sat yawning, still feeling fuzzy after two hours of sleep. "Where's the coffee?" he asked.

"You drink any more coffee and you're going to bounce out of your seat and blow this test. I bought some Thunderbird to calm your ass down."

"You what?"

"You heard me. You can't afford to fuck this up, bud. Drink the damn wine."

"It's 7:00 AM in the morning of a make-it or break-it, six-hour test."

"You're already over-thinking this thing and you're driving me crazy. Drink up."

Bam went silent. He watched quietly as his buddy unscrewed the wine bottles and handed one over to him.

"What's the word?" Buster asked.

"Thunderbird," Bam replied.

"What's the price?"

"Thirty twice."

"Who's da man?"

"Da man with the plan."

They clicked their bottles in a toast. Buster pushed in his Pink Floyd tape and turned onto the back road to take a slow, scenic drive around the bayou. He always enjoyed watching the sunrise over the bayou while he sipped cheap wine.

Thirty miles north, Meadow finished the last of the thick chicory coffee, throwing the Styrofoam cup away as she packed. She got up early to beat the local crowd at the diner across the street for breakfast, returning to the Bumble Bee Hotel to take a bath. Surprisingly, no one had raised an eyebrow in the small town. They assumed she was just waiting to take the Greyhound bus out of town. So far, so good, she thought.

Chapter Fifty-Seven
Reentry

Meadow tightened a cheap motel towel around her naked body as she read the daily newspaper. Bumkin monopolized the front page. Bubba, the son-of-a-bitch, had miraculously lived and Foster's body was missing. Someone had intervened in her plans. Life was predictable only in its unfairness.

She snuffed out the last cigarette in her possession with a sad face. It would be the last nicotine she could have for quite a while. Maggie didn't smoke and surely wouldn't allow smoking in her home.

The injustice that haunted Meadow made her want to scream. Maybe it was hatred. Maybe it was just survival. Maybe she didn't care. Maybe she had no choice. Maybe she had never had a choice. It wasn't fair. Bubba had escaped the revenge he deserved, and she knew down deep that Foster had been killed.

The police and Bubba would be looking for her. The cops were easy, for the moment. She had bedded enough local cops and politicians to ensure that there would only be a half-hearted search. They knew she had their names and phone numbers recorded in her diary. No one would want Meadow to show up unannounced. At least, not alive, she reminded herself, but they would leave her alone if she left them alone.

Bubba was a different matter. He would be merciless, scorchin' the earth until he found her. Nor did she discount their eerie capacity to find each other. They had their own Gris Gris. Her only hope was a place he would never visit.

Meadow dropped the towel and stood naked in front of the mirror. Hers was still a body that men would fight for, some had already died for. She remembered Quinine for a fleeting moment, as she left his body lifeless and bleeding. A good man caught in the wrong moment. She pulled her hair into a bun with one hand, placing the other on slim hips as she twisted in front of the mirror to look at her profile. No more makeup. She would have to soften her expressions some, add layers of clothing to hide her figure. Tone down her language and practice being shy. It wouldn't be an easy transition. The hardest part would be wearing hand-me-down clothes, she sighed.

Hours later she sat in the cab of the eighteen-wheeler next to a burly, Cajun truck driver, parked in a cane field on the back road to Bumkin. It had taken less time than she planned to get reacquainted with a familiar trucker at the diner. The rest had been an easy and welcome respite from the stress of the moment. She liked getting laid in trucks. The vibrations of the big diesel were always fun in the cramped quarters of the cab. She would have preferred to be more adventurous, but you never knew when the wife and kids could recognize his truck in a small town. Besides, it was only a half-mile down the cane row to escape to Maggie's cabin.

It was a bright, beautiful day. Water from the previous day's rain had already evaporated, leaving the ground moist and the grass standing high, rippling different shades like a green sea in the light wind. She walked along the old bayou path avoiding tractors and combines at rest for their lunch break. The white men who drove the equipment rested on their perches with lunch bags, seated high above the black labor who trailed behind them to offload cotton and chop weeds.

Meadow reached the dirt road that led to the cabin, immediately spotting the giant magnolia tree and her namesake meadow. She reminisced about being there just days prior with Foster. Literally a lifetime ago, she winced. His death was too convenient to be coincidental. She would never know what happened to him or his money, but it left more for her. She had been a prostitute, a criminal, and a madman's daughter during the last year. Today she was just a simple, black woman. It was a luxury, a life she could embrace, at least until she got bored. Any passerby would confuse her as Magnolia from a distance. She already felt safer. No one would visit Maggie and Maggie would welcome the company of her new sister.

Maggie looked down the road from the cabin porch, less than a hundred yards away. She held her hand over her eyes to shield herself from the glare of the mid-day sun. She could see the thin silhouette of a stranger walking up the isolated road. Maggie stood up and ran toward Meadow, not believing the image before her. Meadow dropped her bag as the sisters ran toward each other in a tearful embrace that needed no words. They were home. Together. Finally.

Chapter Fifty-Eight
Reconciliation

Sally and Hezekial sat quietly at her kitchen table. She had been working on her latest book and making sure that Bam was adequately packed for college. Hezekial was in his finest black suit with a bright red shirt and black tie. Anyone who knew the Reverend knew that it was his funeral outfit. The worn black bible that was his constant companion sat in front of him on the pine table. Sally noticed it was a little more worn than the last time they had met, just like her and Hezekial, she thought wistfully. A lot had passed their way recently.

"I understand that young Bam is going off to college," Hezekial began with the small talk. It wasn't a necessity for him to break the ice with Sally, but it was a necessity of Southern manners that he try.

"By the skin of his teeth," Sally acknowledged with a wry smile. "He pulled it out in the end, overcame his anxiety, and almost made a perfect score. Now we'll see if he can do the same at college. Of course, he had every prayer in town behind him on the ACT test," she laughed. "It's amazing how everyone in town can pull together to remove a major pain in the ass."

"It's a great quality that he comes by honestly," Hezekial responded with respect, his preacher's voice kicking into full gear. "Young Bam should consider being a preacher one day. I will say a prayer every day that he always remains a pain in the ass for the wrong people and the right conflicts."

Hezekial's contemporaneous eloquence never ceased to amaze Sally. "I will relay that message Hezekial. In the meantime, let's hope education can suppress hormones."

"I take note also that there will be a new principal next year, Mrs. Sally. Mr. Greely is returning to Alabama," the preacher offered.

"Changing tides wash out a lot crap, Hezekial. It is hard to remain principal when half of your student body gets busted for drugs. Looks like Gil finally got what he wanted. Now his schools have a chance, but it's going to be a long, hard battle. With Bubba's school shutting down, there will be a surge of mad, young people from racist families moving back into the public school system."

Hezekial nodded in agreement. "At least the leadership has been purged. Now we can focus on defining education instead of integration in the New South."

"I hope so, Reverend, but politicians still pander to racist voters. Until teachers are empowered to take back their classrooms, I am not optimistic about the future of the public school system. So, tell me, Reverend, to what do I owe the honor of this visit?" Sally asked.

"Mrs. Sally, I just wanted you to know that the black community knows that you took great risk to help us right a wrong. You have always been there for us and we appreciate all you have done."

Sally stared at him with a knowing smile, momentarily choked by the recognition that mattered to her most, knowing there was more to come. She hated compliments and she didn't know when Hezekial had been ordained to speak on behalf of his race, but then, who else was there? Regardless, he was being sincere.

"Why thank you Reverend. I will ask you to remember that we all have our cross to bear. Discrimination is not limited to the black community, nor limited to a crime of color. The pay discrimination against women is the next battle, and without question it is driven by white men. Rest assured I will be calling in favors from you and your congregation in the future. What else do you need, Hezekial?"

Caught off guard, the preacher feigned his intentions. "What do you mean?"

"Oh, give it up, Hezekial, you're not in your church with a bunch of ignorant patrons. If I am truly your friend, tell me why you're here."

Hezekial sighed, embarrassed. "Mrs. Sally, there are times that I wish your reputation for blunt discussion was less evident," he said earnestly. He used the moment to sip some Earl Grey. It was hard to work with a woman who violated all Southern protocol. Ironically, Sally and Ethan White were cut from the same mold. No wonder they didn't get along.

"Mrs. Sally, we have an opportunity to create an inter-racial council to confront racial prejudice in this community, to air our grievances openly so we can get past a hundred years of negative elements."

Sally held up her palm. "Hold it, Hezekial," she said firmly with a stern look. "What you really mean is, you have a chance at another big grant through your buddy in Boston and you need a white female with some credentials to help get it approved."

"Well, not exactly."

"What, exactly?" she persisted, impatient.

The game was up, he knew. It was time to come clean. "Well, yes, Mrs. Sally, you could have a point, but what is wrong with that?"

"Not a damn thing, Hezekial. I just don't have time to guess at what you're really after. Save it for the congregation. What do you want?"

"If you would consider sponsoring the grant, I am sure that we could allocate money for analysis of the underlying historical issues which define the plight of the black race. Most importantly, Maggie has used her influence at the bank to have Bubba's school building donated as a bi-racial juvenile home for the disadvantaged."

Sally was visibly moved. The historian understood the symbolic value of Maggie preserving Bubba's school for better things. "Hezekial, you and I both know no one reads all that historical analysis, least of all the people who need it most. Are you trying to buy me off?"

Hezekial closed his eyes and silently prayed that he would give the right answer. "Yes," he finally affirmed with meek conviction. Small beads of sweat appeared on his forehead as he chose substance over form.

"Then the answer is absolutely 'no,'" said Sally. "But, out of gratitude for a no-bullshit answer for the first time in your ecumenical life, I will sponsor your grant under three explicit conditions." She held up three fingers in front of his face to drive home her point. "First, my share of the money goes to children's education at Maggie's charity, and I keep the publishing rights with no-strings attached. Second, Sadie handles all of the accounting for the grant. If she says one red cent is unaccounted for, I will shut you down," she said bluntly, waiting for a response.

Sally poured more tea as Hezekial considered his options. It wasn't the response he had hoped for, but it was the response he had to have. The opportunity for creative accounting had just been shoved out the window. Perhaps he could find a legitimate way to pay himself, but he hated the thought of paying taxes. Then again, he retained fond memories of Sadie's image in the car… "You have a deal from a grateful congregation," Hezekial confirmed. "What is the last condition?" he asked.

"I want an honest update on Maggie."

Hezekial hung his head to collect his thoughts without falling prey to his emotions. "Sister Maggie seems to have weathered the trauma of her experience," he said in a broken voice.

"And?" Sally stared through his façade. "This stays between us, Hezekial," she assured him.

"She lost the baby," he said sadly. Sally could tell his grief was genuine.

"Lee Esther told me. I am very sorry. How is she?" Sally asked.

"She is very different, Mrs. Sally," Hezekial confided, hesitant in a sudden moment of vulnerability.

"How so?" the professor inquired.

He thought for a moment, looking out the big kitchen window. "In ways I cannot explain," he said plainly. "Perhaps it is the money she has inherited. Perhaps the revelation of her history was just too much for her to handle," he shrugged. "Perhaps she had to admit that it is a very ugly world out there." He did not attempt to discuss her sudden aggression in bed. Where had she learned such things? Not to complain, of course, she had virtually rebuilt the church with Bubba's money.

"She now leads a quiet existence at the old cabin and rarely ventures out. Judge Jim forced a settlement with the Tremblay family on Quinine's land which she inherited. Now she has minimal needs and very significant resources, but she is restless and unhappy nonetheless."

"Did the police ever catch up with Meadow?" Sally asked.

"I don't believe they tried very hard, Mrs. Sally," the preacher complained. "Bubba never pressed formal charges because he didn't relish admitting to his wife what the rest of the world already knows. It's reasonable to expect that a woman as sinister as Meadow held a lot of secrets on a lot of people in positions to help her. Certainly, the Sheriff was not motivated to pursue her," he sighed. "There was a rumor that Meadow returned for a while, but no one has seen her, and Maggie refuses to talk about her. Hopefully, Meadow has departed our lives, although I suspect that Bubba is still looking for her."

Sally considered asking about Hezekial's wife but elected to leave it alone. She shoved a pad and pen to him across the table. "I would like to call Maggie. I miss her visits, but I have been preoccupied with Bam's move, so we haven't talked for several months. Do you know her number?"

"Why yes, of course," he said, writing it down on her legal pad as he stood up to leave. Then with hesitation, he felt compelled to ask, "And do you and Judge Jim still talk?"

It was quid pro quo for her inquisition. "Judge Jim and I will always talk," she said, "we've been friends for almost fifty years, ever since we were kids. He just needs to listen more," she laughed. It was a melancholy laugh that seemed to carry a hint of regret uncommon for Sally. "I hear he will be running for Senator, without Bubba's blessing."

"But will he have yours?" Hezekial asked, curious.

"He hasn't asked—yet," she returned.

Sally walked Hezekial to the door and gave him a hug inside the comfort of her home, not otherwise possible between a large, black man and a small, white woman. They had the same shepherd, she knew, they just came from different flocks. She noticed the big shiny car in her driveway as the preacher walked out. "Isn't that Beverly's car?"

"Not anymore," he said proudly, "she donated it to the church after she took her "ride" with Meadow," he laughed, "guilt by association." Then he headed back to life across the tracks.

Days, then weeks passed slowly as summer receded into the hint of fall and a new school year began. Sally sat at her typewriter, editing her latest book. Life was unusually calm, too calm. She picked up a stack of legal pads and found Maggie's phone number in blue ink, scribbled in Hezekial's handwriting at the top of the pad.

Sally paused momentarily, then swung her chair around and reached for the phone, dialing the number in anticipation, suddenly amazed by the free time she had available now that Bam was off to school. It was time to catch up with Maggie.

Maggie answered the phone, with a terse "Hello," that was not the tender voice Sally expected, but it was still early in the morning for everyone except Sally.

"Maggie, this is Mrs. Sally. It's been a while since I saw you. Lee Esther and I miss our tea time. Rev. Hezekial gave me your phone number several weeks ago and I wanted to see how you were doing."

Maggie went quiet briefly, "Oh, sure. Sally. How are you?" the voice seemed strained, without the familiarity of friends.

"I'm fine, just fine, Maggie. Just starting back to school, you know. I guess you heard that Bam finally got into college. He asks about you every time he comes in," Sally said.

"Well, uh, I didn't know. Tell him hello for me," she replied flatly.

"Hezekial told me about the baby, and I wanted to tell you how sorry I am for your loss. I hope you know you can call me if you need to talk."

There was silence on the phone as "Maggie" pulled aside the covers nervously, leaving the warmth of the man lying next to her. She got out of bed and walked over the polished plank floors to a large window that overlooked the big magnolia tree. A fresh bed of roses grew richly, in full bloom atop a mound of dirt that lay at the base of the big tree. Two small crosses were carved into the tree trunk.

"Well, I put that matter to rest," she said with a sad tone of finality in her voice. "But I have to go now, Sally, I have company and I have things to do. Thanks for the call."

"Why, yes, of course," Sally said, surprised at the terse exchange. "Come visit me, Maggie," Sally said simply.

"Sure, I'll call you for coffee sometime, gotta go." Maggie's voice was aloof and irreverent.

"Coffee?" Sally's shock reverberated over the phone as the line went dead. She stared into the receiver, her eyes wide open.

END

ABOUT THE AUTHOR

Sam Eakin is a financial analyst and venture capital investor. He acquired and restructured troubled companies for forty years. Recently retired, Mr. Eakin is the son of Dr. Sue Eakin, a noted historian responsible for researching and writing the story of Solomon Northrup in *Twelve Years A Slave*. Eakin grew up traveling with his academic mother who had an encyclopedic knowledge of stories from the local culture during the racial friction of the 1960s, which became the background for *Southern Justice*.

Mr. Eakin has been engaged in writing technical analysis for decades as a venture capital investor and is now getting time to focus on his novels which are based on real, rich experiences and characters from his very active life. He has written regular monthly editorial columns for a daily newspaper and his short story, *Hostage* was published by *Tulane Press*. He has recently completed *Section 1983* as a prequal to the classic novel *1984*.

You can contact the author at:
southernsocrates@gmail.com